BL CE

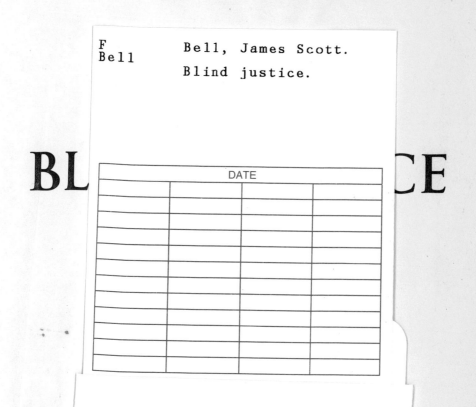

Also by James Scott Bell

Circumstantial Evidence

Final Witness

BLIND JUSTICE

A NOVEL

JAMES SCOTT BELL

BROADMAN & HOLMAN PUBLISHERS

Nashville, Tennessee

Printed in the United States of America

0–8054–2161–0

Published by Broadman & Holman Publishers, Nashville, Tennessee

Dewey Decimal Classification: 813
Subject Heading: CONTEMPORARY FICTION/LEGAL THRILLER
Library of Congress Catalog Number: 99–40602

Library of Congress Cataloging-in-Publication Data

Bell, James Scott.
Blind justice: a novel / by James Scott Bell.
p. cm.
ISBN 0–8054–2161–0 (pbk.: alk. paper)
I. Title.
PS3552.E5158B58 2000
813'.54—dc21 99–40602
CIP

1 2 3 4 5 04 03 02 01 00

DEDICATION

This book is for Marjorie Bruce,
legendary high school English teacher,
who taught me that writing is a discipline,
and learning a passion

Part One

Cruelty has a human heart.

—William Blake

CHAPTER ONE

ON THE LAST Thursday in March, Howie Patino stepped onto Alaska Airlines Flight 190 out of Anchorage, carrying a teddy bear with a little ribbon across the front that read, "Alaska's Cool!" Howie wore a plaid shirt, blue down jacket, and brand new Levi jeans. He also wore, he told me later, a huge smile. "A big, fat, dumb one," he said. "How dumb, stupid, and blind can a guy be?"

His sleep was peaceful on the trip to Los Angeles. Hardly a hint of turbulence. The guy sitting next to him was no trouble at all, chatting amiably without overdoing it. Mostly Howie slept and dreamed of Rae–Rae in a bathing suit; Rae sitting by the pool and offering him a long, cool drink; Rae making kissing noises at him just like she used to.

Howie woke up smiling when the plane touched down at the Los Angeles Airport as smooth as a swan gliding onto a pond at Disneyland. That was one of Howie's favorite places. He and Rae had gone there on their honeymoon. He told me that Rae's favorite attraction was "Mr. Toad's Wild Ride." They went on it five times that night, laughing and screaming like little kids.

The sleep on the plane had removed any creeping hint of fatigue, so Howie wasn't tired when he finally made it to the Greyhound station and boarded the bus. It had all gone so well to this point. Howie closed his eyes and thanked God that he and Rae would be together even sooner than planned.

The trip north, though, took forever.

It was bumper-to-bumper into Westwood and through the Sepulveda Pass. Things opened up a little in Sherman Oaks but tightened again around Tarzana. All the way up, Howie ticked off the towns in his head in a cadence of anticipation: Calabasas and Agoura, Westlake and Thousand Oaks, Ventura and Ojai. Like stepping stones across dividing waters, they were taking him closer and closer to Rae.

It was pure night when the bus finally pulled into Hinton. Moonless. And the town, in its peculiar rustic ceremony, was starting to fold up. Through the bus window Howie saw a few tourists sitting on the outside patio of the Hinton Hotel sipping evening wine and watching the passengers–all three of them–step out into a bit of country California.

The first to alight was Howie, still holding the teddy bear. An older couple sitting at the hotel smiled at him. A good sign. Howie smiled back, snatched his duffel bag from the sidewalk where the bus driver had dropped it, looped it over his shoulder, and started walking west toward White Oak Avenue.

Hinton was both strange and familiar, Howie told me. It seemed, as he got further and further from the town square, unnaturally still. Mixed with the hopeful perfume of orange blossoms and sage, the smell of cows and dry weeds wafted through the air. Howie said later that those were the last smells he remembered, until that final smell, the awful stench of fresh blood that he would mention in the police report.

At White Oak he turned south under an awning of towering eucalyptus trees. It was like walking through a dark tunnel, Howie said, but he knew where the light at the end was–home and Rae, security and warmth. All would be well once again.

When he finally reached the front door of the little house at the end of White Oak, he was dizzy with excitement. He tossed the duffel bag onto the porch and held the teddy bear behind his back as he reached for the doorknob. The door was locked, though, and Rae hadn't given him a house key when he left for Alaska. This was one of her peculiarities, which Howie overlooked through eyes of love. He wouldn't be sneaking in for the surprise he'd planned, so he knocked.

And waited.

And knocked again.

He shouted, "Rae!" and pounded on the door.

No answer. No lights on inside.

He set the little bear on top of the duffel bag and went around to the side gate, finding it padlocked. It had never been padlocked before. Something wasn't right.

"Rae!"

A dog barked in the yard next door.

"Quiet!" Howie ordered as he scaled the wall and jumped into the side yard, knocking over a recycling container. It thudded hard on the walkway, its contents of bottles and cans spilling onto the concrete.

The dog barked louder.

"Quiet, boy!"

Howie slipped around to the back patio. The sliding glass door was never locked. Never a need for it in Hinton. He would get in that way.

But tonight it *was* locked. Howie banged on the glass with his fist. No answer from inside.

Okay, so she wasn't home.

Where was she then? Out with friends maybe. She wasn't expecting him, after all. He'd caught an early flight because he wanted to surprise her. All this was his own fault, Rae would tell him, maybe at the top of her lungs. That was her way sometimes. He'd grown used to it.

Howie considered his choices. He could grab his stuff and go downtown and have a Coke while he waited. He could see if she was at Sue's house, and if not, he could ask Sue to make some calls.

Or he could try to get in the house.

Maybe Rae wouldn't like that though. Maybe she'd yell at him about that too.

But this was his house too. It had been a long flight and bus ride, and now he was tired. He wanted to be inside. He wanted to kick off his shoes and fall into his own bed and wait for Rae. Sure she might get mad, but he could handle that because she would be there with him. That was all that mattered.

With full force, Howie yanked the sliding glass door. The lock snapped, and the door slid open. Later, Howie would say he didn't realize he had that much strength and speculated that his action might have been due to something more welled up inside him, a part of him he never knew he had, like when a mother suddenly gets the strength to lift an automobile when her child is trapped underneath.

Howie entered the house, found a lamp, and turned on the light.

The first thing he noticed was the sofa and the clothes tossed carelessly on it. Rae was never much of a housekeeper, but this was an out-and-out mess. On an end table was an ashtray with a few cigarette butts. Rae had supposedly quit smoking. Had she started up again while he was away?

Howie stood and listened for a few moments, and not hearing anything, walked down the hall to the master bedroom.

He opened the door and turned on the light.

Someone was in bed. The covers moved and then Rae Patino sat up.

"Rae, didn't you hear me?"

Her red hair was messy. With a head toss she whisked the strands out of her face and stared at him coldly. "What are you doing here?"

"I'm home."

"Tomorrow. You said *tomorrow* night."

"Surprised?" He took a few steps toward her, his arms out for an embrace.

Rae recoiled. "You can't stay here."

"Honey, what are you talking about?"

"You just can't, that's all."

"Can't? But–"

"Just leave, Howie."

"But Rae, I'm *home."* He said it like he had to convince himself.

Rae sighed and rolled her eyes to the ceiling. "Look," she said, "you might as well know it now. I'm in love with somebody else."

It wouldn't have been any different, Howie said later, if she had stuck a knife in his stomach and twisted it around. That was the moment things started to go fuzzy on him. He was in and out after that, feeling dizzy half the time and plain lost the other half.

He figured a half hour went by as he pleaded with her, cried in front of her, begged her to see someone for counseling. It seemed to him she was, by turns, cold and caring, obstinate and open. He thought there might be at least some hope of reconciliation, if only she'd try.

And then there was the matter of Brian. During the course of the conversation, Howie asked Rae where their five-year-old son was, and she told him he was at Sue's house, where he loved to visit. It seemed odd to Howie that Brian would be there in the middle of the week, but he paid it no mind. It was more important to talk about their future, the three of them, together.

Howie finally said, "We can all move up there now. I've got a place and a good job. They're building like crazy, and it's a great place for a kid to grow up."

Rae was unmoved. "I'm not going to freeze in Alaska; you can bet on that."

"Rae, please. We need to be together. For Brian."

When he said that, her eyes seemed to darken. Howie remembered that explicitly. It was like looking into two dead pools at midnight.

"What makes you so proud?" Rae said.

"Proud?"

"Yeah, proud."

"Proud of what?"

"Brian." Her voice seemed to spit the name.

"What are you talking about, Rae?"

"I'm talking about Brian, Howie."

"What about him?"

"What makes you think he's yours?"

It was the smile on her face then that unlatched a dark door to some unnamed oblivion. Howie's memories of the next few minutes were short, surreal images, which included that smile twisting her face into a funhouse clown expression, the mockery of it, and her hands clasped behind her head as she lay on the bed as if showing Howie what he would never have again. Then came the blackness followed by the gleam of a blade, a flash almost as bright as a tabloid photographer's camera, a scream, the red stained sheets, the sounds of a woman sucking for breath, and that final image he couldn't get away from, that he kept mentioning over and over. "The devil," the police report stated. "Suspect keeps talking about the devil."

CHAPTER TWO

WHILE HOWIE PATINO was confronting horror he could scarcely have imagined, I was trying hard to come up with one good reason why I should continue to breathe.

Max's Tavern was crowded for a Thursday night. Three ex-jocks–I could tell because I am an ex-jock and know how I used to get obnoxious and annoy people–were fooling around at the pool table near the back. I watched them for awhile as they alternately strutted, posed, and laughed at their own beer-induced hilarity.

I was sitting at a table with a yellow legal pad in front of me. Most people don't approach suicide on a rational basis. It's an emotional decision with, I guess, as many psychological reasons as there are people. Not that I am unemotional, but I do have a certain kind of permanent brain damage known as the "legal mind."

I'd been a lawyer for almost seven years. As such, my mind did not work like that of a normal person, especially after three shots of bourbon chased with two beers. Which is why I was approaching the decision whether to off myself just as I would any other matter, legal or practical.

Here's how I do it.

I divide a piece of paper into two columns. On the left I list all the arguments or facts that lead one way. On the right I list the counterarguments and considerations. When that is all done, I take stock and let my rational mind decide the best course of action.

I had that line down the sheet of paper in front of me, and on the left-hand side I wrote the first argument in favor of checking out of life: *Disgraced.*

Just how disgraced had come home to me earlier in the day when I couldn't even get assigned a drunk driving case from a commissioner out in the sticks of Calabasas. I'd shown up early in hope of getting a case to bring in some badly needed bucks. Court assignments don't pay much, but they can stop financial hemorrhaging when the wallet is thin.

In my case I was flowing red because Gil Lee had asked me for last month's rent on my office and in his own sweet way was starting to make eviction noises.

I went to court on a tip from the Calabasas clerk about a possible conflict case. That meant there was a slight chance I'd get assigned, which also meant a case to nurse along on the county dole. With no other prospects, I snapped at the chance.

I never got it. Commissioner Craig Noonan refused to give me the case. I charged back to his chambers to ask him why. "Because," he said, "you're a disgrace to the legal profession."

Part of my brain began to formulate the insults I would hurl back in Noonan's face–good ones laced with epithets–while in another part of my mind I heard myself agreeing with him. That word, *disgrace,* has a particular history with me. I could hear the voice of my father saying it. I could see myself ten years ago deciding to go to law school so I could show the old man I was better than he ever thought, even though he was dead. There's something immutable about what fathers say to sons. So I was going to be the greatest lawyer the world had ever seen, or at least one of the most successful, with a huge salary, a corner office with a view, and long lines of powerhouse clients begging me to represent them. That would show Dad.

But now I was standing in Noonan's chambers begging him to flip me a scrap off the table of leftover misdemeanors, and he was telling me I was a disgrace to the profession.

That is why the word *disgraced* was the first on my list in Max's Tavern. Noonan was right.

I wrote a few more words on the left side of the legal pad:

No prospects.

No money.

No future.

No wife.

No daughter–maybe.

The last two notations referred to the wife who had divorced me and our five-year-old daughter. Ex-wife had remarried, had custody, and had told me two weeks ago that she and new husband, along with daughter, might move back east to North Carolina where new hubby had a job offer.

That meant my visitations with Mandy would be of the once-a-year variety, if, and this was a big if, I could come up with airfare.

I paused in my ruminations of self-ruin to order another beer. The three ex-jocks were still making a scene around the pool table, laughing at high decibel levels and sword fighting with their pool cues. They were in their twenties. I was thirty-two but felt a couple decades older. I wanted go over and tell them to enjoy their laughter while it lasts because it won't last long.

With the fresh beer served, I decided to write some things in the plus column.

That's when I started to get scared.

I couldn't think of anything to write–not a single, solitary thing. I suppose that if I'd thought hard enough I could have come up with something, even if it was a lie.

But there I sat wondering if I'd actually convinced myself that I had no choice but to do the Dutch.

I sat there for maybe ten minutes, just staring at the list.

Then it hit me, the one thing I could write. And this one thing was powerful enough to tip the scales all by itself. I wrote:

Mandy.

Even in my inebriated reflections of doom, I knew somewhere deep down I couldn't do this to my only daughter. I couldn't saddle her with the lifelong curse of a father who committed suicide.

I tore off the page of legal paper, crumpled it up, and tossed it on the floor. Like it or not, I couldn't check out by way of my own hand. Then my legal mind automatically started considering alternatives–like an accident. . . .

Suddenly I started to laugh. It was a drunk's laugh, the kind that seems like it won't shut off. I got to where I was laughing so hard that the three ex-jocks actually stopped what they were doing and stared at me. I think one of them may have asked me what was so funny.

I was in no condition to explain that I was laughing because I had decided that my only hope in life, the one thing I was wishing for, was to be hit by a truck doing seventy miles an hour.

CHAPTER THREE

WHEN I WOKE up, the talons of a predatory bird were embedded in my head.

Hangovers, I've come to believe, are related to animals and come in various forms, such as the crushing press of an elephant's foot or the sharp report of a woodpecker pounding out a new home in the cerebral cortex. Most often, for me, hangovers came in the form of talons gripping my temples. I groaned, rolled over, and saw an angry red 10:15 on my digital clock. I gripped my entire forehead with one hand. Forget about going into the office; I'll just die here in bed.

As I lay there wondering whether to call the embalmer, the phone rang. The talons dug in harder.

I fumbled for the phone. "Yeah?"

"Jake?" It was my lovely ex, Barb, she of the exquisite timing.

"What is it?" I said.

"How are you?"

"You know me."

"Taking care of yourself?"

"You a doctor?"

"Why do you always do this?"

"What did you call for?"

"Rick and I wanted to go away this weekend."

"I'm thrilled."

"Jake, please."

I said nothing. I pushed a spot on my forehead with my index finger, trying to relieve pressure. It didn't work.

"I was wondering," Barb said, "even though it isn't your weekend, if you could take Mandy. It would be a real favor."

"I just love doing you favors."

"Do it for Mandy then."

"Not for you and Reverend Rick?" That was a low blow, I knew, but I wasn't feeling charitable. Not in the least. I was a mess, so why suffer alone?

"Rick isn't a minister, Jake."

"He just Bible thumps like one."

"Will you take Mandy or won't you?"

"What's it worth to you?"

"Don't do this, Jake. She isn't a bargaining chip."

"Isn't she? Wasn't she just that when you hired that fancy divorce attorney?"

"I thought we were going to move on."

"You wanted custody, you got custody. Now you can live with it."

"Sometimes you can be so cruel."

She was absolutely right, but I wasn't about to admit it. "Fine. I'll take her."

"Thank you."

I said nothing.

"Can I bring her by at noon?"

"Noon!"

"We want to get an early start."

"Oh lovely."

"Well?"

"Bring her."

Again she thanked me without emotion. Then she added, "Um, Jake, one thing."

"Now what?"

"Well, could you please . . . be careful?"

I felt my face heating up. "Careful about what?"

"You know."

"You think I'd do something that would be harmful to Mandy? Is that what you're saying?"

"I didn't–"

"You really think that low of me?"

She sighed. "I won't have this conversation with you every time."

"Okay by me."

"Believe it or not, Jake, I want you to be okay. Not just for Mandy, but for you."

"See you at noon," I said and hung up. Man, I was getting good at being a jerk. I decided not to shave so I wouldn't have to look at myself in the mirror, but I did think it wise to get something in my stomach. I threw on some jeans and a sweatshirt and walked two blocks to Chipper's Coffee Shop, one of the last decent breakfast joints in the Valley. The city was littered with Denny's and IHOPs, not to mention Jack-in-the-Box and McDonald's and all the other temples of culinary mediocrity. At Chipper's they still made their pancakes as big as the plate, didn't slight you on the butter, and knew your name if you came in often enough.

I bought a *Times* from the machine and took a place at the counter. Mary, the waitress who had worked there since Lincoln's second inaugural, greeted me by name. I asked how she was and she said, "Never better." I thought about asking her what her secret was but ordered coffee instead.

The *Times* front page had a story about the overcrowded conditions at the L.A. County jail. A guy from the ACLU was outraged about the "meat locker" atmosphere. A spokesman from the county sheriff's office was outraged that the ACLU guy was outraged. I could smell a class-action lawsuit coming.

In the middle of the page was a story out of Tennessee. A junior-high-school kid had gone berserk and shot several of his classmates with a high-powered hunting rifle.

As Mary served me my coffee, she glanced at the paper. "You readin' about them kids in Tennessee?" she said. She had a southern drawl herself.

"Yeah."

"It was on the TV last night. Terrible."

"Probably drugs or something," I said, "or maybe he broke up with his girlfriend."

"No," Mary said ominously. "It was more than that."

"More?"

"They said he was in a Satan worship group."

"Satan?" I said incredulously. "I can just see that as a defense–the devil made me do it."

"It's real, Jake."

"What's real?"

"Satan."

"Ah, I think the kids just get into those things as an excuse to take drugs, and then they fall off the deep end."

"No, it's a spiritual battle goin' on."

"Well, I believe in evil spirits too, Mary."

"Do you?"

"Yeah. I call them IRS agents."

Mary shook her head and smiled and then slapped me on the arm. I ordered a short stack of pancakes with scrambled eggs and read on about the incident. Sure enough, near the end of the story, there was mention of some kind of occult connection. But the writer seemed as skeptical as I was.

It took me an hour to eat breakfast, finish the paper, and down five cups of coffee. The talons were replaced by a caffeine buzz, and by the time I left, I felt ready to accomplish at least one productive task before my daughter arrived. I had a stack of appellate reports from the *Daily Journal* at my apartment. I needed to scan them for the latest case law to give myself the illusion I was still a practicing lawyer. Then I thought I could find an old movie on TV to watch with Mandy, something from the 30s or 40s, so I could forget about a world where kids kill other kids.

The phone was ringing as I walked through my door. I didn't recognize the woman's voice even though she seemed to know me.

"It's Janet Patino, Jake."

"Patino?" Then it hit me. "Mrs. Patino?"

"Yes, Jake, it's me."

"Wow, it's been a long time."

"Yes it has. How are you?"

"Doing fine," I lied.

"That's good."

"How's Howie?"

There was a pause on the other end. "That's what I'm calling about."

"What is it?"

"He's been arrested."

"Howie?"

"In Hinton. I drove up this morning."

"I didn't know he was back here."

"He moved when he got married about five years ago."

"Howie's married?"

I only heard labored breathing on the other end of the line.

"Mrs. Patino?"

"I'm still here."

"What was Howie arrested for?"

Another short pause. "Murder."

I felt my chin drop. "Who is he supposed to have murdered?"

"His wife." Then Janet Patino started crying.

"Hey, it's okay."

"I can't believe he did it," Janet Patino struggled to say. "He's so gentle. You remember, don't you? Harmless. But they've got him in a hospital."

"Why?"

"He was . . . hurt. I'm scared to death. Jake, could you see him?"

"Has he talked to anyone? A public defender?"

"I don't think so."

I rubbed my eyes. "There's probably local counsel up there who could see him, someone who knows the courts and the prosecutors."

"Can't you see him? Please? I know you're practicing law out here. We always liked you so, Jake. We'll pay you, of course."

The word *pay* sounded nice, but I could have justified a refusal. It was a long drive to Hinton, and Howie would be much better off with a local. I could have done some song-and-dance, but this was the mother of an old friend, a mother who was obviously scared, and I thought I'd already used up my portion of jerk-ness for the day.

So I found myself saying, "Sure, Mrs. Patino. I'll go see him this afternoon. Tell me where he is."

Right in the middle of her doing that, I heard a loud knock on the door and a five-year-old girl's voice shouting, "Lemme in, Daddy!"

CHAPTER FOUR

"NOW DON'T JUST feed her junk food," Barb said.

"Your faith in me is touching."

"Don't."

"You know you're very good with that word."

"What word?"

"*Don't.*"

"Please, Jake."

"That's better."

Mandy was still hugging my leg in exactly the same spot she'd attached herself to the moment I opened the door.

"We'll be back on Sunday," Barb said, handing me a cloth bag with five-year-old essentials in it. "I'll call you."

"You don't have to pick her up. She can spend Sunday night with me."

"I'll call," Barb said. "Mandy, give Mommy a kiss." She squatted, and our daughter ran over and planted a kiss on her mother's cheek.

"Bye, Mommy!" Mandy said in her chirpy voice. Then she ran back into my apartment and went straight to the fun drawer where I kept the crayons.

"Thanks, Jake," Barb said turning.

I didn't respond. I waited until she reached the stairs and then closed the door.

Mandy was already setting up a small play space at the table, complete with a handful of crayons and several blank sheets of white paper, which I also kept in the drawer for her. I looked at her and realized she was the one bright spot in my sorry life. Mandy's auburn hair was in a braid. With her sweet brown eyes focused on her paper, she was the very picture of innocence. There was still some of that left in the world.

"I can draw something, Daddy," she said, not looking up.

"I'd like to see it."

"Okay."

I opened the curtains to give her more light. I had a view of the Van Nuys Airport. This wasn't the best neighborhood in the city, and the vista wasn't of ocean horizons, but I liked looking at the airport. Something about planes coming and going, about life going on normally, had a calming effect. As Mandy worked on her picture, I watched a couple of private planes take off toward the clouds.

Then Mandy said, "Look!" She held up a piece of paper. On it she had drawn three multicolored animals. That's what I took the stick-legged creatures to be. "Horses," she announced. The horse in the middle was smaller than the other two.

"Hey, terrific," I said.

"That's us."

"That's who?"

"You, me, and Mommy."

I blinked.

"Don't you like it, Daddy?"

"Sure, honey, it's just great. If I were a horse, that's how I'd like to look." I took the picture and placed it on the universal forum for all children's art, the refrigerator door. I secured it with a magnet. I knew as soon as Mandy was gone I'd remove the thing and dump it. I didn't want a picture of Barb looking at me, even if she was depicted as a horse.

"Hey," I said, trying to sound cheery, "how about we take a drive?"

Mandy was busy on another picture. "I don't want to."

"We'll drive by the ocean."

"I want to play here."

"I'll make us peanut butter and honey sandwiches, and we can eat them on the way."

"And cookies?"

"Yes, I'll get some cookies."

"And milk?"

"Milk."

She slapped her crayon down on the table, and in her precocious way, the one that made me think of her as twice her age, she said, "Deal!"

A half hour later we were on the freeway heading toward Hinton. I'd made the sandwiches, and then stopped at a convenience store for the cookies and milk. Mandy seemed happy about the cuisine. She gobbled her sandwich and sipped her milk through a straw. I did the same thing, only with one hand on the wheel.

"Where we going?" Mandy asked.

"Just to a little town for a bit. I have to do something there."

"What?"

"See a person."

"Who?"

"A person I used to know."

"What's his name?"

"Howie."

She laughed. "That's a funny name. Is he funny?"

"I don't think so."

"Why?"

"Well, he's just . . . I think he's sad right now. He's in the hospital."

"Is he sick?"

"He's hurt."

"Is he going to die?"

I glanced at my daughter. She was looking at me with extreme seriousness. "No," I said.

She was silent for a moment. I could almost hear the wheels and pulleys in her head. Finally she said, "Are you going to die, Daddy?"

Now that was a left hook out of nowhere. I'd read somewhere that kids start to think about death around Mandy's age. I also knew there was probably something more going on, something that had to do with the divorce. A divorce is like a death to a child. So, perhaps, is a father who drinks too much.

"Everybody dies sometime, Mandy, but I won't be dying for a long, long time."

"What happens?"

"When?"

"When you die."

Why did I have to have this conversation? Why now? Why couldn't I have been prepared? Why couldn't I have been in Australia?

But I wasn't in Australia; I was here in a car with my only daughter. There was a very good chance that I wouldn't be seeing her much after this, and she had just asked me one of those key questions that can shape a kid for life.

I've defended some of the worst denizens of society's underbelly and been asked tough questions by hardened criminals. I've trembled sometimes when I've answered, but never as much as I was trembling now.

What would Barb want me to say? I could just hear her screaming at me. *What do you mean you told her we just go into the ground? Why didn't you tell her we go to heaven? How could you do this to her?*

Barb and I had never really discussed Mandy's religious education. Barb was all for it, of course. After our divorce she had "found Christ," whatever that meant. I had no idea. I also had no faith. So what was I supposed to do now that my daughter was asking the ultimate question? Lie?

I decided to try finesse. I was a lawyer after all. "It's too nice a day to talk about dying, Mandy."

She thought about this for a moment and then shook her head and said, "But what happens?"

"Hey, how about we go get an ice cream cone when I finish my business? Huh? What do you say?"

"Okay!"

"Yeah!"

We smiled at each other, then Mandy frowned. "But what happens, Daddy?"

I sighed. "Have you ever asked Mommy about this?"

"Yeah."

"And what does she say?"

"She says God takes us."

"Well, there you go."

"Does he, Daddy? Does God take us to heaven?"

"Mandy, listen to me. We need to think about life, not death. We need to do our best right now."

"What's God like?"

What God? There is no God! The sooner you learn that the better. The sooner you give up Santa Claus and the Easter Bunny and figure out that Barney is just a guy in a dinosaur suit, the better your life will be.

"No one really knows," I said.

"How come?"

"Because they just don't," I snapped. Mandy flinched. When I got a look at her face, she was staring straight ahead with her lower lip sticking out. That's her mad or sad look. Either way, I'd blown it.

When we finally pulled into the parking lot of the Hinton County Hospital, my head had a steady, Salvation Army drum beat going on inside it.

Now I had to figure out what to do with my five-year-old daughter while I talked to Howie Patino. Mandy did not want to sit in the children's waiting area, even though it had toys, and a nice nurse who looked like Norman Rockwell's idea of a grandmother offered to sit with her. She was just not going to let me go.

The uniformed police officer who was sitting just outside Howie's room thought this was amusing. "Cute," he said. "How old?"

"Five," I answered.

"I got a ten-year-old girl," the cop said. He looked around forty. His ample stomach pressed his pale blue shirt to the limit.

"I'm here to see Howie Patino," I said.

The cop's face changed faster than an auctioneer's patter. He stood up. "Who are you?"

"A friend."

"Nobody can see him."

"His mother asked me to see him."

"I don't care if the pope asked you. He's a suspect in a murder. Nobody sees him."

I looked up and down the hall hoping to spot Janet Patino. I hadn't told her exactly when I would be here and didn't know where to reach her. But I wondered if it would have made any difference to the cop one way or the other.

"All right," I said, taking out my wallet and flipping to my bar card. "I'm a lawyer. I'm here to see him in a professional capacity."

The cop glanced briefly at my card, then back at me. "I thought you said you were his friend."

"That too. Can I see him now?"

"I'm not authorized."

"Mandy," I said, stroking my daughter's hair, "you see that window over there?"

She looked and nodded her head.

"Go over there for a minute and look out of it," I said. "I'll be right over. Daddy needs to talk to this nice policeman in private."

Mandy slowly edged away from my leg, decided it was safe, and went obediently to the window. I turned back to the cop. "Listen, Officer, I don't know you and you don't know me, but I'm an attorney practicing law in the state of California, which has a constitution just like the United States does, and you are bound by both. They say that Howie Patino has the right to speak to a lawyer, which is what I am. And if you don't let me into that room right now, I will personally drag your tail before a magistrate and let you explain to him why an officer sworn to uphold the law decided the law didn't apply to him."

The cop blinked a couple of times. I tried my best not to.

"This is a small town," the cop said finally. "People who come around here with an attitude usually don't get very far."

"I see. So you want to add a veiled threat to this routine? You tell me just how far you want to push it, Officer."

I waited. The cop stared. "All right," he said. "But I know you now."

"My life," I said, "is complete. Mandy!"

My daughter rushed back to my side.

"You can't take her in," the officer said.

"You want to watch her for me?" I said.

"No!" Mandy protested.

The cop threw up his hands. "See if I care." He plopped back into his seat.

Taking Mandy by the hand, I pushed into the room.

CHAPTER FIVE

MY FIRST MEMORY of Howie Patino was back in the third grade when he wet his pants.

It was the end of the first day of school. I was putting my pencils and books away in my desk when Mark Blackmer leaned over and said, "Look at the weirdo. What's he doing?"

I knew who the weirdo was. It was that kid who had the goofy face. He sat in the back of the room. There were empty chairs on either side of him.

Now, in his seat, with two minutes to go before the end of school, the weirdo was squirming around like he had red ants in his underwear. I knew what that was–he was doing the bathroom dance, trying to hold it in. He looked like he was losing the battle. *Why doesn't he just raise his hand?* I wondered. I would soon realize there were many things about Howie I couldn't understand.

One minute to go. Mark kept laughing and whispering. I kept watching. The weirdo kept squirming, his face contorted. Then the weirdo suddenly stopped squirming.

The bell rang.

The other kids in the class got up, scurried for the doors, yapping among themselves–all except the weirdo. He just sat there, motionless now, looking straight ahead. Mark nudged me. We walked up behind the weirdo's desk, and I saw the dripping from the chair to the floor. The kid was sitting in his own water.

Mark burst out laughing. "Look at that!" he yelled. "He wet his pants!"

Some of the other kids heard him and rushed over to see. A chorus of laughter, followed by a clamor of gibes and taunts, erupted. But the weirdo just sat there, frozen. I said nothing, observing instead. I found myself studying the kid's face, wanting to know what was going on inside his head. His face held an expression that was a mixture of desperation and some kind of darkness I couldn't identify.

"Wet his pants! Wet his pants!" Mark was leading the refrain, louder and louder, as a few other kids joined in. The weirdo didn't move his head or change his expression one bit, but tears suddenly started to stream down his cheeks. I watched, fascinated, as the rivulets poured out of the kid's eyes like somebody had turned on a faucet; yet his body didn't move and his mouth didn't make a sound.

Then I heard Mark say, "Hey, baby, need a diaper?"

Without a second thought I spun around, put two hands on Mark's chest, and shoved him backward.

"Leave him alone," I said.

Mark looked shocked and angry, but before he could say anything, I felt a strong hand grab a handful of my shirt. "That's enough!" Mr. McMahon said.

McMahon was our teacher. He was about six feet four inches tall and looked like John Wayne with gas pains. We called him "Mr. McMonster." He threw me to one side and then screamed, "Everybody out!" Every kid in the room hopped to it.

Mark and I made for the door too. Just before I slipped out, I looked back one more time. Howie Patino had finally moved his head.

He was looking at me.

Now, glancing up from the hospital bed, Howie had the same expression as that first day, a sort of lost and sorrowful look. It was amazing to me. Twenty-five years had passed, and he still looked just like that kid who wet his pants.

"Hi, Jake," he said. Howie had the same pale skin with freckles, which went along with his sandy red hair. He was propped up at a forty-five-degree angle on the bed and had an IV attached to one arm. His hospital gown had light blue dots on it.

"Hey, Howie, long time," I said.

Mandy tugged at my leg. "How long do we have to stay here?" she said. I picked her up and held her up for Howie to see.

"My daughter."

Howie smiled. He still had a slight gap between his two front teeth. "Hi," he said.

Mandy put her face on my shoulder. "Shy," I said.

"I know," Howie said as if he understood every emotion in my child's life.

I walked Mandy across the room and sat her on a chair next to a small table. I opened my briefcase, took out a coloring book and crayons, and placed them on the table. "I always come prepared," I told Howie. Mandy obediently sat in a chair. "You just color me some pictures, okay?" I said.

She nodded and began selecting crayons.

I went back to Howie and pulled up a chair next to his bed. I set a legal pad on my lap and took out a pen. "Your mom called me," I explained.

"I know."

"Where is she, by the way?"

"She was tired. I told her to drive home, but she wanted to stay in Hinton to be close, I guess. I think she's at a motel."

"How you feeling?"

"It hurts."

"What did the doctor say?"

"I don't remember. I lost blood, I think. Maybe a lot."

"Can you tell me how it happened?"

Howie looked like he was trying to think and like the thoughts were oppressive. "It's so foggy, Jake."

"Where's your son?"

"Dad took him down to Agoura. I didn't want him to see me."

"Have you talked to anyone about what happened?"

"I . . . I think so."

"Who?"

"I don't know. A doctor, a nurse."

"Police?"

"I'm a little hazy, Jake."

"I know, you must be."

"You used to help me, remember?"

I nodded.

"Remember that time we were in Cub Scouts, and we had to learn how to tie some knots?"

No, I didn't remember the part about the knots, though I did remember the one year Howie and I spent in blue uniforms.

"You remember how I couldn't get it, Jake? I couldn't do a square knot or a loop knot, and everybody kept laughing at me, and I started crying and ran away?"

I started to get a vague recollection. Howie cried and ran away a lot.

"And you ran after me, Jake, and you found me, and you told me to quit crying. And then you sat me down on the curb, and you spent about two hours showing me how to do those knots. You remember?"

"I think so, Howie."

"And I got real good at it, Jake. Because of you, I started being able to tie knots. I know it probably sounds stupid, but it was real important to me. Ever since then, I love tying knots. It's something I can do."

It was so strange to hear this. I hadn't seen Howie Patino in nearly twenty years. After he and his family moved from Florida to California, he wrote me postcards and letters in a childlike scrawl. I wrote him back for the first few years and then gradually let it lapse. Eventually, the letters and cards stopped coming.

When I first moved to California, I'd heard from his parents, Janet and Fred. They were living in Agoura. They'd found out I was a lawyer and wanted to call and congratulate me. At the time Mrs. Patino said, "We always appreciated the way you treated Howie."

I was amazed they brought that up after all those years. I guess the emotional knots of Howie's childhood were still pulled tight around their memories.

"Look, Howie," I said, "your mom wanted me to see you, so maybe you better tell me everything that happened. Then I can talk things over with your mom and dad and figure out the best way to go."

"Will you be my lawyer, Jake?"

"We'll figure out what's best."

"I want you to be my lawyer."

"Let's just start at the beginning, Howie. Why don't you begin by telling me when you got married and go on from there?"

Howie took a breath and stared straight up at the ceiling. Motionless, he lay there for several moments. The strangest sense of déjà vu took over inside me. I couldn't figure out why, and then I suddenly knew.

I knew because tears were streaming down Howie's face. It was exactly like that first day in elementary school when all the kids were laughing at him. I saw the same lostness and the same darkness, which I now understood because I knew that darkness myself. It was my constant companion.

Then Howie let out a wail of such despair I actually shook. "Why'd she hate me, Jake?" he cried. "Why?"

The cop from outside suddenly blew into the room. "What's the deal?" he said.

I stood up. "Do you mind?"

"What's going on?" he insisted, stepping closer to Howie's bed. Howie turned his face away from the cop and buried it in his pillow.

"I'm conducting an attorney-client interview here," I said.

"What's he bawling about?"

"None of your business. Now let me get on with it."

"Ten minutes," the cop said. "You got ten minutes." And then he left.

"Hey, Howie, I'm sorry. It's all right."

Howie turned his face back toward me. His eyes were red and his cheeks blotchy. "I'm scared, Jake."

"I know."

I glanced over at Mandy. She was looking at us, eyes wide with astonishment. "Can we go home, Daddy?" she said.

"Not now, Mandy."

"Please?"

"Keep coloring."

"I'm hungry."

Then I realized that this meeting was not going to be anything like I'd anticipated. I thought I'd be able to talk to Howie a bit, get a rational narrative of events, maybe talk to someone in the district attorney's office, and then get a local counsel assigned–all in an afternoon with my daughter happily silent in her coloring book.

It wasn't going to happen. The emotional crosscurrents were too great, and five-year-olds don't have unlimited stores of patience. This was going to take a great deal more time to figure out. Like it or not, I was going to be Howie's attorney for a while longer.

"Look, Howie, I think we'd better wait until you're out of here before we talk. Let's get you up and around."

"Okay, Jake."

"All right. Now don't say anything to anybody about this case." This is standard legal advice for defendants. Loose lips, as the saying goes. "You got that?"

"Not even my mom?"

"Not even. I'll talk to her."

Howie's face furrowed. He wiped his nose with the back of his hand. "What's gonna happen now?"

"Nothing. They'll patch you up and get you to the point where you can be arraigned."

"What's that?"

"You appear in court and enter a plea."

"Will you be with me?"

"Yeah."

"Then what?"

"Then the process begins."

"Is there gonna be a trial?"

"I don't know."

"I don't want a trial. Just tell them I did it."

A chill ran its icy fingers up and down my spine. "Don't say *anything* to *anybody,"* I said sternly.

Howie's eyes were wide with some sort of horrific vision. "It was the devil, Jake!"

"Hold on–"

"The devil was there. He was in me! And then did it!"

"Howie, calm down."

"I did it, Jake! I did it! I killed her, man! I killed my wife! Oh, God!"

"Howie, will you–" I stopped short, sensing someone behind me. I whirled around and saw the cop, standing smug as you please in the doorway and listening to every word.

CHAPTER SIX

"YOU GOT NO business!" I yelled.

"I hear this guy screaming!" the cop said. "Whatta you want me to do?"

"Stay out of my private conference!"

The cop's face was a deep shade of red. "I got a job; I'm in charge of this guy!"

"You wouldn't know your job if it kicked you in the–" I realized Mandy was listening and shut myself up.

A nurse with squeaky shoes and an expression of extreme prejudice ran up to us. "Excuse me!" she rebuked in a loud whisper. "This is a hospital!"

I motioned Mandy to come to me. I grabbed her hand and walked silently through the door, even though several choice phrases about the cop were competing for space in my head. I headed for the elevators.

"Why did you yell at that man?" Mandy said loudly enough for the nurse and cop to hear it.

Out of the side of my mouth, I said, "I'll tell you later."

When we got out to the parking lot, it was around 3:30. I was steamed, and I wanted a drink, but I had my little girl in tow. This was not a situation conducive to civil behavior. When Mandy asked if we could get something to eat, I snapped at her to be quiet.

Then I backed my car out of its parking space a little too fast, heard the squeal of tires, and felt the impact of being bumped from behind.

I jumped out of my car spitting fire. "What's the matter with you?" I yelled, flapping my arms for added effect.

The door of the other car opened, and a young woman stepped out. She was maybe twenty-five or so and wore a white sweatshirt over light blue jeans. I noticed the jeans were a nice fit.

"I'm sorry," she said.

Not what I expected. I was ready for a fight. I wanted a fight. I wanted her to tell me that I was backing up too fast and should have been watching behind me, so I could tell her she should have kept her eyes open for other cars. I also wanted to ask her when she had taken her last driving test.

She completely disarmed me with her apology. She stepped up closer and looked at the back end of my car. Her hair was blond and hung down to the middle of her back like a swatch of silk.

"Any damage?" she said.

I took a look at my car. I couldn't see anything wrong. The whole episode, it seemed, was a perfect example of how bumpers are supposed to work. "Well, maybe not," I said. "But you really should be more careful."

"I know," she said. "I'm very sorry." Her eyes were a luminescent green. If I had been a normal male in possession of all my faculties, I would have smiled and asked if I could call her for something other than a discussion of auto repairs.

"Forget it," I said.

"Thanks. Look, if there's a problem . . ." she went back into her car, reached inside, and came out with a piece of paper. Then she put the paper on the roof of her car and wrote something on it with a pen. I was enjoying watching her write. She came back and handed me the paper. "Call me if I owe you anything."

I took the piece of paper and put it in my shirt pocket. As an L.A. resident, I guess I couldn't believe someone in today's world was actually acting like a polite human being. Maybe this Hinton was a nice little town.

"Thank you," I said.

She nodded and smiled. I watched as she returned to her car, wishing there *was* more damage to my stupid bumper so I'd have a reason to call her again.

I got back in my car and started out of the lot once again, heading for the DA's office.

"Who was that?" Mandy asked.

"Don't know."

"Did you hurt her car?"

"Hey, she ran into *me*."

"You sound mad."

"Well, maybe we ran into each other."

We drove on, and I started thinking about the Hinton district attorney. What kind of person would he be? How a criminal case is ultimately resolved depends to a large extent on the personality of the prosecutor. Some are reasonable, and some are petty. Some are ambitious, others complacent, and yet others shrewd. In short, district attorneys cover the full spectrum of humanity, with a definite leaning toward pitilessness. I guess it's understandable. When you're the sluice gate for the dregs of society, you pretty soon develop a thick skin and callused ear.

I stopped at a small market–a mom-and-pop type–and bought Mandy a bag of Fritos and a Sprite. My excuse was that this would keep her happy for another hour or two until we could get back home for dinner. I only hoped she wouldn't tell her mommy about this. I'd caught enough flak about my nutritional deficiencies from Barb.

I also picked up a copy of the *Hinton Valley News.* The killing was, of course, front-page material. There wasn't much on Howie, except that he was an itinerant construction worker who had been looking for a job in Alaska and came from Agoura. Most of the story consisted of a quotation from a police spokesperson who said the investigation was ongoing and a profile of the deceased, Rae Patino. The paper said she was a hard-working mom raising a small kid pretty much on her own.

I quickly scanned the rest of the paper, trying to get a little feel for the town. It seemed comfortable with its rural image. There was an ad for a realtor named Dotty who boasted of "planting roots in Hinton for over twenty years." A restaurant called Down Home claimed, "The service is fast, the waitresses friendly, and the food is FOOD, not Mac or Wendy's." And there were several notices of civic pride, which included a story on the renovation of the library and the addition of one hundred new volumes.

Another story caught my eye. The Hazelton Winery, located five miles to the east, had just received a blue ribbon for its Chardonnay. A picture showed a tall, lean, smiling man with a full head of gray hair. He was identified as Captain Warren Hazelton, and his arm was outstretched holding a glass of white wine. Various people were in the background, which gave the impression that this was a reception of some kind. It appeared that Hazelton was toasting the community.

I made a mental note to visit the winery some afternoon and get toasted myself.

With Mandy happily munching, I drove to the Hinton County District Attorney's Office, which was housed in a new, ugly, Spanish-style building near the main highway. The architect must have been a twisted combination of Frank Lloyd Wright and Father Junipero Serra. The mission-style roof and arched entrance clashed with the reinforced concrete and seashell configurations. If any of the prosecutors inside were grouchy, I would understand why.

I presented my card to the receptionist at the front desk and asked to see the deputy assigned to the Patino matter. She told me to wait as she picked up the phone.

Mandy was still munching her Fritos and standing ever close to my leg. On the wall to my left hung a large color photograph of a solemn-looking man in a no-nonsense blue suit. His dark hair, with a hint of gray at the temples, was cropped close to the head, almost like a Marine drill sergeant.

I took a few steps toward the picture and saw the name on a brass plate attached just below it: Benton Tolletson. I recognized the name. He was the big cheese, the county district attorney. Tolletson's expression was like an Old West marshal's, saying with his look, "This town ain't big enough for the both of us."

There was something else about the picture that bothered me so much that I could feel it in the pit of my stomach. It took me a moment, but I finally got it. It was the eyes. The look in Tolletson's eyes was almost exactly like my father's.

The receptionist said, "You can go in now."

"Where am I going?"

"Down the hall two doors. Sylvia Plotzske is the deputy."

Plotzske?

The electric door buzzed. I opened it and took Mandy by the hand down the hall. A young woman carrying several files passed us and smiled. A guy who must have been a prosecutor passed us on the other side and didn't smile at all. He looked at us like we were aliens landing in the middle of his private bog.

The open office door had no name on it. I looked in. The office was even smaller than my own. The woman behind the desk stood up and said, "Come in." She was in her early thirties and plump and looked ill at ease in her gray business suit. Her hair was brown and short, and she wore thick glasses with uncompromising black frames. Her handshake was firm and to the point. "Sylvia Plotzske," she said.

"Jake Denney."

Sylvia looked down and saw Mandy. For a moment she seemed confused and a bit annoyed.

"My daughter," I said. "We drove up from L.A."

"Oh," said Sylvia with as much warmth as a clam. "You sure you want her here?"

"You going to shoot me or something?" I said with a smile.

Sylvia Plotzske did not smile. "We are going to discuss the details of a heinous crime, Mr. Denney. I don't feel comfortable having her here."

Mandy grabbed my leg tighter.

"Let's just see what we can do," I said, sitting in the only other chair in the office. Mandy crawled up on my lap immediately, just like a puppy.

"All right then," Sylvia said. "You're representing Panino."

"Patino," I said.

"Right, right." She sat again behind her desk and looked at her file. "How'd you get connected?"

"His parents."

"You ever try any cases in Hinton?"

"Never. Had one in Ventura once."

Without looking at it, Sylvia Plotzske picked up a rubber band from the desk with her left hand and absently wrapped it around her fingers. "We're a little more laid-back here," she said. "No reason we can't wrap this thing up nice and easy."

Even for a laid-back office, this was a little fast for a plea offer. Sylvia snapped the rubber band with her thumb and said, "We're charging murder in the first, of course."

"Based on what?" I asked.

"The evidence."

I resisted the temptation to roll my eyes. "What evidence?"

"Let's start with twenty-five stab wounds."

That was one little detail I didn't know about. It hadn't been mentioned in the story from the *Hinton Valley News.* It only reported that the victim died of stab wounds. What the prosecutor was describing was butchery.

"Howie was stabbed too," I said.

"Self-inflicted."

"That's your theory?"

"That's the fact."

Mandy squirmed in my lap and pulled my head down toward her. "I have to go to the bathroom," she whispered.

With the watchful and bespectacled eyes of Sylvia Plotzske on me, I whispered back, "Can you wait a couple of minutes here?"

"I'll try," she said with a pained look.

"Problem?" said Sylvia Plotzske.

"What about a plea to involuntary manslaughter?"

She shook her head. "You're not going to get that, not with twenty-five stab wounds. We might consider second-degree murder."

"And I might consider voluntary manslaughter."

"I don't see that happening."

"Have you considered his mental state?"

"You talking heat of passion?"

"Maybe."

Sylvia Plotzske shook her head again. She was good at that. "I don't see that."

"Of course you don't," I snapped. "Why don't you take it up with Tolletson?"

Her eyes widened behind her glasses. "You know him?"

"Just the name. Run it by him."

"I'll have to get back to you."

"Howie's not a bad guy. He's not your America's Most Wanted. This isn't the case to take to the mat."

"Well, that won't be entirely my call. I'll let you know."

I lifted Mandy off my lap, set her on the floor, and stood up. I shook the hand of Sylvia Plotzske and said, "Just one more thing, if I may."

"Yes?"

"Where's the bathroom?"

CHAPTER SEVEN

FINALLY WE MADE it back home.

Before heading to the apartment, we nabbed dinner at Chipper's, which Mandy loved. For some odd reason she liked the liver and onions. That must have come from her mother's side. I can't stand liver, and onions make me sweat.

After dinner I took Mandy to 31 Flavors and got her a scoop of chocolate chip cookie dough ice cream. I was number one on her hit parade.

Then we stopped at Blockbuster, and she picked out a tape from the children's section. Back at the apartment we popped it in the VCR and cuddled up on the sofa to watch it. She was in kid heaven.

It was almost like a scene out of *Father Knows Best.* What Mandy wasn't aware of was the undercurrent of reality. Every now and then I'd get up from the movie–I think it was *The Little Mermaid*–and go into the kitchen where I had a bottle of Jim Beam in the cupboard. I must have taken six shots before the movie ended.

Mandy wanted to play a game after the movie. Because of the drinks, I wasn't in the mood.

"Please?" she pleaded, stretching out the magic word like a musical note.

"No," I said sharply. "Watch more TV."

"I don't want to. I want to play a game."

"No."

"Read me a book."

"Not now. Go color."

Her face grew suddenly dark. "You're mean," she said.

That was a new phrase, something I hadn't heard her utter before. And she was hurling it at me. It stung. "Don't you say that."

"But you are, Daddy."

"You color or watch TV!"

She started crying then and threw herself facedown on the sofa. I closed my eyes and thought hideous things about myself, all true.

The phone rang. I picked up and said, "Yeah?"

"Jake?"

"Who is it?"

"Janet Patino. I'm sorry to call you at home."

"No, no, it's fine." I fought for coherence. My mind was buzzing.

"I just had to know what's happening. I'm sorry."

"Don't apologize. I saw Howie, and I talked to the DA."

"And?"

"Nothing yet. Howie hasn't been arraigned."

"When will that happen?"

"Probably next week. Look, why don't we do this? Come into my office on Monday morning. We'll discuss it then."

"All right."

I gave her the address.

"Jake?"

"Yes, Mrs. Patino?"

"You can help Howie, can't you?"

After a short pause, I said, "Let's discuss it all on Monday."

"Thank you, Jake. Thanks for everything. We do appreciate it."

"See you Monday."

Mandy was still facedown on the sofa. I sat next to her. She kept her head in the cushions. "Hey, Scooter," I said.

She didn't move. I grabbed her around the waist and tried to pull her to me. She stiffened. It was like holding onto a petrified frog. I turned her around and hugged her close, and she finally relaxed.

Stroking her hair, I said, "I'm sorry. Daddy's sorry."

She was still crying softly.

I didn't cry. Real men don't do that sort of thing–or so I'd been taught.

Monday morning came faster than I expected. That's probably because I managed a good Saturday with Mandy. It included the park and miniature golf. Mandy seemed to forget all about the incident the night before.

Sunday we went to the beach. To top it off, my ex-wife actually arrived on time to pick up Mandy in the afternoon. I didn't ask her how her weekend went, so we didn't argue.

I was in a fairly good mood when I arrived at my office in the Lee Law Building in Encino on Monday. I parked my Mustang in the lot and trudged up the stairs. A new girl was at the reception desk again. Gil Lee had a problem with receptionist retention. He paid minimum wage for the thankless task of answering phones, making coffee, and trying to look interested when anyone came to see a lawyer.

"Hi, Marlene," I said.

"*Ei*leen."

"Sorry. Any messages?"

Eileen moved her head in super-slow-motion to check the message tray. She was supposedly a college graduate. I thought she must have majored in sleepwalking.

"No," she said.

I smiled and nodded. Eileen closed her eyes momentarily. I took that opportunity to walk down the hall to the coffeemaker. I poured myself a cup, then went to my office.

It was in the back corner of the building. Normally lawyers look upon a corner office as a sign of prestige and success. They usually have a nice view too. My office looked out on a couple of black dumpsters, an alley, and the rear of Bob's Hot Dog Palace, a one-man operation that was as much like a palace as my office was like a suite. That's probably why I liked to eat regularly at Bob's. We both knew what it was like to operate out of a shoebox.

Once inside, I closed the door and stepped over the boxes and files on the floor. I had developed a sophisticated filing system by this time, one that involved random placement and luck. It usually took me half a day to find something crucial, which didn't matter much at this point because very little on the floor was crucial.

I threw my briefcase on the desk and opened it.

I told myself regularly that I didn't have a drinking problem. I could control it. However, I didn't have any files in my briefcase. I had a pint of bourbon instead.

I opened the bottle and poured some in my coffee, then put the bottle in a drawer.

A quick knock on my door. "Come in," I said.

Gil Lee entered. He was wearing another of his seriously loud ties, this one a mishmash of so many bright colors I was tempted to squint. "Sheesh, this place is a mess," he said.

"I know where everything is, so don't say anything."

"If you know, you know. I only lease the joint. But I hope you don't see clients in here."

"Matter of fact," I said, "I have a couple coming in today. I was just about to clean up a little."

"A little?"

"You wanted to see me?"

Gil stepped around a box and sat in one of my formerly plush chairs. "Look," he said, "I don't want to get into a big thing, Jake. You know me. I like you."

"What's not to like?"

"I've got bills to pay."

"You need a nice, juicy medical malpractice claim, Gil, or maybe a police brutality so you can sue the city."

Gil didn't smile, which indicated that my attempts at charming him off the subject weren't working. "Jake, I need the rent."

I knew that wasn't easy for Gil to say. He liked to look on his tenants not only as lessees but as his charges. He had a tradition of taking each new tenant for a fatherly lunch at Subway where he would informally pass on his wisdom, like Yoda. Gil actually resembled Yoda with his round face, peeper eyes, and gray hair. At our lunch he told me he knew all about my problems and wanted to help me get back on my feet.

That he knew was no surprise. Everyone in the Los Angeles legal community knew about my "problems." They had been splashed all over the front page of the *Los Angeles Daily Journal,* our legal newspaper. How could they avoid the juicy headline, "Lawyer for Drunk Driver Shows Up Drunk in Court"?

I was a deputy public defender at the time working in the San Fernando office. Without false modesty, I can say I was a rising star. My first year I'd gotten three straight acquittals, which is no small feat. In 95 percent of cases, defendants are convicted, either in trial or by plea. For a public defender to get even one acquittal was noteworthy.

My drinking was steady, but I picked my spots. I'd been doing that since I was nine. I thought I could always pick my spots, but soon after I was married, the spots started picking me.

Drinking started to affect my work. I had to be taken off a few cases. The head deputy had me in his office a couple of times to express his concern. I was put on a mild probation.

Then I got handed the case of Mr. Rudy Noble.

A real piece of work, Mr. Noble. He was an electrician who liked to drink and hit women. He had pleaded to one battery a couple of years before but was not above admitting to me, with a smile yet, that they hadn't caught him on several others.

But that was not why Mr. Rudy Noble was my client.

He was my client because he got drunk one night with his buddies, then drove his Chevy pickup through a red light at the intersection of Rinaldi and Sepulveda, and plowed into a Ford Tempo. The Tempo was driven by a man named Julio Sanchez who had his three-year-old daughter, Ines, in the back seat. Mr. Noble and Mr. Sanchez sustained minor injuries. Ines died at the scene.

Noble was charged with vehicular manslaughter while intoxicated under Penal Code section 192. I advised him to plead out, which might have gotten him probation and treatment. If he went to trial, he was looking at state prison.

Mr. Rudy Noble told me he was not going to plead guilty. I asked him why. And he said that he wasn't going to admit any guilt, ever, just for killing a Mexican.

A criminal defense lawyer is obligated, under the Code of Professional Responsibility, to represent his client with zeal even if he appears to be guilty. This obligation had never been a problem with me. I understood and agreed with the United States Constitution and the right of every citizen to a fair trial. The founding fathers knew what they were doing. They just didn't know Rudy Noble.

On the morning of September 12, we picked a jury. My strategy was to contest the breath test that showed Noble had a .13% blood alcohol content, the color of the light, and the observations of the prosecution's witnesses. All standard stuff. I don't really remember the makeup of the jury because I didn't care. I was sleepwalking.

Just before the lunch break, as the deputy sheriff was about to return Noble to the lockup, my client leaned over and whispered to me, "You're the man."

It was a jock phrase, one that is uttered usually by one teammate to another as an encouragement, an expression of common support. Coming from Rudy Noble, it made me physically ill.

I went to a bar for lunch to prepare for my opening statement. I sat on a stool and stared at a blank legal pad for one hour and fifteen minutes. I did not make a single note, but I drank volumes.

The next thing I remember is sitting at the counsel table with Noble sitting next to me and the jury coming in. I had my eyes closed. Noble leaned over and asked me if I was okay. That's when I almost threw up.

I heard the judge ask for the lawyers to state their appearances. I think I heard the prosecutor state hers.

I said nothing.

The judge, an ex-cop and deputy DA, called my name a couple of times.

I don't remember what happened next. From the account in the *Daily Journal,* I apparently told the judge, with the help of a well-known epithet, to leave me alone.

I do remember being hauled back into the prisoner's lockup by a burly sheriff and having an AlcoSensor shoved in my mouth. The AlcoSensor's a handheld breath tester that gives a preliminary reading on the amount of alcohol in the system.

It was all over for me as a member of the public defender's office and almost as a lawyer. Only my admission into an alcohol program and severe groveling kept me from being disbarred.

I might have stopped practicing law altogether if Gil hadn't rented me an office for less than he usually asked. It was my last hope, a life preserver tossed out to a bad swimmer in a choppy sea.

Gil took no pleasure in informing me that he was about to yank the life preserver back onboard his ship.

"I know you need the rent, Gil," I said. "I just got a case."

"What kind?"

"Criminal. A murder."

Gil rolled his eyes. We both knew that criminal cases provided the worst form of income for a private lawyer unless he represented white-collar criminals or the Mafia. "Well, then, remember the first rule of the criminal lawyer," Gil said. "Get the money up front. Because if you don't, they'll stiff you sure as Richard Simmons sweats. If they're convicted, they figure you're worthless. If they're acquitted, they think, 'Why did I need him in the first place?'"

The phone buzzed. Eileen, in a voice that gave new meaning to the word *apathetic,* said, "Some people are here to see you."

With Gil's help, I shoved all the detritus on my floor to one corner and swept off the top of my desk. Gil bowed out just as Janet and Fred Patino entered my office.

Behind them was the last person I expected to see.

CHAPTER EIGHT

"THIS IS HOWIE'S sister," Janet Patino explained. "You remember Lindsay, don't you?"

Openmouthed, I looked at the woman whose car bumped me in the Hinton hospital parking lot. She seemed equally astounded.

I pointed at her. "You're not . . ."

Lindsay Patino nodded and smiled. "Yep. The bratty kid sister who used to annoy you. I guess I still do, with my car."

"I never would have recognized you."

"I've grown up a little bit."

Yes, I thought, *in many good ways.* Fred and Janet looked the same, just older. Fred was stocky, perfect for the lumber business, and still had a rugged complexion. Janet had the same, soft look about her–very motherly–only now her hair was almost entirely gray.

Then I saw something move in back of Fred. A small body was tucked somewhere behind his thigh. "And this," Fred said, "is Brian. He's a little shy."

Fred lifted the little arm and brought Howie's son around in front of him. The boy, sandy-haired and thin, put his face in Fred's stomach. "It's all right," Fred said to Brian, but clearly the boy did not feel like socializing.

"Hey," I said, "would Brian like to see me take off my thumb?"

Smiling, Fred said, "Did you hear that, Brian?"

"I have a little girl," I said, "and she's your age, Brian. She likes to see me take my thumb off, too."

Slowly the tiny head turned, just enough so one eye ventured a look my way.

"Here I go," I said. I held up my left hand with the thumb in the air, then put my right hand over the thumb. Just before closing my fist, I sent the left thumb down into my left palm. I pulled my right hand upward and *voilà,* no thumb!

The boy's head came all the way out, and his mouth dropped wide open.

"I'd better put it back," I said, and with a quick move, I brought my right hand down on my left again and shot the thumb back up. No one will ever confuse me with Houdini, but I'm perfect for a five-year-old audience of one.

Brian broke out in a huge smile. He looked up at Fred and said, "Did you see that!"

"I sure did," Fred said. "Mr. Denney is a pretty clever fella."

"I've got something else for Brian," I said. I reached in a drawer and pulled out a couple of Dr. Seuss books I kept for Mandy. "There are some funny pictures in these." I held them out for Brian, and he took them eagerly. Fred told him to sit on the floor by the door, and Brian did so, spreading the books in front of him.

I motioned for the others to sit. There were only two chairs, so Fred remained standing.

As I spoke, I kept looking over at Brian, making sure he wasn't listening. Fortunately, he was lost in the Dr. Seuss books and had easily tuned out the adult talk.

"How's he taking things?" I said softly.

Fred and Janet exchanged pained looks. "He doesn't know," Fred said. "We just haven't . . ."

A quick sob escaped Janet's mouth. Fred put his hand on her shoulder.

"I understand," I said. "Let me try to lay this out as easily as I can. This is, of course, a serious charge. If we go to trial and lose, Howie is facing twenty-five years to life in prison."

Brian was still looking at pictures.

"That's the punishment for first-degree murder," I continued, "but I don't think they can get that. It's possible, of course, and we'll know more as the evidence comes in. I don't think they can do it, however. The most they can hope to prove, in my opinion, is second-degree murder."

"And what would happen then?" Fred asked.

"That carries a term of fifteen to life."

A thick silence filled my office. Quickly, I said, "But there's good news."

Janet Patino sat up a little in her chair. Lindsay folded her arms.

"I talked to the prosecutor up there, and I think there's a good chance this case can be settled before trial if Howie pleads to manslaughter. Don't know yet whether they'll go for voluntary or involuntary, but either way, it's going to be significantly easier on Howie."

"Will he still go to prison?" Fred asked.

"Depends on what he pleads to, but whatever it is, his term will be a lot less than for murder."

"When will we know?" Janet asked.

"I'll keep you posted as negotiations continue."

Suddenly, Lindsay Patino jumped to her feet. "I can't believe this!" she said. "You're all assuming Howie's guilty!" She turned and faced me directly. "And you're already negotiating like he's some sort of pawn in a great big game!"

"Lindsay!" Fred said.

Brian looked up from his books. "Whatsa matter with Aunt Lindsay?" he said.

"Doesn't this bother you, Dad?" Lindsay said.

"I'm sure Jake knows what he's–"

"This is Howie's *life* we're talking about!"

"Whatsa matter?" Brian repeated.

Janet got up from her chair. "Let me take him outside," she said. She gathered up the books and took Brian by the hand.

"But whatsa matter?" he asked once more as Janet guided him out.

After the door closed, I said, "I understand Lindsay's point." I was going to talk her down. She looked at me like she knew exactly what I was doing. I went ahead anyway. "This is a tragedy, a terrible tragedy for a family to face. Believe me, if there were a better way to go, I would."

"What about he didn't do it?" Lindsay said. The green eyes that had been so friendly and understanding in the parking lot now smoldered.

"As I said, if there were–"

"I'm telling you, he didn't do it!"

I thought for a moment that she had some bit of inside information or a piece of exonerating evidence. But I quickly realized that this was a sister talking more out of love than rationality.

"Lindsay, I–"

"And you're just going to let them take Howie and put him away. He'll die if he goes to prison. He'll die there!"

"No one wants–"

"They'll kill him. He's gentle . . . he's . . . he could never have killed Rae, even though she deserved it."

"Lindsay!" Fred said.

His daughter didn't stop. "I know Howie, and I know he could not have done this thing, never, ever. And if you just sell him out, you're not worth a thing."

"Stop it!" Fred Patino yelled. Lindsay, perhaps realizing she'd gone too far, shook her head and stopped talking. "Jake," Fred said, "I'm sorry."

"No, no," I said. "Forget about it. Look, there's something you should know. When I went to see Howie, he told me he did it. He told me he killed his wife."

I looked at Lindsay. She was glaring at me, the seething emotion still all over her face. Her eyes were moist.

"We just have to deal with that," I said.

Silence filled the room for a few moments. Then Fred spoke. "What about being insane? Is there a possibility?"

"I wish there were," I said, "but it's practically impossible to prove. We would have to show that Howie was incapable–*incapable*–of knowing right from wrong at the time of the act. Is there anything in his recent past that would show this?"

Fred shook his head. "What about, you know, mental retardation?" Fred said.

Nodding, I said, "That would be an issue at trial on whether or not Howie could actually form the requisite intent for murder. It wouldn't be a complete defense though."

"It's all so mixed up," Fred said.

"And traumatic," I said, "for all of us. Howie was my friend."

Lindsay huffed. I was starting to get ticked off at her.

I continued, "I'd like to get him the best deal we can. If we take this thing to trial and lose, his punishment will be much worse."

"Then don't lose," Lindsay said.

"We'll do whatever you say, Jake," Fred said.

"Thank you," I said. "Let's talk after the arraignment."

After they left I poured a healthy shot of bourbon in my coffee cup and drank the whole thing down in a gulp. Then I sat and crumpled blank legal paper into fist-sized balls and tossed them against the door.

All the while I kept thinking about Lindsay Patino.

Mostly I was angry. Where did she get off telling me I wasn't "worth a thing"? I could understand a little emotion, but this was an insult delivered right between the eyes. The fair side of my mind told me she had only said it because she thought I was going to sell out Howie. But I didn't want to be fair; I wanted to be angry.

I wanted to continue being angry because I realized there was more than a little truth in what she was saying. I *didn't* really want to dig deeper into this case. It looked like a dead bang loser, only with a check attached. Janet and Fred Patino had left me a fifteen-hundred-dollar retainer even though Lindsay had protested the payment. She wasn't only questioning my ethics, she was trying to take away my next meal.

There was something else going on inside my besotted brain. It was simple, straight, pure, physical attraction for Lindsay Patino.

She was strikingly beautiful, but there was something else about her. Maybe it was the spark in her anger. She was passionate, and she had perception. She could see right through me and didn't mind saying what she thought.

One thing I knew–I wasn't going to leave things like this. I was going to see Lindsay Patino again soon and set her straight on my motives and abilities.

I was also going to do a little more digging in the matter of the *People of the State of California. v. Howard Patino,* just to show her and to justify the check.

I picked up the phone, flipped through my Rolodex, and dialed. I got the following deep-voiced message: "Hello, this is the office of Carr Investigatory Services. I can't take your call at the moment, but if you'll leave a detailed message, I will return your call as soon as possible. Thank you."

Beep.

"This is the Federal Bureau of Investigation," I said. "We have reason to believe you are engaged in consumer fraud, advertising yourself as a service, when it is well-known that you couldn't find your way out of a paper–"

"Jake Denney!" said Cyril Cornelius Carr on the other end of the line. "Now why'd you want to go and spoil my day like that?"

"Why, Triple C, how'd you know it was me?"

"Who else hath neither wit, nor words, nor the power of speech?"

"Thanks, pal. What's that, *Midsummer Night's Dream?*"

"Julius Caesar. Paraphrased."

"So you want to get off your . . . quotes and do some real work?"

"How much and how much?"

"Not much and what I can afford."

"Meet me at my outside office in half an hour. Your treat."

"Wait a minute!"

"Put money in thy purse. *Othello.* Act one, scene three."

He hung up.

I checked my wallet to make sure I had some bills, then made for my Mustang.

CHAPTER NINE

CYRIL CORNELIUS CARR liked to take his meetings at Sal's Deli on Van Nuys Boulevard. This was partly because his office, like mine, was usually an unsightly mess and partly because only Sal's famous sky-high pastrami sandwiches with Russian dressing could satisfy Cyril's prodigious appetite. Even though he was forty-five years old, he still looked like he could tear through the Green Bay Packers, offensive line.

Cyril Cornelius Carr–sometimes called Triple C, Trip, or just plain C–was one of the more colorful characters I'd ever met, and that doesn't just refer to the loud Hawaiian shirts he favored. He had grown up in south Philly and might have ended up another gang statistic if it hadn't been for his grandmother, Pearl, who raised him after his mother died. She was one tough lady who used the Bible and a leather strap to keep Trip on the straight and narrow. Even when he outgrew her by six inches and 150 pounds, Triple C obeyed her every word.

What he got as a result was a 3.9 grade point average in high school and an academic scholarship to Princeton, even though he had his pick of major football schools offering full scholarships. He was All-Ivy defensive end his sophomore year and was destined for the NFL. An illegal block by a Harvard man blew out his knee and any hope of pro ball.

Cyril Cornelius Carr was not dismayed. Football had really only been a lark for him. He had a hundred different interests, one of which was literature. It just so happened that Princeton's big theatrical production the spring of Trip's injury was *Othello.* Even though he'd never acted in his life, he memorized the entire part in a week, walked into the auditions, and won the lead.

Thus began his love affair with Shakespeare.

After graduation, Trip moved to Hollywood to take up an acting career. A few years later, after being cast as one heavy too many, he gave it up and joined the Los Angeles Police Department. Five years later he was an investigator for the district attorney's office. He was married by this time to a beautiful gal named Victoria, and everything seemed rosy.

Then Victoria died in a terrible accident on the 405 Freeway, skidding into a tanker truck on a rain-slicked road.

Trip had to go on stress leave after that and eventually resigned. It took him a year to get his life back together. He started going to church again, and that, he said, started his turnaround. He opened his own office because he said he couldn't stand the thought of working for anyone else again. He never remarried, and as far as I knew, didn't even have a girlfriend. His work for clients and for the Van Nuys First Baptist Church were everything to him.

Trip was at a table by the window, reading a book. Even though his back was to me, I couldn't miss him. He overflowed his chair and was wearing a yellow Hawaiian shirt with pineapples and *humu-humu* fish on it.

"Whatta you say, Trip?" I slapped him on the back hard enough to make noise.

"You still hit like a girl," Triple C said. He was wearing sunglasses and a gold cross around his neck. "My grandma would take you out."

"No doubt." I sat in the chair opposite him. "You're looking prosperous."

"Can't complain, though I could give a good imitation."

"Anything big right now?"

"Just you, baby."

A waitress came by for our order. For Trip it was the sky-high pastrami. I ordered matzo ball soup and a beer.

"Still drinking, I see," Trip said.

I shrugged. "It's not a problem."

"Don't play me, man."

"Hey, I didn't come here to talk about me."

"I just don't want to see you fall again."

"I won't."

"You tried AA?"

"I don't go in for that."

"In for what?"

"All that 'higher power' stuff. I went to a couple of meetings, but everyone there was into this authority from on high."

"Hey, man, there are more things in heaven and earth than are dreamt of in your philosophy." Trip was the only person I ever met who could go from street talk to Shakespearean verse without missing a beat. "When you coming to church with me?"

"How about when pigs fly?"

"I can arrange that."

I looked at the ceiling. "I've got a case, and I need your help. You interested or not?"

Trip took his shades off and laid them on the table. "All right, gimme the 411."

"It's a murder case. Guy I knew when I was a kid. Killed his wife."

"How?"

"Stabbed her. I mean, really messed her up. Then he stabbed himself."

Trip nodded. "Classic cover-up. Never works though. I had this case once where a guy blew off his own foot with a shotgun after he shot his girlfriend. All that got him was a fake foot and twenty-five to life."

"His sister says he didn't do it."

"What else is new?"

"He says he did."

"He confessed?"

"To me he did."

"You taking it to trial?"

"No way. We'll take a deal."

"So what do you want me for?"

"I'd like you to find out something about the wife."

"Why?"

"His sister, she didn't have too high an opinion of her."

"Maybe that's why the guy O. J.'d her."

"That's what I was thinking. If you talk to somebody who knew her, especially over the last couple of years, maybe something will come up, and I can tell the sister about it."

Cyril Cornelius Carr looked at me through squinting eyes. Then all of a sudden, an enormous smile lit up his face. Triple C had one of those incandescent smiles, like the Cheshire Cat or Magic Johnson.

"Jake Denney! Is this the very ecstasy of love?"

My face took on a little heat. "What are you talking about?"

"You had a certain look. Am I wrong?"

"I told you to leave me out of it."

"It's all over your face, man."

Thankfully, the waitress picked that moment to deliver my beer. I took a long, satisfying pull. Trip watched me with concern, but I didn't care. In fact, I ordered another. Triple C agreed to drive up to Hinton and interview a couple of people. And over the course of the lunch, he didn't lapse into Shakespeare again until just as I was about to leave.

That's when he said, "Thou hast very poor and unhappy brains for drinking."

I didn't stay to applaud.

CHAPTER TEN

ON WEDNESDAY MORNING I arrived in Hinton for the arraignment of Howard Patino in the courtroom of Judge Oswald Mellor. I knew nothing about Mellor except what I picked up from another lawyer in the hallway. Mellor, like most judges in the law-and-order atmosphere of California, was a former prosecutor. He liked to pretend he was the folksy type, this lawyer told me, sort of like Andy Griffith. "He'll sell you crackers and cornpone before he slams your client in the clink," the lawyer said.

Maybe that's why Sylvia Plotzske wore a slight smile as she entered with her files and plopped them on the prosecution table. I didn't give her time to get into them.

"Good morning," I said, with just the right mix of civility and churlishness.

"Give me a moment, please," she said. I merely stood there as she fussed with her files for a minute or two, making herself look busy. Finally she acknowledged my presence again and said, "I spoke with Tolletson about this case."

"Yes?"

"And we really can't offer anything less than second degree."

"You could if you really wanted to."

"This was a shocking crime, Mr. Dennis–"

"Denney."

"–and it just isn't going to go any lower."

I didn't know Sylvia Plotzske well enough yet to know whether this was a bluff or not. My guess was that it wasn't. She didn't seem the type, and she was probably just following the dictates of her boss on this one.

"I'm going to need some time to think about it," I said.

"You can have until the prelim," she answered.

There was nothing more to say. I took a chair and waited for the judge.

At 8:55, three jail inmates were marched in by deputy sheriffs and seated in the jury box. One of them was Howie. He looked pale and scared, or maybe just horribly confused. I walked over to the box and waited for the sheriff to remove the shackles.

"How you doing?" I asked.

"What's going on, Jake?"

"You're going to enter a plea this morning. That gets us on track for the preliminary hearing."

"Do I plead guilty?"

"Not yet. You plead not guilty."

"But–"

"Buy us some time."

"But–"

"Okay?"

Howie looked at his hands. "I'll do what you tell me, Jake, but I want to confess. I want to get this over with. I want to clear my soul."

He was starting to move down the path toward hysteria, so I put my hands up to calm him down. He lowered his voice to a whisper. "I been having dreams every night, Jake. The devil is in them. He's going to take me if I don't confess!"

"Howie, you trust me, don't you?"

"Yes."

"Let's do it my way."

"But–"

Judge Oswald Mellor entered the courtroom. The bailiff called everyone to order as I motioned to Howie to sit down.

"Morning, ya'll," Mellor said. He was graying and in his sixties, with short hair that was a bit unruly. It was almost like the look was studied and intended to portray an air of informality.

He called the first case. One of the other jail inmates stood at the jury box rail as his lawyer joined him. It was a felony battery. Judge Mellor read a litany of rights and asked the defendant if he understood them. He said he did, then entered a plea of not guilty. A prelim was set, and the defendant disappeared back into the bowels of the courthouse lockup.

Then Mellor called our case.

I stood and said, "Good morning, Your Honor. Jake Denney on behalf, Howard Patino."

"Morning, Mr. Denney. Nice to have you here."

"Thank you, Your Honor."

"Hope it stays that way." The judge winked at his bailiff who smiled. "We don't usually get city folks up here."

"Well, that works out," I said. "We don't usually get the rubes down there."

Mellor didn't smile, and I immediately realized my blunder. You don't joke with a judge who wants to be the head comedian. And you especially don't fling humorous insults back at him as if he were a drinking buddy. I felt the other lawyers looking at me like they couldn't believe I could be so dumb.

Quickly, I said, "We'll waive a reading of the complaint and statement of rights, and my client is ready to enter a plea." I joined Howie at the jury box.

"Son," the judge said, "do you understand the charges against you?"

Howie looked at me, and I nodded at him. Howie said, "Yes."

"How do you plead?"

Again Howie looked at me. I whispered, "Not guilty," but Howie shook his head.

"*Not guilty,*" I whispered, a little louder this time.

Howie just looked at me like the proverbial deer caught in the headlights.

"Mr. Denney?" the judge said. "Is your client ready to enter a plea?"

"Yes, Your Honor," Turning again to Howie, I whispered, "Do it!"

Howie looked down and mumbled, "Not guilty."

"How's that?" the judge said.

I glared at Howie. He raised his voice a little. "Not guilty."

"All right," Judge Mellor said. "Preliminary hearing is set for a week from Monday in Judge Abovian's court. You have any thoughts on bail, Ms. Plotzske?"

Sylvia Plotzske stood. "Yes, Your Honor. We request that the defendant be held without bail. This was an act of extreme violence, shocking to this community. The victim sustained at least twenty-five stab wounds. In addition, it's clear that this defendant has no ties to the community. He's been living in Alaska for the last several months. He's a flight risk as well as a danger."

The judge looked at me with a frown.

"Your Honor," I said, "it is not true that my client has no ties to this community. He has his son, Brian. He's not going to abandon him. The boy's staying with Mr. Patino's parents now, and he wants to see him, to be a father to him. He is not going to flee."

The judge kept his frown intact.

"And my client has no prior record of violence. There is nothing in his past to indicate he is a threat to anyone. I don't think the prosecutor has shown by clear and convincing evidence that he is."

"Twenty-five stab wounds is pretty convincing," the judge said.

"Again, look to my client's past."

Judge Mellor said, "Bail set at five hundred thousand. Let's go to the next case."

"Your Honor?" I said.

Mellor looked at me like I'd interrupted his lunch. "What is it?"

"I'd like to request the appointment of a confidential psychiatrist."

"You want him evaluated for mental competency?"

"Yes, Your Honor."

"Denied."

"I think this is a necessary step."

"I don't. If you want him evaluated on your dime, go ahead. But I don't see any evidence of incapacity here."

"That's what the evaluation is for, Your Honor, to–"

"Denied. Next case."

And with that, I was dismissed. I told Howie to hang in there a little longer and reminded him not to talk to anyone. He was just about to be taken back into the lockup when he said, "You only said one wrong thing, Jake."

"What was that?"

"I don't want Brian back. I want him to forget about me. I'm no good for him." He turned around and went with the sheriff.

I didn't say anything to Sylvia Plotzske before I left. There was no need to. We could both read the handwriting on the wall of the Hinton County Courthouse.

Howie was going to do some serious time in prison.

CHAPTER ELEVEN

I HAD TO let Lindsay Patino know the reality of her brother's situation.

I also wanted to see her again.

As soon as I got on the freeway, I took my PCS phone and called the work number she had given me that day at the hospital. A young lady answered, "Agoura Christian School."

I asked for Lindsay. The young lady said she was in class.

"This is kind of an emergency," I said, which was only about one-third true, even though it was an emergency of my own making–I had decided I needed to talk to her *now.*

"Who's calling?"

"Tell her it's her brother's lawyer."

"Oh, I'll get her right away."

A few minutes later Lindsay came on the line. Her tone was frosty. "Yes?"

"Hi, we just finished the arraignment."

"And?"

"I'd like to talk to you about it."

A pause. "When?"

"How about in the next hour?"

"I'm teaching."

"You have to eat lunch."

"It's in a brown bag."

"It's very important that I talk to you. I have a lot of things to explain." I added, "And I thought, why not make it a pleasant experience?"

"All right. I'll meet you in front of the school at 11:45 A.M." She gave me directions and hung up.

For the next forty-five minutes, as I drove south, I was in a very good mood. I found that curious. I hadn't been in a good mood in a year.

The Agoura Christian School was part of a church property in the middle of a residential area. A nicely manicured lawn gave the church itself a homey feel. Lindsay was standing in front of the entrance talking to another woman. When she saw my car, she gave the other woman a pat on the shoulder and walked over.

"Hop in," I said.

She did.

"Is there a place around here you like?" I asked.

"There's an Italian place about a mile from here."

"Italian it is."

Three minutes later we pulled into a mall parking lot near Amato's Italian Kitchen. Lindsay didn't speak a word until we were seated at a table with a black-and-white checkerboard tablecloth.

As soon as we sat down, Lindsay said, "I'm sorry I got so upset with you in your office."

"It's all right."

"It isn't. I was very upset, but that's no excuse. I've got a bit of a temper."

"I've been known to lash out myself."

"But that doesn't mean I'm any less concerned about how you handle Howie's case."

"Understood."

A waiter arrived, and I ordered a beer. Lindsay ordered a Coke. As she did, I swiped a long look at her. She was ravishing, and while it's not the most romantic of memories, I think I fell in love with her the moment she said, "With a slice of lemon, please."

"So you're little Lindsay," I said.

That finally got a smile out of her. "You remember?"

"Sure. You had buckteeth and freckles."

"Major buckteeth."

"You used to follow us around, Howie and me. You had this squeaky little voice."

"Was I obnoxious?"

"Yes." I was relieved when she blushed and smiled. "But it's obviously worn off. And no more buckteeth."

"Orthodontia," she said.

"Now you're a teacher?"

"Fourth grade."

"How long?"

"This is my third year at Agoura Christian."

"Why not public school?"

"Because I couldn't teach about God."

I took the beer from the waiter and sipped. Lindsay Patino didn't fit my stereotype of a religious teacher-type. Admittedly, what I had in mind was a cliché: severe gray hair pulled into a tight bun; a long dress; black, sensible shoes. Lindsay was the very opposite.

"How did you come to this career choice?" I asked.

She shrugged her shoulders. "I felt called to it."

"I guess I don't really understand that."

"Why did you go into law?"

"Money," I said.

"I don't believe that." She was looking at me the same way she did at my office–like she could see into corners I was trying to keep hidden.

"Anyway," I said, "I can certainly think of several hundred other things that probably would have been better to go into."

"Like what?"

"Dog catcher, for instance."

She smiled. "You're a cynic."

"Maybe. But that's the kind of world we live in. At one time I thought the law was a great and glorious thing, able to hold society together and bring justice to people. You get disabused of that notion real quick."

She thought about that for a moment, then said, "Is that why you're so ready to make Howie plead guilty?"

Now it was time for my lecture. "I really want you to understand the way it works, Lindsay. Remember, Howie's my friend from way back. I only want what's best for him. And that means getting him through this with the least possible pain."

She listened, looking skeptical.

"Howie is facing a lot of pain in terms of jail time. Possible life sentence. What I'm trying to do is reach an agreement with the prosecutors that will lessen that significantly. The hard reality is, he'll have to do time. The crime is just too heinous to avoid it."

Lindsay flinched a little. I said, "I don't know why Howie would be driven to do something like that. I mean, who really understands the human mind? But it happened, and we just have to deal with it."

"What about the possibility that he didn't do it?" Lindsay said forcefully. "Has anyone looked into that?"

"Howie confessed, Lindsay. He's admitted it."

"You must know that people have been known to confess to crimes they didn't commit, for a variety of reasons."

"Where did you pick that up?"

"I read, Jake. There was something in the paper not too long ago about this. A study by a couple of psychologists showed that false confessions are a big reason for innocent people being locked up."

"Yes, I–"

"And one reason was what they called 'internalized confessions,' where an innocent person comes to believe he actually did something he didn't do because of police coercion or guilt or something else."

"I think I–"

"And the most susceptible to this type of confession are people who are of lower intelligence, subject to suggestion, and highly trusting of people. All of which Howie is."

Finally, she paused for a breath. "That may all be true," I said, "but there is no evidence of it in Howie's case."

"Have you looked for the evidence?"

I shook my head.

"All I'm saying is I know Howie. I know him better than anyone. He was always innocent and trusting and never violent. Never. He cried once when he accidentally killed a butterfly. He was twenty years old."

That seemed like the Howie I had known.

"There's no way he would kill his wife."

"You mentioned in my office that she might have deserved it."

"I was angry when I said it."

"But it had some truth?"

"She was a terrible person."

"That's important to know. Even a sweet, good-natured dog can bite if provoked."

Lindsay shook her head. "Not Howie."

"Tell me about his wife."

"Oh, boy." She leaned back in her chair as if to gather strength. "I don't know where to start. No one wanted him to marry her, but he fell hard. I mean, Howie never had girlfriends growing up. So when Rae came along and actually made out like she liked him, it was all over."

"If you don't mind my asking, what was in it for her?"

"I don't mind. I've asked myself that over and over. I wish I knew more about Rae's background, where she came from, her family and all that. But she never talked about it. It was like some deep, dark secret. I just got the impression she was pretty messed up."

"Was she good looking?"

"Not particularly, but she made every effort to make herself look . . ."

"How?"

"Sexy, provocative."

"I still don't know how Howie gets involved."

Lindsay shook her head as she looked at the table. "It may be a wild thought, but I think Howie was an experiment for her."

"Experiment?"

"Yeah, like her guinea pig. She wanted to see just how much she could control a man, and Howie was the one she picked."

"She had a child with him."

"That's another thing, the way she was with Brian. It was like she had him, then didn't want him around. She proved she could have a baby, but she didn't want him to get in her way."

"Doing what?"

"Whatever she wanted to do. Howie was working like crazy in construction, trying to give her everything she wanted. But she'd gotten all she wanted out of him. She started talking about divorce. Howie got desperate. Then he got this crazy idea that if he went to Alaska and got a job up there, it would make everything all right."

"Why Alaska?"

"Probably because it represented a fresh start, a totally different world."

"Did Howie ever talk to you about any of this?"

Lindsay nodded. "I was the only one he could talk to. And never once did he say he wanted to kill Rae or wished she would go away or any of that. She was all he lived for."

The waitress delivered our food. I ordered another beer. As I picked up my fork, I said, "I'll look into this, Lindsay. But I can't promise you anything. You've got to believe that I've got Howie's best interest in mind."

She looked at me, this time with a softer expression than ever before. "I know," she said. "Thanks for listening."

And at that moment I fell even deeper for her, desperate about it, wanting her like I've never wanted anything or anyone else before. Disturbed, I tried to shake it off with a long sip of beer. I didn't want her to see anything of this in me, so I switched gears and started talking about other things, trivial matters.

Finally, toward the end of lunch, I took my shot. "I wonder if we might do this again sometime," I said.

"Lunch?"

"Or dinner. How about dinner next time?"

She blushed just a little and smiled. "Thank you for asking, but . . . I don't think so."

I wasn't about to shrug this off. "And why's that?"

"I . . . it's difficult to explain."

Now I was more intrigued than ever. "Try me."

She looked at me half apologetically, which gave me reason to hope. "I made a decision a long time ago not to date anyone that didn't share my faith. I tried it before, and it ended up pretty bad."

"I'm not a bad person."

"I know. But I've thought about it a lot, and I just decided that's what I have to do. It's nothing personal. Really."

She said it, and I believed her. But inside I felt like somebody kicked me. The ache stayed with me as I dropped her back at her school and broke the speed limit back to the Valley.

CHAPTER TWELVE

THE FIREWORKS STARTED early on Monday morning.

I arrived at the Hinton County Courthouse for the preliminary hearing, which was being held in the realm of Judge Armen Abovian. I knew nothing about him and didn't intend to find out. My goal was to settle the case on the best possible terms I could get for Howie and then get out of town and out of the lives of the Patino family once and for all.

I had finally shaken Lindsay Patino out of my mind. I did it with a combination of booze and ill feeling. By working myself up into a lather about her superior attitude–not wanting to date awful pagans like me–I managed to form a negative picture in my mind about her so she wouldn't bother me anymore. I would never have to see her again.

That expectation got shot down immediately when I walked into the courtroom and saw Janet, Fred, and Lindsay Patino all sitting there waiting for me.

Naturally, Janet and Fred wanted to know what was going to happen. I danced around the question, saying this was merely the first big stage of a felony proceeding, where a judge hears the prosecution's evidence and decides if there is "probable cause" to send the defendant to Superior Court for trial.

I didn't tell them I had no intention of conducting a preliminary hearing but was here only to get the quickest and best deal I could before the morning was out.

Lindsay seemed glad to see me. "Why aren't you teaching?" I asked.

"I got the day off to be here. I wanted to support Howie."

"I can't promise any breakthrough."

She put her hand on my arm and said, "I know. I know you'll do what you think is best."

I wished she hadn't said that because it brought back both my longing for her and a fresh sense of self-loathing. I covered both with a stupid smile as I saw Sylvia Plotzske enter the courtroom.

I excused myself and joined her at counsel table. She actually looked pleased to see me. "I've got good news for you," she said.

"Oh?"

"Tolletson will drop this to voluntary manslaughter."

"You're kidding." I was stunned. This was great news, better than I could have hoped. Considering Howie had never been in major trouble before, he would probably end up with no more than three years in prison.

"The only thing," Sylvia Plotzske said, "is that the offer is good now. If we go to prelim, it's off the table, and we go for first degree."

A no-brainer. I was sure the Patinos would understand. At least the parents would. So I told them. Janet and Fred nodded at each other. "It seems the best we can expect," Fred said.

"Yes," I said.

Lindsay looked more disheartened than angry. Maybe she had finally realized the inevitable. But she shook her head slowly and muttered, "He didn't do it. He just didn't do it."

It was now 8:55, and the judge would soon be taking the bench. It was decision time. A sheriff brought Howie in from the lockup and sat him down at the defense table. Howie winced a little, probably because of his side. But then he turned and gave a small smile and wave to his family. Janet Patino started crying.

I was just about to explain the deal to Howie when my cell phone bleeped in my briefcase.

"Hey, man, it's a beautiful day at the beach!" Cyril Cornelius Carr said.

"I'm in court, Trip."

"I know. You're about to strike a deal, right?"

"So?"

"So don't do it."

I looked around as if people could hear him and then cupped my hand over my mouth and turned my back to Howie. "What are you talking about?"

"I got down here early to catch the surfers. Surf's lousy today though."

I could hear the sound of waves breaking in the background. In a vigorous whisper, I said, "What are you talking about?"

"I'm talking about one of the surfers, a guy by the name of Chip Delliplane. He's pretty good on a board. He also saw something the night of the murder."

I couldn't believe this was happening. A surprise witness? Now? "I thought I told you to drop this."

"I just didn't feel good about that, Jake. Something didn't smell right. So I talked to Delliplane. Got his name from a friendly bartender at the edge of town."

"So what's he say?"

"He says he was riding his bike toward the house that night, and it was right around the time of the murder. He heard a scream, stopped, and started to turn around. Just before he did, he saw somebody running from the house."

All breath left me for a moment. I sucked in some air. "Why didn't he go to the cops and tell them all this?"

"Because he didn't want his parents to find out."

"Find out what?"

"That he was having an affair with Rae Patino."

At that moment the bailiff told everyone in the courtroom to rise. Judge Abovian was entering the courtroom. I stood up with everyone else, but I was alone in holding a phone to my ear with my mouth hanging open.

"Jake? Jake?" Triple C said.

"Hold on," I said.

The judge, a man in his fifties who resembled the '40s politician Thomas Dewey, with a good tan, looked at me and said, "I don't allow cell calls in my courtroom."

"Um . . ." I said eloquently, "if, um, I may have just a moment, Your Honor?"

"You may not. Court is in session. Put that thing away."

"Jake!" Triple C cried as if he were being dragged out by the riptide. I disconnected and put the phone away.

"All right," said Abovian. "This is the time set for the preliminary hearing in the case of *People v. Howard Patino.* Is counsel ready?"

Sylvia Plotzske stood. "The People are ready, Your Honor. However, we may have a disposition."

"Is that right, Mr. Denney?" said the judge.

"Your Honor, if I may just confer with my client for a moment?"

"Haven't you done that yet?"

"Not this morning."

"All right, you can have one minute."

I nodded curtly. How generous. One minute to get to the bottom of this thing. I put my hand on Howie's shoulder and leaned in so no one could hear us. "Howie, I want you to tell me, once and for all, if you killed your wife."

He seemed shocked and as if he barely comprehended what was going on. "Yeah, Jake, it was my fault."

"That's not what I asked you."

"I killed her, Jake. I killed her spirit."

Closing my eyes and feeling like I might explode, I whispered forcefully, "I don't give a rip about her spirit, Howie! Was there someone else in the room with you when it happened? Did someone else kill your wife and stab you?"

For a moment, Howie said nothing. Then his eyes went wild, like a character in an old haunted-house comedy who sees a ghost. Only this wasn't funny. This was pure terror.

Howie shot to his feet and started screaming at the top of his voice, "The devil! The devil! The devil!"

That's when everything broke loose.

Howie started running for the exit. Two sheriff's deputies took off behind him.

Judge Abovian started yelling for order, but was drowned out by Howie's screams.

Howie was gang-tackled by two deputy sheriffs and a county clerk just before he reached the front doors of the courthouse. He was dragged back to Abovian's courtroom with a crowd following like flies. By the time Howie was back in his chair, the two burly deputies on either side of him, the small courtroom was filled to capacity.

Abovian came back on the bench and scowled at me as if I were the one who had been screaming. "I hope you will make it abundantly clear to your client," he said, "that another outburst like that will result in his being shackled and gagged. Is there anything about that you don't understand, Mr. Denney?"

With a wan smile and a shaking head, I answered, "No, Your Honor."

"Then, are we going to proceed with the preliminary hearing or not?"

I glanced back at the Patinos. Fred was holding Janet, who was understandably shaken. Lindsay was looking at me as if I was the only one who could offer them any hope. Howie had his head in his hands and seemed spent.

And Sylvia Plotzske, arms folded, looked at me as if I'd better cop the plea right now or I'd be the world's biggest idiot, especially after what had just transpired.

With a gulp, I looked at the judge. "We're ready to proceed, Your Honor."

I thought I could almost hear the sound of Sylvia's jaw dropping. She quickly shuffled through her files, an indication to me that she never thought she'd have to put on a prelim. I was supposed to grab the deal and run. I wondered about my sanity at that moment.

"Call your first witness, Ms. Plotzske," Judge Abovian said.

CHAPTER THIRTEEN

A PRELIMINARY HEARING, for the defense lawyer, is little more than an opportunity to get a cursory look at the prosecutor's evidence. That's why prosecutors will put on as little evidence as possible. Their only goal is to get a judge to send the case to Superior Court for trial, and judges are usually more than happy to oblige.

As a deputy public defender, I'd handled some prelims with as little as fifteen minutes preparation. My preference was more time, of course, but that is a luxury public defenders don't enjoy. When you've got a pile of thirty or forty active files and the fuel of speedy trial rights, you get a fire that burns up your leisure, your relationships, and very often your health.

I was more prepared with Howie's case, though less so than if I'd had this on a trial track to begin with. I'd just have to see what developed.

Sylvia Plotzske said, "The People call Wilburn McGary."

McGary, dressed in his police uniform, stood up in the gallery and came forward. He had a buzz cut, like Tolletson, and a tenacious look in his eyes. He walked next to the witness stand, and the clerk swore him in.

Sylvia began her questioning seated at the prosecution table. "Officer McGary, you're employed by the Hinton Police Department. Is that right?"

"Yes."

"And how long have you been so employed?"

"Three years."

"Before that, how were you employed?"

"I was in the Marine Corps."

"All right. I'd like to direct your attention to the night of March 25. Were you on duty that night?"

"I was."

"And did you respond to a call at approximately 9:30?"

"Yes. We received a report about possible domestic violence. I was in my car, and dispatch gave me the address."

"What was the address?"

"May I refer to my report?"

"Of course. Your Honor, may I approach the witness?"

"Yes," Abovian said. Sylvia took a copy of McGary's police report to him. I glanced at my own copy. McGary looked at the papers and said, "The address was 5035 White Oak Avenue."

Sylvia was back at her table. "Tell the court what transpired when you answered the call."

McGary told the court how he arrived at the house, knocked on the door, and didn't get a response. He went around the side of the house and found the gate padlocked. Concerned about potential victims in the house, he hopped the fence. He found the sliding glass door at the back of the house. It was open.

"Did you think that was unusual?" Sylvia asked.

In a confident and rehearsed manner, McGary said, "Yes. There were no lights on in that area of the residence. It seemed unusual to me that anyone would leave a door open like that at night, unless there was some unusual circumstance."

"What did you do then?"

McGary said he announced his presence again, but getting no response, he went inside. Using his flashlight, he went through the house, eventually coming to the bedroom, where he noticed a light on. Entering the room, he saw blood. Lots of blood. And a body on the bed. "I then heard a noise, like a grunt. I turned and saw the defendant on the floor by the television set."

"Is the person you saw on the floor present in court today?" Sylvia asked.

"Yes."

"Would you identify him, please?"

Officer McGary pointed at Howie. "He's sitting next to the defense lawyer." He said defense lawyer the same way he would have said refuse pile.

"Let the record reflect that the witness has identified the defendant, Howard Patino," Sylvia Plotzske said.

"The record will so reflect," said the judge.

"What was the condition of the defendant?" the prosecutor asked.

"He appeared to be hurt. He had blood on his shirt and was holding his side."

"Did he say anything?"

"No. He made some noises."

"What kind of noises?"

"Like someone who was in pain."

"What did you do next?"

"I quickly swept through the room and the bathroom to see if anyone else was present. No one else was there. I immediately called for backup. I then questioned the defendant in an effort to ascertain what happened."

"Did the defendant talk to you?"

"No. He was either unable or unwilling to talk."

Just so no one would think I was asleep, I said, "Objection. Speculation. It's beyond the competence of this witness to know the mind of Mr. Patino. Move to strike."

Abovian looked annoyed. "All right. We'll strike the last part of the answer. Let's move on."

"No further questions," Sylvia Plotzske said.

"Mr. Denney?" the judge said.

I picked up my legal pad and looked at the few notes I'd written. Some of them I couldn't read. Wonderful.

"Officer McGary," I said, "when you went to the location, you didn't have a search warrant, did you?"

"No, sir. This was an answer to an emergency–"

"Just answer my questions, Officer. You don't need to elaborate. Did you have a search warrant?"

"No."

"You said you were answering a call about possible domestic violence, is that right?"

"Yes."

"Do you know the difference between domestic disturbance and domestic violence?"

McGary shifted slightly. "Yes."

"What is the difference?"

"Well, a disturbance is usually just noise, which can result from loud voices or objects being broken, things like that. Violence has to do with physical contact."

"In fact, there's a chapter in the penal code that defines domestic violence, correct?"

"I believe so."

"Can you cite that code section?"

Looking perturbed, McGary said, "No."

That put us on equal footing. I couldn't cite the section either. But I knew it was there somewhere, and I knew vaguely what it said. "Are you aware that the definition of domestic violence is intentionally causing bodily injury to a spouse?"

McGary shrugged and said, "That sounds right."

Sylvia Plotzske stood up as if she had the goods on me. What she actually had was a copy of the penal code, which she held open in front of her. "Your Honor, counsel is referring to section 13700," she said, sounding like Jack Webb. "It states that domestic violence means intentionally or recklessly causing, *or attempting to cause,* bodily injury to a family or household member, or placing a family or household member in reasonable apprehension of imminent serious bodily injury to himself or herself or another."

"Thank you, Ms. Plotzske," Abovian said. "Continue, Mr. Denney."

I felt for a moment like the judge and Sylvia were a tag team of some sort. Plotzske was sharp enough to know where I was heading, and her reading of the code section was a not-so-subtle transmission to her witness. I started getting a little hacked off.

"Now, Officer, isn't it true that when you got the call you had no idea whether this was a disturbance or violence case?"

"I believe the dispatcher said possible domestic violence."

"Shall we subpoena the dispatch record? Would that refresh your recollection?"

McGary shot a quick glance at Sylvia Plotzske. "It may have been domestic disturbance."

"You're not sure?"

"It may have been."

"That sounds like *not sure,* Officer."

"Without checking the records, I can't be sure."

"But when you testified just a moment ago, you didn't hesitate. You said domestic violence, isn't that right?"

"I thought it was."

"Did you really, or did you just think it would better justify your warrantless entry into the house?"

"Objection," Sylvia Plotzske said. "If this is going to be a suppression motion, the People would point out we have received no written notice."

She was quite right. Under a new statute in California, defense lawyers were required to serve written notice five days in advance of a prelim that they intended to challenge evidence on Fourth Amendment grounds. The problem with that, however, is that most of the time they have no idea until the prelim just what the police did that might be illegal. It was the sort of catch-22 law the legislators in Sacramento liked to pass so they could claim they were tough on law-and-order issues in the next election.

"This line of questioning appears to be irrelevant on the matter of probable cause," said Judge Abovian.

"Your Honor," I said, "I am merely following the lead of the prosecutor in delving into the mind of the officer. You'll recall she asked him what his thinking was when he went around the side of the house. She opened the door, and all I'm doing is walking through it."

For dramatic emphasis, I waved my hand. A clever argument, I thought, and I congratulated myself for thinking so quickly on my feet. I considered it a victory when the judge merely grunted and said, "Move on to another subject, Mr. Denney."

And what subject would that be, Your Honor? How to jump into a dark hole with both feet?

I looked at my notes again and saw the word "weapon" in the margin. "Officer McGary, when you entered the house, did you have your weapon drawn?"

Squinting, McGary said, "Yes, I did."

"I don't think you mentioned that on direct."

"I wasn't asked."

"Why did you have your weapon drawn?"

"I was concerned about a potentially dangerous situation."

"Back to the violence again, eh?"

"Please, Mr. Denney," Abovian said. "This is just a preliminary hearing."

He was right. I was trying too hard. Was I going all out for Lindsay? "When you entered the bedroom, you kept your weapon out, is that right?"

"I was concerned about safety."

"When did you put your weapon away?"

"When I was sure that the scene was secure."

"Did Mr. Patino offer any resistance to you?"

"He wouldn't talk to me when I questioned him."

"He was injured, was he not?"

"He appeared to be, yes."

"Did you call for an ambulance?"

"Yes, I did."

"Did you call for it before or after you started to question my client?"

With a slight shrug, McGary said, "I'm sure it was before."

"Are you as sure as you are about the domestic violence call?"

Sylvia Plotzske stood up, but Judge Abovian said, "You don't have to object, Ms. Plotzske. Mr. Denney, you're out of line."

I took that as a compliment. "No more questions of this witness."

I sat down next to Howie, who was looking at me in a new way. Gone was the wild-eyed fear he'd displayed just minutes before. In its place was a look I remembered from when we were kids. It was, for lack of a better term, admiring.

"That was good, Jake," Howie whispered.

I hoped his sister thought so too.

CHAPTER FOURTEEN

THE REST OF the prelim was pro forma. Sylvia established all the elements she needed, and Abovian set a Superior Court trial date. No surprises.

The Patino family seemed pleased, probably because they finally saw me *do* something. Even Howie was appreciative. He thanked me just before they took him back to jail.

As soon as our little party broke up, I called Trip. He was still at the beach. I could picture him in his Hawaiian shirt, cell phone at his ear, lounging in the sand. Nice work if you can get it.

"Get down here right away," Trip said. "No telling how long our boy will be here."

It took me twenty minutes to reach the little strip of beach just north of Ventura. It would have been shorter, but I stopped off at a liquor store for a six-pack of beer. If I was going to go to the beach, I might as well enjoy it.

This beach was a place the surfers liked. I had passed it innumerable times in the past. As always, a knot of ocean boys in wet suits bobbed on their boards as they waited for a wave to fight over.

Trip was indeed on the sand, leaning back against a large rock and soaking up the rays. He wore shorts and had his shoes off.

I, on the other hand, looked like Richard Nixon, who used to walk the beaches in his suit. I could already feel sand building up in my shoes. I had the six-pack in one hand, my briefcase in the other.

"So, where is he?" I said.

"Hey, man, sit down. Take a load off."

"Glad you're so concerned with my well-being."

"How'd the prelim go?"

"Oh, the usual. Client screams about being tormented by the devil, bolts, tries to escape, gets tackled. Same old."

Trip looked at me through his Ray-Bans and waited for me to laugh. I didn't. He said, "You're kidding, right?"

"Nope."

"Oh, man! I wish I could have seen that! It's boring watching these guys."

"So, which one is it?"

"See the guy third from the left?"

I looked out at the bevy of surfers and counted to three. He appeared to have shoulder length blond hair, which made him indistinguishable from just about every California surfer who ever lived.

I popped a beer and offered it to Trip. He shook his head. "You nuts?"

"Just being sociable."

"When you coming to church with me?"

"When pigs surf." I took a sip of my beer and sat down.

Chip Delliplane was, from the looks of it, a pretty fair surfer. There wasn't much to work with out there, but he made the most of his opportunities. He also had a studied flair. You can pick that up about surfers. They each have a style. Delliplane's seemed less spontaneous. He was still out there trying hard to impress the bunnies, a few of whom lay on towels near the water, watching.

"So, what you got?" I asked.

"Let's hear it from the lad when he comes in," Trip said, his head resting on the rock. "Meantime, I did some digging on the wife."

"What did you find?"

"Not much. Rae Patino has no past. She buried it when she moved here."

"From where?"

"Word I got was she came from the South. I talked to a friend of hers, and I was lucky to get that much out of her."

"Why?"

"Soon as she found out I was working for Howie, she started screaming at me, using language that should not come from a lady's lips. 'She speaks poniards, and every word stabs.'"

"*Taming of the Shrew?*"

"*Much Ado About Nothing,* which is what this turned out to be. She told me to lay off, that Rae's parents had died when she was a kid, and she was just trying to start over out here. I should let her rest in peace."

"Howie didn't know anything about her past," I said. "I think he was afraid to ask. He was so googly-eyed about her that he didn't want to rock the boat."

"Well, from everything I know so far, she smells like a scammer. Howie was probably just another scammee."

I finished my beer, then popped another. We watched the surfers in silence for awhile. I almost lapsed into a nap when Trip suddenly got up. "Let's go," he said.

Chip Delliplane was walking up the beach with his surfboard under his arm. He stopped near a beach towel and stuck his board, nose down, in the sand. The leash that surfers wear around their ankles, connecting board to rider, flapped against the board. Delliplane was just about out of his wet suit when he saw Trip and me approaching.

"No way!" he said. "I don't want to talk to you!" His eyes reflected a certain fear.

"Chill," Trip said. "This guy's the lawyer."

Delliplane looked at me. He was twenty-one or twenty-two, about five-ten, and his body was lean and muscled. To me he said, "I told this guy I didn't want to talk to anybody."

"What's the problem?" I said.

"I don't want to talk, that's all."

"You talked to him though," I said, nodding my head Trip's way.

"Yeah, but I thought he was gonna mess me up!" Delliplane said. "He's crazy."

"Are you crazy, Triple C?"

"I don't know what he's talking about," Trip said like a savage innocent.

"He started talking crazy at me," Delliplane insisted. "I like freaked. I didn't know what he was gonna do next."

"Trip, did you talk crazy?"

"I merely said 'O, thou pernicious caitiff! Torments will open thy lips!'"

"See?" Delliplane said. "See that? Crazy!"

"All right, Chip," I said. "May I call you Chip?"

He shook his head, "I ain't talking."

"What's the problem?"

"The problem is, I can't get involved in this, man. Like I told this dude here."

"Do you realize a man's life is on the line?"

"That ain't my fault."

"Let's sit down, shall we?" I motioned for all of us to lower ourselves to the sand. I had four beers remaining in my hand. I took one out, opened it, and handed it to Delliplane. He seemed too amazed to refuse.

"Chip," I said, "you probably know we can force you into court. But I don't want to have to do that. I respect the fact that you don't want your parents to find out about, well, you know. But I need to know what you do know. You can understand that, can't you?"

"I don't care."

"Let me ask you just a few questions, and we'll decide where to go from there, okay?"

He looked warily at Trip, who was looking Terminator-esque in his shades. "Don't worry, dude," Trip said. "You can trust my man."

"It's you I'm worried about," Delliplane said.

Trip smiled.

"Tell me about your relationship with Rae Patino," I said.

Shaking his head, Delliplane said, "Look, it wasn't a big thing."

"Was it sexual?"

"That's all it was."

"How long?"

"About a month."

"How did you meet her?"

"Oh, man," Delliplane said, shaking his head like he was remembering some weird episode of the *X-Files*. "She comes into The Reef; that's this bar downtown. She comes in one night, and I'm just hangin' with my friends. There's four of us. We were doing shooters, and she walks right up to the table and says, 'Anybody wanna bet?'"

"Like she was challenging you to a drinking contest or something?"

"Exactly."

"What did you do?"

"We all looked at her first. She's wearing this tight, I don't know what it is, this top that's barely covering what it's supposed to cover, and she's got these cutoffs on that are so high up it's almost a belt."

"She was dressed provocatively?"

"She wanted to pop every eyeball in the place. I mean, first thing I think is she's a pro. So then one of my buds tells her to sit down, and she slides in."

"Did she drink?"

"You should have seen her! First she gets us all to buy her one drink each. That's four shots of Cuervo sitting on the table. We're all laughing and watching, and she takes a slice of lime, sucks it, and throws back two shots. Then she laughs, takes another lime, throws back the other two. And we're all, 'Wow! Who is this chick?' "

"Did anyone bother to ask her name?"

"Nah. No one wanted to come off dork-like."

"So what happened next?"

"So we're all kind of watching her, joking around, and then my friend, Sharkey, sitting right next to her, puts his arm around her shoulder and tries to nuzzle her ear or something. And I'm thinking he's gonna be the one, cause Sharkey's pretty smooth, but the next thing we know she's all pushing him away and screaming at him. And Sharkey's all, 'What is *that* all about?' And he pushes *her,* and she goes flying onto the floor. And I'm on the other side, so I jump out and start to help her up, and I'm all, 'Cut it out, Sharkey man!' You know, I'm kind of being her protector."

"And it worked, I guess."

"Yeah. She's all, 'Take me home. Take me home.' So I do."

"You took her back to her house in Hinton?"

"Yeah."

"Did you spend the night?"

"Yeah."

"And you kept seeing her after that?"

"Yeah."

"How many times?"

"I don't know, maybe six or seven."

"Always at her house?"

"One time we came down to the beach."

"Never your place?"

"I live with my parents, dude."

Trip let out a big laugh. I said, “Did she ever talk about her husband?”

“At first she told me she wasn’t married. Then one night she asks me if I wanted to help her smoke her old man.”

“Whoa!” Triple C said.

I felt the same way. “Are you telling me she asked you to help her kill her husband?”

“That’s what I’m saying. But then she starts laughing, so I don’t know if she’s serious or crazy or what.”

“Did she ever bring that subject up again?”

“No.”

It was time for another beer. I popped it and asked, “Let’s get to the night she was killed. You were going to see her?”

“Yeah.”

“On your bike, was it?”

“Yeah. I was on my way about nine, nine-thirty, something like that.”

Trip asked, “Was this by arrangement?”

“No. I just thought I’d go over and drop in.”

“What was your condition?”

“Condition?”

“Were you stoned?”

A little half-smile appeared on Delliplane’s face. “A little, yeah.”

“So, what happened?”

“I’m riding up the street and I’m, oh, about a hundred yards away when I hear this scream.”

“You heard her scream?”

“No, it was a man’s scream.”

Trip and I looked at each other. Delliplane said, “So I stop right there in the middle of the street and listen because I think it came from the house. The house, you know, is kind of angled, and you can see the fields behind it. So while I'm sitting there, looking, I see something moving out behind the house."

"How well could you see? I mean, what was the light like?"

"No lights. It was just a shadow. But I watch, and it's definitely a guy running."

"Fast?"

"Oh yeah. Like he was trying to get away."

"So what did you do?"

"I took off."

I could feel Trip's demeanor changing. He's of the old school, where you do certain things out of duty or honor. Even if it's just some tawdry affair, you don't hightail and run when there's somebody in trouble and you can do something about it. We knew Delliplane hadn't even called the police.

I said, "And you weren't going to say anything?"

"No, man. If this ever got to my parents, I'd be out of the house. Bam. Like that."

"They didn't know you were having this affair?"

"No way. I'm a good liar." Chip Delliplane smiled then, and my stomach turned.

Trip did not look satisfied. "That's not the only reason, is it?"

Suddenly Delliplane dropped his beach-boy smile.

"There's more to it, right?" Trip said.

"Look, I can't talk to you anymore. She was into some bad stuff; there's people out there . . ." His voice trailed off, and he shook his head. "I'm not talking anymore. That's it."

"All right," I said, then turned to Trip. "You got it?"

"Got it," Trip said.

"Got what?" said Chip Delliplane. Triple C pulled the microcassette recorder from his pocket and clicked it off.

"We're going to transcribe this into a statement so you can swear to it," I explained.

Delliplane started shaking his head vigorously. "No way, man! I ain't swearing to anything. I told you I wasn't talking!"

"You just did, Chip."

"I didn't know you were recording me! You can't do that! That's illegal, or something!"

Trip gave him his passive, Terminator stare.

"Isn't it?" Chip asked.

I shook my head. "You're hosed, dude."

"You guys are slime!" Chip said, and then he said a few things nice boys shouldn't say. He finished by grabbing his board and declaring that he would never sign anything, he'd lie and say he was set up if it ever came to that, and he knew people who could hurt us. Then he ran away from us as fast as his surfer feet could take him.

"Well, that was entertaining," I said.

"It was all I could do not to rip his curly hair out."

"What do you think he meant, about other people?"

Trip shook his head.

CHAPTER FIFTEEN

I FINISHED UP an eventful day by getting an earful about Satan.

When Howie was brought into the attorney interview cubicle at the county jail, he looked like he'd been sweating heavily. His hair was matted to his forehead. His blue coveralls were stained. He seemed winded too, as if he'd run a sprint to get here.

The moment he sat down, he put his head in his hands.

"You want to tell me about it?" I said.

"Get me out of this, Jake," he said without looking up. "Help me."

"I can't until you come clean with me. I don't want any more dancing around. Did you or did you not stab your wife?"

Raising his head, Howie seemed lost in a mental fog. "I don't know, Jake. I just don't know."

I heaved a sigh. Having a client who can't remember is worse than having one who lies. You can pick out lies and confront them, but you can't pick out what isn't in the mind to begin with. "Start with the dreams, Howie. What is it about the dreams?"

For a moment I didn't think he would tell me. His face drained of color. Then he said, "The devil."

"What about the devil?"

"Torture."

I waited.

"Beelzebub."

"Come on–"

"I have sinned."

"How?"

"The devil prowls around like a lion. He is devouring me! I can't sleep."

"The devil is in your dreams; is that it?"

"Yeah."

"Join the club. That still doesn't answer my question."

Howie shook his head slowly. "I willed it, Jake. I willed her to die. I wanted her dead. I wanted her to die, and the devil's purpose was accomplished."

"But did you stab her?"

"I don't remember."

"Do you remember holding the knife?"

"I don't know."

I slammed my hand on the table. "Come on, Howie! Get in the game with me. Did you, or did you not, stab Rae?"

Short bursts of breath came out of his mouth rapidly, like his heart was racing. "I must have!"

"Put yourself back in the room."

"No, Jake. Don't make me!"

"Do it."

"No!" He stood up, and his chair went flying backwards.

A deputy sheriff opened the door. "What's going on?" he asked.

"It's all right," I said. "We're finished." I was not pleased. At that point I didn't care about Howie or Lindsay or anything else about this crazy case.

"Let's go," the deputy said to Howie. My client didn't even look at me as he left the room.

I headed back to the Valley and straight to Max's. I took my usual table in the back and began the parade of beers.

Taking stock, I looked at my case. It was getting weirder by the hour. Howie was obviously off his nut, but that would be a tough nut to crack in trial. The key was his mental state at the time of the murder, and there was no evidence he was anything but legally sane. It was only when I had to try to get information out of him that he flipped out. Some client.

Then there was this Delliplane who had potentially startling evidence but was about as credible as a Frisbee. What did he really see that night? Since he was stoned, how sure could he be? If he ever took the stand, even the colorless Sylvia Plotzske would make surfer meat out of him.

Some of the usual crowd wandered into Max's and gave me a few waves. I pretended to be writing notes on a legal pad.

When I was finally in that condition where what anyone thought of me didn't matter an iota, I got up and went to the pay phone in the back. I poured in the coins and dialed Lindsay Patino's number, that is, what I thought was her number. I actually got some woman who spoke Spanish and didn't know any Lindsay Patino.

I dumped in more change and took out the paper from my wallet with Lindsay's number on it. In my inebriated state, my fingers felt like sausages; none of them connected with the others.

"Hello?"

"It's Denney."

"Oh, hello. How are you?" She sounded concerned, not just making conversation.

"Oh, I'm at the top of my game. You like what your brother did today?" I said it with a note of anger.

"He's so scared."

"Yeah? He's crazy too."

"No, he's not."

"He keeps telling me all this about the devil and like that and doesn't remember squat that will help us."

"You sound angry, Jake."

"Look, I gotta talk to you about this case. Now. I'm coming over."

"Wait, tonight wouldn't–"

I hung up. Such was my cheap exercise of power.

As I weaved out to the parking lot at Max's, I realized I hadn't asked her where she lived. I only remembered she had once mentioned the cross streets for the house where she rented the guest quarters. I turned on the lights in my car and tried to find the spot in my Thomas Guide map of city streets. Normally that would be a three-minute process. In my condition it took ten.

I finally found the streets and drove over. My plan was to look for her car, which I had a vague picture of from our little bumping incident. I must have cruised up and down the street four times before I spotted what looked like her vehicle.

I knocked on the front door of the house, and an old man peeked out from behind the chain lock.

"Excuse me," I said, "I'm looking for Lindsay Patino."

"Who are you?" His voice sounded like it came from a gravel pit.

"I'm her lawyer. Does she live here?"

"What's a lawyer doing making house calls?"

"I care about my clients."

"If you're a lawyer, how come you don't have a briefcase?"

I looked heavenward. "She live in the guest house?" I started to walk toward the side.

"Wait a minute!" the old man shouted, but I was gone. I walked down the driveway, which led all the way to the back. I could see the small guest house and lights on in the window.

Before I was halfway there, the old man shuffled out the back door of the main house. "You stop right there!" he commanded.

I turned to explain reality to him and found myself looking into the dark eye of a hunting rifle.

"Whoa!" I said.

"You're trespassing."

"I'm a lawyer!"

"All the more reason to shoot you!"

I put my hands in the air. "Listen, I–"

"Now go out the way you came."

Then I heard Lindsay's voice. "It's all right, Mr. Laguzza." She stepped out of the shadows.

The old man said, "You know this fella?"

"Yes, I do."

"Says he's your lawyer."

"Yes, it's all right."

Old man Laguzza lowered the rifle, reluctantly, it seemed to me. "Strange kind of lawyer," he said.

Lindsay looked at me with some consternation.

"Well," she said, "I guess you better come in."

CHAPTER SIXTEEN

THE LITTLE GUEST house had a country-cottage feel. Without being asked, I sat in a blue wingback chair, like the invited guest I wasn't.

"Where'd you find this place?" I asked.

"Someone at my church recommended it to me," Lindsay said, sitting on the sofa. "She knew Mr. Laguzza, I came to see him, and we hit it off."

"He's handy with a gun."

"Emil Laguzza is a member of the Valley Circle Baptist Church, an association he reveres just slightly ahead of his membership in the National Rifle Association."

"Wow, it must get pretty exciting around here when Jehovah's Witnesses come calling."

I thought it was a pretty decent joke, but Lindsay didn't laugh. So I said, "I talked to Howie earlier, and he got very disturbed again about the devil. Started shouting, going crazy, just like in court. Says he willed for Rae to die and that's how the devil accomplished his purpose. You know anything about this?"

She leaned back and sighed. "Howie has had visions of the devil before."

"Why didn't you mention anything about this?"

"I didn't see any connection before. Then today, when he tried to run out of court, it all came back."

"What came back?"

"Howie's had nightmares his whole life. Terrible nightmares. Waking up screaming in the middle of the night. When he was little, the doctors told Mom and Dad it was just night terrors, something kids get from time to time. They said he'd outgrow them."

"Only he didn't."

"That's right."

"And he would tell you about these dreams?"

"They always came back to the same thing. The devil was out to get him."

I rubbed my eyes, which by this time must have been a nice shade of red. "I never knew that about Howie. I don't remember him ever talking to me about it."

"He was scared to talk about it, except to me."

"That's rough. I've had some doozie nightmares myself, but not my whole life. Why do you think he dreamed about the devil?"

"Because," Lindsay said matter-of-factly, "I think he saw him."

My addled brain was beginning to mellow out, but I still had trouble believing what Lindsay Patino just said. My stare must have been enough because she felt compelled to explain. "Maybe not Satan himself, but a demon, which he has come to feel represents Satan."

Shaking my head, I said, "You actually believe this?"

"Yes."

"That's a little hard for me to swallow, Lindsay."

"I understand that. I know our world today considers Satan to be a myth represented by a funny guy in a red suit. But he's not a myth. He's real."

"How do you know that?"

She stood up, walked across the room, and returned with a Bible. If it had been anybody but Lindsay, I probably would have walked out of there.

She opened the Bible and read. "*For our struggle is not against flesh and blood, but against the rulers, against the authorities, against the powers of this dark world and against the spiritual forces of evil in the heavenly realms.*"

"And that means what?"

"That spiritual darkness exists. That spiritual warfare is real."

"Well, sure, there's a lot of bad stuff out there. But it doesn't necessarily mean a devil."

She flipped some pages and read another passage. "*As for you, you were dead in your transgressions and sins, in which you used to live when you followed the ways of this world and of the ruler of the kingdom of the air, the spirit who is now at work in those who are disobedient.*"

She looked at me. "The ruler is Satan. Now, being a ruler implies having forces that carry out orders and objectives. That's where demons come in."

"Oh, come on."

"He's called other things like that. The prince of demons. The evil one. Jesus called him the prince of this world."

"And you really believe that?"

"Yes."

"You don't strike me as one of those people who sees demons under every rock."

"I believe we have to avoid two extremes. The first is what you say. It's not right to be obsessed with demons. If your car doesn't start in the morning or you burn your toast, that doesn't mean a demon is behind it."

I nodded.

"But there's another extreme, and that is not believing at all. Our culture has become totally naturalistic. It rules out supernatural phenomena, but it has absolutely no reason to do so."

We were quiet for a moment, and I tried to put all this into some perspective. Here was a well-spoken, well-educated woman, someone who could have been a success at just about anything she chose, telling me she believed in actual devils and demons. I was incredulous. The only other person I remember talking to me about the devil with such certainty was a guy downtown who had wine breath and lived out of a shopping cart.

Lindsay Patino did not fit that profile. I wasn't at all leaning toward believing her, but I admit, I was getting intrigued. "Howie said something about a lion devouring him. What's that all about?"

Lindsay flipped through her Bible again. "That's a passage in First Peter. *Be self-controlled and alert. Your enemy the devil prowls around like a roaring lion looking for someone to devour.*"

The image was striking, and I could almost relate. There were times when I'd felt like there was a hot breath on the back of my neck. Usually that feeling came when I was falling into bed after a binge. I always chalked it up to inebriated paranoia.

"Look," I said, "back when the Bible was written, they had a superstitious view of things. I mean, things that happened that were bad were explained away by invoking demons. But that was then. This is now."

"There have always been reports of demonic activity throughout history, right up to today."

I shook my head slowly.

"I'll give you an example. Our church helps support a missionary couple in Kenya. These people are the most levelheaded people you'll ever meet. The husband used to be a marketing executive, and his wife was a consultant. They dropped everything to train and to work with people of a very ancient culture."

I wondered what might have driven a couple to make that sort of irrational decision, but I listened closely.

"There is no separation over there between the natural and the supernatural. Spiritual activity is seen as normal and inevitable. This couple has confronted actual demon possession, talked directly to demons, and cast them out of people. But in our Western culture, we have created an artificial distinction, and then we rule out the supernatural."

She was so sure about what she was saying that it was disconcerting. Suddenly I felt like a lawyer arguing a case and came back with, "Maybe they buy that in Africa. But we are advanced, Lindsay, and we have explanations for phenomena. If you believe in devils and demons, you'll stop the acquisition of knowledge."

"You truly believe that?"

"Yes, I do."

"And that's why the devil is pleased."

"Excuse me?" If this had been a courtroom, I might have voiced an objection. Instead of answering, Lindsay went to her bookcase again and came back with a slender volume. She started looking through it.

"I want you to read something," she said.

"Lindsay, come on . . ."

She looked at me. "Please."

I threw up my hands and nodded. She handed me the open book and pointed. "Read from here," she said.

I glanced at the cover. It was *The Screwtape Letters* by C. S. Lewis. I'd heard of Lewis but never read him. I thought he was mainly a children's writer.

"These are fictional letters," she explained, "written by a senior demon to an apprentice on how to bring people down. He is explaining the methods demons should use to achieve this purpose."

I read:

Our policy, for the moment, is to conceal ourselves. Of course this has not always been so. We are really faced with a cruel dilemma. When the humans disbelieve in our existence we lose all the pleasing results of direct terrorism, and we make no magicians. On the other hand, when they believe in us, we cannot make them materialists and skeptics.

I looked up at Lindsay, and she must have seen consternation in my face.

"Keep reading," she ordered.

Obediently, I went back to the page.

I do not think you will have much difficulty in keeping the patient in the dark. The fact that "devils" are predominantly comic figures in the modern imagination will help you. If any faint suspicion of your existence begins to arise in his mind, suggest to him a picture of something in red tights, and persuade him that since he cannot believe in that (it is an old textbook method of confusing them) he therefore cannot believe in you.

Slowly, I closed the book.

"I know it's difficult for you to believe," Lindsay said, "because you haven't looked into it before."

I bristled but couldn't protest because she was right. I started thinking what a good lawyer she would have made.

"So you think Howie is dealing with some sort of demon possession?"

"That's not a truly accurate concept. The Scriptures talk more about demonic *oppression.* It comes in varying degrees of power. And yes, Howie has been subject to it."

"His whole life?"

"Most of it."

"Has he gotten any help?"

"You mean like psychiatric help? Oh, sure. But that's not the answer."

"What is?"

"Spiritual healing."

My skepticism was returning to full strength. "Are you talking about exorcism here? Are we in Linda Blair territory?"

Ignoring my sarcasm, Lindsay patiently said, "It's not like the movies. But it does call for prayers of deliverance."

"Have you tried that?"

"We did. Once. At our church."

"And?"

Lindsay sat back, looked at the floor, and shook her head. "For this kind of thing, you need some cooperation. We didn't get it."

"Howie resisted you?"

"It was Rae. She told him never to let me or anyone else do that to him again, and Howie always did what Rae said."

"But why would the devil be so interested in Howie? He never did anything to anybody."

Lindsay took a long, slow breath. She leaned forward, resting her arms on her knees. The room seemed suddenly to get smaller. "I'm going to tell you why," she said. "Will you listen?"

"I'm not going anywhere," I answered.

"All right, then," she said. "It was when my parents first moved to Orlando . . ."

CHAPTER SEVENTEEN

. . . AND HOWIE WAS just five years old. Disney World was a blueprint then. Orlando still had a small-town feel. Fred Patino had taken a job with a big lumber and building outfit because along with Mickey Mouse would come boom times.

Janet Patino was pregnant and about to give birth to Lindsay, their third child.

"Third child?" I interrupted.

"I was number three," said Lindsay, "after Howie and my other brother, Mike."

"I didn't know you had another brother."

"He died."

"I'm sorry."

"I only learned about it later on, of course. I had to piece it together bit by bit. Most of it I finally got from Mom after years of her not wanting to talk about it. The pain was just too great. Mike was three years old when I was born."

Howie doted on both of them–Mike and baby Lindsay. This was finally something Howie was good at, being a big brother. If other kids made fun of him for being a little slower than they were, he could always go home and have his two little siblings to play with. Mike was like a puppy, and Lindsay gurgled and smiled at him. It was unconditional love.

Howie always had a vivid imagination. Sometimes too vivid. He woke the family up more than once with visions of boogeymen under the bed, slipping out in the darkness to get Mike, who slept in the same room. Howie was never afraid for himself. He always thought it was some malevolent creature trying to take his little brother away.

He also used his imagination to make up elaborate games to play. At five, Howie's worldly experiences were limited to television's boundaries. Howie liked cartoons about action heroes. He would lead Mike around the yard, searching out bad guys and removing them with extreme prejudice, just like the heroes on the shows he watched.

Mike was a good soldier, always ready to do what his captain told him. Howie made up a code name for their invasion force–Lightning. It sounded fearsome.

Howie eventually began to lay plans for expanding the reach of their missions. Next door to them lived an old man–Howie's parents called him "retired." Howie thought that meant he was extra tired and so he must sleep a lot. In Howie's imagination, that made him vulnerable to bad guys.

One day he led Mike through a loose board in the fence and took a look around the old man's yard.

It was an eerie and wonderful place, full of potted palms and ferns and other plants that made it seem like a jungle. A place where lots of bad guys might hide. Howie made sure he and Mike each had sticks–or rather, high-powered rifles that never ran out of ammo.

The first few times Howie led Mike on an expedition into the yard, they didn't stay long. Mom would be sure to find out, and it was a little scary in this unfamiliar terrain. But each time they returned, they stayed just a little bit longer.

And then one day they stayed too long.

They were on the far side of the old man's yard when Howie heard his mother's voice. It had a sense of panic and urgency. She was calling out for both of them as if they were missing. Trouble was ahead. "Come on!" Howie ordered, and he took off running. He was sure Mike was right on his heels.

Howie ripped his tee shirt slipping back through the fence. His mother was right on top of him, a little angry now, telling Howie he shouldn't have been over there and asking where Mike was.

Howie pointed to the fence, expecting Mike to come through any second.

He didn't.

"Mike!" Janet Patino screamed.

That's when Howie's body filled with a fear and dread he had never known–and would never forget.

His mother ran out of their yard, heading for the old man's house. Howie poked his head back through the fence, yelling for Mike. He was lost, and it was Howie's fault. He knew it. He just had to find Mike and bring him back.

Howie called out "Lightning! Lightning!"

Mike didn't answer the call.

The old man's yard was on a slope. Howie slid on his pants downward toward a fence. He could hear his mother yelling Mike's name, getting closer and closer. He saw her charge into the backyard through the old man's gate.

Howie hit the fence the same time his mother did on the other side. He heard her scream.

Then he saw Mike. He was floating, facedown, in the swimming pool.

"They tried to revive him," Lindsay said. "But he was gone. The old man, I think his name was Harrington, almost died because of it. He had left the pool gate open. My parents never blamed him, but apparently one day he just up and drove away. The house was sold later, and no one ever found him."

"That's awful," I said, shaking my head.

"My parents dealt with it as best they could, I guess. I was never aware that there was any great tragedy that marked them for life, but I didn't have anything to compare it with. When I finally heard the story, I guess I was around twelve or thirteen. That's when Howie told me he'd talked to Mike."

"Talked to him?"

"Sort of . . ."

The nightmares started coming a week after Mike's death. Howie would wake up in the middle of the night, screaming and breathless. Janet and Fred did everything they could to comfort Howie. They would leave a light on in the hallway at night. They even let him sleep for a time on a mat in their room. The nightmares would settle down for awhile, but then another would hit, just as frightening.

Finally, when Howie was seven, his parents took him in for counseling. Howie was given the usual battery of tests, the standard therapies, even medication. Nothing brought relief.

Once, when Howie was around thirteen, the family went on a camping trip. It was then, sitting by a lake with fishing poles in hand, that Howie first told Lindsay he thought the devil was after him. He said it matter-of-factly, but it scared the daylights out of Lindsay.

Howie also told her that he had been trying to bring Mike back from the dead. That scared Lindsay even more. Howie said he would sometimes get up at night, stand in the middle of his room, and try to use a spell to bring up Mike's ghost. He even tried wiggling his nose like that funny witch on the TV show.

Howie made Lindsay swear not to ever tell anyone because the devil might come after her too, and he didn't want that.

The Patinos moved to California and settled in Agoura, where Fred had landed a great job. Lindsay knew her parents had made the move partly for Howie, hoping that moving as far away from the tragic scene as possible would wipe the slate clean.

For a few years, it seemed to work. Howie's nightmares became less frequent. He still had them, and on occasion he woke up screaming, but all in all it was better than before.

Then one night he came into Lindsay's room and woke her up.

"Lindsay," he whispered, "I talked to him."

"Who?"

"Mike."

Rubbing her eyes, Lindsay sat up in bed as Howie told her the story. He'd been over at his friend Barry's house. Barry's mom had an old Ouija Board. Howie told Lindsay about this magical board. You could ask it questions, and it would answer them. It would spell out messages from the spirit world. It could contact the dead.

Lindsay was frightened yet fascinated. Howie was almost crazy with joy. "I asked if I could talk to my brother Mike. The board said yes!"

"How did it say yes?"

"You and another guy put your fingers on this slider thing that moves."

"It moves?"

"Yeah. The spirits move it."

"That's freaky."

"But it told me I could talk to Mike. So I did. I told Mike I was sorry I let him drown."

"Then what happened?"

"Then the board said okay."

Lindsay shook her head. She had, within the last four years, come to look upon Howie as a younger brother. "How do you know this board thing is real?"

"I just do. I wasn't trying to move the slider; neither was Barry."

"How do you know?"

"At first I thought Barry might be trying to fool me. I kept asking him if he was moving it, and he kept saying no. Finally, I thought of a trick. I asked the board a question that only Mike would know the answer to."

"What happened?"

"It spelled something out."

"What?"

"*Lightning.*"

"Now that," I said, "really would be freaky. But those things have been proven to be phony."

"Have they?" Lindsay asked, as if she already knew the answer.

I shook my head. "They have to be," I said, but I didn't sound sure.

"There's more."

Barry's mother, Sonia, was into spiritism. It was a little secret in that family. The people in the neighborhood considered her a little eccentric, but that was it. She managed to function without causing any commotion–until the crack-up. A few years after the incident with the Ouija Board, Sonia was picked up on the 101 Freeway, walking naked and drunk along the shoulder of the highway and screaming at people as they drove by. She was, Lindsay heard, placed in a hospital. She never saw her again.

Before that, however, Sonia told Howie she could help him contact Mike.

Lindsay never heard all the details of the encounter. All she knew was that Howie, without telling their parents, went with Barry and his mother to a room in an old hotel, where they met with several other people for a séance.

For a week after that, Howie walked around the house like a ghost himself. His eyes were blank, like they were staring into a fog. Janet and Fred Patino thought he might be on drugs. They decided to take him to a doctor. That's when Howie ran away from home.

"He took off," Lindsay explained, "hitchhiking. It took us a month to find him the first time. The second time he was gone for half a year."

"What was he doing all that time?"

"We never knew for sure. But he was changed. It was like a permanent shroud was placed over him, and he was resigned to the fact that it would never be removed. I only saw a glimmer of hope out of him two times."

She paused, closed her eyes, and breathed deeply.

Howie was working a construction site in Hinton when he first met Rae Richards. She was serving cocktails in a bar about twenty minutes north, a popular truck stop and biker hangout. When Howie told Lindsay about it, he was glowing like a kid at Christmas. He described Rae as "the woman of his dreams" and a very spiritual person. It was clear he saw her not just as a girlfriend, but as a means of deliverance.

Lindsay and her parents were cautious, and then caution grew to concern when Howie hesitated about introducing her to the family. It was a hesitation that lasted for months. At one point Fred considered forcing his way into the situation, but Janet dissuaded him. Howie seemed happy and was working steadily. Maybe they shouldn't rock the boat.

The boat stayed steady all the way up to the point where Howie announced he and Rae were getting married.

Everything after that was a blur of activity, with Howie rushing headlong into marriage. The family did finally meet Rae, and she had a certain plucky charm about her. But something rubbed Lindsay the wrong way from the start.

"I just didn't trust her," Lindsay explained. "And she knew I didn't trust her. It was the way she looked at me. It was the first time in my Christian life when I felt a sense of evil."

"You just felt it?"

"Sensed it. But I couldn't put my finger on anything. I knew if I tried to stop the whole thing, Howie would be crushed. I guess I just decided to close my eyes and hope for the best. Big mistake."

I nodded as she looked at the floor. "You said there was another time Howie seemed happy."

"Yes, when Brian was born."

It was almost a year to the day after the wedding when Brian Patino–nine pounds, twelve ounces–was born. It was the biggest day of Howie's life, even bigger than when he got married. Here was another person–a living, breathing human being–that Howie had helped bring into the world. It proved once and for all that Howie was not a loser, that he could do something fine and lasting. He told Lindsay it was also a way to make up for Mike. A life for a life.

It wasn't long before Howie's joy reverted to the deep-seated sorrow that had been his before. He wouldn't talk much about it, not even to Lindsay, but it was clear that the marriage wasn't a happy one. Rae was the one calling the shots in the marriage, and she was the one making the decisions about Brian and just what would be done with him. Howie talked to Lindsay about it but never pressed his complaining for fear of Rae's wrath.

At one point Lindsay asked if Howie wanted another child. He said something curious in response: "That's not possible." Lindsay never got an explanation for that.

"That's pretty much how things remained," Lindsay said, "until Rae's death."

I pondered this for a moment, then said, "I never knew Howie had all this going on inside."

Lindsay nodded.

"But doesn't it explain the devil part?" I asked. "I mean, all that guilt and suffering. Wouldn't that result in his imagination coming up with all this?"

"I don't believe that," Lindsay said. "People can open doors to demonic influence. It can be something as little as trying to cast a witch's spell in your bedroom, or it can be a big door, like trying to communicate with the dead."

"Doors? What's that all about?"

"I'm saying there are things that people can do to open themselves up for oppression."

"From demons?"

"Yes. This isn't new." She opened her Bible again and took a moment to find a passage. "In Leviticus, it says, *Do not turn to mediums or seek out spiritists, for you will be defiled by them.* That's what happened to Howie. It fits. All the things Howie has done to try to get to Mike have been open doors."

My head had developed a righteous ache. I wasn't buying any of this. It was too strange. Lindsay believed it and was calm and rational about it. But that wasn't enough.

"I want to have Howie examined," I said.

"By whom?"

"A doctor. A psychotherapist."

"He's been through that before."

"I know. But I want to focus in on the night of Rae's murder. I want to see if we can get into Howie's head, bring back the past, and get a grip on what really happened. Is that all right with you?"

She looked at me steadily. "You're the one defending him. If you think it will be helpful, then do it."

"Thanks."

"But what will you think if it turns out to be true?"

"If what turns out to be true?"

"If Howie really did see the devil? What are you going to do then?"

CHAPTER EIGHTEEN

WHAT WOULD I do, indeed?

If Howie saw "the devil," it was either a delusion or real. I didn't believe it was real. That left delusion, and that meant Howie's mental state at the time of the killing was an issue. While the old diminished capacity defense is no longer available in California, an expert may give testimony about a defendant's background and perceptions and his mental condition at the time the offense was committed.

I had just the expert in mind to do it.

On Tuesday, the day after Howie's prelim and my devilish discussions with my client and his sister, I phoned Dr. Hendrick Brown's office, which also happened to be his condominium near downtown Los Angeles. He wasn't in, so I left a message for him to call me.

Then I called Mandy.

I got Rick.

"Mandy's at camp," he said.

"What camp?"

"A day camp."

"That narrows it down nicely. Thank you very much." I was being a complete jerk, but it seemed by now to be my habitual response to Rick Wilson. He was not a bad guy at all, I knew that, but he was married to my ex-wife. My typical American male pride sat on one of my shoulders, whispering in my ear to make Rick as uncomfortable as possible.

"I can have Barb give you a call when she gets in," Rick said.

"I would just like to know where my daughter is. I would like to be included in the planning stages from time to time."

"Barb felt, I think, that you pretty much leave those decisions to her." He had an understanding tone in his voice that irritated me more. I didn't want my ex-wife's new husband to be right about the situation. He was, though. I palmed off to Barb a lot of the day-to-day stuff concerning Mandy. And I knew why. I had enough troubles getting through each day myself without having to micromanage my daughter.

That didn't stop me from fanning the flames of my irritation. "So now you're an expert in what Barb thinks? And you've been married to her what, a year?"

"I'll have Barb call you."

"Don't you know what camp Mandy's at?"

"It's a nice camp, a church camp."

"Church camp? What's that all about?"

"Our church sponsors it."

An image of Mandy walking blank-eyed down a city street with free magazines in her hand suddenly popped into my head. "What church is that?"

"We're going to Church of the Hill out in Chatsworth."

"What kind of a church is it?"

"Just a regular church."

"That doesn't tell me anything."

"It's just a normal, evangelical church, Jake. If you're unsure about it, come visit."

"No thanks. But you better believe I'm going to find out more about this. I don't want my daughter indoctrinated into some right-wing religious cult. Tell Barb to call me."

I hung up. It took me a few minutes to calm down and realize what a boor I'd been, especially with that last remark. Then it hit me that what I was really doing was lashing out at Lindsay Patino.

She was starting to get to me with the strength of her beliefs, and I was putting up a defense. I didn't want to believe what she believed. I didn't want to believe what Barb and Rick apparently believed. I started thinking in terms of victory and defeat. I didn't want to admit I was wrong.

Anytime I thought about being wrong, I pictured my father. He was not the type to ever admit being wrong. He had an iron will and a steel pride. Not once in all the time I knew him did I ever hear him apologize–for anything.

Once, we were watching a movie on TV, a John Wayne flick called *She Wore a Yellow Ribbon.* At one point in the movie, John Wayne rebukes a soldier, saying, "Don't apologize. It's a sign of weakness."

I remember Dad mumbling, "Right on."

Even after those times he beat me up, he never apologized. I once overheard him arguing with Mom about it. She said something about his being unfair to me, and he said that didn't matter; it was going to toughen me up, and I needed toughening because I was a "mama's boy."

But I would gladly have taken more of the physical punishment if once, just once, Dad had told me I'd done a good job on something. Anything.

He never did.

I was thirteen when he died. He hung on to life for a week in the hospital before his heart stopped for good. I only saw him there once. He was gaunt and weak. I was sure–and I'm sure he was too–that this would be the last time we spoke to each other.

As I look back on it now, even though I was uncomfortable around him, I was waiting for the grand gesture. A hug. A plea for forgiveness. Some parting words of affirmation.

Instead, I got mostly silence.

Just before I left, he said "Don't mess things up for your mother."

Those were the last words he ever said to me. Four days later he was dead.

The night after the funeral I decided to sneak out of the house and get rip-snorting drunk. And I decided to do it with the only friend I had at the time.

Howie Patino.

He was more than willing, as was the wino who hung out near the liquor store and bought us the bottle with the money I gave him, along with an additional buck for his trouble.

Even though I was sick the next day, I remember that night as one of the happiest of my life.

It was like a huge weight had been lifted off my shoulders, and with each sip of wine I became lighter and lighter, like I could fly from Orlando to Los Angeles and back again with barely a flap of my arms.

Howie and I began making plans for our futures. For once I was able to think about it without wondering how Dad was going to put me down.

Howie said he wanted to be a jet fighter pilot. He wanted to go to war against the Commies and blast them out of the sky.

I said I wanted to become the biggest millionaire in the world. I was going to have my own fleet of yachts and go to all the great spots in the world where millionaires go. I was going to drink champagne all the time and own my own football team, and then people would know that Nick Denney's kid had so far outdone his old man that nobody could remember the dead guy anymore.

As I said more and more, Howie sat there slapping his legs and saying, "Yeah, man! Yeah, man!"

Well, I didn't make my millions. I became a lawyer scouring for clients just so I could afford a place to live and drink. I wondered if the old man could see me and wondered what he would think. Sometimes the only thing that would make those thoughts go away was a drink.

I spent an hour in my office making disjointed notes on Howie's case, then got a return call from Dr. Hendrick Brown.

"You were an expert on a case I tried," I told him.

"Yeah," he said. "Attempted murder, wasn't it?"

"That's right. The guy who shot his wife and said he couldn't remember it."

"As I recall, she was somebody who deserved to be shot. Kind of a big lady with a mouth to go with it."

"Doc, that kind of opinion is inadmissible in a court of law."

"I'm talkin' about my world now, which is the court of reality. Anyway, Jake, what can I do for you?"

"I'd like you to examine a client of mine."

"You name the time and place; I'll name the fee."

We haggled about the fee part, but I set up a tentative date for him to see Howie.

At one o'clock Triple C came to my office. We had the names of two people we were going to interview in Hinton. I was going to take the old lady who lived across the street from the Patino house. Trip would see the bartender at the place where Rae had most recently worked. Maybe one thing would lead to another. I was hoping that all this would lead to something, anything, because at this point we didn't have a lot.

And we were just about to find out we had even less than we thought.

CHAPTER NINETEEN

DAPHNE BARTH'S EYES were filled with suspicion as she peeked at me past the chain lock on her door.

"My name is Jake Denney, Miss Barth."

"Who are you?"

"I'm investigating the murder."

"I already talked to you."

"I'm not from the police, Miss Barth. I'm the lawyer representing the defendant."

Her face came close to that hideous countenance I feared. "I am not going to talk to you!"

"Now, Miss Barth–"

"You leave decent people alone!"

There were two ways to handle this. The first way, the hard way, was to threaten her with a subpoena and the prospect of being dragged into court–dragged would be the actual word to use–and grilled on the witness stand. I'd probably get her scared enough to talk for awhile, but how much good information I'd get would be another story.

I chose the other way. "You're right, Miss Barth. Absolutely right."

She looked puzzled. "Excuse me?"

"You're right about decent people needing protection from our system. There's only one way to do that, and that's to make sure the truth comes out."

"I believe that's right."

"Now, if I could get at the truth quickly, at the facts, there might be a way to protect you in court."

"How?"

I took a little step closer. "Would you mind if I came in?"

She hesitated. "I'm not supposed to talk to you."

"Who told you that?"

"Somebody from the district attorney's office. They said I wasn't to talk to the defense. You seem like a nice young man, but I have to do what I'm told."

A jolt of electric excitement shot through my body. There was a real possibility here of witness interference. A witness for the prosecution is not considered to be represented by the prosecutor and can be directly approached by the defense. An attempt to interfere with communication with defense attorneys or investigators is an ethical violation. If I could nail this down, it might come in very handy at trial.

"Miss Barth, are you sure this is what you were told?"

"Well . . . yes."

"Do you remember the name of the person who told you this?"

She shook her head. "It was a nice young lady."

"Does the name Sylvia Plotzske ring a bell?"

She thought for a moment. "Yes, I think that's it."

"I know Sylvia."

"You do?"

"Sure. Miss Barth, if I could come in for just a moment, I won't take up much of your time. And I promise that if you get uncomfortable with anything I say, you can ask me to leave. Fair enough?"

The cogs and wheels turned inside her head. Then she unlatched the door and let me in.

Her house was Victorian–in size, decoration, and smell. It had an eerie sense of time standing still. The little woman took me into what would have been called the drawing room many years ago, and we sat on furniture that could have come from Mark Twain's home.

"This is all so upsetting," Daphne Barth said. "I don't want to get into any trouble."

"You won't, Miss Barth."

"It's *Mrs.* Barth, young man. My dear Oscar and I were married for fifty-four years."

"I'm sorry."

"What's that?" She cocked one ear toward me.

"I said I was sorry."

"You'll have to speak up, young man. He was a rancher, you know."

I nodded and smiled.

"He helped build Hinton. He was the first city commissioner."

"Was he now?" I wanted to keep her talking. The more she talked, the easier it would be to transition into discussing the case.

"Oscar first came out here in 1936. We were living in Kansas then, but my dear Oscar was never one to be fenced in."

"A real pioneer type, eh?"

"A free spirit, Oscar was. He was the smartest man I ever knew." She described, in protracted detail, Oscar Barth's acumen in the cattle business, his meeting with Franklin Delano Roosevelt–"Gave him a piece of his mind, my Oscar did"–and several other highlights of Oscar's life.

Before I got her around to the night of the murder, my neck was almost sore from nodding and my cheeks from forcing a smile.

"I don't remember anything about it," Daphne Barth explained. "It was a night like any other night. I always make myself a pot of tea at nine o'clock or thereabouts. I like to drink it out on the porch when the nights are pleasant."

"Was it pleasant that night?"

"Not that I remember. I drank my tea inside. I watched the television."

"Did you hear anything from across the street?"

"I did hear a loud voice, like I told the police, and I think he shouted her name."

"You mean Rae's name?"

"Yes."

"Who?"

"I assume it was him."

"Her husband?"

"That's your client, isn't it?"

"Yes."

"I think it was him."

"But you're not sure?"

"That's all I remember."

"Anything else?"

"No, that's all."

I scratched my forehead, not because it itched, but because I was trying to figure out why the prosecutor would be advising this woman not to talk to me when she had only one item of relevant testimony, which probably wouldn't even be needed at trial.

I had just sat through a half hour of the history of Oscar Barth, and I was not about to let that investment go with such paltry returns. "How well did you know Rae Patino?" I asked.

"I never saw her very much. She was a night crawler." She whispered the last two words.

"What, exactly, do you mean?"

"Oh, you know."

"Help me out."

She leaned a little forward, as if someone else might be listening. "She was *fast.*"

It was an old-fashioned term, but I'd heard it used in the South by some of the older ladies. "You mean she had rather loose morals?"

Daphne Barth nodded.

"What makes you say that?"

"Oh, I've been around the block, sonny."

"Did you ever observe Rae Patino with other men?"

She shook her head. "But I know it just the same. The way she dressed."

"Did you ever hear anything going on at her house? Any parties? Things like that?"

Again she shook her head. "Nothing wild, if that's what you mean."

I didn't know what I meant. I was fishing for something, anything. "So, no noise," I said offhandedly.

Oscar Barth's widow frowned at that, like she suddenly remembered something. "There was a time," she said, "when I heard a strange thumping."

"Thumping?"

"Yes. It was loud. It was so loud, it rattled my windows and woke me up."

"What was it?"

"It sounded like someone pounding on my front door. I was frightened. I didn't dare get out of bed."

"Someone trying to break into your house, maybe?"

"It was so loud, but then it suddenly stopped. I stayed in bed waiting for it to start again. When it didn't, I got out of bed and went to the window. I peeked out."

"What did you see?"

"Nothing."

"Nothing at all?"

"Just a car driving by."

"What kind of a car?"

"A big one, more like a truck."

"Was it a truck?"

"No, it was more like a car than a truck. But it was *like* a truck."

I almost laughed at the massive waste of time this had turned out to be. The pounding on the door might have been relevant, but without some identification tied into some incident at Rae Patino's, it was useless.

I stood and thanked Daphne Barth. She asked if I had to go so soon. She probably wanted to fill me in on Oscar Barth's childhood. I told her I had to get over to the jail and talk to my client. She asked if I would need to speak with her again.

"No, Mrs. Barth. This was all I needed."

She looked disappointed.

Triple C was breathless on the phone, like he'd been jogging. I was in my car, driving to the jail.

"You ready for this?" he said.

"For what?"

"Something weird's going on down here."

"You talk to the bartender?"

"Yeah, I talked to him."

"You get anything useful?" I was anxious for a bit of good news.

"Maybe. But that's not the weird part."

"Why don't you tell me the weird part?"

"Our boy Delliplane? The surfer?"

"Yeah."

"They fished his body out of the ocean this morning."

CHAPTER TWENTY

THE HINTON COUNTY medical examiner, Chet Riordan, was a portly man with a bristle-brush mustache. He looked like he'd be some kid's favorite uncle, not someone who spent his days around dead people. But it was clear that this guy loved his work.

"Your drownings, you see, can't be proven by positive evidence," Riordan said. We were sitting near his desk, which was in a cubicle in a small office a short walk from the courthouse. The ME munched Rye Krisp crackers as he spoke. "You eliminate other options, see, and then you look at the circumstances, and if they involve a lot of water, you got your drowning."

"And that's what we've got here?" I asked.

"More'n likely. You got your surfer out there a little too long, gets a little too tired; the others have gone in for the day. It's happened before. You mix in some beer, some marijuana, you got yourself the big dive."

"Big dive?" Trip said.

"That's what I call a drowning. The big dive. I made that up myself." His mustache moved, making me believe he smiled. Trip looked at me like he couldn't believe this guy's rap.

"What other details can you give us?" I asked.

"Well, you got your wet drownings and your dry drownings, and then you got–"

"Excuse me," I said putting my hand up. "I mean about the victim. What about the victim?"

"He's dead."

I started to fantasize about pulling the guy's mustache out hair by hair. Riordan laughed at his little joke, then continued. "Here's the deal. I looked him over real good, and there was no sign of foul play. No cuts or abrasions, and no blows to the head, nothing like that. The guy looked in pretty good shape, so I doubt he had a heart attack or a stroke. The guy probably got out a little too far or got a little too tired; then he fell off his board, and a wave took him down."

Riordan took a bite of Rye Krisp. A few crumbs jumped into his mustache and held on for dear life. "When a drowning victim goes under, you see, he reaches a point where his body tells him to take a breath, or it's bye-bye. He instinctively sucks in, but instead of air, he gets water. And then he gets desperate, sucks some more, gets more water, and his respiration stops. Cerebral anoxia sets in. And that's the big dive, gentlemen."

"So, you're treating this as an accident?" Trip asked.

"I'm just your humble ME," Riordan said. "I report the facts. The police do what they want. If they want my opinion, I'll give it to them." He held up a one-page report sheet in his hand.

"May I see that?" Trip asked.

Riordan shrugged and handed him the sheet. I said, "Did anybody find his surfboard?"

For a moment Riordan seemed surprised, as if he would never have considered such a question important. After all, surfboards don't take the big dive. Then he said, "Yes, I believe the officer said his board was found on the beach."

"Which officer would that be?"

"I'm sorry. I don't remember."

Trip handed the report back to Riordan and gave me a little slap on the shoulder. "Let's let Mr. Riordan get back to work," he said.

That was a signal. Trip wanted to talk. I stood and thanked Riordan. He seemed a little disappointed we were leaving. He probably had lots more to tell us about causes of death.

We got in Trip's car and just sat. "What's up?" I asked.

"I got a hunch."

"About what?"

"Something is rotten in the state of Denmark."

"You mean Hinton."

"Same thing."

"And that rotten thing is?"

"If I tell you now, and it doesn't turn out, that might make you disappointed."

"Come on!"

Trip smiled his wide, teasing smile. "Steady, knave. You remember the first time you saw Delliplane?"

"Yeah, I was with you."

"On the beach."

"Right."

"What was he doing?"

"Surfing."

"And what was he doing when we talked to him?"

"Not surfing?"

"Think."

"Come on, man, I'm tired." But I knew my protests were in vain. Triple C liked the Socratic method.

"Think back. What was Delliplane doing?"

I closed my eyes and tried to picture the scene again. I got bits and pieces. I saw Chip Delliplane stick his surfboard, nose down, into the sand. "He stuck his surfboard in the sand," I said.

"And then what?"

Eyes still closed, I looked again. And then I saw it. I opened my eyes and sat straight up. "His wet suit!"

"You're warm."

"He was getting out of his wet suit. Don't wet suits make you buoyant?"

"Good guess, but no. Stuff they use now's too thin. Keep looking."

I was out of images and ideas. "That's enough. Just tell me."

"This is why you're the lawyer, and I'm the gumshoe. It's the little things. Like that little detail Riordan gave us. He said they found the board on the beach; you remember that?"

"Yeah."

"When we talked to Delliplane, did you notice the little dangling thing on his surfboard?"

I thought back again and did see it. It was what surfers call a leash, which attaches to the board on one end and to the surfer's ankle on the other. "So, if the board was supposed to be attached, why'd they find it on the beach instead of on his ankle?"

"You'll make it yet, Einstein," Trip said. "It's possible the thing came off, but unlikely. I'm thinking there's a good chance our boy was knocked off."

"Because?"

"Because he talked to us."

My case was getting stranger, but the next day things went nuts.

I took Dr. Hendrick Brown to see Howie.

Dr. Brown was in his sixties, his closely cropped black hair flecked with gray. He was tall and trim, with a salt-and-pepper mustache setting off sparkling eyes. He looked more like a storyteller than a psychiatrist, someone you could imagine sitting lankily around a pot-bellied stove telling tales about frogs and hound dogs.

I knew Brown from my days in the public defender's office. He'd been employed as an expert a number of times by our office, because his price was right, and, as an African American, he had a natural affinity with our minority clients. His practice was aimed primarily at the poorer demographic areas of our fair city. He viewed his calling as a mission as much as a profession. Because he was not one of those fancy, Westside practitioners, he was treated with some disdain by others in his trade and by the prosecutors who had to cross-examine him.

But juries loved him.

When we were about twenty miles from Hinton, Brown asked, "So, do you want a theory, or do you want an explanation?"

"What's the difference?" I said.

"It's what you want out of this exam. I can question him about it and then try to figure out a theory of his mental state at the time, or we can go deep and try to get him to remember every detail of what happened."

"I want to know as much as possible. Howie thinks he saw the devil. I want to know if that was something in his own mind, or if there was another person present. Is there any way we can get to that?"

"Hypnosis would be my first preference, but we won't have the time or conditions for that."

"What's your second preference?"

"Bend the rules a little."

I shot him a quick glance. He was smiling at me like a boy who was suggesting some mischief. "What, exactly, do you mean?" I asked.

Brown patted the medical bag he'd brought with him. "Sodium pentathol."

"You want to shoot him up?"

"That's an option."

"But where? At the jail?"

"Unless they're going to release him."

"But we can't. I think we have to give notice."

"That's why I said we bend the rules. Not break, bend. We make the exam, make a report, then give it to the prosecution in discovery. That's notice."

"After the fact."

"But you'll have an idea about what really happened that night."

Another possibility was that I could be facing the wrong end of an ethics charge if the prosecutors got angry enough. But I was running out of time. I had to know what happened. It was as much my own curiosity as it was anything else now.

"Let's do it," I said.

CHAPTER TWENTY-ONE

THE JAIL DEPUTY on duty recognized me, though not in a warm fashion. I was still the outsider. Worse, I was the big-city lawyer, even though my big city was a small office at the rear of a building, and my only client was a resident in his pokey. His look changed from contempt to suspicion when he noticed Dr. Hendrick Brown with me.

"Who's he?" the jailer asked.

"This is a doctor," I explained. "He's going to examine my client."

A temporary cloud of confusion came over the jailer's face, which he blew away with bluster. "He's not going to examine anybody here. You need a medical transfer. Now you go on down to the–"

"Excuse me. This is Dr. Hendrick Brown; he's a psychiatrist. This isn't a medical examination; it's a mental evaluation. We don't need any transfer for that."

The jailer gave Brown a quick up-and-down, as if he was skeptical. "He got some ID?"

Brown reached in his coat and produced a card, which he placed before the jailer. The jailer looked at it, shrugged, and tossed it on his desk. "Doesn't tell me anything."

So the jailer, perhaps to break up a monotonous day, or because his supervisor chewed him out that morning, or maybe because his wife packed him a bologna sandwich for the third straight day, decided to play some hardball.

I took a swing. "Look, I can go over to the courthouse if you like, disturb Judge Abovian's lunch, tell him they're not cooperating down at the jail, and ask him what to do. But that'll only mean you'll have to process a bunch of paperwork while your supervisor asks you to explain why a judge is calling him up and screaming at him over the phone about interfering with the attorney-client relationship. We don't want that, do we?"

The jailer thought about it. "You guys are all the same, aren't you?"

I nodded. "Every one of us is here to make life miserable for somebody else."

Next to me, Dr. Hendrick Brown suppressed a laugh. The jailer barked, "Go to the first conference room."

As we made our way toward the door, Brown whispered, "That man needs my help. He's suppressing a lot of anger."

"He's got your card," I said. "Maybe he'll give you a ring."

We entered the small conference room, which consisted of four blank walls, a barred and screened window, and a metal table with two chairs. A few minutes later, a deputy sheriff opened the door and led Howie in. After waiting until Howie was seated, the deputy left, closed the door, and locked it from the outside.

Howie did not look well. He seemed tired but also something worse than tired. Defeated? I wondered for a moment if he should be put on suicide watch. I'd keep that in mind.

"Howie, this is Dr. Brown," I said. Howie looked at him with ambivalence.

"How are you, Howie?" Brown extended his hand. Howie didn't take it, nor did he move.

"Dr. Brown is here to examine you, Howie."

"Why?"

"To help us figure out what happened that night."

"You already know what happened," Howie said, his head slumping slightly.

"This will just help make things a little clearer," I explained. "For me."

Shrugging his shoulders, Howie said nothing.

"Shall we begin?" Dr. Brown asked.

Howie shrugged again. Brown nodded at me, which meant he was ready. I took out a handheld tape recorder from my briefcase and set it down on the table. Howie looked at it suspiciously. "What's that for?" he said.

"I'm going to record our session, Howie. It's just for me."

"I don't like this."

And if he didn't like that, he was really going to hate the next part. I put on my soft voice. "Howie, listen. Dr. Brown knows what he's doing. He needs to give you a little injection first."

Suspicion glimmered in Howie's eyes. "Injection? You mean like a shot?"

"Yes, Howie. It won't take a second."

Shaking his head, Howie said, "I don't want a shot. I don't like shots."

"I won't hurt you," Brown said. "I promise. If I do, you can slap me. Is that fair?"

This wasn't typical bedside manner, but it had an effect. Howie actually smiled. It was startling, but Brown had somehow found the right thing to say and the way to say it. No wonder juries ate him up.

"Will it help?" Howie asked me.

I nodded.

"Okay." Howie sat back as Brown prepared the syringe. I kept glancing nervously toward the door, afraid that several armed guards would burst in at any moment and arrest the lot of us.

Brown injected Howie's left arm with sodium pentathol. It's a fast-acting barbiturate that puts the subject into deep relaxation. It was first used as anesthesia for surgeons and dentists, but they found along the way that it had a way of bringing up suppressed memories, which is why it is sometimes called "truth serum."

It took only a few minutes for Howie to go into what looked like a trance. His lids closed heavily over his eyes, and I had to sit near his side to keep him from falling over.

Finally, Brown said he was ready to begin questioning Howie. I turned on the tape recorder.

"Howie?" Brown said.

"Hmm?"

"Can you understand me?"

"Yes."

"You're relaxed now, aren't you?"

"Yes."

"Do you know where you are?"

"Sleeping."

"Where are you sleeping?"

"Chair."

"Are you comfortable?"

"Yes."

"All right. I want you to listen very carefully to me. Are you listening?"

"Yes."

Brown leaned a little closer to Howie and spoke softly. "I want you to remember the day you flew down from Alaska. It's March 25, and you're getting on a plane. Do you remember that?"

"Yes," Howie said. I watched for any change in his passive expression. There was none.

"Where are you going?"

"Home."

"Where's home?"

"With Rae."

"How do you feel?"

"Happy."

"Why are you happy?"

"Going to see Rae." Howie smiled. It was the same goofy grin he'd always had. At that moment he looked about ten years old.

Taking his time, Brown led Howie step-by-step through the events of the twenty-fifth. Later he told me this was essential to the examination. Reliving as much sensory detail as possible would make the crucial sequence come alive with greater clarity.

And that's what it seemed Howie was doing–reliving the events in a dreamlike fashion.

As the recollection unfolded, Howie grew more voluble, even animated. He sat up a little, and though he had his eyes closed, his face played out the emotions in a hypnotic masque.

"The air is cool," Howie said with a smile, recalling stepping off the bus onto the main street of Hinton. "I like the cool air. It reminds me."

"Reminds you of what?" Brown asked.

"Rae. She's warm. She will keep me warm. I like the cool air because I know Rae will keep me warm."

Howie was almost laughing now, and for a moment I considered calling the whole thing off. I knew what was coming, and I knew Howie's insides would be ripped out once more. But Brown had prepared me for this. He said Howie would not recall the trauma once the examination was finished and the effects of the drug wore off. He'd be very tired and would probably feel some physical discomfort, but he wouldn't know that he had virtually experienced again the worst moment of his life.

"I like my street," Howie said as he recalled walking toward the house. "It's quiet and peaceful. Rae is going to be surprised. She might get a little mad, but then she'll be glad to see me. She'll know how much she missed me."

It hit me then why Howie would have been lost in delusion when he finally did get to Rae. The poor guy had constructed a fantasy for himself. He actually thought Rae, who was by all accounts an abuser of persons and interested in no one's welfare but her own, would be glad to see him. He'd gone away; now he was coming back, and everything would be all right. They'd live happily ever after. It was Howie's last hope for happiness in this world, at least in his own deceived mind.

Howie recalled reaching the house and how excited he was. His face was lit up like a kid at Christmas. "I try to open the door, but it's locked. I don't have a key with me. I knock. No answer. I knock again and I call out, 'Rae!' No answer."

That's when his face started to change, reflecting his sense at the time that something was not right. Howie narrated how he went around the side, scaled the wall, found the sliding door in the back locked, and broke it open. The house was still. No one seemed to be home.

But someone was. In the bedroom he found Rae. She sat up in bed. She wasn't happy to see him. And then she said she was in love with somebody else.

Howie paused. Brown didn't ask another question. He seemed to be waiting for something. I looked at Howie's face and saw a tear squirming down his cheek.

After a short pause, Dr. Brown asked, "What do you say to her?"

Howie gave his next responses in dialogue form, alternating between his voice and a slightly higher voice with a hard edge, which was obviously Rae's.

Who is it?

I can't tell you that.

Why?

That's just the way life is.

Please, Rae, don't do this to me.

I'm not doing anything to anybody.

I'm a better person. I can get a good job in Alaska. You'll see.

That's enough, Howie. It's over. It's been over for a long time.

Please, Rae! Oh, please, please!

The tears were now flowing freely down Howie's face. He raised his hand in front of himself and moved it in the air slowly, rhythmically. In the "Rae voice," he said, "There, there. Don't cry." I realized he was reenacting what Rae had both said and done. She had suddenly become loving and understanding. She had allowed Howie to rest his head on her shoulder while she stroked his hair.

Howie had released a volley of words then, which he now repeated to Dr. Brown and me. "You'll see, Rae. You'll see. You'll see how great it is up there. Really, you'll see. It's like a whole new land, Rae, and we can start all over. We can have a piece of land someday up there, a real good one. Brian can grow up there, and it will make him strong. You'll see."

Then, Howie's voice changed instantly. He sat up straight and stiff. In my mind's eye I could almost see Rae shoving him away, becoming surly again, playing him the way a cat toys with a half-dead mouse.

They exchange more words, Howie doing everything he can to get her to change her mind. She softens again for awhile, then goes back to cruel anger.

Watching Howie go through this was like watching someone with multiple personalities changing this way and that like a psychometric kaleidoscope.

Then it turned ugly.

Howie played both parts again, giving Rae voice to say, "What makes you so proud?"

Proud?

Yeah, proud.

Proud of what?

Brian.

What are you talking about, Rae?

I'm talking about Brian, Howie.

What about him?

What makes you think he's yours?

Howie's expression became a horrific grimace. From deep within him came a guttural moan like the sound of a rusty door creaking open. Then it flew up into his mouth and turned into a wail of agony. Howie's head began rocking back and forth, his eyes still closed.

Brown jumped in quickly. "What do you see, Howie?"

"Rae!"

"What is Rae doing?"

"Laughing." Howie's voice was tight, strained, and tortured.

"Why is she laughing?"

"At me."

"How do you know?"

"She's pointing."

"Is she pointing at you?"

"Yes!"

Then Howie became perfectly still, every muscle in his body seeming to tense.

"What do you see, Howie?"

No answer.

But now Howie's eyes opened. They were wide eyes, eyes with fear in them, eyes beholding something terrible.

"Howie, what do you see?"

"A knife."

"Where is the knife, Howie?"

"In front of me."

"What do you do?"

"Grab."

"You grab for the knife?"

"Yes."

"What happens?"

"I miss."

"What do you do?"

Howie's face contorted into another variation on a dread theme. "It hurts!"

"What hurts?"

"The knife!"

"Where does it hurt?"

"In me!" Howie put his hands on the right side of his stomach.

"You stab yourself?" Dr. Brown asks.

Howie shook his head.

"Who stabbed you, Howie?"

Eyes widening again, Howie says, "He!"

"Who is he?"

"The devil!"

"What does the devil look like?"

"Black."

"Black? Black skin?"

"Dressed in black."

"What color is his skin?"

"Dark."

"Can you see his face?"

"His eyes."

"You can see his eyes?"

"Yes."

"Can you see their color?"

"Hate."

"What color?"

"Hate!"

I noticed that Dr. Hendrick Brown was starting to sweat. He wiped his forehead with the back of his hand. "What is he doing?"

"Rae!"

"What is the devil doing?"

"Killing Rae!"

"Is he stabbing her?"

"Yes!"

"What do you do?"

"I'm getting up."

"Can you get up?"

"Rae! Rae!"

"What is happening?"

"She's screaming! I can't get up! Rae!"

Howie raised his left arm in the air and reached out toward the image he was seeing in his mind. He sucked in a labored breath and held it. Then suddenly his eyes closed, and his head fell on his chest. For a moment I thought he'd died of a heart attack. I reached for him, but Dr. Brown put his hand on my shoulder and pushed me back, shaking his head slowly at me.

"Howie," Brown said, "it's over. You're back in the conference room with me and Jake. Remember?"

Howie's head didn't move at first; then it lifted slowly. It reminded me of some movie where a corpse rises from the grave.

CHAPTER TWENTY-TWO

". . . AND HOWIE HAS transferred the guilt onto himself," Hendrick Brown finished explaining as we drove back to my office. "He has convinced himself that he was responsible for Rae's death because at that moment he wanted her dead. And there appeared at the right time an angel of death. Only this was no angel."

"So why didn't he kill Howie too?" I asked.

"I've been thinking about that. And I'm thinking it's more transference."

"How so?"

"The killer transferred the killing to Howie, right? Howie's the one who got arrested, Howie's the one with the motive, and Howie's the one with the knife in his hand."

"What about that? How did that happen?"

"You remember at the end when Howie looked like he passed out?"

"Yeah."

"He did. On that night he blacked out from his wound, from the trauma. He fainted. I figure the killer put the knife near Howie's hand. The whole scene was made to order."

It made sense in an Alfred Hitchcock sort of way. But this wasn't a movie, and I wasn't a director who could change the script to come up with new evidence.

"I don't know," I said.

"What don't you know?"

"I don't know how I'm going to get you up on the stand and get the judge to allow you to share your theory with the jury."

"Well, son, that's your department. I just do the figuring. I don't do the lawyering."

But I do. And it is a defense lawyer's job to sow reasonable doubt in the collective mind of the jury. That's the system. And the system in California dictates that reasonable doubt is not "mere possible doubt," but where, after consideration by the members of the jury, the evidence leaves in their minds less than an "abiding conviction" in the truth of the charge.

I played these words over and over in my head as I sat in my office, the sun setting on another day outside my window.

Did I really have anything other than "mere possible doubt"? Would the jury, after comparing all the evidence, really have enough to say that they didn't feel an "abiding conviction" of the truth of the charge?

Not likely. Without some corroborating evidence, Brown's theory was as fragile as my legal future.

I scoured my mind for possibilities. Daphne Barth was not going to be any help, and the one guy who could have given us a link was dead.

Nothing else.

I poured myself a drink from the bottle I kept in my drawer, took off my shoes, and put my feet up on my desk. I placed my handheld tape recorder on the desk and replayed Howie's examination.

I just sipped and listened, hoping something would jump out, some clue or suggestion that would give me some direction to turn.

And then it happened.

It was near the end, just before Howie went into the blackout. Howie's voice, playing two parts, came through again:

Proud?

Yeah, proud.

Proud of what?

Brian.

What are you talking about, Rae?

I'm talking about Brian, Howie.

What about him?

What makes you think he's yours?

When I heard that last comment in the interview room, I had assumed it was something Rae said just to make Howie go nuts.

But what if it was true? What if little Brian Patino was not Howie's son?

Then somebody else was the father. And could that person be the killer?

My phone rang. It was Lindsay Patino.

"Did you see Howie today?" she asked.

"Yes."

"What's the latest?"

"I'd rather not go into this by phone," I said.

"Can I come to your office? I can be there in fifteen minutes."

I checked my watch, which seemed absurd as soon as I did it. I had no plans, no appointments, nothing to get to. "That's fine," I said.

It took me ten minutes to clean up the office a little bit, take another drink, and hide the bottle. And it was almost fifteen minutes to the second when Lindsay walked through my door and sat down.

She looked more beautiful than ever, which only got me angry.

"Thanks for seeing me," she said. "I'm here for Mom and Dad. It's so hard on them. And they have Brian too."

I said, "I had Howie examined by a doctor, someone I've worked with before. He's good, very good. He put Howie under medication to help him remember what happened."

"What kind of medication?"

"Sodium pentathol."

She looked surprised. "Does that work?"

"I think we got somewhere."

"What happened?"

"The doc walked Howie through the night of the killing."

"And?"

"He saw someone. He says it's the devil. It may be more mundane than that. It may be the real killer."

Lindsay thought a moment and nodded. "Howie may have sensed something, the presence of evil."

"Or he may have dreamed it up in his own mind."

"I don't think so."

"Because if he did, we may have a mental defense."

Shaking her head, Lindsay said, "That's funny."

"What is?"

"Just the fact that if Howie did sense demonic influence, it would be viewed as a type of insanity."

"Well, you've got to admit it's not normal."

"Isn't it?" She looked at me without so much as a flinch.

"Look, Lindsay, I'm not one to run down what you choose to believe, but we're dealing with the real world here."

"How do you know what's real?"

"Excuse me?"

"How do you know that the real world doesn't include the supernatural?"

Once more I felt on the defensive with her. That didn't help my disposition. I felt myself drawn toward her with even greater strength than before. But there was a wall around her, something she had erected, and it was something I didn't understand.

Or maybe I did understand it but didn't like it.

"I just don't believe in a personal God," I said. "The universe is obviously *impersonal.* Things don't happen because of the will of some Supreme Being. That's just the way it is, and the sooner we come to terms with that the better off we'll be."

With a slight shake of her head, and looking almost personally hurt, Lindsay said, "I see it just the opposite way. Coming to terms with our Creator is the only way to get to reality."

"That's a delusion."

"Is that what you really think?"

"Yes."

"Why?"

The question caught me by surprise. I was not ready with a quick answer. "That's just what I believe."

"But you must have a reason. You must have thought this through. I'm very interested."

And I believed she was, which somehow just added to my irritation. Having a spiritual discussion was the last thing I wanted, especially with Lindsay Patino. At that moment, all I wanted was for her to go away.

But she had asked a fair question, and as I thought about how to answer, I remembered a pivotal incident in my life. It came flashing back to me in vivid colors, almost demanding to be let out. It was deeply personal, something I wouldn't have told many people, let alone a near stranger. But somehow, I didn't feel reticent about telling Lindsay.

"When I was ten years old," I began, "there was a kid in our class named Danny . . ."

He was a skinny kid with glasses, not what you'd call the athletic type. We called him a nerd. He was the object of wedgies and pantsings, ridicule and jokes–the same way Howie was from time to time. While I'd come to be sort of a protector of Howie, Danny was a different case. I participated occasionally in the pranks because of peer pressure. I didn't want my friends to think I wasn't a regular guy.

Then one day I was walking home from school and it started to rain, one of those instant Florida cloudbursts. I began to jog, turned a corner, and saw a small group of kids up ahead. I couldn't see too clearly, but it was evident that one kid was being singled out for juvenile abuse.

I kept jogging and watching. The kids dispersed. All but one. When I got closer, I saw it was Danny. His school books lay all around him, soaking in the rain. He got down on one knee and started picking them up.

Without thinking about it, I stopped to help him.

When we both stood up, Danny looked at me with astonishment. It was hard to tell what else he was feeling because raindrops covered his glasses, and I couldn't really see his eyes. But I sensed a certain stoicism in him, almost a reserve of strength in the face of the humiliation of getting his books knocked out of his hands.

"Thanks," he said.

I shrugged my shoulders. "We better get out of this," I said and motioned for him to follow me as I jogged toward a large tree half a block away. We found some shelter there.

We were silent for awhile, listening to the rain. Then I said, "I know those guys. They're just jerks."

"It's okay," Danny said.

"You ever thought about boxing lessons or something?"

Danny laughed. "No. I'm not supposed to fight back."

"How come?"

"Because Jesus said to turn the other cheek and love your enemies."

Those were both foreign concepts to me and sounded weird coming from a skinny, ten-year-old kid. "Where'd you pick that up?" I asked.

"The Bible."

"You read the Bible?"

"Sure. It's the Word of God. The King James Version, of course."

"What's that?"

"The King James Version is the only true, inspired translation of the original texts."

I didn't have any idea what he was talking about or how to respond, so I didn't say anything. We waited for several minutes, and then the rain started to let up. Silently, we both started walking in the same direction.

There was definitely something different about Danny. When we got to his house, I learned why. His father was in the front yard fixing a shutter on the house. He looked exactly like Danny, only bigger. When he saw us, he smiled and waved.

Danny said, "This is Jake from my class."

Danny's father put out his hand. "Hello, Jake. Nice to meet you."

"We were talking about the Bible," Danny said, his voice full of excitement.

"Well!" Danny's father said. "Are you a Christian?"

"No, sir," I said with a shrug.

"Are you interested in the Bible?"

Not wanting to sound rude, I said, "Sort of."

"Well, come on inside. Let me get you a lemonade."

I felt strange about it, but I went in anyway. Danny's father, whose name turned out to be Irv Dickerson, poured us lemonade. Then he started talking.

Over the next half hour, I found out some things about Danny Dickerson and his father. They were fundamental Christians, and Danny's father was the pastor of a local church. Before I left, Danny's father gave me a small Bible as a gift and invited me to church the following Sunday.

I got home and told my mom about it. She thought it was very nice of Mr. Dickerson to give me a Bible. I asked her if I could go to church one Sunday. She didn't look certain. "I'm not sure what your father would think about that."

Not much, as it turned out. When Mom broached the subject, he yelled at me to stay away from Danny, his father, and "that church." He also took away the Bible I'd been given.

When I told Danny about it, he said God would take care of me. All I had to do was pray. If I was ever scared of anything, Danny said to just pray about it.

It wasn't long before I was scared. Irv Dickerson called my house to speak to my father. I suppose he was trying to be reasonable, but Dad was full of beer at the time, and I heard him screaming at Mr. Dickerson to leave us alone.

Then he yelled for me. I was trembling in my room. He yelled my name again. I quickly put my hands together and prayed for God to protect me from a beating.

I went to see my father. "I thought I told you to stay away from that kid," he said.

I was too scared to answer. The look in his eyes was frightening. Then he suddenly slapped me hard. "I'll teach you to listen to me!" he yelled.

My mom screamed at my dad to stop, but he didn't stop. I got one of the worst beatings of my life.

"And as I sat crying in my room," I explained to Lindsay, "he burst in and pulled me up by the hair. He screamed at me to stop bawling. 'Only wimps and pansies cry,' he yelled in my face. 'You're going to be a man if I have to knock those pansy tears out of you myself!'"

Lindsay's face looked pained.

"I decided I would never cry again," I said. "I wasn't going to give him that satisfaction." My hands were actually shaking as I finished telling the story. "And I decided something else."

Lindsay's eyes asked what that was.

"I decided this God stuff was bogus."

After a long pause, Lindsay said, "I'm so sorry."

"For what?" I snapped. "It isn't your fault."

"No, I'm sorry you feel that way. Maybe we could talk about it again another time."

"Not interested. Right now the only thing that interests me is defending your brother."

"Jake," she said with pronounced earnestness, "what's going to happen? What's really going to happen to Howie?"

I looked her in the eye, couldn't hold the gaze, then looked at the floor. "To be quite honest with you," I said, "I don't know. I just don't know."

CHAPTER TWENTY-THREE

THE ONE MAN who did seem to know was Benton Tolletson.

He practically ordered me up to his office. He didn't want to discuss the case with me on the phone. I was wondering why he wanted to discuss it with me at all. Sylvia Plotzske had been doing a creditable job on her own.

Visions of what would transpire danced in my head as I drove up to Hinton. I'd never met Tolletson; I'd only seen his brooding presence from the picture hanging in the Hinton DA's office. I knew a little bit about him from a murder case that made the papers a few years before.

A couple of teenage bodies, both female, turned up in the cabbage fields of north Hinton. Naturally, it sent shock waves through the rural town. The girls were both cheerleaders at Hinton Valley High and best friends. They attended the First Baptist Church. One of them had been named Asparagus Queen at the county fair.

Suspicion finally centered on the quarterback of the football team. He was known as a wild kid. It was also known that he had designs on the Asparagus Queen, but she did not reciprocate.

The two cheerleaders were last seen leaving the football field one Friday night after a game. A witness reported seeing them getting into a black Camaro, which was the kind of car the quarterback drove.

Blood matching one of the victims was later found on the carpet of the Camaro.

The case seemed open and shut. Benton Tolletson, then a deputy DA transplanted from San Jose, got the case.

It took him one week to order the arrest of the Hinton Valley High School football coach.

The town erupted. Art O'Connor was a town legend, a family man, and perhaps most important to the citizenry, a consistent winner. Only two years before, the Eagles had gone undefeated. And now this new, zealous prosecutor was dragging the beloved football coach through the mud.

Tolletson was a decorated Vietnam War vet, and he handled life like it was his own personal battlefield. Even with all the pressure against him and with a case built almost entirely on circumstantial evidence, Tolletson proved that Art O'Connor was indeed a double murderer and a planter of evidence.

When the shock finally wore off, the people of Hinton looked at Benton Tolletson as a true hero. The next year they elected him district attorney.

As far as I knew, Tolletson hadn't tried a case since his election. He was content to oversee the office and move his deputies around like chess pieces. That's why it was so odd to be on my way to see him face to face.

Maybe he liked what he was hearing about me. Maybe he was going to offer me a job.

Any thoughts about the largesse of Mr. Benton Tolletson disappeared the moment I stepped into his office.

The place was neater than any office I'd ever been in and cleaner than most hospital rooms. I got the feeling that Tolletson walked around with a white glove, testing for dust. It was impressive and ominous at the same time. My favorite professor in law school was an ex-judge. His office was always a mess with open books everywhere and unfinished cups of coffee on the shelves. He once told me, "Never trust a man whose office is too neat."

I didn't trust Benton Tolletson.

His handshake was "the crusher," the kind that tries to stop the blood flow of the other fellow's hand. His hair was clipped in the same tight military style he had in the portrait downstairs. He wore a vest that was buttoned up against a frame that looked hard and lean.

"I've heard some good things about you," Tolletson said. I was sure he was lying. What would Sylvia Plotzske have told him that was good? And any information he may have gleaned about my career down south was anything but exemplary.

He offered me a seat on a chair that was absolutely devoid of any dirt or stain. I was almost afraid to sit in it. He took his big executive chair behind an enormous desk. "How do you like our little town?" he asked.

"Nice," I said.

"You bet it's nice. A little bit country, but not out in the boonies. My wife and I love it here. We have a place in the north valley. Beautiful."

I nodded. This was just the salad before the meat and potatoes.

"The Patino case," Tolletson said, swiveling slightly in his chair. "You really want to take this thing to trial?"

"I haven't heard a reason why I shouldn't."

"We gave you a good reason before the prelim. Voluntary manslaughter. I was pretty amazed you passed that up."

"Well, some people just can't appreciate a gift."

Tolletson snorted a laugh. It was a laugh I'd heard many times before, the condescending fluff of the prosecutor who thought he held all the cards. It wasn't much different from the schoolyard bully who wants to shame you before he lays you out. In our system, prosecutors wear the heavy gloves. The power of the state is like the horseshoe inside the glove. When a prosecutor knows he's facing someone without much clout, he laughs like Tolletson.

"It's against my better judgment," Tolletson said, suddenly becoming ever generous, "but I'm willing to put that back on the table once more. Plead him out and let's all avoid a very bad situation."

"What's so bad about it from your standpoint?" I asked.

"Time. That's all. It would take up some of my time."

"*Your* time?"

"Yeah. I'm going to try this case."

Now there was a shot, like a left hook I didn't see coming. I knew that was his big blow as soon as he said it, the one he had called me up here to deliver in person.

Benton Tolletson himself, the local legend, the man who was in it to the death once his steel jaws clamped shut–he was going to step into the courtroom against me.

Any false bravado I might have had walking into the office melted away like a thin layer of frost under the morning sun. Sylvia Plotzske I could handle. Tolletson was another matter entirely.

I tried not to swallow or let my face give away my feelings. Tolletson looked at me, waiting for a reaction. I tried to think of something casual or clever to say to show him I could deflect his best punch. Nothing came to mind.

"Well," I finally said, "that doesn't really change anything."

"I think it does," Tolletson said. "Look, Jake, I'm very serious about trying your client for murder. And you know, the people around here just don't like murder."

"I can move for change of venue."

"Never happen."

"It might."

"Come on, Jake. You ever moved for change of venue before?"

"There's always a first time."

"Where's the evidence of adverse publicity? You claiming the *Hinton Valley News* has a vendetta against your client? You see an angry mob clustering outside the jail?"

"I can get a hearing."

"What'll that do? Delay? You want a continuance? I'll give you a continuance. You can try all you want to put off the inevitable. But sooner or later you and I are going to square off in the Hinton County Courthouse. And you know what? That's when the publicity will kick in."

There was something going on behind his eyes. He was the proverbial gambler with a winning hand.

"What publicity?" I asked.

"Oh, people interested in me stepping back into the courtroom again. I have some friends in the media who would be very interested in that. You know, we've never had a camera in the courtroom here in Hinton. This case would be the perfect debut."

He had some connection, if he wasn't bluffing, that meant the trial would get far more media exposure than it otherwise would have. That would mean putting the entire Patino family through a publicity wringer. Not to mention yours truly. The background stories on me would be wonderful–just what Mandy would like to see on TV.

"So what do you say, Jake?"

Tolletson was starting to remind me of someone.

"I'll have to think about it," I said.

"I'd like your answer now."

"I can't give it to you."

Benton Tolletson let out a huge theatrical sigh. It was a breath of exasperation, a signal of utter annoyance at someone very stupid–me. Then I realized who Benton Tolletson reminded me of.

My father.

He was treating me as if I were a fool, and that is exactly what my father had been so good at. It was probably one of the reasons I drank, maybe the main reason. So when the picture of my father merged with the presence of Benton Tolletson, all rationality left me. It was replaced by a range of emotions bubbling up from the distant past but still alive somewhere inside me.

I stood up and said, "My answer is no. We're going to trial."

For an instant Tolletson looked shocked, as if he couldn't believe I had turned him down. He recovered quickly, and his face became rock hard. "I'm going to put your client away for a long, long time. You can leave now."

I felt like a naughty child as I left the office, the same way I used to feel when leaving my father's bedroom after getting yelled at.

I handled it the same way now as I did then. I looked for somewhere to get a drink.

CHAPTER TWENTY-FOUR

THE FIRST AVAILABLE pub was a place called Frisbee's, just about a mile from the main highway.

It was spacious and cool inside with two large-screen TVs at either end. Both were blaring a baseball game for the afternoon crowd, which appeared to be young locals and a few older professionals.

Surprised at how tired I was, I took a seat at a small table. There was some sort of psychic combat going on between Tolletson and me. It went beyond the usual sparring between prosecution and defense. It had something to do with reminders of my father, but it also felt like something deeper. I didn't know what. All I knew was that I had to beat Benton Tolletson.

But how?

My case was extremely weak. Although the defense doesn't have to prove innocence, it's an unwritten rule that in fact, it does. Ninety-five percent of the time, the prosecution wins either through plea agreement or verdict. Occasionally, a strong case of reasonable doubt takes the verdict away. However, when the defense wins a not-guilty verdict, it's almost always because it has proved to the jury's satisfaction that the defendant is innocent.

A young waitress in a Frisbee's tee shirt asked what I wanted. I almost said, *A friendly person around here to talk to.* I ordered a beer instead.

The TVs were carrying a contest between the St. Louis Cardinals and the Chicago Cubs. I watched the game half-heartedly for awhile, ordered another beer from the pretty waitress, and got a little drowsy. In fact, I started drifting toward slumber, snapping my head back to upright every time it started to droop.

In this state, I had a vision.

I'm not talking about a bright, bold movie before my eyes, but merely the hint of a dream, or a nightmare.

In this scant hallucination I saw a courtroom hallway. I was looking through my eyes as if I was actually standing in this corridor and waiting to go inside a courtroom. People walked up and down the hallway silently, looking more like the walking dead than real folk.

Then I saw Benton Tolletson walking toward me. He had on a three-piece suit and held a briefcase and walked in slow motion. He walked with purpose, his face set like a stone god. Then he came right up to me and stopped. I looked at his face. It was frozen for an instant.

Then it changed, transforming from the stern but benign visage of the local district attorney to a horrible, monstrous face–with hungry, lupine eyes and sharp, fanged teeth that dripped blood.

I sat bolt upright, my heart pounding. I may have said something out loud, something like, "What in the . . ."

For a moment I sat there like a person coming out of a coma who had to readjust his vision for a minute or two to get his brain back to working order.

As I felt my way back to awareness, I heard the fight start.

Someone was yelling at the far end of the bar. I couldn't make out the words, but the tone was unmistakable. Whoever it was, he was ready to take on all comers.

Then I saw two bodies wrestle each other off their bar stools and onto the floor. Almost immediately, they were surrounded by other patrons and a bartender pulling them away from each other. The shouting drowned out the din of the ballgame.

The pretty waitress arrived with my beer and set it down on the table even as she watched the commotion.

"Is it always like this?" I asked with a laugh.

"No," she replied. "It's just Darcy."

"Darcy?"

"Hazelton."

I thought a moment. "Where have I heard that name before?"

"The winery," she said. "He's the captain's kid."

That was it. Captain Warren Hazelton. I'd read a story about his winery in the local paper.

The bartender and a couple of other patrons were showing Darcy to the door. "He come in here often?" I asked the waitress.

"All the time. Never a dull moment."

"What do you mean?"

"He gets that way when he's had a few."

"Likes to make a scene?"

"You got it."

"Spoiled rich kid?"

"Something like that. His parents . . ." She shook her head and made a face like she smelled something distasteful.

"What about his parents?"

"Weird."

I heard the sound of a car engine angrily revving up, followed by the din of a radio station cranked all the way up and booming some sort of urban beat right into the bar and my chest.

"Nice sound system!" I shouted to the waitress. We listened as tires squealed and the blaring music did a Doppler effect away from the bar. I noticed the waitress was smiling. "In what way are his parents weird?" I asked.

"What? Oh, just weird. His mom's really his stepmom."

"What happened to his birth mother?"

"No one knows," she said in a conspiratorial whisper. "I mean, one day she just wasn't there."

"She left?"

"Some say. When I was little, my friends and I used to say the house up there was haunted by the ghost of Darcy's mother."

"Is it?"

"Maybe," she laughed, then scurried away to take care of another table.

For the first time I felt as if I'd finally gotten to know this town, the way you do when you hear about the skeletons in someone's family closet. Maybe it was just my morbid curiosity, but I suddenly wanted to find out more about this particular set of bones.

I motioned for my waitress and asked her to send the guy over who had scuffled with Darcy Hazelton. She looked puzzled but did it for me. I watched as the guy at the bar looked my way, hesitated, then grabbed his glass of beer and walked to my table.

He was a big man in his mid-twenties. He wore a tank top that gave ample room for his muscles to show. On his upper right arm was a tattoo of a cobra ready to strike. His head was shaved, and he had a stud in his right ear. I was immediately sorry I'd asked for his company.

"Who are you?" he said coldly. His face was flushed, an obvious aftereffect of the scuffle. More than that, his eyes were red, a classic sign of some sort of substance abuse.

"Sit down a second," I said.

He didn't move. "What do you want?"

"I want to buy you a beer," I said.

"Why?"

"I'm a lawyer," I said.

"So?"

"I'm working on a case up here."

His eyes seemed glassy now, unfocused. His voice was low and thick. "What's that got to do with me?"

"Please, have a seat." I motioned for him to sit down. As he sat, I said, "My name's Jake Denney."

"Cool."

"You have a name?"

"Yeah."

"Would you like to share that with me?"

He had a dumb half-smile on his face, as if the littlest thing might amuse him. "Hang Creswell," he said.

"Hank?"

"Hang. As in loose, man. Or noose."

I raised my hand for the waitress. "What'll you have?"

"Bud. Wise. Er." He laughed.

After I ordered two of them, I said, "That's an interesting first name you have. Where'd it come from?"

"Nickname. My real name is Chaney. Now wouldn't you want a nickname if your first name was Chaney?"

I shrugged. "Beats some names I know."

"I hate it. I surf. Hang is short for 'Hang Ten.' Get it?"

"You live around here?"

"A few miles. What's this all about, man?"

The waitress returned with the beers, and Hang happily accepted.

"I want to get a feel for the town. I may be picking a jury here soon, and it pays to know the personality."

"Personality?"

"All jury pools have a certain personality."

"Cool. How do you find out?"

"Well, you can spend a lot of money and hire what is known as a jury consultant. Jury consultants study a certain demographic area and tell you what kind of people live there and what kind of person you want to sit on your jury."

"That work?"

"When the lawyers on the side that hires a jury consultant win, they say it works."

"What about when they lose?"

"They say they hired the wrong consultant."

Hang Creswell laughed.

"My way," I said, "is the product of necessity. I can't afford to hire a consultant. So I try to talk to people in the area, get a feel for what they might think, who they are."

"That why you're talking to me?"

"Partly. The other part is that little scuffle that just took place. What happened?"

Smiling, Creswell said, "Oh, Darcy. He gets a little out of it sometimes."

"You know him?"

"Sure, man."

"So what was the fight about?"

"He said something about my sister. See, he likes the ladies. And he's got money, family money, so he thinks he can say what he wants. I smacked him in the face, and he screamed and jumped me. That's all."

"That's all? You make it sound like a friendly game of badminton."

"You expect that from Darcy, that's all. Anything else? I wanna get back to my friends."

There wasn't any reason to ask him the next question, but I did anyway, like a stab in the dark. "Did you know Rae Patino?"

Hang Creswell's face, which had been sort of macho friendly, suddenly changed to macho cold. His eyes slowly widened. "You the lawyer for her husband?"

"That's me."

Creswell stood up quickly. "Thanks for the beer, man, but I ain't talking to you."

"Hey, why . . ."

"Forget it."

I stood up and faced him. "Listen to me then. Did you know Chip Delliplane?"

Hang's red-rimmed eyes turned serious and had a hint of sadness about them. "Oh, man, yeah. We surfed."

"You think he drowned?"

"What are you talkin' about, man?" He took two steps toward me and raised his right hand in a fist.

"Easy," I said, "I'm just asking questions."

"Well, you better not ask around here again, you got it?"

Before I could say another word, he turned and headed back to the bar.

I started to sense an undercurrent.

High-profile cases usually create an undercurrent, some unspecified but real feeling that permeates a community. When the community is small like this one, the undercurrent has greater palpability.

The problem is, you can't predict the direction of the undercurrent. And, if you get caught in it, you don't know where you're going to end up.

Back at my apartment, I was assaulted by the angry blinking of my answering machine. It was Barb, and her voice was not friendly. "Call me the minute you get in."

I called her.

"How could you do this, Jake?"

"I was up north. On a case."

"Really?"

"Do you think I'm making this up?"

"I don't know anymore, Jake. I really don't. One of the things a drinker will do . . ." She didn't finish.

"What's that supposed to mean?" I said.

"Have you been drinking today?"

My first instinct was to lie, but I knew she wouldn't believe a denial. She had my number, in multiples. So I went into attack mode. "Is that an accusation of some kind?"

"Jake–"

"Because if it is, I'm not going to sit here and listen to it. I've got too many other things to deal with, like making a living."

"Jake, will you–"

"Now why don't you just settle down and bring Mandy over here right now."

"No, Jake."

"What do you mean, *No, Jake?*"

"Mandy's with Rick's mom."

"I don't want her with Rick's mom. I want her here."

"She's not coming."

My face was getting hot, and my rationality was getting kicked downstairs by my anger. "You can go pick her up and bring her over here."

"Jake, we have to talk."

"Did you hear what I said?"

"I'm not going to bring her, Jake."

"Then I'll go get her myself."

"No, you won't."

"Watch me!"

"Listen, Jake," Barb said softly, "there's something I have to tell you."

I waited, hardly hearing her, aware of my own breathing.

"I'm going to change the custody arrangement," she said.

My head erupted with rage. "You *what?*"

"You're a danger to yourself and to Mandy," my ex-wife said coolly, as if she had the whole thing rehearsed. "I can't have her in that environment."

"Spell it out for me, Barb."

"You need help."

"About Mandy!"

"No unsupervised visits."

"There's no way."

"It's already that way, Jake. I'm going to get a restraining order."

I suddenly felt like a blind man in an avalanche, not knowing which way to turn and powerless before the onslaught. "You really thought this out, didn't you?"

Her tone sounded apologetic. "How else can we get through to you?"

"We? Who is this we?"

"Mandy and me."

"Does she know about this?"

"Yes."

"And I suppose she agrees with you?"

"She knows you need help."

"She's five years old! She knows what you tell her to know, and what you've told her is pretty obvious! Well, I'm going to report that you've kidnapped her, that you're using her, that you're an unfit mother. I'll fight you every step of the way!" Specks of sweat popped out on my forehead.

"I'm sorry you feel that way, Jake. I had hoped we could talk about this like adults."

"I won't forget this, Barb. I'm going to make your life miserable. I'm going to get you."

No answer this time, just a click on the other end of the line.

For a long moment I just stood there, frozen in an emotional vice, not sure where the pressure was greatest. Images of Barb flashed into my head, setting off more rage, but they were quickly followed by a picture of Mandy, at a distance, beyond my reach, maybe forever.

The next moments were like a waking dream. I watched myself yank the phone off the wall and hurl it at the window, hearing the sound of breaking glass and the small shower of shards on the floor and feeling in that disembodied state what we sometimes feel in dreams–a sense of falling, falling, falling, toward the impact of a dark, certain death.

Part Two

The law hath not been dead, though it hath slept.

—Shakespeare

CHAPTER TWENTY-FIVE

THE MURDER TRIAL of Howie Patino began on a Monday morning in the Hinton County Superior Court, Judge Adele Wegland presiding.

It was the biggest show in town.

Judge Wegland's courtroom was stuffed. I'd made sure there were seats for Janet and Fred Patino and Lindsay, and all three were there. Behind them were two rows reserved for the press. Judge Wegland apparently was not taking any chances. She was going to make sure that any member of the media who wanted to report on the drama in her courtroom would be sure to have a spot. This was her big moment.

Small-town judges do not normally get such moments. When they come, however, they can be career makers–or breakers. Judge Wegland was going to turn this moment into a maker, and that was bad news for me and my client.

At fifty-two, Judge Wegland was ready for a move up the legal ladder. She was a former prosecutor, naturally, with black hair pulled back so tight it looked like she had an ongoing face-lift. Her small, thin-lipped mouth seemed incapable of the physiological strain of a smile.

She was, I'd heard, looking for an appointment to the court of appeal. And with the tenor of the times the way it was, that meant showing she was tough on defendants, giving them no quarter and tolerating no "nonsense." Nonsense in this case meant a defendant pressing his legal rights under the Constitution of the United States.

That is exactly what I was doing this morning–running a motion to suppress evidence.

Howie was seated at my counsel table. There was also a chair for Triple C. He was running late, but I didn't need him for my pre-trial motion. Benton Tolletson and Sylvia Plotzske sat at the prosecution table.

After Judge Wegland called the proceedings to order, she said, "Mr. Denney, I understand from your papers that you take issue with two items of evidence. The first is the defendant's confession. Is that right?"

I stood up. "It's not a confession, Your Honor. It's a statement uttered under the protection of privilege."

The judge waved her hand. "It doesn't matter."

"But it does," I insisted. "A confession is a full and unequivocal acknowledgment of all the facts necessary to establish guilt. That's not what we're talking about, and it matters very much that Your Honor sees the distinction."

The heat from Judge Wegland's glare was no doubt palpable to everyone in the courtroom. I had determined I wasn't going to roll over in front of this or any other judge in Hinton. While this was a minor point, I was right about it. But it meant that from the very start the judge and I were not dancing in unison. I was stepping all over her feet.

"If you want to play legal games," Judge Wegland said icily, "I suggest you do it elsewhere. We all know what we're talking about, and we don't need to spend twenty minutes figuring it out. We have a statement by your client, and you want me to rule on its admissibility at trial. You indicate in your motion that you want to call a witness."

My witness was going to be the police officer who had stood guard at Howie's hospital room and heard Howie cry out, "I did it, Jake! I did it! I killed her, man! I killed my wife!" I'd subpoenaed him but hadn't seen him in the courtroom. Before I could even say his name, which was Cheadle, Benton Tolletson was on his feet.

"Your Honor," he said, "in order to expedite matters here, we'll stipulate to the facts as laid out in Mr. Denney's moving papers. This is a purely legal argument."

"I don't agree, Your Honor," I said quickly. I wanted this officer on the stand. I wanted the judge to see him testify, to look into his beady eyes. It might not be enough to move her, but it would surely be better than a cold legal dispute. I also hoped the officer wasn't around, so I could look with anguish at the judge and say that the other side was obviously not cooperating.

But Judge Wegland said, "Well, I do agree, Mr. Denney. There is no dispute about the facts if Mr. Tolletson stipulates to them. It's a legal matter only. So, let's go over the arguments."

I looked at Tolletson. He had what appeared to be a slight smile on one side of his face. I also glanced at the Patinos, all three of whom were leaning forward as they listened to this first legal scuffle. The prosecution had landed the first blow, and everyone seemed to know it.

"Fine," I said to the judge, trying to sound like I hadn't lost any breath. "The issue is one of attorney-client privilege, pure and simple. A defendant in custody has the absolute right to privacy in consulting with his attorney. Denial of this right is a violation of the Sixth Amendment to the Constitution. I cite *Barber v. Municipal Court* for that proposition."

"Yes, yes," Judge Wegland said, "I've read it."

"Mr. Patino was in custody, Your Honor–in the hospital. I was consulting him as his attorney. The officer knew that, but he purposely opened the door during the consultation and heard the statement my client made. He violated the privilege, Your Honor, and the People cannot benefit from that violation."

The judge nodded slightly, which to me was a major victory. It was impossible to tell what she was thinking, of course, but the fact that she made a slight gesture of affirmation was heartening. She turned to Tolletson and said, "Your response?"

Tolletson stood up confidently and looked like a marine holding fully-loaded twin carbines aimed at some cowering enemy lying weaponless in a swamp.

"Mr. Denney has stated the legal basis quite adequately, Your Honor, both in his papers and in his statement. However, he is seeking to assert a privilege where there is no privilege."

I almost didn't believe what I was hearing. No privilege? How could any sane lawyer make that statement? I had cases in my motion papers stating unequivocally that defendants in hospital rooms enjoyed the privilege. I had expected Tolletson to try a flank attack by distinguishing the facts of these cases from ours, and I was sure he wouldn't succeed. But this was an all-out frontal assault.

Judge Wegland seemed almost as surprised as I was. "Your argument is that there is no privilege here, Mr. Tolletson?"

"That's right, Your Honor. The privilege was waived."

"It certainly was not," I objected.

Shuffling papers in front of her, Judge Wegland said, "I don't see that here, Mr. Tolletson. When was it waived?"

"At the very moment the consultation commenced."

"That's just not true, Your Honor," I said with as much moral indignation as I could muster. Tolletson was making a big mistake, I was sure, and I was determined to play it for all it was worth.

"I still don't see it," Judge Wegland said in a tone that suggested she wished she *could* see it.

Tolletson paused and picked up a paper that had been lying on his table. "It's not in our opposition papers, Your Honor, because I just learned more about the facts this morning. As we all know, for the privilege to apply, the consultation has to be confidential."

"Which it was," I interjected.

Tolletson went on as if he didn't hear me. "That means, if the participants knew that another person was able to hear what they were saying, they cannot claim privilege because they knew there was no privacy."

"But Your Honor," I said quickly, "I did address that point in my papers. Officer Cheadle was seated outside the room. There was absolutely no indication that he would be listening to us."

"That's not who I'm talking about, Your Honor," said Tolletson. He glanced at the paper in his hand. "Officer Cheadle informs me that Mr. Denney had his daughter with him in that hospital room. That waived the privilege."

You could have knocked me over with a parking ticket. I'd forgotten. Mandy's presence in the room that day had melted into the fabric of my memory.

Now it was blowing a hole in my case. A big one. I stammered a response. "Your Honor, Mr. Tolletson hasn't offered . . . any proof . . ."

"Is what he is saying incorrect?" Judge Wegland asked.

"No. . . ."

"Well, then, how do you respond?"

"She's my daughter, Your Honor. She's five years old."

"Is that legally significant?"

"No," Tolletson said. "It isn't. Under section 952 of the Evidence Code, a confidential communication means the client discloses no information to third parties unless those parties are there to further the interest of the client in the consultation. I don't think there is any way to conclude that a five-year-old child is filling that requirement."

Tolletson had done his homework, and it was now clear that I had been sandbagged. He'd kept this information under wraps until this moment, waiting for me to wander into his trap.

I hunted around my brain for something, anything, to say. "This is a little girl, Your Honor. How can she possibly be deemed competent to understand what was going on?"

"Is there a competency requirement, Mr. Tolletson?" The judge was relying on my opponent as the legal authority! I was cooked.

"I don't believe so, Your Honor," said Tolletson. "Besides which, a five-year-old child is certainly capable of understanding simple language, such as 'I killed her.' I don't think Mr. Denney is here to assert that his daughter is mentally challenged."

I could have punched him then. That was a needle he didn't need to stick in me. But I decided that it was time to lick my wounds, move on, and preserve the issue for appeal.

"Your Honor," I said, "I'll submit the question. It's my opinion that the attorney-client privilege has not been waived in this case."

Without hesitation the judge said, "Your motion to exclude the statement is denied. Next issue."

That was the motion to suppress the knife. I had not been able to run the motion at the preliminary hearing when Officer McGary was on the stand. Now I could.

Under the Fourth Amendment, police are required to have search warrants before they enter a home. There are a few exceptions to this, but if a search is warrantless, the burden to justify the entry shifts to the prosecution, which is why Benton Tolletson was forced to call Officer McGary to the witness stand to testify.

Tolletson led the officer through the events of that night. McGary basically repeated his testimony from the prelim, with one little change. Now McGary was "sure" that the call he got was for domestic *violence.* That one word, *violence,* as opposed to *disturbance,* was all-important. If Tolletson could convince the judge that

McGary had acted like a reasonable, well-trained officer, the "exigency" exception to the search warrant requirement would apply. Officers who respond to certain emergency situations, like a possible victim inside a residence, don't have to wait for a warrant.

I was convinced that McGary was embellishing, but it wasn't going to be a walk in the park to establish that through the testimony of an unfriendly police officer.

"Good morning, Officer McGary," I said when it was my turn to ask questions.

McGary looked at me with cool suspicion. "Good morning," he clipped.

"You recall my asking you questions at the preliminary hearing?"

"Yes."

"We talked about the call you got on the night of March 25. Do you remember that?"

"Yes."

"I asked you if it was a call about possible domestic disturbance, or possible domestic violence. Do you remember that?"

"Yes."

"And you weren't sure, were you?"

"I'm sure now."

"Are you telling the court your memory is better today than when you testified at the prelim?"

"I've had a chance to think about it."

"Did anyone help you think?"

"I don't understand."

I motioned toward Benton Tolletson. "The district attorney, for instance?"

McGary shook his head. "He didn't help me think."

"You didn't go over your testimony with Mr. Tolletson before your appearance this morning?"

"Sure I did." McGary wasn't intimidated by my question. Sometimes rookie officers will get the heebie-jeebies when asked that question, thinking that going over testimony is some evil act that will show their bias.

What I wanted was a hint that Tolletson had suggested the change. "Did Mr. Tolletson help you refresh your recollection?"

"Objection," Tolletson said.

Surprisingly, Judge Wegland said, "Overruled. The witness will answer."

"No," said McGary. "I refreshed it myself."

"Oh? And what memory refresher did you use?"

"I just thought about it, that's all." McGary sounded like a kid with cookie crumbs all over his face. *They just appeared there, Ma. Honest!*

I decided that was a good place to stop. Tolletson had only one more question to ask. "Officer McGary," he said, "did I at any time suggest to you that you do anything but tell the truth here today?"

"No," McGary said sitting up straight.

Then came the legal arguments. Since Tolletson had to come up with a justification for the warrantless entry, he argued first.

"Your Honor," he said, "this case clearly falls under the exigency exception, and we have a case on point, *People v. Higgins.* Officers responded to a domestic violence report. The court held they had a reasonable belief that domestic violence had happened, and therefore, going into the house to make sure everything was all right was permissible. It's the same here, Your Honor."

"Mr. Denney?" Judge Wegland said.

I was caught off guard. Tolletson had just cited a case I'd heard of, but I couldn't remember the facts of the case. If I didn't say something in response, I'd lose for sure.

I remembered I'd tossed into my briefcase a copy of a book called *Points & Authorities on Searches & Seizures,* a handy reference to the law. I fished it out and looked up the summary of the case Tolletson cited.

"Your Honor," I said, "it appears that in *Higgins* a woman came to the door looking frightened. It was that observation that made the police suspicious, and that's why the court held it was an emergency. In the present case, Your Honor, there is no such observation. In fact, there was no answer at the door at all, nothing even to indicate anyone was home."

I knew I'd done well when Judge Wegland looked back at Tolletson almost rebukingly. And I must say, I enjoyed watching him squirm a little.

"Well," Tolletson said, "that may be. But there is another difference. We have the open back door. That is an indication that something was amiss. Surely a reasonable officer would want to at least take a look."

Flipping through the *Points & Authorities,* I said, "But the entry violated knock-notice provisions, Your Honor. Under the U.S. Supreme Court case of *Sabbath,* just a knock and a wait of a few seconds before entering was not valid."

Tolletson was ready. "In *Sabbath,* Your Honor, the door was *closed.*"

I could feel the judge looking back and forth at us, like this was a tennis match between Sampras and Agassi. And it was exhilarating to be standing toe to toe with Tolletson and looking for an ace.

I flipped another couple of pages. "But it doesn't matter if the door is open or closed, Your Honor. The California Supreme Court, in *Bradley,* ruled that a no-knock entry through an open door violated the Constitution."

"These are minor distinctions, Your Honor," Tolletson insisted.

"They are distinctions recognized by both the United States and California Supreme Courts!" I answered. "And I object to the district attorney calling the rights of all people 'minor.'"

I thought for a moment that Tolletson actually snarled at me, but the judge interrupted. "All right, all right. Anything else?"

"No, Your Honor," I answered, feeling confident for the first time. I'd done well. If the judge was at all open-minded, there was a slight chance I could actually win this thing.

Benton Tolletson had nothing more to say, and we both sat down. We then watched as Adele Wegland shuffled through papers and thought for about five minutes.

Then she looked up and said, "Motion denied."

I felt like I'd gotten a Doc Marten to the stomach. Wegland called a recess until 1:30, at which time we would begin selecting a jury.

Howie had been silent, almost motionless, throughout the morning. Now, as I gathered up my papers, Howie said, "We didn't do too good, did we?"

"No, Howie. We didn't."

He didn't say another word as the deputy led him back to lockup.

CHAPTER TWENTY-SIX

JANET AND FRED asked if they could buy me lunch. I demurred, making some noises about wanting to do some preparation. In reality, I wanted to get a quick drink.

I decided to return to Frisbee's. Somehow it seemed like my home away from home, or my tavern away from Max's. Maybe I'd see the pretty waitress again.

I didn't. This time I got a not-so-friendly waitress with an empty-eyed look I'd begun to notice in a lot of young people. A few sociology types I'd read said this was a new "lost generation." Maybe I'd join.

After I'd ordered beer and a hamburger, I took out the *Hinton Valley News* I'd bought at the courthouse.

I was stunned by what I saw on the front page.

"Disciplined Lawyer Defends Local Killer," the headline shouted. My throat clenched as I read, in lurid detail, the record of my life as a drunken lawyer. Just about everything was there, as if I'd given a detailed confession myself. Only I hadn't. The reporter got the information from someone else.

I suspected Tolletson. In fact, I was beginning to suspect Tolletson of being capable of anything, of engaging in almost any tactic in order to win.

My imagination got to work on me. Were the people in the bar looking at me? Were they whispering to one another, giving each other surreptitious jabs with their elbows, nodding toward the sad-sack lawyer at the far table?

My mood darkened to the point where I thought I could give my waitress a run for her money in the angst department.

That's when I saw Lindsay Patino enter the bar.

At first I was sure it wasn't her, that it had to be some look-alike. Lindsay in a bar? But then she saw me and came to my table.

"What are you doing here?" I asked.

Her hair was beautiful with the light behind it. "Are you all right?" she asked.

I put my hands out in a gesture of disbelief. "Of course I'm all right. How did you know I was here?"

"May I sit down?"

"Look," I said, "I'm trying to get my head together for the afternoon."

She sat down and looked from my eyes to my half-empty beer glass and back up to my eyes. "Why are you doing this, Jake?"

"Doing what?"

"Drinking."

"I'm having a beer. Who are you, my mother?"

She pretended not to be hurt, but I thought I saw a pained expression flash across her face, then disappear. "No," she said, "but I am concerned."

"About what?"

"About Howie. About you."

"I don't want your concern," I snapped. "I want to be left alone to do my job."

"You don't have to be alone, Jake."

That was a strange answer, and I was not entirely sure what she meant. Was she offering me her company? Or something else? Regardless, in my mood it sounded patronizing.

"I have work to do. Okay?" I said.

The brush-off didn't work. "I saw the story."

"In the paper?"

She nodded.

"So?"

"I didn't know, Jake."

She said it sympathetically, but that was the last thing I wanted. "So now you know. I had a drinking problem, messed up a case. You want to fire me?"

"No–"

"You want to have me put away so I can't do your brother any harm?"

"Jake, I–"

"What do you want, Lindsay?"

"To help."

"I don't need your help."

"Everyone needs help."

"I don't. If I get falling-down drunk and can't make it to court, then you can help me. Until then I'll thank you to keep your concerns to yourself." I was just this side of all-out nasty, leaving in just enough cruel to get her to leave. She didn't, and for a second I felt a grudging admiration for her. She had some inner strength keeping her seated across from me. But admiration or no, I didn't want her here. I didn't want her to see me drinking. I didn't want her to see me fighting back the darkness.

"I remember one time," Lindsay said, "when we were kids and I was following you and Howie around, like I did, and it was summer. You guys were going down to the 7-11 for a Slurpee, and I wanted one too, but you and Howie tried to get me to buzz off."

She paused for a moment, maybe to see if I had any recollection. I didn't, though I did have a general recollection of Lindsay, the little sister, hanging around.

"Well, my mom told Howie he had to take me with him, so I got to go. After we got our Slurpees, we were walking down the street, and we came to this liquor store."

I remembered the liquor store. It was the little one where my dad usually bought his supply.

"As we were walking by, this man stumbled out. He had a paper sack under his arm, and I remember he had red eyes, the reddest I'd ever seen, and I was scared. I thought he was a vampire or something. And he was dirty. His face was dirty, and he smelled bad. I could smell him even from where I was, which wasn't that close."

Slowly, I started to remember.

"And you and Howie were right next to him when he came out, and he said something to you. He said something like, 'Hiya, kid!' He said it like he knew you. And then you stopped and said something back to him. Then he said, 'Tell your old man he owes me money! You hear me? Tell him!' He yelled this at you. Then he stumbled away, my way, and I got up against the wall to let him pass because I was scared of him."

Now it came back.

"I went up to you and said, 'Who was that man?' I said it because I was so amazed that you knew him, and I'd never seen any man like that before. It was an innocent question, like a little girl would ask. And then you–"

"Screamed at you to get out of there," I said.

Lindsay nodded. "Or else you'd sock me in the nose."

"Thanks for the little stroll down memory lane."

"I'm sorry, Jake, I didn't mean to upset you."

"Then why bring it up?"

"Because I felt something then that I'm feeling now. You didn't just scream at me, Jake. Your face got so red, and your eyes were wild. It was like you were screaming at the world."

"So that's what you think I'm doing now?"

"Maybe."

"Thanks, Dr. Brothers, but you can save that stuff for the talk show circuit."

"May I tell you something?"

"No."

"I'm going to anyway," she said, and there was that inner strength again. That's when I felt myself pulled in two directions at once regarding Lindsay Patino.

"I don't know all you're going through," she said, "and I've been through some things I don't think you'd believe. But Jake, I've got to tell you that I was pulled out by God."

A rock-solid wall shot up in my mind. "Get out of here, will you? Just get out . . ."

"I want you to know–"

"I don't care."

"I do."

My eyes must have told her that enough was enough. She got up and walked out, and as she did, I felt like the last light of day had just disappeared.

I have a fatalistic attitude toward juries. Some lawyers say that jury selection is the most important part of a trial. Others–a minority, I should add–pretty much go with the cards they're dealt. That's me. All I hope to do is get rid of any obvious bad eggs with my peremptory challenges, then move on.

It took us just three hours to seat a jury. I only used three challenges. The first was against an older woman whose daughter was a waitress–too much identity with the victim.

My second peremptory was used against a fireman whom I bumped for no reason other than that he looked too much like Benton Tolletson.

The third juror I got rid of was a deacon at a Presbyterian church. Why? Because Clarence Darrow once wrote an essay on jury selection and explained that he always bumped Presbyterians. I wasn't about to argue with Clarence Darrow.

Adele Wegland seemed pleased. We had a jury in very short order, and the trial itself could start tomorrow morning. In addition to being tough on the defendant, she would be viewed as running an efficient and orderly court. I could feel the choke chain growing tighter around my throat.

As I was packing to leave the courtroom, Benton Tolletson strode over to me. The man never strolled. He seemed to march wherever he went. "Last chance for a deal," he said. "Once the jury is sitting in that box, I'm going all the way."

What happened next was my own sorry fault. I admit that. But I was ragged. I was tired from the day in court, drowsy from three beers at lunch, and drained from my little visit with Lindsay Patino. My motion to suppress evidence had been summarily denied, and I was facing the prospect of a trial that was going to be nearly impossible to win.

In other words, the rational thing was for me to grab whatever scraps Benton Tolletson was tossing out to me and go home.

I did not, however, take them.

Instead, I looked at the man who still reminded me of my father, an officer of the court whom I had a sneaking suspicion was not all open and aboveboard, and I said, "Benton, you can take your offer and stick it where the lights of Hinton never shine."

He reacted like he'd been slapped. Red blotches appeared on his cheeks like emerging land masses from receding ocean waters. I could almost hear the snapping of synapses in his brain as he searched for a response. Then it came. "I'm going to drag you through the dirt, Denney," he said. "I'm going to make you bleed."

CHAPTER TWENTY-SEVEN

AT 9:15 ON Tuesday morning, Judge Adele Wegland turned to the twelve jurors and two alternates seated in the box and said, "Good morning, ladies and gentlemen."

"Good morning," they answered like kids in an elementary school classroom.

"You have been selected and sworn in as jurors in the case of the *People of the State of California v. Howard Patino.* I want to start by thanking all of you for accepting your duties as jurors. This is what people used to call a civic responsibility, and I, for one, still feel that way."

Bully for you, I thought as I sat at counsel table. A judge who still believes in responsibility. I glanced back at the gallery. Janet and Fred Patino were seated there. Lindsay was not.

Triple C was seated on one side of Howie and I was seated on the other. Howie was looking down at the table. Triple C did not look like himself. He was wearing a coat and tie.

"This is a criminal case. The defendant has been charged with murder in the first degree. I'll be telling you later on about what that means and what the law is that applies here. But it is your duty, and yours alone, to decide what the facts are. That's not my job, and it's not the job of the lawyers. It's yours. That's one of the cornerstones of our judicial system.

"Now, it's my job to see that this trial runs smoothly. I'll be called upon by the lawyers from time to time to make a legal judgment. I will also need to make judgments about time and scheduling and about the all-important lunch break."

The judge paused like a comedian, and the jury, as if on cue, delivered polite laughter. I wondered how many times Judge Wegland had used that line.

"I'll do my best in that regard. But when I make a ruling on an objection, or when the lawyers come up for what we call a side bar, you are not to speculate about the reasons. Don't draw any conclusions because I sustain or overrule an objection or yell at the lawyers."

The jury laughed again. Wegland knew how to play to the crowd.

"Let me tell you a little bit about the trial process. First of all, each attorney has the opportunity to address you with what is called an opening statement. That is their chance to give you an overview of what they believe the evidence will show after the trial is through. It's important for you to remember that nothing the lawyers say to you is itself evidence, and you are not to take it as such. You are to judge the facts solely on what is admitted by me into evidence.

"After the opening statements, witnesses will be called to the stand, where they will testify under oath. There will be an opportunity for cross-examination of any witness. Exhibits and documents may be offered into evidence as well. The important thing is that you all keep an open mind about this case until all of the evidence has been presented, the lawyers have given you their closing arguments, and I have instructed you on the law. Do not form any final opinions about this case until you go into the jury room together and begin your deliberations."

Inside, I laughed. Most jurors form strong opinions well before entering the jury room. Everyone knows this, including the judges who admonish them.

"And do not, under any circumstance, discuss the merits of this case amongst yourselves. During those times when court is in recess or adjourned, do not allow anyone to discuss the case with you. If anyone attempts to discuss the case, tell the person that you are a member of the jury and can't talk about it, and ask the person to stop. If the person keeps talking about the case, leave the conversation and report the incident to my clerk, Ms. Wagner. She'll bring it up to me, and I'll decide what to do about it."

A ritual hanging, perhaps? I wondered what awful justice Adele Wegland would mete out.

"You are not being sequestered in this case, which means you get to go home at night. Do not listen to any reports about this case on the TV or radio, and do not read any accounts in the newspapers or on the Internet. Don't even talk about the case with your spouse or significant other. Let him or her give you a back rub instead. You'll probably need it."

The jurors laughed. Jurors like to laugh when judges make jokes.

"Now, in every criminal case the accused party is presumed innocent. To overcome that presumption, the burden of proof of guilt is placed on the prosecution. They must prove to you every element of the charge beyond a reasonable doubt. I'll tell you exactly what that means when I explain the law to you. Also, in a criminal trial the accused has the absolute right, under the Constitution, to remain silent. He does not have to take the stand to testify. You are not to draw any inference of guilt if the accused so chooses. That must not influence your verdict in any way."

Then why did I have the impression that Judge Adele Wegland was silently telling the jury she thought my client should go away for a long stretch in the pen?

"Again, I want to thank you for accepting the role of juror in this case. We will take a ten-minute recess, and when we come back, the lawyers will proceed with their opening statements."

As the judge went back to chambers, Triple C said, "The show is about to begin. You ready?"

"Sure," I said. "Why not?"

"Then speak the speech, I pray you, and fit the action to the word, the word to the action."

"Hamlet?"

"You got it."

"Nice literary reference," I said. "But only one thing bothers me."

"What's that?"

"Hamlet ends up dead."

Because the state has the burden of proof, the prosecutor gets the first word to the jury. Benton Tolletson took that and more.

He seemed to own the courtroom. I was beginning to suspect he really did, along with all the judges in Hinton County and maybe a handful of the jurors too.

"Good morning," he said to the jury. "As you know, my name is Benton Tolletson, and I am the People's representative, the county district attorney. I'm standing before you today to speak on behalf of one of our own, Rae Patino, a young woman, a young mother, a working mother, who was trying to forge a new life for herself and her little boy here in the town of Hinton. You're going to hear her story from those people who knew her, but mostly what you're going to hear about is a jealous husband, one so jealous it drove him to plan the murder of his wife."

Pausing for a moment in front of the jury box, Tolletson looked up and down the two rows of rapt jurors.

"You see, the defendant over there"–Tolletson pointed at Howie–"thought about how he was going to do it, how he was going to dispose of his wife, while he was five thousand miles away. He thought about it on the plane trip to Los Angeles, and he thought about it on the bus ride from Los Angeles International Airport up here to our town. He thought about it when he got off the bus, and he thought about it as he walked up White Oak Avenue.

"This defendant, you see, knew that Rae Patino had decided to move on with her life. This sometimes happens in a marriage. We all know that. And in this country, at least, when that decision is made by one party, the other party has to accept that.

"But this defendant couldn't accept that. Wouldn't accept that. And he decided Rae Patino was not going to get away with it."

Tolletson was pacing up and down now, like a panther in a cage. His hands were clasped behind him, his head bowed slightly. I could see his neck turning a faint shade of red.

"The defendant knocked on the door and shouted out Rae's name. There was no answer. There's a reason for that. Rae Patino was scared of her husband. She recognized the voice and refused to answer the door.

"That did not stop the defendant. He went around to the back of the house where he was able to break in. Once inside, he made for the bedroom where Rae Patino lay in bed, no doubt afraid of the confrontation. Did she beg for her life? Perhaps. We don't really know. What we do know is that the defendant got a knife from the kitchen and proceeded to stab"–Tolletson made a stabbing motion with his fist–"and stab and stab and stab"–he pumped his arm–"over and over again, until Rae Patino bled to death."

Howie was motionless beside me. It was almost like he was in a coma. Maybe he was, in a way, lost in a catalepsy of torment.

"You will hear a lot of evidence in this case, ladies and gentlemen, but nothing you hear will be as important as what came out of the defendant's own mouth. You will hear the words, 'I did it! I killed her! I killed my wife!' You see, the defendant had a moment when he just couldn't hide the truth any longer. That's because the truth just won't go away."

For another twenty minutes or so, Tolletson went over the evidence he was going to present. If this had been any other prosecutor and any other venue, I would have said he overplayed his hand, promising too much to the jury. When that happens, the other lawyer can usually do severe damage to his opponent's case by reminding the jury about how much was told them during opening statement, and how the guaranteed evidence never materialized.

But we were in Hinton, where the people had elected Benton Tolletson to the office of the district attorney. Maybe the jury would believe him if he said pigs flew.

I heard my name called by Judge Adele Wegland. After a quick look at Triple C and Fred and Janet Patino, I stood up.

And almost fell down.

I don't know what it was, or how it happened. A wave of nausea washed over me so suddenly and completely that I thought I was going to faint. I was either temporarily blinded or else had my eyes closed. Either way, I was in momentary darkness.

It was the darkness that scared me more than anything. Maybe it can be explained psychologically; maybe it was something more. Much more. But in those few moments, I was oblivious to everything except myself, feeling like I might pass out, but also something far worse–feeling I was in a blackness from which I would not emerge.

And then I heard a voice.

What happened next may have only taken a few seconds in real time in the Hinton County Courthouse, but it seemed like an hour in my head. The voice was audible in the way dream voices are, sounding in my brain without passing through the ear canals, without the physiological requirements needed to make an actual sound.

It's all over, the voice said.

Where was it coming from? A pickled part of my brain?

It's all over, so why don't you just give up?

I felt Triple C take my arm. "Jake, what is it?"

"Mr. Denney," said the judge, "are you all right?"

"Water," I said. Triple C poured me a glass from the pitcher on the counsel table and handed it to me. I could feel the eyes of everyone in the courtroom, including the jurors, and could only wonder what they thought. Poor sap attorney can't even get out the first words of his opening statement.

"May we have a short break, Your Honor?" I asked.

After a terse pause, Judge Wegland said, "All right. Fifteen minutes. And I want to see counsel in chambers."

She got up and left the courtroom.

CHAPTER TWENTY-EIGHT

"JUST WHAT HAPPENED out there, Mr. Denney?"

Adele Wegland's office was a study in contrasts. Even with the lights on, it seemed darker than it should have been, and the dull browns and blacks of the interior only added to the brooding feeling. Yet on her desk, in a small vase, was a single, hopeful flower–a red rose. It reminded me of blood.

"I apologize, Your Honor," I said. "I don't know what hit me. Maybe it's all the excitement."

Benton Tolletson huffed.

"Do you feel ill?" the judge asked.

"I think I'll be all right."

"I don't want to call a halt if I can help it."

"You won't have to." I was feeling my forehead, which had a thin layer of sweat across it.

"I wish I could be sure, Mr. Denney. Do you need a doctor?"

"I don't think so."

"Do you need something else?" Benton Tolletson said.

I looked at him sideways, wondering what he meant. The judge said, "What do you mean, Mr. Tolletson?"

"I'm not one to speculate," the prosecutor answered. "But we all know Mr. Denney has had his troubles in the past. Drinking, you know."

I wanted to shout some choice epithet to express my outrage, but two things stopped me–my stomach and the judge. Adele Wegland was looking at me like she was in complete agreement with Tolletson. If I'd been a conspiracy buff, I might have said they had gotten together before the trial to plan this very thing–a tag team match, two against one.

Shaking my head, I said, "That's . . . ridiculous."

"Is it?" Tolletson said like a cross-examiner. "When was the last time you had a drink?"

I looked at the judge. "I don't have to answer that."

I might as well have been looking at a poster of Uncle Sam, the one where he is scowling and pointing at you. "I think you do," said the judge.

Tolletson was sitting there with a half smirk on his face. I could read his thoughts as if they were words appearing on a computer screen. *You're out of it, Denney. You have no business being here. You're a loused-up lawyer with a loused-up life. You thought you could come up here and take me on, but you can't even say a few simple words to a jury. I don't even want you around my town, stinking up the place . . .*

"I asked you for a response, Mr. Denney." The judge had her firm-lipped look, like a mother superior with tight shoes.

"My personal habits aren't your business," I said.

"If you can't handle this case," she said, "then it is my business. I have to make sure your client gets competent counsel. And if your alcoholism is going to make that an impossibility, I'm going to have to remove you."

"Alcoholism? That's ridiculous."

"Are you an alcoholic, Mr. Denney?"

"No!" I snapped, sounding to myself like one of those classic dipsos who say *I can quit anytime I want to . . .*

"Maybe we need a medical opinion," said the judge.

Tolletson shrugged his shoulders. That's when I decided to fight back. "You try that, and I'll have you up before the Commission on

Judicial Performance. I'll make the biggest stink of your professional life."

"That," Tolletson interjected, "I can believe."

"Now, now," said the judge, "you don't need to fly off the handle. My only concerns are your client and the twelve people sitting in the jury box. I just want to know if this sort of thing is going to happen again."

"I'm not planning on it," I said. "And I'm not going to be replaced."

"Then you go give us an opening statement."

"All right," I said, standing up. My legs felt like spaghetti.

"But, Mr. Denney," said the judge, "I'll be watching you very carefully."

Yeah, I thought. You and everybody else.

"You look like the walking dead," Triple C said when I got back to the courtroom.

"Thanks. You're a real pal."

"I mean, you don't look healthy."

"I'm okay."

"You don't want to scare the poor people on the jury. Why don't we put this off until tomorrow?"

"Judge wants to get on with it."

"Oh, man."

I put a hand on Trip's shoulder. "Don't worry. Maybe the jury'll have such sympathy for me they won't possibly convict."

Trip laughed, but it was muted laughter. I suddenly felt very alone. As the jury marched in, I wished that my little girl was in the courtroom giving me a big hug. If there was one person in the world who wasn't ready to condemn me, it was Mandy. I wanted Mandy.

Instead I got the jurors, and I could tell they had questions in their minds when I finally started speaking.

"I must apologize, ladies and gentlemen," I said. "Opening night jitters, I guess."

At that point I had absolutely no idea what I was going to say next. I had an outline written down, which went over the evidence, but I felt I had to tell the jury something else. Just what, I didn't know.

"I guess I'm a little nervous here. It's a big responsibility defending a man accused of murder. A big one. And I want to make sure I do the best I can, not only for him, but for you. You are the ones who will ultimately decide this case, not me, not the judge, and not the prosecutor. It's my job to get you the evidence you need to make that decision, and that's just what I'm going to do. I only ask that if I seem a little shaky on my feet you don't hold it against my client."

"Your Honor," I heard Benton Tolletson say. "This is not a proper opening statement."

I spun around, and if I'd had anything in my hands, I probably would have thrown it at his square-jawed face.

"Sustained," said the judge.

No lawyer likes to have an objection sustained against him, but especially not during opening statement. It makes the jury think you're trying to pull something and got caught. Not a great way to start a trial.

I walked over to counsel table and looked down at my outline. The words were there, but they didn't seem to make any sense. They were a jumble, like the scribblings my daughter made with crayons when she was three years old.

I looked back at the jury. "Ladies and gentlemen, there are two sides to every story. What the prosecutor told you a little while ago was only one side, his side. But what he said is not evidence. The evidence is going to come to you from that witness box and through exhibits. All I ask you to do is keep an open mind, as you have sworn to do, before making your decision. Thank you."

As I sat down, Judge Wegland said to Tolletson, "Call your first witness."

The witness was none other than Officer McGary, and Tolletson walked him through the events for the benefit of the jury. Starting off with the dramatic action was a smart move by the prosecutor.

Jurors, like just about everyone else in society, are TV trained. They watch cop shows, and that's just what Benton Tolletson was giving them. With rehearsed adroitness, McGary spun his tale, and Tolletson led him up to the point of greatest dramatic interest–the introduction of the murder weapon.

Juries love the introduction of the murder weapon. It's just like show-and-tell.

When Tolletson held up the knife, Howie's eyes widened with a look of abject terror. If you didn't know him–and the jurors didn't–the look would have signaled just one thing: conscious guilt. That's why I leaned forward in my chair, trying to keep Howie's face from being flashed to the entire jury like a neon *I DID IT* sign.

Fortunately, most of the jurors were watching Tolletson, which is just what he wanted.

After McGary finished identifying the weapon, Tolletson turned him over to me. "Go get him," Trip whispered as I stood up.

"Just a few questions for you, Officer," I said walking to the edge of the jury box. Some lawyers like to ask their questions from a lectern, giving them the appearance of professional authority. Others, like me, stand so as to make the witness look past the eyes of the jurors, the ones who sit in judgment on credibility. I wanted them looking into McGary's baby blues.

"When you got to the house," I said, "you didn't hear any screams, did you?"

"No," McGary answered brusquely.

"Well, how about voices? Did you hear any loud voices?"

"No, I did not."

"Sounds of something breaking?"

"No."

"A gunshot?"

"No."

"A television set?"

"No."

"A radio?"

"No."

"In fact, Officer McGary, you did not hear anything from inside the house, did you?"

"Which is why I had some concerns."

"Just answer the questions I give you, if you don't mind."

Tolletson shot to his feet. "The witness may answer as he sees fit, Your Honor."

Nodding, Judge Wegland said, "As long as it's responsive. Continue, Mr. Denney."

I said, "How many times in your career has the absence of evidence been evidence of a crime?"

"Excuse me?"

"You say the lack of any sound raised concerns for you. Sir, if you were following a car that was driving straight at a normal rate of speed, you wouldn't pull it over for drunk driving, would you?"

"Objection," said Tolletson. "Argumentative."

"Sustained," said the judge

"Officer McGary, this was at night, correct?"

"Yes."

"Around 10:45 or so; is that your testimony?"

"Yes."

"At 10:45 at night, sir, is not the absence of noise consistent with people sleeping inside their homes?"

McGary scowled slightly, then said, "But that's not what was going on."

"You didn't know at the time that anything was going on, did you?"

"Not when I knocked on the door, no. But later–"

"Just answer my questions, sir. At no time did you hear any noise from within that house. Isn't that a fact?"

"Yes."

I could see the backs of all the jurors' heads, which was a good thing. At least they were watching the witness.

During the direct, Tolletson had placed a diagram of the Patino home on an easel so McGary could refer to it. I approached the diagram, which the jury could see as well.

"Now, Officer, let's turn to your testimony about what you saw in the bedroom. I believe you testified you saw Mr. Patino lying on the floor here, at the spot where you earlier placed a red D, for defendant. Is that correct?"

"Yes."

"And you described Mr. Patino as being 'out of it.' Were those your words?"

"Yes."

"Meaning he was not rational."

"I didn't say that."

"That's what you meant, though, isn't it?"

"No, I meant he was 'out of it'; that's all."

He had wandered into the thicket of meaningless distinction, a place jurors don't like witnesses to go, so I hammered on. "Come now, Officer McGary, what does 'out of it' mean if it doesn't mean irrational?"

"Well, what I mean . . . what I'm saying is he looked like he had just gone through some major deal and was upset."

"Isn't part of being upset that you don't think straight?"

Tolletson stood up to protect his witness. "Your Honor, Officer McGary is not testifying as an expert on mental state."

"He was expert enough to offer his opinion on direct," I said. "I should be able to cross-examine."

After a short pause, Wegland said, "You've made your point, Mr. Denney. Move on."

Be a good little boy, and don't try to show up this fine, upstanding officer, Mr. Denney. We can't have that now, can we?

Trying to keep my composure, I said, "At the very least, Officer McGary, my client did not appear normal, did he?"

"Depends."

"On what, sir?"

"On what you mean by normal. Somebody who has just killed his wife; maybe it's normal for him to be out of it."

"I object to that answer, Your Honor, and move to strike."

"All right," said the judge reluctantly. "The witness's last answer will be stricken, and the jury is instructed to disregard it."

"You say you saw the knife," I continued. "On the diagram, that's where you've placed a small K; is that correct?"

"Yes."

"And it was how far from my client?"

"Just about arm's length."

"But he wasn't holding it, was he?"

"No."

"You never saw it in his hand at any time, did you?"

"No."

That's when I asked the question that Benton Tolletson had conveniently ignored during his direct. "Did the police lab find any fingerprints on this knife?"

McGary paused, looked slightly confused, then said, "I don't know."

"You don't *know?*"

"I haven't seen the report."

"Would it surprise you to know there were no fingerprints on that knife?"

"Objection," said Tolletson.

"Sustained."

It was good place to stop. The jury would be wondering about the fingerprint issue, and I wanted them to wonder. I said, "No more questions," and sat down. Tolletson asked a few more questions on redirect, but I added nothing further. Things had gone about as well as could be expected.

My entire strategy was one of basic, reasonable doubt. I had to raise enough red flags in the minds of the jurors to convince them to reject the prosecutor's case. It was a long, long road, but at least I'd taken a step in the right direction.

CHAPTER TWENTY-NINE

DURING THE LUNCH break, I strategized with Triple C on a park bench in the center of Hinton. We plotted between bites of roast beef sandwiches, courtesy of Trip. I was starting to go over the afternoon schedule when Trip said, "This town gives me the creeping willies, like one of those places in a horror novel where evil things are going on beneath the surface."

"Where'd that come from?" I asked, agreeing with him more than I cared to admit. The truth was, I'd had a similar feeling from the moment I first got here but dismissed it as nothing more than my own insecurities.

"Just a feeling," Trip said. "Sort of a Scottish play thing."

"Huh?"

"You know, the Scottish play."

I shook my head.

"By Shakespeare. The Scottish play . . ."

"You mean *Macbeth?*"

"Don't say it!"

"What is wrong with you?"

Trip put his half-eaten sandwich on his lap, I suppose so he could motion with his hands, which he did, wildly. "You never call it that, man! It's a theater superstition. See, that play is about witches and spells and all that, and theater folk believe there's dark forces at work whenever there's a production of the Scottish play."

"Oh, come on."

"No lie! Things happen. Accidents. Actors have died. Look it up."

Trip was sounding serious, which made the whole thing a lot more disconcerting. I found myself believing that something like that might possibly be true.

"It's like that here," Trip continued. "I feel like there's some stuff going on we don't see. I felt like that in the courtroom."

"When?"

"When Tolletson was questioning that cop. There was something going on between 'em."

"That's usual for a prosecutor and a policeman."

"No," Trip insisted. "Something more."

"Like?"

"Don't know."

"Very helpful. Don't quit your day job."

"I don't have a day job. I work for you."

I laughed, but it was a short one. A long silence followed.

"What is it?" Trip asked finally.

I shook my head. "I don't know, exactly. You feel like there's weird stuff going on in town. I feel like there's weird stuff going on with me and this case."

Trip looked at me. "I think I know what that's about."

"Yeah?"

"Booze."

"Oh come on, will you?"

"Just my opinion, as a friend."

"I don't need your opinion, as a friend." I was too sharp with him and wouldn't have blamed him if he threw his sandwich in my face. He didn't. I sensed his shoulders hunching a little, and he looked straight ahead, pushing the rest of his lunch into his mouth.

After a minute or so, my anger subsided, and I felt terrible. Trip was maybe the last friend I had on this earth. I pulled myself together enough to say, "Look, I just know one thing."

Trip waited for me to tell him.

"I've got to win this case."

Trip leaned back slightly, as if to give himself room to look me over. "Man, you can't put all your eggs in this basket," he said.

"I am."

"Because he's your friend?"

I shook my head. "Really, that doesn't have anything to do with it. I care about him, sure, but that's not it."

"So why?"

"I don't know. I just have to win this one, that's all."

Triple C nodded and put one of his big, strong hands on my shoulder. He gave it a little squeeze and said, "Okay, then. Let's go win it."

It's no wonder I self-destructed on the cross-examination of Daphne Barth. During the afternoon session, I was nervous and jittery. I kept trying to concentrate on what was going on in the courtroom but kept thinking about a bunch of other things, including getting a stiff drink.

Tolletson took his nice-little-old-lady through her story, how she heard a loud voice across the street and called 911. She testified in a calm, grandmotherly fashion, occasionally saying something that drew a sympathetic laugh.

She was, in short, a great witness for the prosecution, which left me with a dilemma.

Trial lawyers will tell you that there are two kinds of witnesses you have to approach with extreme caution in cross-examination—old folks and children. The jurors side with them and don't like lawyers getting rough with their questions. Another rule is that if you can't get something extremely worthwhile out of a witness on cross, it's best to leave that witness alone.

I should have left Daphne Barth alone.

I didn't.

"Do you recall," I asked her as I rose to my feet, a note pad in my hand, "an occasion when I visited your home?"

"Yes, I do," Daphne Barth answered directly, without fear.

"We spoke about this case, didn't we?"

"You asked me some questions about it. I'm afraid I wasn't very helpful."

"But you do remember, don't you?"

"Oh, yes."

So far, so good. I was laying a foundation to retrieve from her some of the information I'd extracted on that earlier visit.

"Now, you testified here today about hearing a voice shouting from across the street; is that right?"

"That's what I told Mr. Tolletson, yes."

"And the jury."

She looked at the jury and nodded. "Yes," she said. I caught a glimpse of a few jurors' faces. It was like they were listening to their own mother.

"You have no way of knowing whose voice that was though, do you, Mrs. Barth?"

"It was a man's voice."

"Right, but you don't know whose."

"How could I know, young man? I just heard the shouting."

I noticed my right hand shaking slightly. I stuck it in my pocket and tried to assume a casual pose. "Mrs. Barth, do you recall at our meeting that you asked me to speak up?"

Daphne Barth frowned, thought, and shook her head. "No, I'm afraid I don't."

"You don't recall that?"

"I just told you that."

"I said something to you, and you didn't hear me clearly, and you asked me to speak up. Do you recall that?"

"I'm sorry, young man, but I don't. We had a pleasant conversation, and I heard everything you said."

"Mrs. Barth, don't you recall that when I came into your house we began discussing–"

"Objection," Tolletson said. "The witness has told him three times she doesn't recall any such event."

"Sustained," said the judge.

There was nothing I could do. I hadn't memorialized the conversation with Daphne Barth in writing. She had not signed any statement. If she didn't remember now, it was like it never happened.

"Well, then," I said, feeling frustrated, "how *is* your hearing?" That was a mistake. I was starting to sound like a bully.

"My hearing is just fine, young man!" Mrs. Barth snapped.

"Let's move on, shall we? Do you recall telling me that the prosecutor's office had instructed you not to talk to me?"

She paused then and looked toward Benton Tolletson. I did the same. He was looking calmly at his notes. Then she said, "No."

"Wait a minute. Don't you remember telling me that Miss Plotzske had given you that instruction?"

"Objection!" Tolletson blasted. "May we approach the bench?"

Adele Wegland waved us up so we could talk to her out of the jury's earshot. Benton Tolletson's eyes were ablaze with righteous indignation. "I can't believe what I just heard, Your Honor. There is no basis at all for that question. He asked it to prejudice this jury."

I could manage no better response than, "I did not!"

"Keep your voices down," Judge Wegland said. Like an aggravated school marm, she looked at me and said, "Mr. Denney, do you have any foundation at all for this question?"

"I do, yes," I said. "The fact is, she told me that Sylvia Plotzske of the district attorney's office told her not to talk to me."

"That's an outrageous falsehood. The witness denies saying that to him. I don't want him asking that question again because it is just too prejudicial."

"I agree," the judge said. "Unless you have some impeachment document of some kind, Mr. Denney, I don't want you to ask that question again."

"What is this?" I said, looking back and forth between my adversary and the judge.

"This is a court of law," Judge Wegland said, "and it will be conducted as such. Now go back to your places."

Like a rebuked dog, tail tucked between legs, I shuffled back to my spot. And I started getting the same feeling Triple C had told me about, a sensation that things were going on beneath the surface, that I was bobbing on a dark ocean with my head barely above water.

I was angry, and that's a bad thing for a trial lawyer to be. When you're angry, you lose some control. The jury knows it too. But I found myself not caring.

"Your memory of our meeting," I said, "seems to be a little foggy. Is that right?"

"I don't know what you mean by foggy, young man. I'm still pretty sharp for my years."

"Do you recall us speaking about your late husband?"

"Oh, yes, I do. My Oscar. Married fifty-seven years. He was a rancher."

"Thank you, yes. So you remember that at least."

"I do, yes."

"But you somehow don't remember other parts of our conversation."

With a disgusted huff, Daphne Barth said, "Young man, I remember what I remember. That's what I'm telling everybody here. Now if that's not good enough for you, I don't know what is."

This drew some laughs from the gallery and a couple of jurors too.

"Well then, let me ask you this," I said quickly. "You told me you heard a thumping noise at your house, didn't you?"

"Objection," said Tolletson. "Vague as to when."

"Sustained."

I ran my fingers through my hair. "First, do you recall telling me about a thumping noise?"

"I believe I do, yes."

"You told me that on an unspecified night, fairly close to the events in this case, you heard this noise. Is that right?"

"Oh, yes."

"And you said it was like someone pounding on your door."

"It was like that, but I can't be sure."

"You were sure when you talked to me."

"Objection. Argumentative."

"Sustained."

My face flushed, so I turned my back to the jury. I pretended to think. In reality, I was trying to calm myself down. It didn't work. "Are you hiding something from us, Mrs. Barth?"

I shouldn't have asked that. It was accusative, and there was no basis for the accusation, except in my own mind. The question certainly wasn't going to help me with the jury. And I suppose that's why Benton Tolletson didn't object. He knew how bad I was looking.

"That's awful!" Daphne Barth said, like a grandmother accused of stealing candy from her own grandchild. "I would never!"

I was in deep and should have cut my losses. But I was running on some strange autopilot, as if I'd turned over control of my brain to someone else, someone without any training in civility, trial tactics, or just plain common sense. I turned and looked at Benton Tolletson, letting the jury see me look at him, and said, "Oh, wouldn't you?"

That got the prosecutor to his feet again. "Objection!" he shouted.

Adele Wegland wasted no time. "Court will be in recess," she said. "I'll see counsel in chambers."

Things could not have ended any worse if Benton Tolletson had written the scene himself. Here is what the jury saw: a desperate defense lawyer piling on a nice old lady, refusing to let up on her, finally ending with an insinuation so low that the judge had to call a halt to the proceedings and summon the lawyer to her chambers to give him a sharp, legal spanking.

Which is exactly what I got.

"You are this close to being held in contempt," Judge Wegland said, even before she closed the door to her office. "I don't care to try your case for you, and if you want to go down in flames, that's your business. But I will not tolerate questions that have no basis except to cast unwarranted aspersions on the People's representative or this court."

Tolletson stood smugly to the side, no doubt enjoying every moment. He kept silent, waiting to see if I would hang myself. I didn't let him down.

A defense attorney in his right mind would have apologized and tried to recover. He would have taken anything the judge had to say, considered it with all due respect, and moved on. He would have put the interests of his client ahead of his own pride.

Naturally, I did nothing of the kind. "I don't have to explain my strategy to you or anyone else," I said. "Least of all with His Holiness over there."

Tolletson stiffened slightly, then relaxed, content I'm sure to let me keep wrapping the rope around my own neck.

"I won't have that kind of offensive wordplay in my courtroom," Wegland snapped.

"Is the First Amendment suspended in your courtroom?"

"Mr. Denney, I've had just about enough of you."

"Fine. Then appoint me counsel, and let's go at it. Let's go back on the record and have a full on contempt proceeding. I don't care."

"I think that's it, Mr. Denney," said the judge. "You just don't care. You're a lawyer who has a client on trial for murder, and you don't give a rip about him or yourself. I could hold you in contempt, but you're beneath contempt."

At that moment I had no argument to offer. She was right. If we had been on the twelfth floor of a courthouse in some large city, I might have seriously considered walking to a window and stepping out.

Tolletson broke the silence. "Perhaps we should give Mr. Denney the option of withdrawing from the case. Under the code of ethics, if mental incapacity renders him unfit to represent his client, he should move to be released from the case. That would be the honorable thing to do."

An incredible sense of déjà vu took over. I'd had this conversation before, this set of circumstances. Even the voice was oddly familiar, like my father's voice from the distant past.

"I'm not withdrawing from anything," I said. "I'm taking this to the jury."

Shaking his head, Tolletson said, "Why they let you still practice law, I don't know."

"I'll be paying very close attention to you, Mr. Denney," said Judge Wegland.

"Well, that's just fine, Judge," I said. "I hope you enjoy the view."

With that, I walked out.

CHAPTER THIRTY

WE HAD TWO more witnesses that afternoon.

The first was Garth Watts, lead detective on the Rae Patino murder. He was a big man, whose ample stomach poured over his belt even as it fought the restraint of his shirt. He had bushy eyebrows and thinning hair that once must have been red. What was left on his head now was a dull, orange fuzz.

Tolletson led him through his qualifications and then to the murder scene. He asked Watts to walk through his preliminary investigation.

"I arrived with the photographer at approximately 11:35 P.M.," Watts explained. "Officer McGary was at the scene and had placed the defendant under arrest. I immediately examined the victim."

"And what was her condition?" asked Tolletson.

"Dead."

"Did you determine the cause of death?"

"Knife wounds. She had been stabbed numerous times, with great loss of blood."

"What did you do next?"

"I tried to interview the defendant."

"Where was he at the time?"

"Officer McGary had him sitting in a chair in the living room."

"What was his condition?"

"He was bleeding but in stable condition. A paramedic was seeing to his wound."

"What was your opinion at that point as to how the defendant sustained the wound?"

I objected. "This is mere opinion, Your Honor."

"Overruled," said Judge Wegland. "The witness is qualified to answer."

"I at first thought he might have been a victim too. But that changed when I asked him what happened."

"Why did that change, Detective Watts?"

"Because he wouldn't talk, even though he was capable of it. I started to wonder about that. Why wouldn't a guy who'd been attacked himself want to help us out? That's when I Mirandized him."

"You informed him of his right to remain silent and to have a lawyer present?"

"That's right."

"What did you do next?"

"I returned to the murder scene and began my sketches." Watts explained a little bit of police procedure–the making of sketches, the taking of photographs, the collection of physical evidence. Tolletson lingered over this line of questioning to give the jury the impression of a very careful veteran detective doing his job.

When Tolletson turned the witness over to me, I felt like the proverbial salmon heading upstream, looking for any current of reasonable doubt I could catch.

"Detective Watts," I began, "you sound like you try to be very careful at crime scenes."

"That's my job."

"Of course, it is. We all understand that. You want to make sure you get everything you can out of the scene, don't you?"

"Sure."

"To help you find the person who committed the crime, correct?"

"We did that in this case."

"That's your opinion."

"It's my professional judgment." He was not giving an inch, and he was good at holding the line. But I was just getting started.

"Detective Watts, when you got to the crime scene, the sliding glass door at the back of the house, was it open or closed?"

"It was open. Officer McGary reported that it was open when he arrived at the scene."

"I see. An open door at the back of the house, allowing anyone access to the inside."

"That's right."

"How about to get out of the house?"

"Excuse me?"

"Isn't it true that an open door also allows people to get out?"

"Well, sure."

"Like a perpetrator, for instance?"

"If he chose to leave. In this case, he did not."

"You're assuming the defendant is guilty, aren't you?"

"That's why we arrested him."

"But he is not guilty until the evidence proves it to the jury, is he?"

Adele Wegland did not wait for Tolletson to object. "Mr. Denney, I will state the law to the jury at the end of the testimony. Confine your questions to the facts, please."

Another rebuke from the judge in front of the jury. I was a wayward child, not a lawyer, and I felt some of the heat of impatience arising from the jury box. Two things a trial lawyer must never do–bore or annoy the jury. I felt I was starting to do both.

So I raised my voice a little, hoping the volume change would make things more interesting. "Isn't it a fact, sir, that you never considered the idea that another person committed this crime?"

Watts hesitated before he answered. Then he dug in his heels. "It's a fact because there was absolutely no evidence pointing to anyone except Howard Patino."

"That's because you didn't look for it, did you?"

"Detective work isn't a fishing trip, Mr. Denney. We don't waste our time. We go where the evidence points us."

"Didn't the fact that the defendant was stabbed himself give you even a slight suspicion that another party might be involved?"

"Like I said, I had that idea at first, but not after I tried to question the defendant."

"How did Mr. Patino look to you, Detective?"

"Look? What do you mean?"

"I mean, look. Was he calm, cool, collected? Or was he agitated in some way?"

Watts thought a moment. "He looked guilty."

The courtroom erupted with laughter. Watts looked surprised at first; then he himself started to laugh. And I was being buried by it. Laughter at a lawyer's expense is not a good thing. It chips away at any authority you hope to establish. When you get up for closing arguments, you don't want the jury to think of you as a hapless fool.

So I took the gloves off. "You're an expert at judging guilt or innocence just by looking at people?"

"No, sir. But you asked for my opinion."

"I'm interested in the facts, sir. And isn't it a fact that you did not follow any other leads?"

"As I said, there was nothing to point us anywhere else."

"Not even the fact that the knife had no fingerprints?"

"That is consistent with the perpetrator trying to stage his own attack."

"And it's also consistent with someone wearing gloves to keep fingerprints off the weapon, isn't it?"

"Anything is consistent with anything if you have a big enough imagination."

"Is the open bathroom window a product of anyone's imagination?" It was a small fact that I had noted in one of the reports.

Watts seemed momentarily disarmed. "Well, that again, like I said before, there was no reason to consider that."

"Did you even look at the window?"

"I personally did not, no."

"Never even gave it a thought, did you?"

"Again, there wasn't a reason."

"So your answer is *no?*"

"That's my answer."

I scooped up a copy of Watts's report, which had been provided to me during discovery. It contained one minor detail that I decided to try to upgrade to major.

"Detective Watts, you testified earlier that you tried to talk to Mr. Patino and that he did not talk to you. Is that correct?"

"He was uncooperative, yes."

"That's not entirely true, is it?"

"Yes it is. He did not cooperate with any questioning."

"In fact, though, he did say something. Do you have a copy of your report in front of you?"

"Yes."

"On page 2, in the middle, do you not say that the suspect mentioned the devil?"

Watts took his time looking at his report, giving himself the chance to formulate an answer. "That was not in answer to any of my questions," he said finally.

"But it *is* something he said. In fact, didn't my client keep mentioning the devil over and over again?"

"I remember a few instances, yes."

"And you didn't ask him about that?"

"Mr. Denney, I don't really think the devil is a suspect in this case." The answer drew more laughter from the courtroom.

"But what if my client believed that, Detective? Wouldn't you think he was crazy?"

Tolletson didn't give his witness the chance to answer. "That is beyond the competence of this witness, Your Honor. He's a detective, not a psychologist."

"Sustained," said Judge Wegland.

"May we approach the bench?" I asked.

"No," the judge answered. "Move on."

I had nowhere to move. I was beginning to think that all I had going for me was the defender's desperate last hope–that the jury would think I was so obviously being ganged up on that they would start to feel sympathy for me. They would see that I was so out of it that they would think to themselves, *His client deserves better; maybe we better let him go.*

Yes, it was desperation time. As I walked with wobbly knees to the counsel table, Triple C was looking at the far wall. He couldn't bear to make eye contact with me.

The only look of encouragement I got was from my poor client. "It's okay," Howie whispered to me as I sat down. "You're trying."

I hoped to do better with Tolletson's next witness, Hinton police officer Donald Cheadle, who heard Howie's blurted statement at the Hinton County Hospital. This was potentially the most damaging testimony of all and an admission from Howie's own mouth that he killed his wife.

Tolletson and Cheadle seemed to be having a grand time with this testimony. It's not often that a prosecutor gets such a juicy statement, even though in my opinion it should never have been admitted into evidence. It would be a good ground for an appeal.

That night I couldn't sleep, even with the help of the bottle.

I'd taken a room at a Motel 6 near the freeway so I wouldn't have to make the long drive back to Hinton the next day. That way I'd be fresh.

But not if I didn't sleep. Not if I stayed up half the night fighting visions.

They came fast and furious, and for awhile, I actually thought I might be going insane, losing my already tenuous grip on reality.

My first vision was of a lost girl drowning in the black ocean. No life jacket, no boats.

In my mind's eye, I watched, and at one point almost screamed for someone to save her, but who would hear me on a moonless night that existed only in my imagination?

I kept seeing her, this little girl, and then a horrible realization hit me.

The girl was Mandy.

She was going to be lost. Lost to me. Lost forever.

As was my custom, I fought back with a drink and a vow of anger. I would make Barb pay, some day, some way, for making me have visions like this.

That was not the only vision I had. I paced the room, the TV blaring, not listening or watching it but hoping it would push out the maelstrom of images. It didn't work, and I was hit with another vision–this time, a vision of myself.

I was in a bare field, and it was night. The only light came from the flickering flames of torches held in the hands of faceless people. I was tied to a post, and my back was bleeding from open wounds, red and raw like I'd been whipped. There was a man standing there with a whip, and it was my father.

None of this made sense, but alcoholic dreams seldom do.

The walls of the room began to close in on me, so I went outside, to enjoy its sweeping vista of the motel parking lot. If you're looking for inspiration, ever in need of a visual to fight off thoughts of self-destruction or deep depression, do not go to a Motel 6 parking lot.

I couldn't see the mountains I knew were behind me or the ocean, which was miles from view. The sun had set long ago, and there was no moon. For all I knew, I could have walked out to the parking spot of cave dwellers.

Lindsay Patino popped into my mind. I wished she was here. I wished she was here so I could point out to her what a meaningless existence this was, that in the end the only thing to look forward to was a darkness much like this one, a darkness that would last forever and we wouldn't know anything about it because we wouldn't be conscious. I wished she was here so I could look her in the eye and tell her I couldn't share her sweet delusions because I was too rational, too stuck on reality to escape life through deception.

Why I had the need to tell her all that I don't know. I wouldn't really find out until the next day, when everything caved in.

CHAPTER THIRTY-ONE

IRONICALLY, THE DAY started out pretty well for us.

Tolletson called Randy Crowley, the man who sat next to Howie on the flight down from Alaska. The calling of this witness was proof that Tolletson was dead serious about winning this case because it must have cost a lot in time and money to track this guy down.

When I got the witness list in discovery, I asked Howie about this man. Howie remembered him vaguely but couldn't remember anything he'd said to him. His mind had been elsewhere.

Mr. Crowley seemed to have a great memory of his conversation with Howie.

"What was the first thing you recall the defendant saying to you?" Tolletson asked.

Crowley, who was thin–Ichabod Crane thin–and wore glasses, wasn't a magnetic witness. He had a reedy voice that annoyed me and, I hoped, the jury.

"He asked me where I was heading to," Crowley said.

"And you answered?"

"Toluca Lake. That's where I live."

"What, if anything, did he say next?"

"He told me he was going to catch a bus and come up to Hinton."

"Did he tell you why?"

"He said he had to see someone."

"Were those his exact words?"

"Yes, sir. He said, 'I have to see someone.'"

"How did he say it?"

"He just said it in a matter-of-fact way."

"Did he say he was going to see his wife?"

"No. He said, 'Someone.' And he had a faraway look when he said it."

"Objection," I said. "Non-responsive and speculation."

"Sustained."

Tolletson asked, "What, if anything, did you say next?"

"I asked him if this was regarding business."

"What did he say?"

"He shook his head and said, 'No, I'm going to deliver a message.'"

"What was his demeanor like when he said that?"

Again I objected. This time Wegland overruled me. Crowley said, "He was very serious and looking straight ahead."

"He wasn't talking directly to you?"

"No, sir. He just looked straight ahead, sort of faraway."

Once more I objected, since the same speculative answer had come in again. Wegland said the answer would stand this time. "He's explained it," she said.

"Did he say anything else?" Tolletson asked.

"Only one more thing," Crowley answered. "He said, 'She'll never forget it.'"

"Again, were those his *exact* words?"

"Yes. 'She'll never forget it.' And he was still looking far away. I got a little spooked."

"You were afraid?"

Crowley squared his shoulders. "Not afraid, just spooked. Like this guy was a little weird."

"Objection!"

"Overruled."

Tolletson said, "And did you have further conversation with the defendant?"

"No. That was it. I was glad when the flight was over and he would go away."

"Your witness," Tolletson said to me.

"Good morning, Mr. Crowley," I said. He nodded at me. "What was my client wearing that day on the plane?"

The question surprised him, which was exactly my intent. Crowley looked at the ceiling a moment, then said, "He had on a red shirt, I think."

"Can you describe it a little better than that?"

"Well, I wasn't really studying him. I think it was a red shirt of some kind."

"What about pants?"

"I believe they were jeans."

"Light blue? Dark blue?"

"I believe they were dark."

"You believe? Can you be sure?"

"Again, I wasn't studying his clothes."

"I see. Did you have a meal on that flight?"

"Yes, I believe so."

"Do you remember what you ordered?"

Crowley smiled and said, "It was probably rubber chicken." His attempt at humor fell flat. No one in the courtroom laughed. That shook him. He looked nervously at the jury, then back at me.

"This is a serious question," I rebuked. "What did you have to eat?"

Sighing, Crowley looked up at the ceiling again. Maybe he was looking for an escape hatch. "I think it was chicken, or maybe some sort of beef."

"Do you know the difference between chicken and beef?"

"Objection," Tolletson intoned.

"I'll withdraw the question, Your Honor. Mr. Crowley, did you order any drinks on that flight?"

"Yes," he said confidently. "I always order a Coke when the flight attendants come around."

"And what did my client order?"

"I'm not sure."

"Did he order anything?"

"He may have. I wasn't paying attention."

"I see. Now Mr. Crowley, you've just testified that you aren't sure, that you 'think' or 'believe.' Yet when it comes to what my client said, you have no such uncertainty, do you?"

Now fully aware of what my questioning was about, Crowley began to fidget. He put his bony hands together on his lap, and one of his thumbs started flicking up and down, up and down.

"I remember what he said, yes."

"It's more than that, isn't it? You remember his *exact* words, don't you?"

"Yes, I do."

"You even remember the details of his facial expression, for heaven's sake."

Tolletson objected at this point, which didn't bother me. My point was made. Judge Wegland sustained the objection.

"Mr. Crowley, can you search that sharp memory of yours and tell us if you remember that Howie Patino was carrying anything with him on that flight?"

"I seem to remember a carry-on bag."

"Seem to?"

Crowley snapped, "I do remember."

"Was he carrying anything else?"

"Um . . . I think he might have been."

"Was he by any chance carrying a stuffed bear?"

"Yes. That was it. He had a stuffed bear."

"You remember now. Is that it?"

"Yes."

"It was, in fact, a little teddy bear, was it not?"

"Yes, I believe it was."

"One last question, Mr. Crowley. Do people generally take stuffed teddy bears to people they are going to harm?"

"Objection!" Tolletson said, but once more I didn't care. I had the witness right where I wanted him. Even as the judge was sustaining the objection, I said, "No more questions."

I knew I'd done well and felt pretty good.

Then Tolletson called his first expert.

Criminal trials increasingly depend on the testimony of expert witnesses. You've got the forensic experts working for law enforcement, uncovering grand stories from such minutiae as clothing fibers and fingernail scrapings. Then there are the microbiologists, who can go even smaller, and the population geneticists, who can apply all this to the entire population of the world. Every conceivable medical niche is filled by innumerable people with advanced degrees who love nothing more than telling jurors how much they know.

These people generally work for law enforcement and the prosecution. Unless the defendant has money or wealthy relatives, all he generally ends up with is one court-appointed doctor who gets ripped on cross-examination.

I had Hendrick Brown, who was about as good as I could get for the resources at my disposal.

Benton Tolletson began the forensic part of his case with Chet Riordan, the chief medical examiner of Hinton County, the man who liked Rye Krisp with his cadavers.

He had an avuncular appearance, which no doubt served him well in front of juries. His down-home style of answering was straight Andy Griffith. That was a counterpoint to the details of his testimony, which involved multiple stab wounds and a whole lot of blood.

After ten minutes of testimony, Benton Tolletson showed Riordan a color 8 x 10 glossy of Rae Patino's body. After Riordan identified it, Tolletson asked if he could show it to the jury.

I objected, and the judge asked us to approach.

"That picture is highly prejudicial," I said. "We will stipulate to the cause of death and the number of wounds. But showing that picture to the jury will just get them all worked up. Against my client."

"Murder is not pretty, Your Honor," said Tolletson.

"Neither is this attempt to sway the jury."

Wegland held up her hand and looked closely at the photo. "No, it's not pretty, Mr. Denney, but it is evidence. Your motion is denied."

"I object vigorously to this."

"Noted," the judge snapped. "Now go back to your chair."

So Tolletson got to show the jury the photograph. As the wide-eyed jurors passed it from hand to hand, I could almost feel a sense of frontier justice rising in them. It's impossible to see a picture like that and keep a sense of objectivity. One juror, a woman in the second row, glared at me.

I tried to keep a poker face attempting to prevent the jury from seeing my inner agony at this ruling. I'd had years of practice at this but still wasn't very good. My jaw muscles start to twitch. But with a few deep breaths and some strategic placements of my hands on my face, I managed to keep cool.

That is, until the bombshell.

Every trial has at least one surprise for a lawyer, no matter how well prepared he is. If he's lucky, it will be a minor thing, easily handled with a little clear thinking. If he's not lucky, it will explode in his face and threaten to blow his case right out of the water.

That's what happened as I sat there, trying to calm my quavering jaw muscles as Benton Tolletson continued with his direct examination. I was only half listening as I jotted some notes for the imminent cross-examination.

"Was there anything else unusual about the body of Rae Patino?" Tolletson asked.

Riordan calmly answered, "Yes."

That stopped me. I looked at the witness.

"And what was that?" said Tolletson.

"The victim was approximately three months pregnant."

The shock waves were immediate. It was like one of those TV moments, when the crowd gasps together in collective horror. I gasped myself. All thought left me. It was only out of instinct that I shouted, "Objection!"

At that very same moment, Howie Patino stood up and screamed.

He screamed as loudly as any person I had ever heard, and it didn't help that he was only a foot or so from my left ear.

The bailiff, a portly deputy sheriff, ran over to Howie and wrapped his arms around him to restrain any further movement. Howie struggled for only a second before going almost completely limp.

Out in the gallery, people were scuffling, talking, and exchanging looks.

I practically raced Tolletson to the bench.

"I was not provided this material on discovery!" I said through clenched teeth. "This is the first I've heard about any pregnancy."

"You certainly were informed," Tolletson said.

Almost crying with indignation, I said, "I went over every inch of Riordan's report, and that was not in there."

"It was the subject of a supplementary report," Tolletson said.

"Do you have that?" Judge Wegland asked me.

"No, I do not," I insisted.

"He does, Your Honor," said Tolletson. "Ms. Plotzske can tell you she delivered it herself."

Sylvia Plotzske had handed me several items of discovery over the past few weeks, but surely I would have noticed a supplementary medical report on the victim of this murder.

Wouldn't I? Or had my drinking affected my short-term memory that much?

"Mr. Denney," said Judge Wegland, "Mr. Tolletson and Ms. Plotzske are well known to me, and if they're sure they delivered you this item, then I'm sure they did. Frankly, I think the more realistic possibility is that you misplaced it."

"But I–"

"Your objection is overruled."

I could sense, rather than see, the smile on Benton Tolletson's face. He was enjoying this. I'm sure that if he ever mowed down Viet Cong with an M-16, he enjoyed that too. This was a slaughter.

I made it back to my counsel table in a daze. Tolletson asked Riordan a few more questions. The judge called on me to cross-examine.

For a long moment, my head was blank. I heard the judge's voice call on me again. It was like a distant echo.

Then I heard Trip whispering in my ear. "Ask about the blood," he said.

"The what?"

"Ask him why he never tested the blood."

I remembered. Trip and I had discussed this point during preparation, but I had forgotten about it. Not a good thing for a trial lawyer.

I stood up. "Dr. Riordan."

"Yes, sir."

"How many stab wounds did the victim receive?"

"Twenty-five."

"You counted them yourself?"

"Part of the job."

"I see. That's a lot of stab wounds, isn't it?"

"It sure is."

"Were there any slash wounds?"

"There were, yes."

"How many and where?"

Riordan reached for the papers in front of him. "May I refer to my report?"

"Please."

After a moment's reading, Riordan said, "Three deep lacerations. One to the jugular, another to left cheek area, and a third to the left shoulder."

"Is it safe to say that the laceration to the jugular would have resulted in a massive loss of blood?"

"Yes."

"In fact, Dr. Riordan, isn't it true that a wound of this type would have blood spurting forth?"

"That would be consistent with such a wound."

"And so, isn't it also safe to assume that a killer inflicting twenty-five stab wounds, including a laceration to the jugular, would be covered with the victim's blood? Isn't that true, Dr. Riordan?"

For a moment, Riordan hesitated. "In the usual case, yes."

"And is there anything unusual about this case?"

"There may be. I don't know."

"You *don't know?* You're the medical examiner, aren't you?"

"Objection," Tolletson said. "Argumentative."

"Sustained."

I didn't skip a beat. "Dr. Riordan, did you test the blood on Mr. Patino's clothing?"

"No, sir. I wasn't asked."

"And you didn't think it was important enough to conduct a test?"

"The facts as given to me didn't lead me to believe that it was necessary."

"So there is no way of knowing, is there, how much of the blood on Mr. Patino was his own or the victim's, is there?"

Riordan paused, and said, "Not without a test."

That was enough. A smart cross-examiner has to know when to stop. At one time I had been a smart cross-examiner. So I stopped. I was hoping that I planted some questions in the minds of the jurors, at least enough to dilute the shock of the pregnancy testimony.

How much of a dilution it would be, I hadn't a clue.

After court adjourned for the day, Howie said he wanted to talk to me. The deputy took us to a small conference room in the courthouse and said I could have ten minutes.

Howie was an amazing sight as I entered the room. He sat almost serenely in a chair, his manacled hands folded quietly in his lap. His eyes were red-rimmed but soft. It was a look almost of . . . peace. *Surreal* is the word that occurred to me.

"Howie," I said, "I want you to know I didn't have any idea–"

Howie stopped me with an upraised hand. "I want you to know it doesn't matter, Jake," he said.

"What doesn't matter?"

"The trial."

"Why doesn't it matter?"

"Because it's God's will," he answered. "I know that now."

"Look, Howie–"

"He wants me to go to jail."

"Howie–"

"That's the way it has to be, Jake. To make up for killing Rae and the baby."

"I don't think–"

"You're trying, Jake, and I appreciate that. You're my only friend in the whole world. But God wants me to go to jail forever. That's where I can repent. He'll take care of me there."

"Will you stop it!" I fairly shouted. Yes, the trial was going badly. That was no secret. But in the short walk between the courtroom and the conference room, I had decided I wasn't ready to throw that towel in. After all, I hadn't presented my evidence yet.

"Get off this kick right now," I demanded.

"It's God's will, Jake. I killed a baby. I know it wasn't my baby, Jake. I know that. Rae and I didn't . . . I mean she and I . . . not for a couple of years." His head fell toward his chest. "But a baby, Jake. I killed a baby."

"What if you didn't?"

"It's God's will."

"Will you shut up!" I blurted out of frustration as much as anything else. This trial, this client, were nightmares. "Forget God! It's just you and me and that courtroom in there."

With an incredulous look, Howie said, "How can you say that, Jake? How can you forget God? You take that back."

"We've got to face reality, Howie."

"Take it back, Jake!" He was still a little boy being picked on by a bully.

"Fine! If it will make you happy, I take it back. Okay? But you can't give up on me, not now."

Howie smiled. It seemed to hold more peace that any smile I'd ever seen. "It's in God's hands, Jake. You just watch and see."

That was the end of our conversation. Watch and see, he said. Okay, I would. I'd watch and see just what God was going to do with his hands.

CHAPTER THIRTY-TWO

TOLLETSON FINISHED AFTER three days of testimony. His presentation had been crisp, clean, and deadly. Grudgingly, I had to admire his work, though in much the same way as a condemned man admires the way the executioner swings his ax.

Now it was my turn. My case would rise or fall with the jury's understanding of Howie's mental state. I had to prove that he did not have the mental state necessary for murder, namely, malice aforethought. That meant the jury had to get to know Howie.

That's why my first witness was Janet Patino. I knew the jury would listen carefully to her. She was his mother, and she was credible.

In a calm voice, broken only occasionally by a short sob, she told the jury about Howie's childhood, about his struggles in school, and how he was always "just a little slower" than the other kids. Tolletson let her testify without objection up to the point where Janet met Rae for the first time.

"He called you and told you he wanted you to meet her. Is that right?" I asked.

"Yes," Mrs. Patino answered, "and we decided to have them over for dinner."

"When was that?"

"I don't remember exactly, but it was in the summer."

"And did they come over for dinner?"

"Yes, they did."

"What was your impression of Rae when you first met her?"

"Objection," Tolletson said. "Relevance. The witness's impression doesn't go to anything at issue here."

"It does, Your Honor," I said.

"I don't see it, Mr. Denney," Judge Wegland said. "The character of the victim is not relevant. Nor is the state of mind of the witness. What other issue does it go to?"

"It just gives a fuller picture to the jury, Your Honor."

"I'm bound by the rules of evidence, Mr. Denney. Only relevant evidence is admissible. The objection is sustained."

So the jury was not going to know anything about what kind of person Rae Patino was unless Howie took the stand and testified about it. And that was a gamble I wasn't prepared to take. Yet.

Tolletson asked only a few questions of Janet Patino. He was all charm and deference with her.

"Mrs. Patino, you love your son, don't you?"

"Oh, yes."

"You'd like to see him walk out of this courtroom a free man, wouldn't you?"

"Of course I would." She wiped away a small tear from her left eye.

"But you also would want him to be held accountable for any wrongdoing on his part, wouldn't you?"

A brilliant question. There was no way she could answer it so that it wouldn't be helpful to Tolletson. If she said no, the jury would discount her testimony as biased. If she said yes, Howie would stand condemned by the words of his own mother. So it was, from a trial lawyer's standpoint, a great move. But I hated Tolletson for asking it.

The tears started flowing freely down Janet Patino's cheeks. She trembled visibly. Her mental strain was obvious as she attempted to formulate an answer. At one point she looked at Howie as only a mother in torment could.

Tolletson said, "That's all right, Mrs. Patino. I withdraw the question. That's all I have."

As Janet Patino stepped off the witness stand, I tried to read the jurors' faces. Most of them were looking down, as if they couldn't stand to look at poor Janet because they knew what anguish she was suffering–the agony of a mother with a guilty son.

Next up was Dr. Hendrick Brown.

As he took the oath from the clerk, I could sense the tension in the courtroom. Everyone seemed to know this was a crucial moment. The defense expert was about to take his shot. From both Brown and myself, it would have to be the performance of a lifetime.

I spent a good fifteen minutes having Dr. Brown go over his education and credentials. I wanted a solid, credible foundation for his testimony. Another reason for the *bona fides* was that he didn't look the part of the traditional psychiatrist. He did not dress sharply or speak with an Ivy League accent. If seen on the street, most people would not even think of him as a professional. He seemed more like somebody's neighbor, one who liked to work in his rose garden. That impression was magnified by what he wore to court–a sweater over his shirt and tie. So I made sure the jury knew of his extensive education, writings, and work with patients.

Then I turned to his examination of Howie at the Hinton County Jail. "Can you describe for us, please, the procedure you used to examine my client?"

"Certainly," said Dr. Brown as he expertly turned toward the jury box. "I injected Mr. Patino with sodium pentathol, which is commonly called truth serum. It's a medical device that is often used to help patients recall traumatic events. In this case, I thought it necessary to break through the mental wall Mr. Patino had understandably erected concerning the death of his wife. After the injection, Mr. Patino went into a mild, trancelike state, and I proceeded to ask him questions."

"And did he answer those questions?"

"Yes, he did."

"Was a transcript made of those questions and answers?"

"Yes."

I fetched a copy of the transcript from my briefcase, but before I could hand it to Brown, Tolletson spoke. "At this point, Your Honor, I'm going to object on *Kelly-Frye* grounds."

Tolletson was referring to two cases governing the admissibility of certain scientific evidence. I had expected that and was ready. "Your Honor, I don't think we'll have to dismiss the jury for a hearing. If we may approach?"

Wegland waved us up. For once, Tolletson seemed caught off guard. It was like fresh air blowing through a stuffy basement.

"This is not a *Kelly-Frye* issue," I said. "We're not talking about a new scientific method here at all. Sodium pentathol has been used for decades."

"But we don't know how reliable it is," Tolletson protested.

"That's something he can offer evidence on," I said. "Besides which, this is medical testimony. *Kelly-Frye* does not apply to expert medical testimony, as held in *People v. Rowland.*"

I had done my homework. Judge Wegland, taken aback, reached for a California evidence book and started leafing through the pages.

Almost five minutes went by. People shifted in their seats. One of the male jurors yawned.

Finally, Judge Wegland took off her glasses and said, "I have to agree with Mr. Denney on this one. The objection is overruled."

For a second I wasn't sure I heard right. Had I actually won a ruling? When I saw Tolletson's dark expression, I knew. I really had won, and on a crucial point.

Now I was free to have Dr. Hendrick Brown tell the jury about Howie's examination, which he proceeded to do. I took my time with it, allowing the full impact to be felt by the jury.

At the end of the testimony, I asked Brown if he had an opinion about Howie's mental state at the time of the murder.

"I do. It is my opinion that Mr. Patino did not harbor any malice regarding the victim. He was delusional and completely removed mentally from the events that transpired."

Thanking Dr. Brown, I returned to my seat.

Tolletson wasted no time. "Dr. Brown, as a competent psychiatrist, you have to admit that your field is not one known for scientific precision, don't you?"

"It is precise in its own way."

"Well, you don't have any instruments to measure mental capacity, do you?"

"We can now get a picture of the brain through magnetic resonance imaging, if that's what you mean."

Impatience was evident in Tolletson's voice. "Did you use an MRI to examine the defendant, Dr. Brown?"

"No, I did not."

"So you didn't measure his brain in any way, did you?"

"No, sir."

"In fact, you have no instruments, even including an MRI, that give you measurable data about mental state. Isn't that true?"

"Psychiatry is a distinct science."

"Please answer my question, Doctor. You cannot measure mental state with any instrument, can you?"

"That is correct."

"You can't observe a mental disorder in the same way you can observe, say, a cut or scratch, can you?"

"No, you cannot."

"It's all opinion, isn't it?"

Sitting up a little, Brown said, "Opinion based on training and experience."

"But isn't it also true, Dr. Brown, that opinions differ widely in the field of psychiatry?"

"I don't think I'd agree with your use of the word 'widely.'"

At that, Tolletson spun around like he'd been slapped on the back of the head. "Then you're telling the jury that everybody in psychiatry agrees?"

"No, that's not what I'm saying." Brown was growing defiant.

"Then what *are* you saying, Doctor?"

"All I'm saying, Mr. Tolletson, is that psychiatry is like any other discipline. The more experience one has, the better one is able to make a diagnosis."

"I see." Tolletson walked to his counsel table and picked up a book. He held it in his hand for a moment, so the jury could see it, then placed it back on the table. "You do recognize, do you not, that there is quite a body of respectable authority in this country that would not agree with your conclusion?"

"I recognize there is some room for disagreement, yes."

"And do you recognize, sir, that there are some experts out there who would say you were wrong?"

"Perhaps."

"In fact, some would say you were way off base?"

"That would be their opinion."

"As experts."

"Perhaps."

My witness was hedging now, not a good thing. Tolletson was doing a masterful job in this area of expert cross-examination. He swung a mean ax. I could only hope that after he was finished, Dr. Hendrick Brown wouldn't be chopped to pieces.

"Let's talk about this, Doctor," Tolletson continued. "Are you aware that there are at least eight experts who have criticized, in books or articles, the very standards you relied upon in this case?"

"Well, there are also others who agree with it."

"That's not my question. I'm talking about eight, at least eight, highly respected authorities in the field who would call you wrong on this."

"I don't know the number."

"Let me help you. Are you familiar with Dr. Elizabeth Trevisano?"

"Yes, I am."

"Would you agree that Dr. Trevisano has abundant experience in the field of psychiatry?"

"Yes."

"She would be considered one of the leaders in the field of mental disorders, would she not?"

Brown nodded. "I would agree with that."

Tolletson again picked up the book that had been on his table. "And are you familiar with her book *Diminished Capacity and Mental Defenses?"*

"I've heard of the book."

"Ever read it?"

"No, I can't say I have."

"Would it shock you to learn that Dr. Trevisano disapproves of the very method you used to examine the defendant in this case?"

"Nothing shocks me anymore, Mr. Tolletson."

"If she called the method 'quackery,' would that shock you?"

"That would be her opinion."

"Ever heard of Dr. John Carlino?"

"Yes."

"Ever read any of his articles?"

"Some, I think."

"He disagrees with you, doesn't he?"

"He may, I don't know for sure."

"He's an expert, isn't he?"

"Certainly."

"Dr. David Caldicott?"

"I know of him."

"Dr. Helen Meyer?"

"Yes."

"Both disagree with you, don't they?"

Brown scowled now, and that was in stark contrast to the easygoing demeanor he had exhibited before. Part of Tolletson strategy, I'm sure, was to get Brown's goat, make him lose his cool, the better to show him as biased. It was about to work.

"Mr. Tolletson," Brown said, "perhaps I can save us some time. You can go out and find people who disagree with anybody on anything. Eventually a consensus emerges. I maintain I'm perfectly in line with the accepted wisdom in this field."

"Is that right?"

"Yes."

"And how many books have you written, Dr. Brown?"

Brown paused and glared at Tolletson. I could see in the doctor's eyes a glint of the young street fighter he had been in his youth. "I work in the field with people. I'm not an academic."

"So your answer is, none?"

"That's correct."

"Have you written any articles in any leading psychiatric journals?"

"No, sir. But that is not my focus."

"Well, my focus is the truth, Doctor."

"Objection!" I virtually shouted.

"Sustained," said the judge, with little enthusiasm.

There was more Tolletson could have done with Dr. Brown, but one of the best things a good cross-examiner can do is quit while he's ahead. Apparently feeling he had done adequate damage, Tolletson sat down.

I did my best to rehabilitate my witness. I threw him some softball questions, which gave him the opportunity to explain again how and why he had reached his conclusion. Actually, considering the harm Tolletson had done, I thought I did a pretty good job.

But not good enough to win the case. If Brown had been a knock-out punch for me, maybe I could have rested. Not now.

Now there was only one way to save Howie.

He would have to take the stand.

CHAPTER THIRTY-THREE

COURT BROKE FOR the weekend, giving me a chance to think things over. Only I couldn't think about them. My mind was split into too many segments.

Largest segment–my daughter. I couldn't believe how much it hurt not to see her. I thought I would be able to stand it for awhile, at least until after the trial, when I could go and fight for custody. I figured I could wait that long. But I couldn't. It was torture.

On Saturday I went into the office. It was usually deserted there on the weekends, and I could at least pretend I was doing some legal work. I could also drink in peace.

My office was too cramped, so I spread out my stuff on the conference table in the library. Gil Lee kept a pretty good stock of legal books there. He even had a computer set up for his tenants, and for a small fee, we could do online research.

In about two minutes the conference table was covered with legal papers, notepads, transcripts, and discovery items. There was no order to the material, fitting perfectly with my state of mind. A man's desk, someone once told me, reflects his inner life. At this moment, I had to agree.

Was there anything in this jumble that could possibly help me? Something I hadn't seen before?

I remembered the supplementary medical report, the one that concluded Rae Patino had been three months pregnant when she died. Where was that? I couldn't remember ever seeing it. Surely I would have remembered something that important.

I found a copy of the report. It was two pages long. And there, in the middle of the second page, was the information that had surprised me at trial.

The report was signed by Chester A. Riordan.

For five minutes I looked at that thing and tried to recall when I'd received it. I could not. No memory. Blank screen.

Could I have seen it and not remembered? A scary thought hit me. Maybe my short-term memory was damaged in some way. Worse, maybe I hadn't registered this in my memory at all, being juiced at the time I first got it.

Alone and lost in the library, I shook. If there had been another L.A. earthquake, I probably wouldn't have noticed.

To calm myself, I took a swig from the bottle I'd brought with me. It was warm and soothing, like always. I knew I would be comforted soon.

Next thing I knew I was being jostled awake by a hand on my shoulder and a voice repeating my name. Slowly, like a boat being dragged out of mud, my mind came back into reality.

"You sleeping on the job?" Triple C said. "That why you don't answer your phone?"

I rubbed my eyes and looked at my watch. I'd been out for forty-five minutes. "I must have dozed off."

"Yeah, right," Trip said, holding up my half-empty bottle. "I got a mind to smash you over the head with this."

"Maybe it'd do me some good." My temples were pounding, and my neck was sore.

"You're losing it."

"Is that why you tracked me down?"

"No, I was actually doing some work for you, though for the life of me I don't know why."

Trip took off his shoulder bag and sat in a chair on the other side of the conference table. He was wearing his signature Hawaiian shirt. "My dad was a drinker," he said. "He ended up on a slab at sixty, with no liver and a heart like Kleenex."

"Don't lecture me."

"Don't do this to yourself."

"Do we have a chance?"

"For what?"

"To win."

Trip took a long time before answering, watching me from behind his sunglasses. "All you need is one," he said, referring to the possibility of a hung jury.

"Have I got that?"

"Probably not."

I couldn't disagree.

"You putting Howie on the stand?" Trip asked.

"I don't see as I have a choice."

"That's tough. Tolletson might take him apart."

"That's what I'm hoping."

Tapping his sunglasses with a finger, Trip said, "You're *hoping?* What's that all about?"

Amazingly, I had thought through this part of my case pretty clearly. "I want Howie to be taken apart," I explained, "because I want him to crack up in front of the jury. I want them to see just how much of a fruitcake he is. I want him babbling away about God's will, so the jury can see this is not the kind of guy who would plan and then carry out a murder. And this is the one way I'm going to get in some of Rae Patino's background. Since Howie's state of mind is an issue, he can tell the jury just what he thought about Rae."

After a pause to reflect, Triple C nodded. "You really can think when you give yourself a chance."

"Yeah, maybe. Anyway, this is my last chance."

"Why?"

"I'm through after this." Until I said those words, I had not made any decision like that. I was almost surprised to hear this coming out of my mouth. But it made perfect sense to me. "This is my last trial."

"What are you talking about?" Trip said. "What else could a washed-up hack like you do besides practice law?"

"I don't know. I haven't thought that far ahead. I only know I haven't got anything to hold me here anymore. I can't see my own daughter. I owe my landlord money. I'm getting my butt kicked in a little podunk town. Why should I hang around?"

"Don't ask me. I'm no doctor. But I have tracked down my share of skips in my time, and I can tell you this. You don't find the answers by running."

"Ah." I waved my hand in the air in the universal sign of dismissal.

"Let's forget about that for the moment," Trip said. "I just thought you'd like to know something."

"How generous."

"Not. I'll bill you for the time."

"So, what is it?"

"It's that podunk town. You remember I told you I felt weird about it?"

"Yeah."

"I think I know why." Trip finally took off his shades and threw them on the table. "You have any idea how the little town of Hinton got its start?"

I shook my head.

"I spent yesterday afternoon in the Hinton Municipal Library."

"They have any books?"

Snorting, Trip said, "Several. Anyway, I asked the librarian for a history of the place. She got me one. The Chamber of Commerce actually published a history of Hinton on its centennial, back in

1990. The official version of the story is that the land that is now Hinton County was won in a poker game in San Francisco. The man who won it was a ne'er-do-well who'd been chased out of polite society in the East. You know what his name was?"

"Gandhi," I said.

Trip shook his head. "Come on, man. You need to hear this."

"Sorry."

"The man's name was Solomon Hazelton."

"Hazelton Winery?"

"Not then. Not yet."

Now Trip had my attention. One thing he knew how to do was tell a story. He'd baited the hook, and I was biting.

"The unofficial version," Trip continued, "is that Solomon Hazelton killed a man to get that land. Whatever happened, he moved down here and started building a town. By the twenties the place was thriving, and Solomon Hazelton was a very rich man. He owned most of the land in the county, and everything was great up until 1929 and the crash. Solomon Hazelton died, and his son took over the crumbling family holdings. The son's name was Victor. Victor is the father of Warren, better known as Captain Warren."

"The winery guy."

"The very same."

"Who looks to have revived the family fortune."

"He's done well."

I shrugged. "Sounds like a typical American success story."

"That ain't all." Trip smiled mysteriously, the way he did when he was about to tell something he'd uncovered through dogged detective work. "As I was reading this book, an old guy comes up to me. He's not smelling too good, and his clothes are from the Salvation Army. I figure him for one of these guys on Social Security who hangs out in the library because it's cool inside. He says to me, 'I heard you ask about the history of Hinton. You want the real story?'

Well, I'm a PI. I don't turn down any offer of information. I say, 'Sure,' and he takes me outside. . . ."

The old gentleman, whose name was Morris, asked Trip for a cigarette. Trip told him he didn't smoke. Morris said he would not reveal what he had unless he got a nail. So Trip walked him around the corner to a liquor store and bought him a pack of Camels. That was all it took for Morris to get started.

He told Trip he had once been a city councilman, back in the sixties, which was the heyday of Hinton. He also owned a restaurant downtown, a place frequented by the power players of the time.

The most powerful of the bunch was Captain Warren Hazelton. He was called Captain because of his fondness for racing yachts, two of which he had docked in the Ventura Marina. The appellation had a dual significance. He was a man who not only liked sailing the ocean but was used to giving orders.

His other passion was wine, and he had built Hazelton into the best winery in the region. Naturally, he expected the local establishments to carry a full stock of Hazelton wines.

"But I wouldn't do it," Morris told Trip, "because he wanted to overcharge me. Told him I'd run my place my way. He didn't like that. He said he'd ruin me. And he did."

Morris took a deep drag on his cigarette and looked at the hills above Hinton. "I could have been up on that mountain instead of him, but he unloosed the powers on me."

"What powers?" Trip asked.

Squinting through the languid smoke, old man Morris said, "The powers of darkness."

Thinking he'd been conned out of a pack of Camels by some homeless nut, Trip was about to leave. But there was something in the old man's eyes that made him stop–a depth of feeling that told Trip either the guy was telling the absolute truth or else believed absolutely that he was.

"They practice the magic arts," Morris said. "They call on the powers of darkness."

Trip thought immediately of the Scottish play. "You mean like witchcraft?"

Morris nodded with a wry smile. "You want to see?"

"He starts leading me," Trip said, "and I thought about getting out of there, but something kept me going."

"Your morbid curiosity?" I said.

"Maybe your skin," he answered. "Why I do these things for you, I don't know."

"So what did you find?"

Morris led Trip to a dilapidated guest house on the back property of a shabby house in the less desirable section of town. The railroad tracks were literally across the street. Scrub brush sprouted from every crack in the sidewalk, and the eucalyptus trees lining the street were in various stages of decay.

Morris's place was a one-room, windowless shack that might have originally been designed to store tools. Now it was lined, floor to ceiling, with the detritus of a lifetime.

Old man Morris was a classic pack rat. Books, newspapers, vinyl record albums, shoes–including two pairs of red and white bowling shoes, Trip noted–closed the quarters into a bizarre theater-in-the-round, with a small living space in the middle. A solitary mattress with an old Army blanket was the only piece of furniture, if one could call it that. The air inside was stale and heavy.

"Sit down," Morris said.

"Where?" said Trip, looking around.

"Right there." Morris motioned to a stack of newspapers bound with twine. "On 1977."

Indeed, the top newspaper, a *Hinton Valley News,* was dated August 16, 1977. Trip noticed the headline and realized he was about to sit on top of the death of Elvis Presley.

Fitting, he thought.

Morris was digging through a pile on the opposite side of the room. "I'll have it for you in a minute," he said.

"Some filing system," said Trip.

"I know where everything is," Morris said. "I know where the bodies are buried."

For a moment Trip wondered how many bodies were buried inside, or underneath, this freakish hovel. But he reasoned Morris must be speaking figuratively. He hoped he was.

"Ah!" Morris said, returning to Trip with a shoebox. Trip saw it was filled with newspaper clippings, a haphazard jumble of yellowing paper. Morris started sifting through it, like a mouse scratching for hidden cheese.

Presently, he pulled out a clipping and held it up. "Take a look at that!"

Trip took it. The story, dated September 15, 1968, described the nuptials of Warren Hazelton and one Heather Epstein. The accompanying photo showed Hazelton with a young woman who appeared to be about twenty years old. She wore a garland of daisies in her hair in the classic "flower child" style of the time. Her smile was bright and hopeful, yet also, it seemed to Trip, a touch naive. Warren Hazelton was not smiling.

"So, this is Mrs. Hazelton?" Trip asked.

Morris nodded. "Now take a look at this." Morris handed Trip another clipping, this one some sort of feature story from the mid-'70s, a local profile of Heather Hazelton. Her marriage to the Captain had apparently bestowed on her instant social standing. Yet, she retained her hippie pedigree, the story noted, especially with regard to her love of the earth.

"I'm into the Goddess," she was quoted as saying. "The Mother of All was first, and I merely practice an ancient form of religion that worships Mother Nature. I use visualization, chants, candles, amulets, and meditation to tap into my power. It's wonderful. It's really what this whole generation is searching for."

"Do you see that?" Morris said, pointing to that section of the story with a yellow-stained index finger.

"So?" Trip said. "A lot of hippies were into weird stuff back then. It was pretty harmless."

"Harmless! Look at me!" Morris shouted. "You think I brought this on myself? Do you?"

"Look, man–"

"I'm giving you the whole story right here!" Morris held up a clutch of clippings in his fist and waved them around.

Trip started to fear the old coot would grab a gun and start shooting. But just as quickly as it had come on, the outburst passed. In a suddenly quiet voice, Morris said, "They cast a spell on me. That's when I lost everything. That's when the fire broke out."

"Fire?"

"My place. My business. Everything I worked for." Morris stepped back and sat heavily on another stack of papers.

"How do you know this?" Trip asked. "About the spell, I mean."

"Because I know," Morris said.

"But she–Mrs. Hazelton–seems harmless enough."

At that point Morris began to laugh. It built from a guffaw to an out-and-out convulsion, the kind of uncontrolled hilarity usually reserved for cheap horror films.

Trip shifted on Elvis and waited. This old man was crazy all right, but Trip had seen enough crazy people in his line to know that they sometimes spoke the truth. Just because someone is paranoid, the old joke went, didn't mean that everyone wasn't after him. There could very well be a basis for what Morris was saying. The trick would be in figuring out what that kernel of truth was.

"Boy," Morris said finally, short of breath from his laughing jag, "you don't know much, do you?"

Trip shrugged. "Some say."

"You'll see. If you stay long enough, you'll see."

"See what?"

With a demented smile, Morris reached behind a stack of papers and came out holding a dark red cylinder. He waited for Trip to react.

Which he did. "That's not . . ."

"Dynamite."

Trip took one look at the fuse, and at the lit cigarette in Morris's other hand, and he quickly stood up. "You better be careful, man."

"You think I'm certifiable, don't you?" Morris said.

"You're a fire hazard; let's put it that way."

Morris held up the dynamite. "I'm going to purify the land once more."

Trip nodded, forced a smile, and quickly started for the door.

"Solomon is the key," Morris called out. "He's the one who had the line to the big boy."

Trip turned around. "Big boy? Who is that?"

In the swirl of cigarette smoke, slightly hunched over, and wearing a knowing half-smile, Morris looked like the twisted assistant of some mad scientist.

"Satan," Morris said.

I sat there for a long time, digesting the story and trying to put the information into some coherent form. "You think he's serious about using that dynamite?"

"Nah," said Trip. "One stick isn't going to do more than take out a mailbox. I think he's more likely to blow himself up."

"What about this deal with Solomon. You think there's something to that?"

"If the guy was into Satan worship, there might be."

"So what am I supposed to do, call this loony Morris as an expert witness on Satan?"

"Maybe we should follow this up."

"We haven't got time! On Monday I've got to put my client on the witness stand. The case is almost over. I'm not going devil hunting. There's no relevance here anyway. What Hazelton does with his private life has no connection with this case."

"Oh," Trip said gently, "there may be a slight connection."

I shook my head. "Where?"

Trip smiled and reached into his shoulder bag. He removed a newspaper and tossed it on the table. "Recognize that?"

I did. It was the copy of the *Hinton Valley News* I picked up on my first trip to Hinton, with the story of the murder on the front page. I'd given it to Trip, along with other materials, to help him prepare his investigation. I'd forgotten all about it.

"Take a look at the picture at the lower left," Trip said.

It was the picture of Captain Warren Hazelton holding a glass of wine at a reception. He had just won an award for his Chardonnay. "I remember this," I said.

"Take a close look."

I leaned over and scanned the photo more closely. Nothing jumped out at me. I looked at Trip and shrugged.

He pulled a rectangular magnifying glass from his shoulder bag and handed it to me. "Take a real close look," he said, "right there." He tapped the left side of the picture with his finger.

I did as I was told. That part of the photo showed several people gathered in the background, apparently chatting. I figured this was what Trip had in mind for my scrutiny, so I scanned carefully. And then one of the faces in the background jumped out at me. "That's not . . ."

"Oh, yes it is," Trip said.

I looked again, and there was no doubt. It was Benton Tolletson.

THERE WAS STILL no connection to my client. The fact that a prominent citizen like a district attorney was at a party with a prominent local winegrower was nothing unusual. But I couldn't help feeling there must be a thread somewhere. It was all too bizarre.

But I came up with nothing by Monday morning, the day Howie testified.

I met with him briefly before we marched into court, and if anything, he had become more resolute in his conviction that God wanted him to go to jail for a long, long time. He did not want to take the stand. In fact, he told me he wanted to change his plea to guilty.

"No, Howie," I said firmly.

"Aren't I allowed to, Jake?"

Of course he was allowed to. A defendant has the right to do whatever he wants in terms of a plea. And, ethically speaking, the lawyer is not to stand in his way. But I didn't give a rip about ethics at that point. All I wanted to do was beat Benton Tolletson by getting at least a hung jury.

"We've come too far, Howie."

"But I can change my plea. A guy in jail told me I could."

"What are you listening to him for? Huh? I'm your lawyer. I'm your friend."

"It's what God wants me to do."

"Look, Howie–" I put my hand on his knee as I tried to think of an argument against divine intervention. I found myself saying, "What if *I'm* God's will?"

"Huh?"

"Yeah. Listen to me. What if God put me here to see that justice is done for you? What about that?" I didn't believe a word of this, of course, but at that moment, all I was trying to do was get Howie to change his mind.

"I didn't think of that, Jake."

"Well, you've got two minutes to think about it now. I'm telling you, don't do this. Don't do this to your mom and dad. Your sister. Your son."

Howie's eyes went sort of blank. "My son . . ."

"Trust me. Will you, Howie?"

"Do I have to take the stand, Jake?"

"For a little while. Can you do that?"

"I . . . think so. Will he try to trick me, that Mr. Tolletson?"

"I'll be in there with you, Howie. Don't worry. And just one more thing."

"Yeah?"

"This is very important."

"Okay."

"Do not, under any circumstances, say you did it. You don't know if you did it. And that's what the prosecutor has to prove. When we get to the point about talking about what happened, you don't really know, except that you're sure someone else attacked you and killed Rae."

Howie shook his head. "I'm awful foggy on that, Jake."

"You'll be fine. Just answer my questions, okay?"

"Can we pray?"

His request was so innocent, like a child asking a parent to kneel down before bedtime, that I was surprised at my hostility. "You pray," I said. "I'm going inside."

As I left the lockup, Howie bent his head to his chest.

As always, court was packed. And for the first time in days, Lindsay Patino was sitting with her parents. I don't know if it was intentional or not, but she did not look at me. Fred Patino, however, gave me a thumbs-up sign. The poor guy didn't have any idea what we were all about to go through.

Judge Wegland took the stand, the members of the jury marched in, and the judge greeted them. I tried to read their faces. They were about as expressive as aluminum siding.

"Call your next witness," said the judge.

"Call Howard Patino," I said. Howie didn't move. It was like he was lost in a daydream. I had to gently prod him out of his chair.

I could sense the whole place watching his every move. Was this a cold-hearted killer about to take the stand? Or just some tragic figure in a farcical soap opera?

After the clerk administered the oath, she asked Howie to state his name for the record and spell his last name.

"Howie Patino," my client said. "P-A-T-I-N-O."

"Is it Howard?" the judge asked.

"Everybody calls me Howie."

"But Howard is your given name?"

"I don't like Howard."

Exasperated, Judge Wegland said, "I'm not interested in what you like, Mr. Patino. What is the name on your birth certificate?"

Howie shrugged. "I don't know."

Apparently sensing this was not worth further effort, Judge Wegland shook her head and motioned for me to ask my questions.

For the first half hour I had Howie testify about his life, letting him tell the jury in his own, distinct way about growing up. I wanted to the jury to see Howie for what he was–a harmless innocent man who would not preplan a murder. And then I wanted them to believe that Howie really saw someone else in that room, someone who was the real killer. Failing that, I at least wanted them to think that if Howie did do the killing, it was in the heat of a delusional passion.

I took Howie to the point where he met Rae Richards for the first time.

"I was here about a job," Howie said.

"In Hinton?"

"Yeah. At the lumberyard."

"How did you hear about this job?"

"My dad," Howie said, and as he did, he looked out at Fred with a mixture of sadness and love. It was almost as if he was apologizing to his father for the mess things were in now.

"Your dad arranged for a job interview?"

"Yeah. He was always doing stuff like that."

"So then, how did you meet your wife?"

Howie's eyes got a faraway look, as if searching for a distant memory. "Well, it was a hot day; I remember that. And I wanted to get something to drink. I drove into the town and stopped at a place."

"What kind of a place?" I interrupted.

"A bar kind of place. It was dark and smoky inside. But I kind of liked that."

Howie paused, and I asked, "Why did you like it, Howie?"

"Because," he said slowly, "it made me feel kind of grown up."

I hoped the significance of that wasn't lost on the jury. Howie was my age, and the incident he was describing had taken place only a few years ago. That he had a need to feel "grown up" in his twenties was a strong indication of his mental state.

"Go on, Howie."

"I sat at the bar and ordered a Coke. I don't drink alcohol, see."

Unlike your attorney, I thought. "What happened next?"

"Nothing much. I was drinking and listening to some men talk about the Dallas Cowboys"–Howie turned to the jury–"that's a football team," he told them, as if he was sharing inside information. "And then somebody tapped me on the shoulder. Like this."

Howie tapped his right shoulder with his left hand. "And I turned around and saw Rae. She had a tray in her hand with some glasses on it. And she smiled at me. And she asked me if I needed anything like a sandwich or something."

"So, she was a waitress?"

"The prettiest one there," Howie said proudly.

"What happened then?"

"Well, I told her I didn't need anything, and then she asked me if I was new in town because she'd never seen me in there before. And that's how we sort of got talking."

"How long did you talk?"

"For hours, it seemed like. She kept on asking me questions."

"What kind of questions?"

"Just about what I did and where I grew up and all that. Man, could she ask questions."

"And when you were finished talking, what did you do?"

"I didn't do anything. Rae asked me if I'd like it if she showed me around the town sometime. Boy howdy, did I ever say *yes!*"

"She was the one who asked to see you?"

"Yep. That was Rae. She was always real outgoing with people. Sometimes that made me mad."

That was a little addition I hadn't expected and didn't want the jury to think about. Quickly, I asked, "How long until you got married?"

"Oh, not too long."

"Tell us about it."

As Howie recounted the wedding, his face took on a soft glow, as if he was describing the high point of his life. It was perfect. He finished by saying, "I still don't know why Rae would choose somebody like me, but I figured it was a gift from God."

"And you have a son?"

Howie smiled broadly. "Brian Anthony Patino."

"How old is he?"

"Five."

"You love him, don't you?"

Before Howie could answer, Tolletson objected on relevance grounds. Wegland sustained it and asked me to move on. I wasn't upset by the ruling. Howie's testimony was powerful, completely lacking the dissembling almost every criminal defendant engages in. It was almost as if Howie seemed incapable of lying, and I was sure the jury picked up on that. Tolletson's objection merely underscored Howie's effectiveness as a witness.

But I heeded the judge's admonition and began moving to the crucial night. As I did, I watched Howie carefully, reading his face. I had to be ready to move quickly if things started getting too far out of hand. The jury could not for a moment think Howie was *trying* to appear crazy.

When we got to the part where Howie went around to the back of his house, his expression began to darken. No, that's not it. *Depart* is more like it. He was beginning to withdraw himself from what he knew was coming. It was, I realized, a defense mechanism.

"What were your thoughts when you got to the sliding glass door and found it locked?"

"I figured Rae was at a friend's house or something."

"And you decided to go inside and wait for her?"

"Yeah."

"So you broke into your own house?"

"Yeah."

"Why?"

"Cause I wanted to be inside my own home. I wanted to see my wife."

"What did you see when you got inside? Was there a light on?"

"Um, no. I turned on a light."

"And what did you see?"

"Not much. It looked like Rae hadn't cleaned up in awhile."

"Why did you think that?"

"Because of the clothes on the chairs and stuff."

"What were you thinking then?"

"Just that I wanted to see Rae."

That was a good place to shuffle my notes. It's a little trick when you want the jury to get the full effect of an important answer. I wanted them to see a man who wanted nothing more than to be with his wife, not a man who had murder on his mind. Howie was doing fine.

I returned my notes to the exact order I had before. "What did you do next?"

Howie thought a moment, and it seemed to me he was almost afraid to continue. His voice was even more detached when he began to speak. "I walked down the hall to the bedroom and opened the door."

"Was the light on?"

"No."

"Did you turn it on?"

Tolletson stood. "Objection. He's leading the witness."

"Sustained," Judge Wegland said tonelessly.

I cleared my throat. "What was the next thing you did, Howie?"

"I turned on the light." Someone in the gallery laughed. It sounded like Howie was just repeating the answer I'd already implied in my previous question.

"And what did you see?"

"Rae."

"Where was she?"

"In bed. She sat up."

"What, if anything, did she say to you?"

Howie's eyes narrowed in a mixture of emotion and troubled memory. "I don't remember exactly. I just remember we started to talk."

"Can you remember any of the conversation?"

"Only some. She wasn't very happy to see me, I guess. Maybe because I woke her up."

"Do you remember anything else?"

"Not much. It's all kind of dark. I'm sorry, Jake."

He was childlike in that moment, and that's when I began to feel very confident about my chances. There was no way all twelve jurors would think this man a cold-blooded murderer.

"You just have to tell us what you remember, Howie, that's all. You just tell this jury what you absolutely remember, okay?"

"Okay."

"Listen carefully. Did you, at any time, pick up a knife?"

Howie gently shook his head. "No."

"Did you, at any time, strike your wife?"

"You mean hit her?"

"Yes."

"No, I didn't do that. I would never do that. Not to Rae. I loved her."

I took in a deep breath, then said, "All right. Do you remember anyone else being in that room with you and Rae?"

This was the biggie. I well remembered Howie's hysterics at the preliminary hearing, when he began to scream about the devil. With an emotional outburst of that magnitude, you just never know what the jury is going to think. But it was a question that had to be asked.

Howie's eyes became blank screens, and he sat motionless for a long moment. Then, in almost a whisper, he said, "The devil."

I responded in a quiet tone. "You think you saw the devil, Howie?"

"Yeah."

"Could it have been a person?"

"The devil is a person."

"Yes, Howie, but you're sure you saw someone else in that room?"

"I think so."

It was perfect. Howie wasn't ranting and raving, but he was clearly going through an emotional wringer. Even if I'd been able to coach him, I couldn't have come up with anything better than this.

"And then what do you remember?"

"Pain."

"What kind of pain."

"Here." Howie pointed to his side.

I said, "May the record reflect Mr. Patino is indicating his right side, approximately two inches above his waistline?"

"The record will so reflect," said Judge Wegland.

"What happened there, Howie?"

"I guess I was cut."

"With a knife?"

"That's what the doctors said."

"You don't remember being stabbed with a knife?"

"No. I just remember the pain. I think I passed out or something."

"And what's the next thing you remember after that?"

"Sitting. I was sitting in the living room in my house. I was bleeding. Some men were asking me questions. From the police. Jake, do I have to answer any more questions? I'm tired."

He was no longer my witness but only my childhood friend, looking to me for help. I looked at the judge. "Maybe this is a good time for our recess, Your Honor."

"All right," said the judge. "We'll be in recess for half an hour."

CHAPTER THIRTY-FOUR

DURING THE BREAK I talked to Janet and Fred. They were supportive, saying they thought I did a good job and to hang in there.

I hardly heard what they were saying. I was looking for Lindsay, who had apparently slipped out of the building. I was surprised at how much I wanted to see her.

But she had made the right decision, I had to conclude. I had treated her shabbily, and why should she put up with it? What would an atheistic drunk have that would be in any way attractive to her?

Still, the longing was there inside me.

When court got back underway, Lindsay was once again seated with her parents. She was here for the big show.

In the universe of trials, there is nothing as stirring as the cross-examination of a defendant. Here is where it all hangs out. The defendant, by taking the stand, declares his innocence of the charges and challenges the prosecutor to prove otherwise.

The prosecutor must face up to the challenge. It is make or break. If the defendant holds up, the case is lost–or at the very least, the jury hangs.

And everybody knows it.

So Benton Tolletson, standing up to examine Howie, walked to the lectern like Wyatt Earp approaching the O.K. Corral. He looked fully armed.

The first words out of his mouth were, "Why did you kill your wife, Mr. Patino?"

No warm up, no preliminaries–just an in-your-face question designed to put Howie on the defensive immediately.

It worked.

Howie looked stunned and confused and hurt. He started to open his mouth a couple of times, but nothing came out. He shook his head. Tolletson just let him squirm.

Finally, Howie managed to say, "I don't know."

"You don't know why you killed your wife?"

"I . . . don't know what I did."

"You killed your wife, didn't you?"

"I . . ."

"Let's go back a bit, Mr. Patino. Maybe this will help us. You testified that Rae sometimes made you mad. Do you remember that?"

Howie shook his head.

"Please answer out loud," said Judge Wegland.

"No," said Howie.

Tolletson picked up his legal pad and looked at it. "You don't remember testifying that Rae was very outgoing and that this sometimes made you mad? You don't remember that?"

"Oh," Howie said quietly. "Okay."

"Okay *what,* Mr. Patino?"

"I remember."

"That's good."

I objected at this point, just to show Tolletson I wasn't going to let him say whatever he wanted. The judge sustained me.

Tolletson didn't miss a beat. "You were mad that Rae was outgoing because you were jealous. Isn't that it?"

Frowning, Howie said, "I don't know."

"Come now, Mr. Patino, try a little harder here. Isn't it a fact that you did not like it when Rae gave attention to anyone else?"

"I . . . guess."

"We don't want you to guess, Mr. Patino. Yes or no?"

"Sometimes." Howie flashed a small hint of anger at Tolletson.

"Such as when she might talk to another man, right?"

Howie hesitated.

"Right, Mr. Patino?"

"Sometimes!"

The entire courtroom seemed to snap to attention at this outburst. Tolletson let the tension build, waiting before he asked his next question. On the stand, Howie was breathing hard, his eyes darting back and forth across the courtroom like a kid who'd been backed into a corner by the school bully.

The picture was pitiful, and I thought that if Tolletson pushed it too far the whole thing could backfire. As if he sensed my very thoughts, Tolletson framed the next question softly, almost soothingly.

"Mr. Patino, isn't it true that you just didn't feel good about Rae ignoring you, especially when she would talk to another man?"

Nodding, Howie said, "Yeah."

"That's understandable," Tolletson said, suddenly playing good cop to his previous bad cop. "And wasn't that what ultimately drove you to kill your wife?"

Howie shook his head like he was trying to clear out cobwebs. "I don't know," he said weakly.

Tolletson turned to another page of his notes. "Something you said on direct confused me. Do you recall testifying that when you came to your house that night and no one answered, you thought that Rae might be at a friend's house?"

"Um, yeah."

"And that's when you decided to go in and wait for her. You recall that?"

"Yeah."

"But then when your lawyer, Mr. Denney, asked you why you broke into your house, you answered, 'I wanted to see my wife.' Do you recall that?"

"I . . . no."

"You don't recall that?"

"No, I don't."

Tolletson set his notes on the lectern and made a half turn toward the jury. "During the recess I asked the reporter to find that portion of the direct testimony and mark it. Your Honor, with your permission, I will have the reporter read it back to us."

"Wait a minute!" I said, jumping to my feet.

"Is that an objection?" Judge Wegland asked.

"Yes, it is."

"On what grounds?"

I had no idea what grounds, so I said, "That's impermissible."

"Do you mean inadmissible, Mr. Denney?"

"Both," I said.

"This is the official court record," said the judge. "Sometimes we have the reporter read back a question. I see no reason why she cannot read back an exchange. Go ahead."

The reporter, a middle-aged woman who up to this point had been all but invisible, suddenly took center stage. She lifted the folds of transcription paper from her tray, holding them in front of her like ticker tape, and began to read.

"Question: What were your thoughts when you got to the sliding glass door and found it locked?

"Answer: I figured Rae was at a friend's house or something.

"Question: And you decided to go inside and wait for her?

"Answer: Yeah.

"Question: So you broke into your own house?

"Answer: Yeah.

"Question: Why?

"Answer: Cause I wanted to be inside my own home. I wanted to see my wife."

The reporter lowered the paper back into the tray.

"Does that refresh your recollection?" Tolletson asked.

"I guess so," Howie said.

"Isn't that really why you broke into your house, to see your wife?"

"I wanted to see her."

"You knew she was inside all the time, didn't you?"

"No."

"You wanted to see her because you wanted to kill her. Isn't that right, Mr. Patino?"

"No." Howie's face was almost pleading with Tolletson to stop.

Tolletson turned bad cop again. "You wanted to kill your wife because she was pregnant with another man's child. Isn't that right, Mr. Patino?"

"No!"

From the gallery, a woman's voice shouted, "Stop it!" I turned and saw it was Janet Patino. She had her hands pressed hard over her mouth, her eyes wide and wet. Fred and Lindsay put their arms around her.

Judge Wegland said, "I won't have that kind of interruption here. If this is too much for you, please leave the courtroom. Otherwise, control yourself."

Janet buried her face in her hands.

Tolletson did not let up. "You went to your house with the intent to kill your wife, didn't you, Mr. Patino?"

Howie hesitated. "No."

"When you confronted her, she told you your marriage was over. Isn't that right?"

"I . . . don't remember exactly."

"And when she told you that, it made you mad, didn't it?"

"There was . . . I was . . ."

"What were you, Mr. Patino?"

"Confused."

"Angry?"

"Maybe some."

"Maybe a lot?"

"Mostly I was crying."

"Were you crying when you got the knife?"

Howie looked like he'd been slapped in the face. "No."

"No *what,* Mr. Patino?"

"I didn't."

"You didn't *what,* Mr. Patino?"

"Knife."

With an exasperated sigh, Tolletson said, "What about the knife? What are you hiding?"

I shot to my feet. "Your Honor, please!"

Wegland was unmoved by my emotion. "If you have an objection, state it, Mr. Denney."

"All right," I said. "This is just harassment, Your Honor, argumentative–"

"I withdraw the question," Tolletson said.

"–intended to inflame the jury–"

"The question is withdrawn, Mr. Denney!" said the judge.

"–a blatant attempt–"

"Sit down!"

I sat down slowly. I wanted the jury to know I was outraged. I was hoping Tolletson had overstepped.

"Isn't it true," Tolletson said, "that you stabbed your wife repeatedly, then stabbed yourself to cover up the crime? Isn't that true, Mr. Patino?"

The emotion of the moment seemed to engulf Howie like a poison gas paralyzing him.

"What is your answer, Mr. Patino?" said Tolletson.

"No . . ."

"No *what,* Mr. Patino?"

Howie looked at me, pleading with his eyes for me to do something.

"No *what?"* Tolletson repeated.

"I don't remember."

"Isn't it true, Mr. Patino, that after stabbing and killing your wife, and after inflicting yourself with a wound, you made up a story about seeing the devil?"

"I . . . did . . ."

"You *did* make up such a story?"

"No, I mean . . ."

"*What* do you mean, Mr. Patino?"

"I saw . . ."

"*What* did you see, Mr. Patino?"

"The devil!"

There it was. If Howie was going to explode, this would be the moment. I realized I was gripping the sides of my chair like a roller-coaster seat.

"You saw the devil?"

"Yes."

"Did he have a tail?"

"What?"

"I'm sure the jury is interested in what the devil looked like, Mr. Patino."

"Objection," I said.

"Overruled," said the judge.

"Well, Mr. Patino? Describe the devil for us, will you?" Tolletson leaned against the lectern with his arms folded.

"I can't."

"You can't because he wasn't really there, was he?"

"I thought . . ."

"This is a product of your imagination, isn't it?"

"No, I thought . . . I'm confused."

"Of course you are. Because you're making this up. Isn't that right?"

Howie looked completely lost.

"Isn't that right, Mr. Patino?"

"I . . . don't know."

"Of course you don't," said Benton Tolletson, gathering his notes and returning to his chair.

I did a double take. He was finished so soon? This was a gamble but a well-considered one. Tolletson was showing the jury that he didn't need to spend any more time with the defendant, that he was obviously guilty, and his guilt should be clear to everyone.

He caught me unprepared. Judge Wegland asked, "Any redirect, Mr. Denney?" I had to decide whether to ask Howie more questions, to try to rehabilitate him.

I could leave things alone and hope the jury members were more sympathetic toward Howie than they were toward the prosecutor.

If I did ask some further questions, it was possible Tolletson would come back with some dynamite, maybe something he was holding back. He could have been sandbagging me.

"Mr. Denney?" asked the judge.

I heard myself say, "No more questions, Your Honor." The examination of Howie Patino–and essentially the trial–was over.

Judge Wegland set the next morning for closing arguments and recessed the court.

CHAPTER THIRTY-FIVE

I SPENT A sleepless night at the Motel 6.

Nights before closing arguments are always like that for me. My mind is filled with thoughts about what I'm going to say, what I shouldn't say, what happened during the trial that I may have overlooked, and whether I'm up to the task of speaking on behalf of a human being facing years in prison.

I was never one of those lawyers who could hold a courtroom spellbound by the pure power of his golden tongue. Mine was more of the aluminum variety. But I was adequate when I had the facts and the law on my side. This night I wasn't sure about either. I tried to rehearse a little but gave up around eleven and tried to go to sleep.

At midnight I decided to go out for a drink.

Frisbee's was unusually crowded, I thought. Maybe this was the social center of Hinton. This was what the people had to look forward to. Up here there was no Hollywood Bowl or Dodger Stadium, just the multiplex, 7-11, and Frisbee's.

I took what was becoming my usual table, near the back, where a big screen TV tuned into the Classic Sports Network was playing a tape of the first game of the 1988 World Series. The Oakland A's were supposed to win that one, with a one run lead in the ninth over the Dodgers and Dennis Eckersley on the mound. But with two out and a man on, Kirk Gibson came limping up to the plate to pinch hit. He had two bum legs and hadn't played the entire game, but now he was going to give it a go.

As I drank a beer, I watched that moment of high drama again. Eckersley, the best reliever in baseball, got two strikes on Gibson right away. Gibson worked him, getting the count to 3 and 2.

You couldn't have designed a better scenario: Bottom of the ninth, full count, two down, man on, one run lead, great pitcher, gutsy hitter. Eckersley delivered the pitch. Gibson swung, and as the ball took off toward the right field bleachers, Vin Scully, calling the game for NBC, said, ". . . she is *gone!*"

A round of cheers erupted from the Frisbee's crowd, as if the home run had just happened. I had seen it on TV when it *did* happen and felt the same elation as I had then. It remains, for me, the most exciting sports moment I've ever witnessed.

As I watched Kirk Gibson limp around the diamond again, pumping his fist in elation, getting mobbed at home plate by his teammates and the elfin Dodger manager, Tommy Lasorda, I had an amazing insight.

I was Kirk Gibson.

Tomorrow I would be limping into a courtroom for one last at bat. Could I come through? Hit it out of the ballpark? Set Howie free?

It was both exhilarating and frightening.

On the TV Bob Costas was interviewing Gibson. Gibson was talking about how he'd wanted one more at bat and then said something about "the good Lord" coming through for him.

I snorted and looked into my beer. "All right, Lord," I said to the foam, "let's see what you can do for me." And then I drank my prayer.

A couple of minutes later, after ordering another beer, and as I was mentally rehearsing my closing argument, I felt something in my chest. It was a vibration but not a steady one. Pulsating. A thumping.

It grew stronger.

I then realized it was the sub-woof of a car stereo. It continued for another second or two, then shut off. I watched the front door and somehow knew it would be him.

Darcy Hazelton swaggered in. He was greeted by some buddies with whoops and hollers and joined them at the bar.

Suddenly, through that mysterious mental alchemy that sometimes happens, diffuse thoughts and images began to coalesce into an odd semblance of order. Connections were made in my mind . . .

Darcy Hazelton . . .

Warren Hazelton . . .

Tolletson . . .

Daphne Barth . . .

Thumping noises . . .

Murder . . .

Did any of this make sense? Daphne Barth had reported a thumping noise, thinking it was someone trying to break into her house. Could it have been a car stereo? *This* car stereo? What was it she had said? She looked out her window and saw a car. No, she said, more like a truck than a car.

Could it have been Darcy Hazelton's? And could he have possibly been the one Howie saw in the room?

I had no evidence of that. This was all a patch of thin reeds. But having nothing else to weave a story from, I stood up, drained my beer, and walked over to the bar where Hazelton was sitting.

He was bracketed by two guys who looked like they spent a lot of time in the gym. The one on his right had a tank top on, exposing a snake tattoo just below the neck. The other one didn't have any distinguishing marks, but he did have biceps that looked like croquet balls. The two guys were laughing hysterically. Darcy

Hazelton, who wore a cream-colored silk shirt, appeared to be shaking with laughter too.

When the guy on the right saw me standing there, he stopped laughing. He nudged Hazelton on the shoulder, then nodded my way. Hazelton twirled on his barstool and faced me.

"Darcy Hazelton?" I said.

He had an angular face, one that narrowed from a prominent forehead down to a sharp chin. His skin was pale, blending almost seamlessly into the colorlessness of his shirt, and his eyes were narrow in a weak sort of way. His hair, what was left of it, was black and combed straight back.

"Who are you?" he said. His voice was about as friendly as a syringe.

"My name's Denney. I'm here on business."

Hazelton's eyes thinned a scintilla more. "Denney?"

"That's right."

"The lawyer?"

"People seem to know me, don't they?"

"What are you doing here?"

"I was having a drink."

"Then drink." He clipped the words dismissively.

"Can I have a word with you?" I asked.

Hazelton looked at his buddy on the right, the one with the snake. "Can you believe this guy?" he said. Mr. Snake half-smiled and shook his head.

Returning to me, Hazelton said, "You got to be kidding."

"I'm not."

"I got no reason to talk to you."

"If I could just have a sec–"

He started to spin back around.

"It's important."

Hazelton stopped midway and half-turned his head toward me. "Don't you know you're a cockroach?" He spun back so he could look at me directly. "You're a cockroach. You know that?"

His two friends cracked smiles, and I noticed a few others at the bar looking at me, no doubt wondering if I'd scurry away like the unsanitary bug I'd just been compared to.

"Sure I know that," I said. "It's like the old joke."

"Huh?" Hazelton looked genuinely confused.

"What's the difference between a cockroach and a lawyer?"

Darcy Hazelton turned to Mr. Snake, who shrugged.

I said, "One is a dirty, ugly, crumb-sucking pest. The other one's an insect."

The guy with the biceps snorted a laugh. Hazelton shot him an angry look, and he clammed up.

"Why don't you get lost?" Hazelton said to me.

I half considered it. In a macho bar like this, I was a perfect target and outnumbered to boot. But Hazelton's hostility told me I was on to something. I didn't move.

"What kind of car do you drive, Darcy?" I loaded my voice with mock conviviality, giving the question a sarcastic spin.

"You better get out of here now," Hazelton said. I half expected the two muscle boys to stand simultaneously, like thugs in a 40's *film noir,* and escort me out.

I stood my ground like Victor Mature. "You've got a nice sound system."

Blinking, Hazelton seemed momentarily baffled. I congratulated myself on a small victory. "I told you, I got nothing to say," he finally offered.

"That's what he said," Mr. Snake added, looking at me with macho eyes of menace. He was reveling in this.

"How would you like to be called as a witness, Darcy?" I said.

"What?"

"Yeah. How would you like me to drag your sorry butt into court tomorrow? I have a feeling you could tell the jury some things."

His narrow slits widened enough so I could see his eyes. Just as quickly, they closed down. Mr. Snake said, "Let's do him."

Darcy Hazelton put his hand up to stop the thought, much to my relief. "Outside," he said.

He got up from his stool and walked toward the door, leaving his two companions to give me the testosterone glare. I smiled, nodded, and followed Hazelton outside.

The midnight air was crisp. The moon was nearly full, giving the parking lot a faint, silvery wash. Young Hazelton stood near the first row of cars, his back to me, looking down the road that led here to the social center of Hinton.

I saw a Range Rover a couple of cars down and walked toward it. "Yours?" I said.

Hazelton gave me a half-turn look. "You know who my father is?" he asked.

"Sure."

"Then why are you being stupid?"

"I don't follow you."

When Hazelton turned to face me, the moon gave his pale face a moonlike quality of its own, dull light reflecting off it–a ghostly luminescence. It was hard to make out, but I thought I saw a touch of fear.

"Look," he said, "you don't mess with my father."

"I don't care about your father. I care about you."

"Why?"

"What do you know about the murder of Rae Patino?"

For a long moment he stood and stared at me, a fleshy statue in this eerie automotive garden. "I just know what everybody else knows," he said finally.

"That's all?"

"That's all."

"You ever go out with her?"

"You're crazy."

"You ever go over to her house? Spend time with her?"

Darcy Hazelton took a step toward me. The look of fear had given way to anger, but not just any anger. It was . . . twisted. Like he'd lost control. Now he seemed truly dangerous.

"I don't know what you think you're doing," Hazelton said, "but if you come near me again, I'll get you messed up. I'll get you messed up, and then I'll kill you."

Quickly he turned and charged back into the bar, leaving me to wonder what I'd just witnessed. Was it consciousness of some sort of guilt? That was possible, but only if Darcy Hazelton was playing with a full deck, something I was doubting seriously. It could have just been the reaction of a spoiled and somewhat off-kilter, rich kid who was not used to threats or insinuations.

All I knew for sure was that what had started as a simple inquiry had turned into an oddball scene with a manifestly dangerous man. The sooner I got out of Hinton, the better, I decided.

I returned to the motel and didn't fall asleep until sometime after 3 A.M.

CHAPTER THIRTY-SIX

TOLLETSON SEEMED FRESH as a Tic-Tac.

As is the rule, the prosecution got the first word in closing argument. Tolletson spoke without notes for two and a half hours–and he was masterful.

He used charts to fully explain the jury instructions the judge would give. Visuals are always a good idea for the jury.

He stopped at emotional points, letting it all sink in with the jury, his voice rising and falling as appropriate. He painted Howie in broad strokes as a jealous husband and Rae as the helpless–and pregnant–victim.

"This is a case of first-degree murder," he said in conclusion. "No more, but certainly no less. The very nature of the crime proves it. Twenty-five stab wounds to the body of a young mother carrying a child inside her even as she cared for the one child she had. And you heard the defendant declare how much he loved that child. Was it love to deprive him of his mother? Was it love to kill the only mother he knew as well as the baby brother or sister she carried in her womb? Was it, ladies and gentlemen?"

He stopped here and let the jurors answer in their heads.

"Then you heard the defendant, faced with incontrovertible evidence against him, come up with this story that he saw the devil in that room. Well, ladies and gentlemen, if he saw the devil, he must have been looking in a mirror because the devil who committed this crime is sitting right over there."

Tolletson pointed at Howie, looked at him for a long moment, then returned his gaze to the jury. "When the defendant's lawyer gets up to argue, I plead with you not to let him obscure the issues. His client stabbed an innocent victim–two innocent victims, really–to death. In cold blood. After planning the crime. It is your job to hold him accountable for this horrific act by bringing in a verdict of guilty on the charge of first-degree murder. Thank you."

Judge Wegland thanked Tolletson, then informed everyone that I would begin my closing argument after lunch. It was eleven-thirty, and she ordered us back by one o'clock.

I wondered where to go during the break. My brain felt like oatmeal, due to lack of sleep and an alcohol bath the night before, and what I really wanted was a bed. Trip asked me if I wanted to be alone to prepare. I told him yes without really knowing why–maybe so he wouldn't lecture me.

I decided to find a far corner in the courthouse cafeteria and try to down some soup. Before I could leave though, I was stopped–by Lindsay Patino.

She was waiting for me in the aisle. "I just wanted you to know something," she said.

Her face was gentle, as if she'd forgotten about the nasty things I'd said to her a few nights back. She was beautiful.

"What is it?" I snapped.

"I'm going to be praying for you."

Yeah. That and fifty cents will buy me a bad cup of coffee.

"That's nice," I said and quickly stepped past her.

She said nothing more.

Sometimes you can read juries; other times you can't. Or you can get a partial read while the rest of the panel remains obscured.

Then there's the worst scenario, where you think you have a certain juror or two in the bag, ones who are absolutely for you, and it turns out they lead the charge against you in the jury room.

This jury was a complete puzzle. It might have been the fact that I was barely able to remember what I wanted to say, let alone read the minds of twelve Hinton citizens. The only ray of hope was juror number seven, a middle-aged woman who looked, if you can believe it, slightly like my mother. When I stood up to give my argument, she smiled at me in a way that made me feel reassured.

I spoke with my legal notepad in my hand. At least I had a good outline of the points I wanted to raise and felt like I hit them, one by one. My brain was still warm cereal, but halfway through the summation I began to hit a stride. It was something I just felt, like an athlete who reports being in "the zone." I was there, I thought, right there–fully in tune with my argument, my client, the jury, and even the judge.

"Ladies and gentlemen, as jurors you fulfill the most important civil duty in our system of justice. You stand between the government and a fellow citizen accused of a crime. That's the way our founding fathers wanted it. They knew full well what it was to be paraded into court on trumped-up charges, so they put protections for all of us into the Constitution. This isn't like other countries where there is no jury, where it's the prosecutor or a policeman who sits where you're sitting, where there is no burden of proof beyond a reasonable doubt."

Turning slightly, I pointed at Benton Tolletson. "In this country, it is not Mr. Tolletson who tells the judge what the facts are. No, here in the United States he is required to prove his case to you, twelve citizens, and to prove it beyond a reasonable doubt. Mr. Patino doesn't have to prove anything to you. What you the jury say to Mr. Tolletson and all the power behind him is, 'You prove these charges you've brought. You call this man a murderer; well then, you prove it to us beyond a reasonable doubt.' That is a jury's solemn duty, ladies and gentlemen."

Now I swept my hand toward Judge Wegland. "In a little while the judge is going to read you several important instructions on the law. When you were picked as jurors, you gave an oath. You swore that you would follow the law as the judge gave it to you, whether you agreed with it or not. You are sitting on this jury because we believed you. We believed and we trusted that you would follow the law as the judge gave it.

"She is going to tell you that any defendant in a criminal trial is presumed innocent. That presumption goes right into the jury room with you, and it remains unless the evidence convinces you beyond a reasonable doubt. Let's talk about that a moment."

I tossed my legal pad on the counsel table. I didn't need it anymore. What I was going to say from now on was from memory and instinct.

"If you go back into the jury room, ladies and gentlemen, and you discuss this case, and if after that discussion you say to yourselves, 'You know, Howie Patino probably did it,' your verdict must be not guilty. That is the law because *probably* is not enough to convict anyone in this country.

"And know this: a verdict of not guilty, based upon your reasonable doubts, doesn't hurt us. It doesn't hurt society or the government. Indeed, society always wins. We all win. You are protecting all of us from being convicted of crimes without evidence. Without that protection, we cease to be the country we are."

I then spoke about the evidence and the witnesses and the weaknesses in the prosecution's case. I spoke for roughly two hours, and when I concluded, I faced the jurors squarely and gave them the bottom line from the depths of my being. "Ladies and gentlemen, I just ask you to look at Howie Patino. I say to you, you cannot look at this man, you cannot hear him testify and believe in your hearts that he is a murderer. Putting aside all the problems with the investigation in this case, the sloppy handling of evidence, the fact that the police failed to even consider that another person committed this act–put all that aside, ladies and gentlemen, and listen to your gut instincts."

I was spent, physically and emotionally. Somewhere inside me I had the thought that I should keep talking, talk till I dropped, but I knew I couldn't. I'd laid it all out there. I'd done the very best I could. There was just no more to give.

All I had left to say was this. "Return Howie Patino to his son, ladies and gentlemen."

My head was throbbing as I took my seat. There was silence in the courtroom for an extended moment; then Adele Wegland asked Benton Tolletson if he had more to say. He did, of course. The prosecutor always gets the last word.

But I hardly heard a word he said.

The drama was over.

All except the waiting.

CHAPTER THIRTY-SEVEN

I COULD HAVE avoided the big blow-up if I'd just gone home. I was an emotional wreck after the trial. All I wanted was a drink, a series of drinks. But Trip insisted on taking me to dinner. If I'd known what he was going to talk about, I would have said no.

We hit this steak place near the ocean. I immediately ordered a beer from the waitress and told her to hurry it up with it.

Trip didn't flinch. Not then. "You done good," he said. "I didn't know you had that in you. Great speech about this country and all. Sounded almost like you believe it."

"I do," I snapped. Part of me knew he was joking. The other part wanted to blow off steam.

"Most people don't anymore," Trip said. "Most people think tricky lawyers go around getting guilty people off."

"Yeah, well most people don't know anything about what goes on in court, that 98 percent get convicted, and that a guy with no money, even if he's innocent, is probably going to the slam."

"Because he gets a public defender like you." Trip smiled.

"What's up with you?"

"Nothing, man. It was a joke."

I didn't say anything. The waitress appeared with my beer and I drained about half of it. There was silence for a couple of minutes.

"The jury was listening," Trip said. "I watched their faces."

"You can't tell much from faces."

"You think they'll have a verdict tonight?"

I shook my head. "Too soon. And the longer they stay out, the better."

"Why's that?"

"Means they're arguing. Means we've got some on our side. When juries come back quick, it's almost always for conviction."

"Unless it's O. J."

"Don't start."

I looked out the window and saw late afternoon light falling over the hills and creating a golden radiance. I thought about Mandy. Where was she right now? What was she doing? I wanted to know that more than anything in the world, even more than I wanted to know what the jury was thinking.

Would I ever see her? There was no way Barb could keep her out of my life completely, but she could certainly make things difficult. It would just be another fight. There would always be fights. That's what I was thinking, anyway, and maybe that's why what happened next happened.

I finished my beer and waved to the waitress. She came to the table, and I ordered another. But Trip said to the waitress, "Wait a second." To me he said, "Why don't you hold off?"

I looked at him openmouthed. "I want another beer."

"Let's talk a second."

And as my chin dropped a little further, Trip told the waitress to give us a couple of minutes.

"What are you doing?" I said.

"I just want to talk to you about something before you get all souped up."

"Come on, man."

"Just listen, will you?"

"What, what?"

Trip leaned forward. "I want you to come to church with me."

I reacted by leaning back and rolling my eyes. "Will you get off that?"

"No." Trip's face was resolute.

"Look, I'm not going to church with you, so give it up." I wasn't going to give an inch, not in the mood I was in.

"What are you always being so pigheaded for?"

"Knock it off, will you?"

"The trial is over. You've done a great job. I can see how much it took out of you. Now it's time to put your own house in order."

"My house is fine the way it is."

"It isn't. Anybody can see that."

Something snapped inside me then. I slammed my hand on the table, rattling the silverware. "Butt out! Just butt out of my personal life, Trip!"

The old football player must have come out in Trip because he was going to hold his line. "What're you so ticked off about, huh? I'm trying to help you."

"I don't want your help. Can't you get that?"

"You need it."

"Not from you! I'm ordering another beer, so just keep out of my face."

Shaking his head, Trip stood up. "Uh-uh. I'm not going to sit here while you drink yourself to death."

"Good. You're lousy company anyway."

"That's what you think?"

"You bet that's what I think. I just wish everybody would leave me alone."

"You got it." He turned and walked out.

I should have called to him, gone to him. But apologizing was a sign of weakness. I wasn't going to show him weakness.

Instead, I showed it to myself. I had two more beers before I left the place and drove back home. Once in my apartment, I opened a new bottle and surrendered myself to the warm arms of inebriation. When sleep finally came, I dreamed of witches. At least I think that's what they were–dark figures off on the edge of some smoky cliff, looking at me with yellow eyes that glowed. They seemed to be planning something.

My pager woke me at 10:30 A.M. It was Judge Wegland's clerk. I called her back, and she told me the jury had a verdict.

I didn't bother to shower. I threw water on my face, ran the electric shaver over my cheeks, and put on a rumpled suit–the only kind I seemed to own. I called Janet Patino and told her I'd meet her at the courthouse. I thought about calling Trip but didn't.

When I arrived at the courthouse, it was teeming with cars and onlookers. The word had gotten out. Two mobile TV units, their antennae jutting from van roofs, formed bookends at the courthouse entrance. I had to park on the far side of the parking lot and slog through a muck of the curious to get to the courthouse.

When I finally made it to the front doors, I got a microphone in my face. A fresh-faced reporter identified himself as somebody-or-other from KEYT in Santa Barbara and asked if I knew what the verdict was.

My first media interview had finally come. I was not prepared. In fact, I was annoyed. What was the big deal here? Didn't these people have real stories to cover?

"How would I know the verdict?" I snapped.

The young reporter, whose styled black hair seemed to pose, blinked. "I mean, what do you think it will be?"

"You can't tell."

"Will you appeal?"

"If I win?"

He blinked again. "I . . . why would you appeal if you won?"

"Because I'm a masochist." I brushed past him and went inside, wondering what the guy was going to do with this scintillating footage.

Benton Tolletson was already at his counsel table when I entered the courtroom, sitting next to Sylvia Plotzske. All eyes turned toward me. Apparently I was the last of the principals to arrive. It was show time.

A deputy marched Howie into court. He glanced over at his parents and Lindsay, sitting in the front row. A faint smile, that goofy grin he'd always had, played across his face. The guard unshackled him, and Howie sat down next to me.

"Hi, Jake," he said, as if it was the start of another ordinary day.

I patted his knee and wished with all my heart that we would soon be walking out of the courthouse together.

Wegland's clerk picked up a phone and spoke into it. One minute later Judge Wegland strode into the courtroom and took her seat. She wasted no time in calling for the jury.

Even though it's a fool's game, I tried to read faces as the jury filed in. I was looking for a smile from any one of them, a look of encouragement, even a nod. I only got a glance or two, both with serious looks. They were all business. I noticed my palms were sweating.

"Good morning, ladies and gentlemen," Judge Wegland said.

The jury answered in kind.

"Have you reached a verdict?"

The foreman of the jury, a middle-aged African-American man, someone I picked as possibly leaning toward acquittal, stood. Without emotion, he said, "Yes, we have."

"Hand the verdict form to the clerk, please," Wegland said to the foreman. Wegland's clerk crossed the courtroom, surrounded by dead silence, and took the piece of paper that held my client's fate. She handed it to the judge.

Wegland looked at it, nodded slightly, then handed the form to her clerk. Then she looked down at us. "The defendant will rise," she said. I stood up with Howie, and we both faced the jury box.

"Read the verdict," said Judge Wegland. Her voice sounded like a bell tolling at midnight.

In a monotone, the clerk read, "To the charge of violation of Penal Code 187, the crime of murder, we find the defendant guilty."

I closed my eyes. The clerk continued her flat condemnation. "We further find the act was committed with deliberation and premeditation and that the defendant is guilty of murder in the first degree."

I sensed, though I didn't see, Janet Patino slump against her husband. Or maybe it was just my insides doing it for her. As a seasoned defense lawyer, I knew that *guilty* was the word most often heard at the end of a trial. But I'd been hoping on this one, really hoping.

In front of me, Benton Tolletson was shaking Sylvia Plotzske's hand. His back was to me, but I could discern his expression just the same. It was self-satisfaction, smugness, pride. He'd whipped me. Over his right shoulder, I saw half of Sylvia's face. She glanced at me for a second, and I thought I saw through the dark frame of her glasses an eye filled with a hint of sympathy. Was she feeling sorry for me? She quickly looked away.

Wegland thanked and dismissed the jury. When they were all gone, she set a sentencing date. Then court was adjourned. I gave the usual spiel to Howie about how this wasn't over yet, how we had grounds for appeal, *yadda, yadda, yadda.* After he was taken out, I made the same speech to the Patino family, but I couldn't look any of them in the eye.

Janet Patino patted my arm and said, through sobs, "Thank you."

Lindsay started to say something, but I turned quickly back to the counsel table. I couldn't get out of there fast enough. I ducked out through the rear door of the court and down the judge's hallway to a side exit. I actually walked around the entire block to get to my car and avoid the TV cameras.

No one saw me drive off.

I remember stopping at a liquor store about a mile away. I vaguely remember buying a bottle of Jim Beam. A big one. And a can of Coke.

Then I drove around the corner and pulled over on a commercial street. I opened the bourbon and started throwing down shots with the cola chaser. There was almost an anger in it. In your face, Hinton, you hick town with kangaroo courts and walking dead. In your face, Tolletson. Here's what I think of your city and you and the horse you rode in on.

I also remember planning a fanciful revenge. There was some sort of commercial complex half a block from where I was parked. Dynamite could be planted there very easily. I could get that old guy, Morris, to put it there. Or maybe at city hall, or somewhere under Tolletson's desk.

I laughed and drank.

Then I vaguely remember starting the car again and trying to get back on the freeway. Later they told me I'd found the off ramp and was trying to get on where the cars were getting off.

I remember the sound of a car horn, the flash of blue metal, and the sound of screeching tires.

And after that, blackness.

Part Three

In all of my years, one thing does not change . . .
The perpetual struggle of Good and Evil
—T. S. Eliot

CHAPTER THIRTY-EIGHT

THIS TIME THE talons in my head were accompanied by a spike stuck through my brain.

As the slow warmth of consciousness began to pull me back into life, I could sense myself asking if life was worth it. The pain was intense, like nothing I'd ever felt before, and I knew it would be with me for a long time.

I became aware of an antiseptic smell, the odor of sterilization. A soft light cast its hazy illumination from a distance. I realized I was lying down, and when I tried to move my head the spike in my brain twisted, its red hot point causing me to cry out.

A moment later a face was hovering over me. "Take it easy, Mr. Denney."

The thoughts came in a jumble.

Hospital.

Nurse.

Accident.

Why am I not dead?

"Dr. Chen will be here in a moment," the nurse said.

"Where . . ." Even that word was a struggle.

"You rest." I felt a pat on my arm and the sense of someone leaving.

How badly was I hurt? I tried to lift both my arms. They felt like sandbags, but I managed movement. A tube was taped to my left arm, but at least my arms were up. I wiggled my fingers.

Legs next. They rippled under the sheets. I tapped my feet together and felt it.

A huge sense of relief filled me just before another shot of heat zapped through my head.

My tongue was thick, my mouth dry–unmistakable reminders of heavy drinking.

Then I heard a voice. "Jake?"

I rolled my head, slowly, to the right. A fresh jolt of pain was followed immediately by a picture of Lindsay Patino standing next to my bed.

"What . . ." I said in complete bewilderment.

"Shh," Lindsay said softly. She pulled a chair from near the wall over to the side of my bed and sat.

"Where am I?" I said.

"The hospital. In Hinton."

"Why?"

"You were in an accident."

Like an amnesiac, I struggled to remember. Some of it came back to me–the verdict, the drinking, the driving. "How bad?"

Lindsay looked down at her hands.

"How bad?" I said.

"Jake," she said slowly, "you hit another car."

"Anyone hurt?"

She didn't answer immediately. I blurted, "Killed?"

"No, no one killed. The other driver, a man named Ruben Azario, was hurt."

At that point the room started to tilt, like a boat listing in a treacherous current. I closed my eyes and wished Lindsay would go away. I did not want her to see me anymore.

Then Lindsay said, "I brought you something."

All I wanted was a new head. But I was curious. She leaned over and pulled something out of a tote bag that sat on the floor next to her. "I'm giving you an assignment, as soon as you're feeling up to it." She held up a paperback book for me to see, but before I could read the title, she placed it on my bed table.

"What is it?" I asked.

"Some thoughts."

"About what?"

"Oh, just life, the universe, and everything."

Despite my condition, despite the fact that I was sorely tempted to let go of the effort, this mystery intrigued me. I wanted to find out what she was talking about. And then I realized how good it was to have her here.

"I'll be back to see you," she said. "I expect you to read that and report back to me."

"You sound like a teacher," I joked, amazed that I had the capacity to be frivolous.

"That is exactly what I am," she said, standing. "And I'm a tough grader. Bye."

And then she was gone.

I tried to watch her go, but the pain smacked my head back to the pillow. After a few minutes of reflection, I realized I wasn't sure what just happened, especially the last part with talk of an assignment. Why had she come here? I couldn't think about it now. Like Scarlett O'Hara, I would think about it tomorrow.

I drifted off to sleep.

I was awakened by the sound of my last name. It was being spoken over and over again. When I came to, the voice that had been saying my name switched gears and said, "Well, well, well."

Then I saw the face. It was a cop's face and a familiar one. I didn't know why it was familiar until he said, "Ain't this one of life's twists?"

He smiled coldly, and then I remembered him. It was Officer Cheadle, the same cop who'd been guarding Howie in this same hospital when I'd first come to see him.

"Yep," Cheadle said, "it sure is funny how things work out. What goes around comes around."

He took out a flip book and opened it. "It's my pleasure to tell you that you're under arrest for driving under the influence of alcohol and causing bodily injury. You have the right to remain silent. Anything you say can and will be used against you in a court of law. You have the right to an attorney"–he smirked when he said that–"and if you can't afford one, one will be appointed for you at no charge before any questioning. Do you understand your rights, Mr. Jake Denney?"

With a heavy breath I said, "Sure."

"Then why don't you tell me what happened?"

"I'm not talking."

"You want a lawyer?"

"I've got one."

"You?"

I said nothing. Cheadle flipped the cover of his booklet back to the front and slipped it into his shirt pocket. "That's perfect," he said. "You got yourself a loser for a lawyer."

My eyes closed heavily.

"I'll be outside," Cheadle said, adding with a lilt, "if you need anything." He lumbered out.

My eyes still closed, I saw the immediate future in bright colors. Imprisonment. Disbarrment. Humiliation. Even homelessness.

Congratulations.

I was now ready to pull the plug. Call Kevorkian. Get me out of the nightmare. I'd been low before, but never this low. The bottom of the barrel. Time to check out.

For no particular reason, I turned my head at that moment. In fact, it was almost as if my head turned itself for lack of anything better to do. When I did, I caught sight of my bed table, which held a plastic water pitcher, a Styrofoam cup, and a paperback book. At first it seemed oddly out of place, then I remembered Lindsay's visit. She had left it for me. I grabbed it.

The book had a funny name–*Penseés.* I had no idea what it was about. I flipped the book over and read about it. The author's name, Blaise Pascal, was vaguely familiar, as if I'd run across it in a college class once. The book cover copy gave the essentials–seventeenth-century mathematician and physicist who underwent a dramatic conversion to Christianity and set out to write a defense of the faith. He died before finishing, but his notes survived and were collected here.

It all sounded a bit dusty, but Lindsay had bothered to bring it by. I wasn't going anywhere, and I had a choice. I could read the book or watch *All My Children* on the hospital TV.

I started to read.

CHAPTER THIRTY-NINE

WHEN I WAS in law school, I used to go out to the undergraduate plaza and eat Christians for lunch.

That's the way I looked at it, anyway. In the hallowed halls of law school, I was learning to argue, to destroy with words. These undergraduate Christians were like a shooting gallery for me. Easy pickings and good practice. I sought them out.

Various student groups set up tables in the plaza to hand out literature and invite people to join. One group was a campus Bible study. I got to know the leaders of this group pretty well. Not by name, but by look.

One of them was a guy who looked like Barbie's dream date. I called him GQ because he seemed to have stepped right off the cover of *Gentleman's Quarterly.* The other was a girl, a serious, intelligent-looking type. I called her Pickles, though not to her face.

The first time I approached their table, they put on a little dog and pony show. I let them. GQ explained to me what a "great fellowship" they had and how they were getting into "God's Word." Pickles nodded silently beside him. They obviously thought I was a prime prospect.

I waited until GQ finished his pitch and said, "There is no God."

Their expressions changed from hopeful-friendly to reserved-defensive. GQ said, "Of course there's a God."

"Prove it," I said.

The poor guy tried, but he was no match for me. I was sharp, precise, cutting, and pompous. I had the arrogance of a first-year law student and the anger of a confirmed atheist. GQ didn't have a chance.

After that encounter I would visit the table from time to time and look for new blood. When I didn't get it there, I'd go listen to the occasional speaker in the open forum area. Whenever a Christian was speaking there, I'd heckle him and put him on the defensive. It was all great fun for me.

One thing was certain. I had never heard what I considered a compelling argument for the truth of Christianity. I thought all who tried to make one were fools.

Pascal, I learned as I read the book in the hospital room, was no fool.

"This present life is momentary," he wrote, "but the state of death is eternal. . . . Seen from this angle, how absurd it is for people to go through life without regard for their eternal destiny."

Bam.

Immediately my lawyer's mind tried to formulate a counter argument. There wasn't one. The facts were against me. Death *is* going to last a rather long time. In that view, if you don't give eternity some considerable thought, it *is* absurd.

Was this my time now? I'd had a death wish for a long time. But that was only to escape life. What more should I be thinking about?

As I read on, I got the surreal impression that Pascal was alive and speaking directly to me. "There are only three sorts of people," he wrote. "Those who have found God and serve him; those who are busy seeking him and have not found him; and those who live without either seeking or finding him. The first are reasonable and happy, the last are foolish and unhappy, those in the middle are unhappy and reasonable."

My attempts at refutation failed once more. Pascal had us all pegged, and I knew I had spent my life in the last category.

I read on, fascinated. Thought after thought came zapping out of these pages like laser beams burning into my brain. It was almost unbelievable how much insight into humanity this man from the 1600s had. He didn't have television news and stories of children shooting other children on almost a nightly basis, and yet he wrote this:

> *When we see the blindness and misery of man, when we look upon the whole universe in all its dumbness and upon man without light, abandoned to his own devices, without knowing who put him there, what he has come to do, or what will become of him when he dies, and is so incapable of knowing anything, I am overwhelmed by fear. I am like a man carried off in his sleep and left on some terrifying desert island. There, he wakes up without knowing where he is and with no means of escape. I am amazed that people are not driven to despair over this condition.*

"Well, Blaise," I said out loud in my hospital room, "I'm on that island right now. What are you going to do for me?"

I kept reading, thinking and reacting, and arguing in my head, all the while feeling like a fool. I was glad I never had to face Pascal in court. He would have held a jury spellbound.

And he was getting to me. At one point I put the book down and said to myself, *Look, Jake, you're in a terrible situation here. You messed up big time. You know that. Fine. You're at the bottom, buddy boy. So don't go flying off the handle here. Don't go making any big decisions. Because if you do . . .*

I stopped that voice and willed another. *But what better time, Jake? What better time?*

Still I resisted. Reasons, that's what I wanted, the reasons I'd never gotten before, the proof that I demanded.

I went back to the book, and two pages later I read, "The heart has its reasons of which reason knows nothing."

For a long time I stared at the ceiling, feeling uneasy. I realized that for the first time in my life, I was entertaining the notion that there might be a God. I hadn't planned on this and certainly hadn't sought it.

But Lindsay Patino, by way of Blaise Pascal, was making it happen.

I suddenly got very scared.

And for some reason I remembered Danny Dickerson, the son of the preacher, who once told me that if I was ever scared about anything, all I had to do was pray.

I had never in my life uttered a sincere prayer. But now, with my back on a hospital bed, I made a first, feeble attempt. It wasn't much, but at least I meant it. "All right," I said, "if you are really there, show me."

That was it. And there was no immediate answer, no thunderclap, no voice from the sky. But there was something like relief, like a heavy coat being lifted from my body. And then I realized that the pain in my head was gone. It had been there all morning, since I had awakened, but it wasn't there now.

Two days later I was discharged and taken immediately by police car, courtesy of Officer Cheadle, to the Hinton Courthouse. There I was marched before a familiar face, Judge Armand Abovian. Only this time I was a defendant in a serious criminal case. And Sylvia Plotzske, my former adversary, was now my prosecutor.

Abovian looked at me from the bench and shook his head. "I must tell you, Mr. Denney, this is a sad day for the law."

I nodded. What could I say? He was absolutely right.

"How do you plead?" he asked.

"Your Honor," I said, "I think if you give me a moment to discuss this with the prosecutor, perhaps a disposition can be reached."

Looking at Sylvia, Abovian said, “Is that all right with you, Ms. Plotzske?”

She shrugged. To me it looked like a practiced shrug, not entirely natural. “I can’t promise anything,” she said.

“Well, see what you can do. I’ll call the case again in a few minutes.”

I sat down at Sylvia’s table. “So,” I said, “how about I plead out to a misdemeanor and take my medicine? I want to enter a program. I know I need it.”

She shuffled some papers on the table. “I’m afraid not.”

“You’re going to push this as a felony?”

“Yes.” She did not look at me.

“But the guy was just observed and released,” I said, hitting on the main issue. Prosecutors have the discretion to charge drunk driving with injury as a misdemeanor and usually will if the victim’s injury is not too severe. “I was hurt worse than he was.”

“I’m sorry. I can’t deal on this one.”

That was more of an admission than she may have realized. “Is that the word from Tolletson?”

Once more, Sylvia busied herself with papers, file folders, and rubber bands.

“Sylvia!”

She jumped slightly and turned to me with a look of anger. “Don’t yell at me, Mr. Denney.”

“I just wanted to get your attention.” I also wanted to look her in the eye. Behind her thick lenses, the eyes were trying to avoid my gaze.

“I can’t do anything for you,” she said.

“You can, but you won’t.”

“I can’t.”

"You looked at me after the verdict," I said quickly, holding steady on her face, watching for any kind of reaction. I got one surprise, but the sort of surprise when someone is caught in a lie.

Sylvia didn't say anything, so I added, "After the guilty verdict, you looked at me in the courtroom. I remember it clearly. I could tell something. I could tell you weren't comfortable about it."

Trying to keep to her busywork, Sylvia said, "I have a bunch of cases to–"

"It's true, isn't it?" I was closing in like a good cross-examiner, sensing a crack in the barrier. "What aren't you telling me, Sylvia?"

"Nothing."

"I don't believe that. We're talking about a man's life. Not just Howie Patino's, but mine too."

"I have to get back."

"Sylvia, please!"

For a brief moment, I thought she would tell me. I thought, in my Perry Mason fantasy way, that she would gush forth with some dark truth. Just as quickly, the moment passed.

"I have nothing more to say to you," Sylvia said as she stood up. She walked toward the side door where a beefy bailiff stood like a statue of Hercules.

I turned toward the gallery and saw Lindsay. I was surprised to see her and ashamed. But she just smiled and nodded at me. I went to the rail, and she came to meet me.

"What are you doing here?" I said.

"I heard you were being arraigned."

"You came for that?"

"I had to check up on you. I gave you an assignment, remember?"

"Don't you have to be at work?"

"We're on break this week. Now, did you read the book, or didn't you?"

"Sort of."

"And?"

"I think you're very clever."

"Me?"

"Putting Pascal on my case."

"He convince you yet?"

"Let's just say he's a worthy adversary."

Lindsay smiled, and a warmth filled me. Then I heard my name called by Judge Abovian. I turned around. "Has the case been resolved?"

"No, Your Honor," I said. "Miss Plotzske is being told to charge this as a felony."

Sylvia immediately shot back, "Your Honor, I haven't been told . . . I have the discretion here, and we are proceeding with a 23153 felony. Mr. Denney is free to plead guilty to that."

"Mr. Denney?" Abovian said.

"Not guilty," I said. "Let's set it for trial."

"Very well," the judge answered and gave us a date to do our dance in court.

"Why did you plead not guilty?" Lindsay asked.

We were in the outer court of McDonald's, where I had generously sprung for coffee.

"Because I'm not guilty," I said, "of a felony."

"But that's what they're charging you with."

"It's what they call a wobbler. Certain offenses can be charged as either a felony or a misdemeanor, depending on the circumstances and the discretion of the prosecutor. Usually if a victim goes to the hospital with a severe injury, they'll go felony."

"Didn't that happen?"

"To *me* it did. But the guy I hit wasn't hurt that bad. I think there's something more going on here."

Lindsay lifted her coffee cup with two hands. They looked soft yet strong. The bright, morning sun hit her red hair and made it shine. "Thank you for coming," I said. "I didn't expect it."

"You know something? I didn't expect it either."

We looked at each other for a beat, and I almost reached out for her. But I held back, as if I didn't have the right to touch her.

"Would you mind telling me something?" I asked.

"Sure."

"Why the effort with me?"

A faint blush came to her cheeks, turning soft white to pink. "For Howie, for his appeal. You'll handle that, won't you?"

To that point I hadn't planned on it. I said, "Of course. Is that all?"

"I do care about you, Jake. And maybe I can help in all this."

"How?"

"You know I believe Howie's case has had spiritual overtones from the start. You don't see it. You resist it. Now Howie's in jail for something he didn't do."

That was like a blow to the stomach. She hadn't meant to accuse me of incompetence, but it felt like the same thing.

"What I want to do is help you see," she said. "There is more to this, and whoever killed Rae is still out there."

"What do you mean by *more?*"

"What I've always told you. Dark power. I'm sure of it."

For a moment I paused, a part of me still resisting her. But it was a weaker resistance than before, and I overcame it by sheer force of will. I no longer wanted to resist. I wanted Lindsay.

Suddenly she reached out and took my hand. It was warm, soft, and comforting. "Let's work on this together," she said.

A feeling of peace filled me then. I felt myself falling into a place I had never been, but wanting to fall.

Before I made a fool out of myself with some sort of starry look, Lindsay said, "Do you want to hear my plan?"

CHAPTER FORTY

AND WHAT A plan it was. I was impressed with her moxie. Lindsay Patino, whatever else she was, was not afraid.

She drove while she explained. "There is something called spiritual discernment," she said. "It's like a sense. It's understanding and being aware."

"Of what?"

"Spiritual things. Christians have that through the power of the Holy Spirit. That's why I want you to take me up there."

She was talking about the Hazelton Winery, which was exactly where we were heading. I had been planning to go there myself, so when she suggested it, I didn't argue for one very obvious reason–I no longer had my driver's license. It had been temporarily suspended, pending a review by the DMV and the outcome of my case.

"Well, what do you do to make it work?" I asked.

"It's not like a magical power that you make work. In fact, it's the opposite. It's listening to God. That's why I wanted to go with you. To listen."

"Like my spiritual investigator?"

"Exactly. We're dealing with the occult here."

"You make it sound like some sort of conspiracy."

"The occult doesn't have any formal order to it. But it does have a common source."

"The devil?" I said, almost as if I was starting to believe it. But I did a quick mental shake and said, "But that's so . . . outlandish."

"Is it?"

"I mean, I just don't see it in everyday life."

"Do you know what the word *occult* means?"

"Dark forces?"

"No. It literally means to hide, to cover up. Satan isn't going to go around making himself public."

"That's really what it means?"

"Yes. But this hidden world can be uncovered by those who seek it. It can also overwhelm those who open the door."

"What door?"

"Dabbling in the occult, you open up your soul. And the devil is not shy about coming in."

For a minute we drove in silence. I was trying to come to grips with this, trying to figure how much of this I really believed. "But how widespread is this occult business?"

"Some people estimate that neo-paganism is now the fastest growing religion in the world."

"Neo-paganism?"

"That's the umbrella term. The occult is part of that."

"This is all very confusing."

"Because there's no central authority or teaching."

"And yet all this is the fastest growing religion?"

"Yes."

"How can that be?"

"Dark power again."

I shook my head, wondering what we would find at the Hazelton Winery. Dancing neo-pagans ready to put me to the stake?

"Many neo-pagans," said Lindsay, "don't realize that the power behind all this is demonic. They try very hard to make it seem sweet and nice. A worship of the earth, of the goddess, of the mother of us all, that sort of thing. But the evil one is behind it all."

"Do they worship Satan?"

"Not formally. In fact, they reject the idea of Satan. They believe Satan is a Christian corruption of a good god. Remember Pan from Greek mythology?"

"Sure."

"Neo-pagans say Christians turned him and others gods like him into Satan to frighten people and gain converts."

"So Satan doesn't really have anything to do with them."

"That's the lie. See how it works? The more they deny his power, the easier it is for him to use them."

"If they're not organized, where do they get their teachings?"

"They have a loose network, especially now on the Internet."

"And what exactly do they believe?"

"That there are no absolutes."

"None?"

"Except that everyone has his or her own truth within."

"That's it?"

"They reject one truth."

She almost missed the turnoff from the main road but managed to catch the sign that read "Hazelton Winery Left" and made the turn. We were heading upward into the hills on a road with lots of twists.

Once she had her bearings, I asked, "Do they kill people?"

"Most of them say they don't believe in doing harm. It's part of what they call their pagan ethic. If you harm no one, you may do what you will. At the same time, what they practice becomes an opportunity for the evil one to influence them. In extreme cases, that can lead to murder. Many times it leads to suicide."

"Where did you learn all this?"

Lindsay spoke softly. "I had a roommate my first year in college who got into the occult. It started off innocently enough with some dabbling in role playing. There was a bunch of that going on, you know, *Dungeons and Dragons* type stuff."

"That's a game; isn't it?"

"It's no game. At the end of the second semester, she jumped off a ten-story building."

A quick chill ran up my back.

"Ironically," Lindsay continued, "her death spurred me on to look at my faith seriously and to find out what it was that drove her to do it."

She spoke with simple conviction. It was beginning to sound believable.

When we turned up the road that led to the winery, I may have gotten a jolt of that discernment she spoke about. I felt the immediate creeps. Not because of the look of the place. The vineyard that blanketed the land to the east and the tree-lined road leading up to the winery were all nicely preserved.

In fact, there was no objective reason for the feeling at all. It was just there.

Like most wineries in California, Hazelton had a visitor center, where samples are served and wines and accessories sold. As we pulled in and parked, I saw in the distance a Spanish-style mansion tucked in behind a grove of oak trees. No road led there.

The visitor center was immaculate. Seascape oil paintings decorated the walls, underneath which were finely polished wood racks sprouting seemingly endless bottles of wine. A small tasting bar was in front of a huge bay window, which looked out upon the vineyards and beyond to the mountains. It was idyllic, very California.

"Folks like to try some wine?" A rotund, smiling server was placing two wine glasses on the bar. He looked a little like the skipper from *Gilligan's Island.*

"Maybe later," I said. "I was wondering, is Captain Hazelton around?"

The smile faded and I got a serious look from the man. "Oh, he only comes in here occasionally. You wanted to meet him?"

"Yes."

"Any particular reason?"

"Not really. He's kind of a celebrity, isn't he?"

"Locally, maybe. He makes a fine wine. Can I pour you a glass?"

"That his house up there?"

"One of them," the server said. "Can I start you off with a white?"

"I'm not much of a wine drinker," I said, which was true. Beer and hard stuff were my poison.

"Then you won't find much of interest here," he said, "this being a winery and all."

I got the distinct impression he was asking–no, telling–us to leave. I could feel my lawyer's blood rising while my head searched for some too-clever response. Then I felt Lindsay's hand in mine.

"Let's go look at the gourmet section," she said, pulling me toward an alcove that led to an adjoining room. Without protest I went with her, casting a quick glance back at the server. He was still looking at me.

The new room was stocked with specialty foods and condiments, sauces and mixes, overpriced crackers and high-end cutlery. There were also several people milling around, which made us a tad less conspicuous.

Lindsay picked up a jar with something yellow in it and held it up. "Mustard?" she said.

I laughed. "Smooth, very smooth. You didn't like that guy either."

"He got very nervous when you mentioned Hazelton."

"Good eye."

"So let's buy the mustard, go out to the car, and then take a little stroll."

"Where?"

"To see Mr. Hazelton, of course."

It was almost like we were kids again, engaged in a conspiracy of two, sneaking into the forbidden zone of some building construction site or empty warehouse. Lindsay was that mischievous little girl again with the sparkle in her green eyes. I loved it.

We did buy the mustard, and I waved at the server on the way out.

"Come again," he said in a tone that conveyed the opposite.

Lindsay and I walked to the car, and I deposited the gourmet mustard in the back seat. Then Lindsay said, "This way."

She led me to the end of the visitor's lot and around the back of the building. The back wall was windowless, and only a dumpster leaned up against it. The hill dropped off severely into a ravine about a hundred feet down. On the other side it rose again, covered with native brush and high, brown grass. That's what we would have to climb if we were going to get up to Hazelton's.

"What if it's fenced off?" I asked as Lindsay started down the hill.

"We'll see when we get there. Come on!"

I followed her down, the dirt on the hill kicking up after me. Pain shot through my legs and back. Lindsay was athletic, and it was hard to keep up with her.

We reached the bottom and started up the other side. Scrubby bushes reached out to scratch us, and loose rocks fell underneath our feet. But we climbed, and it was, in an odd way, pure joy.

At one point, winded, I stopped for a moment. Lindsay laughed and came back down to me. "Come on, chum," she said with a laugh and reached out her hand. I took it, and she pulled me along after her.

At the top of the hill, the land flattened out and held the unmistakable signs of professional landscaping. Fresh green grass and manicured shrubs offset a stark, wrought iron fence jutting up from the ground, black and unfriendly. Through the fence we could see a large swimming pool and one side of the Hazelton mansion.

"Some setup," Lindsay said as I tried to catch my breath.

"Fence . . ." I said between breaths. "What . . . now?"

"We find the front gate."

"Just . . . like . . . that?"

"You need some first aid. Maybe we can ask for help."

"Funny," I panted. "Very . . . funny."

I heard a crackle to the side and looked over. A thick man in a dark uniform, mirror sunglasses, and combat boots was holding a serious handgun at his side.

"Don't move," he said.

We were marched like prisoners into the huge, Spanish-style mansion, our heels clicking on the tile floor, creating a tiny echo. The security officer had holstered his weapon and was speaking now into a small handset as he took us forward.

Two turns and a huge corridor later we entered a cavernous room. There was a large fireplace on the left, active with a crackling fire. To the right, an oak-paneled wall lined with books–fine, leather-covered volumes–stretched upward to a second story, where more books were evident. A small, winding staircase led up to the second level.

Directly in front of us was a huge desk made of some dark wood, almost black, with ornate, carved designs on the corners. At first glance the room seemed empty. No one sat at the desk. Then I noticed a figure standing by the curtained window, almost blending into the dark scarlet curtain itself. From what I could see, this figure was tall but rather hunched over and almost skeletally thin. He wore some kind of robe. Thin wisps of smoke trailed outward from his left hand.

"That's all, Simon," the figure rasped. Our security guard walked quickly from the room, closing the heavy door behind him.

The man at the window took a step toward us. More light was cast on him. His hair was white and unkempt, and the skin on his face sagged. *Cadaver* was the word that popped into my head. "What do you want?" he said in a low, coarse voice. "You're trespassing."

Lindsay, I sensed, was watching him very closely. I said, "Captain Hazelton?"

"I asked, what you are doing here?"

Now I saw what the smoke was about. He held a lit pipe in his hand. "Why do you have security guards with guns?" I asked.

"You're the lawyer, aren't you?" He opened his thin lips, put his pipe through them, and clamped down with his teeth.

"I'm curious about that guard," I said. "He licensed to carry?"

"You don't understand." A sucking sound came from the pipe, and Hazelton issued a stream of smoke from the corner of his mouth. He removed the pipe with a shaky fist. "I'm a very wealthy man. One never knows who might wish to take advantage."

"Do I look like a threat?"

He turned his face toward Lindsay. "Who is the woman?"

"A friend," I said quickly.

Hazelton shuffled around to his desk, moving with what looked like painful steps. He turned his pipe over and tapped it on a brass ashtray a couple of times. "I shall have to press charges."

"You won't do that," I said.

"And why not?" He left his pipe on the desk and faced me squarely. His eyes were sunken, deep and dark under drooping lids.

"Because you don't want the publicity." When he didn't answer immediately, I knew I was right. "You don't want the publicity because you know that things get messy when you go to court. Things come out. I don't think you want that."

An odd smile crept across Hazelton's mouth. "You're a smart young man," he said, almost with admiration. It struck me then that there might be a subtle implication in Hazelton's reaction, as if he was disappointed in his own son for not being a smart young man.

"I admire intelligence," he continued. "It's what makes this"–he motioned around the room with his bony arm–"possible. It builds. But it can also be a nuisance. I don't think you want to be a nuisance, Mr. Denney."

So he knew my name. All that pretense of whether I was "that lawyer" or not was just that, a pretense. Clearly Howie Patino and I had made an impression on the Hazelton family.

"I'm just interested in the truth, that's all," I said.

"About?"

"What happened to my client's wife."

"That was decided in court; was it not?"

"A jury reached a verdict. We all know that doesn't mean it was right."

"Unlike you," he said, "I have faith in our legal system."

"And in the district attorney?"

He squinted at me. "Benton Tolletson is a friend."

"Anything else?"

"I don't know what you mean."

"Mr. Hazelton, can you account for the whereabouts of your son on the night of March 25?"

For a long moment the only sound in the room was the crackling of the burning logs in the fireplace. They snapped like gunshots. "Am I to understand that you are accusing my son of complicity in this matter?"

"I'm not making accusations," I said. "I'm just asking questions."

"You'll please leave."

"Can you answer me that?"

"I'll have you removed if you don't leave now. And if you ever come back, I'll have you arrested."

"Even if I want to buy a good bottle of wine?"

"Not even then."

I turned to go, thinking Lindsay would come with me. She didn't, and before I could stop her, she said, "Mr. Hazelton, do you practice magic?"

A jolt of electricity seemed to rip through the room, bouncing off the wall and snapping everyone to attention. I was stunned at Lindsay's boldness.

So, apparently, was Hazelton. He looked like someone had sprayed cold water on his ashen face. "Young lady," he said, "my practices are none of your affair. How dare you!"

Lindsay answered with an air of confident assurance that amazed me. Maybe she didn't know to whom she was talking. Or maybe that didn't impress her at all. "I thought," she said, "your beliefs were a matter of public record."

Hazelton's face was reddening.

"Do you follow the ways of your grandfather, Solomon Hazelton?"

"Get out, both of you!" Hazelton exploded, which led to an immediate coughing fit. Hazelton doubled over, hacking and holding his sides.

The security guard bolted into the room, saw Hazelton bent over, and rushed to him. Hazelton waved him off, and between coughs, said, "Get . . . them . . . out . . ."

The guard walked to us and didn't have to tell us what to do. We headed out the door, the guard behind us. I opened the door of the house myself. The guard stayed with us all the way down the path to the winery parking lot. He watched us until we drove out of sight.

"That," Lindsay said as we got back on the main road, "is one weird place."

No argument from me. We headed back to L.A.

"There's got to be some connection," Lindsay said.

"Maybe, but I don't know how to find it."

I think she realized this too. We drove in silence most of the way back.

She dropped me at my office–I didn't want her to see where I lived. "You going to be okay?" she asked before I got out of her car.

"Like the man falling off the Empire State Building," I said.

"Huh?"

"At each floor they could hear him say, 'So far, so good.'"

Lindsay laughed, and it was intoxicating. She said, "Keep reading Pascal."

"And if I don't?"

"I'll come after you."

"That's not an entirely bad thought."

She smiled, and I detected a blush.

"Lindsay?"

"Yes?"

"One of these days, very soon, I'm not going to be responsible for my behavior."

"What do you mean?"

"I mean, I'm going to put my arms around you and kiss you for all it's worth."

Now her cheeks turned bright red. They twitched too, in response to an evanescent smile. "I, um . . ."

"Thanks for the ride," I said as I walked away.

CHAPTER FORTY-ONE

I BOUGHT A spicy polish and a bag of Fritos from Boulevard Weenies and brought it back to my office. The lights were out in the building, save for the watery glow from the fish tank near the receptionist's desk.

I took my glorious dinner into my office, flicked the radio on to The Wave, and prepared to eat in easy listening comfort. Only then did I realize I hadn't ordered a drink to go with the meal.

There was, in the kitchenette around the corner from my office, a small refrigerator for the tenants. I knew Sharon McGuire, another attorney, kept a good stock of Coke in there. I could tap one and pay her back later.

But something stopped me. I knew I had a half bottle of bourbon in my desk drawer.

I tried not to open the drawer. Then I knew I had to.

When I did, I saw the inviting liquid lapping inside the bottle. My mouth, my tongue, and my brain all sent me relentless messages about how I needed a drink at that very moment.

And I knew, absolutely, that I was going to finish the bottle. I had been down this hillside before. Once you start, you slide to the bottom. No stopping.

Then something did stop me–Lindsay. The image of Lindsay Patino's face popped into my head and kept me, for the moment, from touching the bottle.

It's what they call in AA a motivating incident. Then I surprised myself by saying out loud, "God, please help me."

With sudden resolve, I grabbed the bottle and literally ran out of my office as if I were being pursued by some demon. I charged to the back exit of the building, threw open the door, and stood at the top of the back stairs that looked out over the dumpsters below.

I threw the bottle to an open dumpster and heard the shatter sound that told me I'd scored.

I stood there for several minutes, breathing heavily and noticing some sweat breaking out on my forehead.

I went back into the building, took one of Sharon's Cokes, and ate my sausage with a minor case of the shakes.

Then, with my eyes burning and head throbbing, I threw down a couple of aspirin I got from the kitchenette and went into Gil Lee's office. It's naturally the largest one and has a comfortable couch by the door.

I lay down on it and went to sleep.

I awoke before seven, and the first thing I realized was that I was without a car. In Los Angeles that's like having no legs. But I was in Gil Lee's office, and I knew Gil kept an old Chevy in the garage that he sometimes used for little errands. He didn't like taking his Corvette out to the post office or store, where somebody could open a door into it.

All I had to do was find the key and write a note.

Finding note paper was easy, but it took me twenty minutes to find the key. Gil kept it in a cigar box on his credenza. Silly me. I thought it would have had cigars in it.

I took the car back to my place and cleaned up. Then I went to Chipper's for breakfast. Mary, the waitress, greeted me like always. I found comfort in that, something familiar that kept me rooted to reality.

After that I headed to the beach at Santa Monica. I just wanted to spend a few hours alone, without anyone or anything hammering on me. Maybe I'd get a brainstorm or a vision.

I almost got run over by a rollerblader. But I finally found some shade and sat and listened to the ocean. The ocean has always meant peace to me. Whether it was the Atlantic in my childhood or the Pacific out here, I could always find some degree of comfort from the waves.

As I sat there I began to ask myself a question that engendered a distinct sense of déjà vu. The question was: Who made all this?

Why was this question familiar? I knew immediately. I had sensed the same question when I was four or five years old and standing on the shoreline of the Florida coast. I remembered vividly my sense of awe at the whole thing, the bigness of it.

I was feeling that same awe now as I looked out at the blue waters with a topping of whitecaps under the morning sun.

I sat there for three hours, until I finally got the urge to get a hot dog. That's when I noticed something else strange–I had no urge to get a beer. None. It was gone.

Gone! I couldn't believe it. With me, beer went with hot dogs like Gilbert went with Sullivan. It had for as long as I could remember.

Not now. And that made me giddy. I actually broke out into laughter. If this hadn't been L.A., I might have gotten some strange looks.

That giddiness turned to a new sense of purpose. I suddenly got an idea and knew what I was going to do.

I was going up to Hinton to see a prosecutor.

I reached the Hinton County Courthouse at around 3:45. For an hour and a half, I sat in Gil's car at the edge of the courthouse parking lot. The courthouse square in Hinton was fairly small, which made what I was about to do easier. I spent the time thinking about

Lindsay and listening to the only station–Country–that I could get clearly.

In between thoughts of Howie's sister and the warbling of various honey-toned singers, I kept an eye on the courthouse doors.

At exactly 5:17 Sylvia Plotzske walked out of the courthouse, ambled down the small flight of steps, and started across the parking lot. I watched her all the way to her car, which turned out to be a yellow Volkswagen Beetle, one of the new ones. That was going to help.

I am no expert in surveillance, but I'd been on a tail with Trip once, and all the while he lectured me on what he was doing. He told me how to keep from getting too close, what to do if a light suddenly changed color, how to anticipate, and what to do if you temporarily lost someone.

There was also a factor here that was both an asset and a liability for me. Hinton was a small town with few streets. That would make following the yellow car easier, but it would also make me more conspicuous.

Sylvia backed her Beetle out and actually burned a little rubber heading for the parking lot exit. On top of everything else, she was a speed demon. I set off after her.

I followed her easily for a good couple of miles, keeping a buffer of at least ten car lengths between us. There was one intersection I had to speed through before the yellow light turned red. As I did, I noticed a cop car waiting in one of the opposite lanes. I was sure he was going to pull me over to ask for a license I didn't have. But he stayed put.

I hardly had a chance to enjoy my relief when I saw Sylvia speed through the next major intersection. This time I didn't make it.

My eyes stayed with the yellow Bug, but I was sure I was going to lose her. My red light was staying red, content to let the leisurely commuters of Hinton have a long wait. Then, about half a mile up the road, Sylvia turned into a lot.

The light changed, and I sped up to the point where I thought she had turned. It was a shopping center with a Ralph's prominent in the middle. The after-work crowd had filled the parking lot. I made a quick scan and didn't see Sylvia's car.

But then I saw Sylvia. She was heading into Ralph's.

I took a parking space at the far end and waited.

The sun was setting on Hinton, and lights were starting to come on. It seemed to me an apt metaphor. My life had been in the dark for a long time, but there was just an inkling of light now. Lindsay was part of it, and Pascal was too. But there was still plenty of darkness surrounding Howie's case, and that's why I was tailing Sylvia Plotzske.

About twenty minutes later I saw her emerge from Ralph's carrying two plastic shopping bags, one in each hand. She put them in her car and headed for the side-street exit.

Following her this time was not a problem. She lived only two blocks away.

It was an apartment building, not too big nor too small. Even though this was small-town Hinton, it still had a security garage, which is where Sylvia pulled in.

I parked halfway down the block and went to the front door of the building. There were ten numbers listed on the keypad but only nine names. None of them was Plotzske. That figured. As a prosecutor, she did not want to advertise her location.

Would she be surprised to see me?

The front door was secured, so I decided to wait for someone going in or out. In short order, a middle-aged woman with too much makeup and a Pomeranian on a leash opened the door from the inside and walked past me.

I caught the door before it closed.

"You can't do that!" the woman said. I turned and saw her glaring at me.

"It's okay," I said, "I'm an attorney." The absurdity of that answer was immediately apparent to me, but inexplicably the woman's face softened and she said, "Oh, all right." And then she walked off into the night.

Score one for the profession nobody likes.

I entered the building and took the stairs to the second floor. My calculation, based on the number pad, was that Sylvia resided in number 210. That door was the end of the hall. I knocked.

And then, like a school kid or criminal, I put my back against the wall so Sylvia couldn't see me through the peephole.

The silence seemed full of confusion. Then I heard her voice. "Who is it?"

I didn't answer. Then a curious Sylvia Plotzske opened the door and stuck her head out.

Simultaneously, at the very moment she saw and recognized me, I spun around to face her and put my hand on the door. Her attempt to close it ran right up against my palm.

"You can't–" she started to say, but I pushed her back, jumped in, and slammed the door behind me.

Immediately she bolted, like I was a serial killer. And, in keeping with the role, I ran after her, shouting, "Wait a minute!"

She was in the kitchen, grabbing the phone, fingers flying over the keypad looking, no doubt, for a nine and two ones. I hit the plunger with my finger. "Listen to me, will you?"

"Get out of here!" She dropped the phone. It hit the floor with a loud *clack.*

"I have to talk to you."

"You can't! I could get . . ."

"What? In trouble? From your boss?"

"You just broke into my apartment," she said incredulously, as if the full import of my action had only now hit her.

"Yes, another felony. You want to charge me?"

"You have to leave."

"Not until you talk to me."

"You walk out now, I'll forget this ever happened."

"Sylvia, listen to me." I picked up the phone by the dangling cord and replaced it in its casing. "I'm not here to threaten you. Can we just talk?"

She shook her head.

"I'll make you a deal."

She looked amazed, and who could blame her? Here was a defense lawyer and criminal defendant, all rolled into one, standing in her kitchen, which she had every reason to believe was a private refuge protecting her from the nasty outside world. I was an intruder.

"Just listen to me," I said. "That's all I ask. Just listen, and when I'm through, I'll leave if you tell me to. Is that fair?"

"If anyone ever knew you came here . . ."

"No one will know. I won't say anything. I promise you as a colleague."

She thought about it a moment. "All right," she said with a shrug, adding, "But only for five minutes."

"Thank you." I looked to the side and motioned toward the kitchen table. "Can we at least sit?"

She did not hesitate. She obviously wanted to get this over with as soon as possible. We sat at the modest table, next to peaches-and-pears wallpaper.

"Sylvia, you're a good lawyer. A solid one. And I think you have a great career ahead of you. I also think you're honest."

Her face, a moment before defensive, softened a bit. "I'm not saying that to flatter you," I added. "I really believe it. I've dealt with prosecutors all my professional life. You get to know the way things fall. You're a straight shooter."

"I try to be." She had both her hands on the table in firm little fists.

"Which is why I think you aren't entirely comfortable with the Patino case."

She looked at her hands then. "What do you mean, uncomfortable?"

"Obviously I don't know the facts. But my sense is that you know things about the case and about Tolletson's role in it that you've gone along with. Not because you're dishonest, but because you're junior in the office. Tolletson has control, and he's not above using it. Am I right?"

"Benton Tolletson is one of the finest lawyers I've ever known."

"That's not what I asked you."

Her eyes, behind the thick lenses and black frame of her glasses, scanned my face. "I don't know what you're asking."

"I think you do. But something is holding you back. Why did Tolletson take this case from you? He doesn't try cases anymore."

"Sure he does. Only last year–"

"As a rule, I mean. This wasn't a complex trial. Why him instead of you?"

"I don't know."

"Come on, Sylvia."

She pounded her right hand on the table. "I *don't know!*"

"But you have an idea. You've got to."

She turned her head to the side as if looking for a way of escape. "I'm not going to speculate about Benton Tolletson for you."

For a long moment I stared at the tabletop–gold flecks on a red background. "Sylvia," I said softly, "I haven't done too well as a lawyer, I know that. I've screwed up my life and done a lot of things I shouldn't have. Ramming into Ruben Azario is only the latest, and I'm going to pay the price. But Sylvia"–I leaned forward, both my arms on the tabletop–"Howie Patino did not kill his wife. But he's in for life, and that's my responsibility. Tolletson went out of his way to make sure Howie got nailed for this. I think you know why, Sylvia. That's what I'm asking you for. Please."

She would not look at me, but I got the feeling she was fighting a war inside her. I waited.

Finally, shaking her head, she said, "You have to go. I have nothing to say."

It felt like my chest caved in. "Sylvia–"

"Go. I listened. Now leave. Please."

She slumped slightly in her chair. Whatever she knew was going to stay inside her, where it was already acting like an acid on her basic decency. She had reached a crossroads and decided her direction. I felt sorry for her.

I stood up and walked toward the kitchen door. Sylvia's voice stopped me. "A word of advice, Mr. Denney."

"Yes?"

"Let it go. Things can only get worse for you if you don't let it go."

"Thanks a lot, Sylvia," I said sarcastically. "See you in court."

CHAPTER FORTY-TWO

I HAD ONE last crazy idea, crazier even than driving without a license in a town, as they say, without pity.

Frisbee's was hopping as always. I parked at the far end of the lot and used the moon and whatever light spilled out of the saloon to search the other cars. I didn't see Darcy Hazelton's car, but that's not why I was here.

I popped my head inside and looked around. The blonde waitress I'd met my first time here was serving a station of tables, all full. I went in anyway.

Though there was a lot of noise and activity, I still felt like I was in one of those cartoons where the eyes are staring at you from a dark forest.

The waitress, holding a tray of drinks by a table, looked up and recognized me. I could tell by the smile. The smile quickly faded, and she shot a glance at the bar. Then she glanced back at me with a nod of her head toward the back. She wanted me to go there.

I walked to the back of the place near the bathrooms and waited. I scanned the whole place from where I was.

She joined me and pulled my arm toward the back exit. Next thing I knew we were out in the night air in relative quiet.

"You shouldn't come around here," she said.

"Why not?"

"Look, there's people who know about you. I've heard them talk. You're a big deal."

"I needed to ask you some questions. Are you on break?"

"I shouldn't talk to you."

"Then why are you here?"

"I don't know what's going on, but I think you're in some kind of trouble. I don't really care one way or the other, but I don't want to see anybody hurt, you know? Why don't you just leave Hinton?"

"Why would anyone want to hurt me?"

"You should just go."

"I don't even know your name."

She hesitated and looked me in the eye. "April," she said.

"I need to ask you about Darcy Hazelton."

"No."

"Are you afraid of him?"

"That whole family's crazy. I don't want my name in this. I don't want to have to go to court."

"I just need some information, that's all. I won't call you as a witness or anything."

She appeared to be thinking about it.

"Please," I said.

"Hurry."

"I think Darcy Hazelton killed Rae Patino. I think he was having an affair with her, and she got pregnant. He went to see her to talk her into having an abortion. That just happened to be when Howie Patino showed up. Darcy heard all this, got a knife from the kitchen, and then hid in the bathroom while Howie was pleading with Rae about his marriage. When Rae started talking about the kid to Howie, Darcy came in and shut her up. He got to Howie too, then escaped through the bathroom window."

April's mouth fell open slightly. "Why are you telling me all this?"

"You know this town pretty well. People say things. Maybe you've heard something. Anything."

"Not about this."

"Nothing?"

"Sorry." An empty feeling opened up inside me, and I was about to pack it in and head home when April said, "Just one thing."

I snapped at it. "What?"

"About what you just said."

"Yes?"

"I don't think it happened that way."

"Why?"

"Because," she said, "Darcy Hazelton is gay."

"What?"

"Sure."

"I was told he was a ladies' man."

"By whom?"

"Somebody who knew him . . . Hang Ten or something."

"Hang Creswell?"

"That's the guy."

April laughed dismissively. "Hang Creswell hardly knows his own name, he's so out of it. His brain should be sent to Harvard for marijuana research."

"How do you know all this?"

"The way you know things. This ain't a large town, in case you haven't noticed. I got to go. You should take off. Leave things alone here."

I reached in my pocket and pulled out a five-dollar bill. "Can I tip you for your time?"

She smiled and shook her head. "It's okay. You probably need that more than I do."

I waited until she disappeared inside, then walked to the edge of the dark hillside at the rear of the place. Out in the distance was the highway that led to and from the town of Hinton. A sparkling of headlights was moving toward the town, and a stream of red taillights was moving away.

Suddenly an odd feeling hit me, as if I had finally come to an understanding of some deep, mysterious secret. It felt like one of those word problems I had in elementary school. They never came easily to me, and I'd agonize over them until that moment when, all of sudden, everything was clear.

Looking down at the cars below, I knew it was all meaningless. Every car had a person inside it. Every person was driving somewhere. But it didn't matter where, because this was a world, a life, that would end, and it was empty without some meaning that was above it all. I realized then that this is what Pascal had said in different ways, and now I knew he was right.

So what should I do now? Jump off the hill? Pascal had also written that we must all choose sides in this question of God. For or against. And if you looked at it like a bet, which would be the better choice? Choose God, and if you lose, if there is no God, you lose nothing, really. Choose against God, and if you're wrong, you lose everything.

My body filled with a longing to choose something that would be the final answer. Before I could think of anything else, I heard the crunch of gravel from behind me.

Turning, I saw three dark figures. They were shadows, backlit by the lights of the tavern. But there was no doubt about their intentions. That's when I knew.

"Hello, Darcy," I said.

"You shouldn't be here," he said.

And just how did he know I *was* here? I mentally fingered that the bartender or some other regular who knew Darcy and also me told him. My face was now well known in these parts, thanks to local TV and the *Hinton Valley News.*

"It's a great country, isn't it?" I said. "Free."

"Not here."

The outlines of the other two showed weight-lifter arms and V-shaped bodies. This was going to hurt. I had to think fast. "What were you doing visiting Rae Patino at night?"

The silence was testimony to confusion. Then he said, "What are you talking about?"

"A witness can testify about your car being at Patino's house. Now what about it?"

"You got no witness."

"You weren't having an affair with her, we all know that."

One of his man friends made a move toward me, but Darcy stopped him. "You better tell me everything you think you know," he said.

"I intend to," I said. "Maybe you were seeing her to protect somebody. But who?"

He waited like a coiled spring.

"The Captain," I said, revealing the information to myself the moment I said it. "It was your father who was having the affair with Rae Patino."

"You don't–"

"Did you kill her to keep her quiet? Or did your father do it?"

His response was a scream, then a charge. All three converged with a dark fury.

I made a move to the right, slipping on the tiny rocks, but with enough force to get clear of the initial thrust. A hand grabbed my left arm for an instant before I ripped free.

I headed for the front of the building, hearing grunts behind me. Then I went down.

Someone had hold of my legs.

I hit the ground hard. Tiny jags shot into my forehead. I could feel the warmth of blood drops appearing. Then I was lifted up like I was a mannequin.

My arms were held behind me tightly. I could see Darcy standing off to the side. The other muscle boy was right in front of me, and then he punched me on the side of the face. It felt like a brick.

"Hold it," Darcy said.

There was a clanging in my head like the bells of Notre Dame. And I was sure my soon-to-be reworked face would make me look like Quasimodo. I sensed Darcy's face next to mine. "You don't know nothing," he said.

"Maybe I do," I answered, having no idea what I would say next. I just wanted to delay the inevitable beating as long as possible.

"I could snuff you," said Darcy.

"You won't."

"Why not?"

"Too many witnesses know you don't like me. Why don't you like me, Darcy?"

"You got no idea what I could do. You got no idea what goes on in this town. You're nothing here. I could make it look like an accident."

"Or set somebody up, like you did with Howie Patino?"

The goon who held me yanked me upward. I'd been slumping. Darcy's breath was hot on my face, his breath sour like he'd had a few beers. At that moment I felt a double shot of disgust–for Darcy and for myself, for having smelled like Darcy too many times to count.

"You know what I'm gonna do?" Darcy said. "I'm gonna use you as an example. I'm actually gonna do it, and that'll show him."

"Show who?"

At that moment the goon who had hit me across the face said, "Hey, Darce?"

"What?" Hazelton snapped.

"You're not really gonna off him, are you?"

Whirling with obvious rage, Darcy said, "We'll do what I say!"

"I thought we were just gonna mess him up."

"You listen to me!"

"No," I said, "don't listen to him."

"Shut up!" Darcy slapped me across the face. It didn't hurt anything like the fist I'd gotten. "Carl," he said softly, "I'll take care of it. You know I can."

"I know," Carl said, "but I don't know if I'm ready for this."

I felt just the faintest loosening of the grip on my arms. The still unnamed muscle boy who held me was probably just as fascinated with this debate as I was. Darcy was losing control of his little world.

And I might not have another chance. Using the only weapon at my disposal, I snapped my head back as hard as I could. The crushing feeling told me I'd hit paydirt in the form of a nose. The guy who had me screamed–actually screamed–and let go of my arms.

Out of old schoolyard instinct, I kicked out as hard as I could. I didn't get Carl where it counted most, but I did get him in the knee.

Darcy tried to grab my arm, but his grip was not nearly as strong as his buddy's. I yanked away and pushed Darcy in the chest, and then I broke into a sprint, heading for the hillside.

I figured that was my only hope.

I heard Darcy yell, "Get him!" followed by the scuffing of feet on gravel. I didn't bother to look behind me. Instead, like a long jumper, I took a leap over the edge and into the cold darkness below.

CHAPTER FORTY-THREE

PAIN IS A great clarifier. It forces you to think about survival–even while you're rolling down a rocky hillside in the dark. Especially then.

I hit rocks, brush, sticks, and possibly several nocturnal animals on my way down to the road. The only thing I didn't hit was a tree, which is why my descent was not interrupted. All the way I kept trying to think of a way to keep from impaling myself on some limb, and I came up with no answers.

By the time I thudded onto the shoulder of the road, I was warm with blood and numb with pain. But I was alive and apparently didn't have any major injuries. At least I wasn't aware of them. I lay there for a moment on cool grass and gently felt around my body. I'd be hurting for a long time.

Light flashed around me. Headlights. A car coming. Could it be Darcy and his friends? No, it was too soon, but I was sure they'd be heading this way in no time.

Knowing I was not going to make it on foot, I brought myself to my feet, fire shooting up my legs, and stumbled to the edge of the road. I waved my arms like a wild man at the oncoming car.

But who was going to stop for the likes of me in the dead of night? Still, I had to take a chance.

It was the right one. The car was a police unit. Even though it was the Hinton police, it was a welcome sight at the moment.

The headlights stopped. Through the glare I saw a shadowy figure emerge and walk toward me. A terrible thought hit me. What if it was my old friend Officer Cheadle? He'd probably cuff me to a tree.

"You all right?"

The voice wasn't Cheadle's, and it sounded young.

"No," I said. "Can you give me ride?"

The young policeman stopped, and I could tell he was in a ready position. I couldn't blame him. I must have looked like Swamp Thing.

"What happened?" the officer asked. "You're hurt pretty bad."

"Can I explain it to you in the car?"

"Where'd you come from?"

"There's some guys who want to mess me up."

"Did you come off that hill?" He sounded incredulous. Down the road I saw another set of headlights looking our way, like eyes.

"Quick," I said, limping toward the squad car. The young officer, who had probably never trained in confronting the walking dead, wordlessly followed.

The headlights of the other car were almost upon us.

"Man, you look bad," the officer said. He was a sandy haired, freckled kid, no more than twenty-two or three. He would have looked perfectly at home behind the counter at Dairy Queen. "I'll get you to the hospital."

"Just go," I said, glancing behind me.

He followed my glance. "You think those are the guys?"

"I don't know. Do we need to find out?"

"I guess not," he said, sounding a little confused. With a shrug, he started up the unit and took off.

The headlights behind seemed to stop dead in the road. If it was my fan club, they'd wait for another time.

"Maybe you'd better tell me about it," the officer said.

"I want to tell Tolletson."

"The DA?"

"Take me to the station."

"But you're–"

"Just do it. Radio ahead. Get Tolletson down there. Tell him it's Jake Denney."

I washed up as best I could in the station's public restroom. At least it was clean. My face was another story. I looked like I'd been in a scratch fight and lost. And a big, ugly, blue spot was breaking out all over the right side of my face. I had various points of pain up and down my body, and my clothes were caked with blood and mud. I wondered what they were saying out at the station desk.

I didn't have a chance to find out. As soon as I emerged, I was met by Benton Tolletson himself.

He was wearing a crisp blue polo shirt and sharp slacks–the picture of country-club casual. Out of a suit, he looked almost human. But he had his usual expression of contempt on his face.

"What's this about, Denney?"

"Nice to see you too."

"Come with me."

He led me past the leering eyes of a few Hinton police officers, and the kid who'd given me the lift. He still looked utterly confused.

Tolletson opened the door to a small meeting room and in we went. Metal folding chairs were scattered around in haphazard fashion. A large whiteboard held a mishmash of officer names and assignments scrawled in blue marking pen. Was "arrest Jake Denney" one of them?

"I get a call at night about you, I'm intrigued," Tolletson said. He didn't bother to sit or offer me a chair.

"I know what you think of me, and at the moment, I really don't care."

"Did you ever?"

"No."

"Go on."

"But you're the DA. You still have the obligation to see that justice is done."

"This about Patino?"

"You bet it is."

"Then I'm not interested. You can take it up on appeal." He made a slight movement to leave.

"Will you knock it off!" I yelled, surprising myself. "Quit making everything a game, a competition, and listen to me for a change. Darcy Hazelton tried to kill me tonight."

A look I could not read registered on Tolletson's face. That didn't surprise me. What was going on behind those eyes was always anyone's guess. "Darcy Hazelton?"

"Yeah, and his two buddies."

"They did this to you?"

"They gave me this"–I pointed to the left side of my face–"and the rest was provided courtesy of your Hinton topography."

"Stupid."

"What?"

"Darcy Hazelton's always been stupid."

"And I thought he might be the guy who killed Rae Patino."

"Why?"

"Several reasons. But I don't think he did it. I think it was someone else."

"Who?"

"Are you really interested?"

"I'm listening, but I know you're desperate. You've always been desperate."

That I could not argue with. Desperate is exactly what I was. "I called you in good faith. I want you to listen to me."

"I'm listening."

"I think it was Darcy's father."

"The Captain? Whatever gave you that idea?"

"The fact that Darcy's gay."

Tolletson scowled, and for the first time looked like I'd made an impact. "So what?"

"So I don't think he was having an affair with Rae Patino. But his father was. In fact, he was paying her for it. There's no other way to explain that rack of skin and bones getting together with her. And when she got pregnant, she thought she'd hold out for a little more money, but he wasn't buying."

Shaking his head, Tolletson said, "This is screwball. You have any proof?"

"No, but you do."

"What's that supposed to mean?"

It was a shot in the dark, but I took it. "I think you know more about all this than you're telling me. I think you know things about the Hazelton family and a possible connection to the murder. And I think you never followed up on any of it because, frankly, you had a winner with Howie Patino, and you just went for it. You went for a notch on the belt rather than the truth."

His jaw muscles twitched. "You're nuts."

"Am I?"

For a long moment he glared at me, wheels turning in his head. "I'll prove it to you."

"How?"

"You're coming with me."

CHAPTER FORTY-FOUR

IT WAS A bizarre situation.

Here I was riding in a new black Cadillac with a man I loathed and who felt the same way about me, on a mission of criminal justice. At least that's how Tolletson had put it. He said he wanted to clear things up tonight.

We were going to see Warren Hazelton.

It was unorthodox, yes, but Tolletson convinced me this was the right thing to do. I would stand in the room with him while he put the questions to Hazelton. Tolletson said he wanted me there to watch Hazelton's eyes, as I would with any witness I was confronting in court. That would be enough to convince me, Tolletson said.

Strangely enough, I believed him. He was, after all, the DA of a small county. That gave him tremendous power. And even though he had socialized with Hazelton, I didn't think that would prevent Benton Tolletson from trying to get to the bottom of things. He didn't strike me as a man who would let a minor item like social graces get in his way. The fact that he had made his reputation bringing down another local hero, the football coach, made it seem plausible that he'd do it again.

There was another reason this was so strange. Technically, I was a criminal defendant in a drunk driving case that Tolletson's office was prosecuting. It's not often that a defendant rides around town with the DA. It was almost comical.

As we made our way toward the Hazelton estate, Tolletson's mood was far from frivolous. "If there isn't anything here," he said, "you better be ready to face the music."

"What sort of music?"

"Hazelton has money. He can make your life hell. He might sue you for defamation, for starters."

I huffed. "He's welcome to go after my deep pockets. Maybe he'll get my VCR."

"What went wrong with you?" Tolletson said, taking a sharp turn into the personal. "You were a good attorney."

Suddenly I was in the car with my father. The disapproval and disappointment were heavy in his voice.

"I'm still a good attorney, Benton. I just have to find my way back."

"You got a long way to go."

"I know that."

"We're almost there," Tolletson said. I'm sure he didn't want to go any deeper with me. What had started as an attempt to establish superiority had turned into a discussion about the meaning of life. Benton Tolletson was not ready to go there, especially with me.

At the large, black iron gate Tolletson pressed a keypad and announced himself through the speaker. Apparently he had called ahead because the gates slowly swung open without any further comment.

The same security guard was waiting for us as the front entrance. He showed us in. The Hazelton mansion looked familiar, but at night it was oddly dark, even with the lights on. Sort of like a medieval castle illuminated with torches. I started to wonder where the torture chamber was.

We were shown into the same library where Lindsay and I had confronted the captain before. It had the same, musty smell.

Hazelton himself seemed not to have moved or changed clothes since that encounter. Even the fire in the fireplace seemed perpetual.

"Benton," Hazelton said in his raspy voice. He was standing by the mantle tamping tobacco into his pipe. He said nothing to me, giving me only a glare.

"Thanks for seeing us on such short notice," Tolletson said.

"Of course. Anything to help the DA's office. Sit down." He motioned us to the leather chairs in front of his desk and then sat in his own chair. He lit his pipe with a wooden match.

"Warren," Tolletson began, "you know Mr. Denney, I believe."

Squinting at me through a veil of smoke, Hazelton said, "Oh yes."

"That's the reason I'm here tonight. Mr. Denney thinks he has some information on the murder of Rae Patino."

I had no idea where Tolletson was going with this, but I was surprised he would be so direct. A good prosecutor doesn't show his cards while the investigation is going on.

"And what sort of information would that be?" Hazelton asked me, appearing unconcerned.

"Maybe Mr. Tolletson can tell you," I said.

"No, Jake, why don't you go ahead?" Tolletson said. I felt like he was leaving me out to dry.

But I didn't care. "All right," I said. "What was your relationship with Rae Patino?"

For a moment Hazelton's sunken eyes quivered. They quickly resumed impassivity. "Who is he?"

"Come off it, you know who I'm talking about."

"Benton?" Hazelton said with seeming confusion.

Tolletson turned to him. "The young woman who was murdered."

"Ah, yes," said Hazelton, the liar. I hoped Tolletson wasn't buying this sham. "I didn't know the girl."

"This is a pretty small town," I said.

"Quite so."

"You're a pretty big wheel."

"True."

"And you claim you didn't know her at all?"

"Mr. Denney," Hazelton rasped, "there are two worlds in existence. There is the world I occupy, which has very few people in it. All the rest live down there." He motioned toward the window with his bony hand.

"You mean you're sort of like a god, up here on Olympus."

"In a way," he said with complete seriousness.

"Pardon me if I find that a bit deranged."

The remark did not amuse Warren Hazelton, even though a demented half-smile edged across his face.

"Maybe we can start by asking where you were on the night Rae Patino was murdered."

Hazelton looked at Tolletson and said, "That's enough."

Tolletson looked at his feet.

"Enough what?" I asked.

No answer. And then it hit me. "You're in this with him."

Tolletson raised his head and looked at me. His eyes were dead.

Hazelton stuck out an osseous finger, pushed a button on a small console, and said, "Bring Mrs. Hazelton in."

A moment later Heather Hazelton walked into the library.

She looked older than I'd expected. I had a picture in my mind of the youthful hippie tromping through the flowers with skin like milk. What I saw now was a middle-aged woman, dressed completely in black. Her dark hair was streaked with white lines and fell to the middle of her back. Most striking was her face. It was not that of an innocent flower child. She had a darkness about the eyes. Around her neck she wore a large, silver pentagram.

"We're ready," Hazelton said tonelessly.

Heather walked to the middle of the room, staring. The look held more than contempt. It was deadly and chilled me to the spine.

I turned to Tolletson. "What are they talking about?"

"Sorry, Jake," he said.

"Sorry about what? What is this?"

At that moment the security guard, as if on cue, walked through the door. His gun was in his hand, and in two seconds it was at the base of my neck.

Heather reached up on the mantle, pulled down a black box, and held it out to Tolletson.

Stunned beyond belief, I watched as Benton Tolletson, district attorney of Hinton County, pulled from the box a set of handcuffs. He then pulled my arms behind me and locked them there.

"You're all crazy," I said.

"Silence," said Heather.

Tolletson pushed me to a chair and sat me down. A rope was looped around my body. The security guard was tying me to the chair.

"Benton," I said, "I can't believe this."

Tolletson said nothing.

Warren Hazelton walked to his wife and stood with her in front of the fire. They joined hands. Then Warren Hazelton closed his eyes and said, "*A diaboli et Rege!*"

It was more a chant than anything else.

"*Adeste diaboli!*"

It sounded Latin to me.

Heather said, "Receive this sacrifice, O father."

Sacrifice?

Me.

"Benton, this is insane!" I said.

"Shut up," he said.

Heather reached up to another box on the mantle. She opened it and pulled out something of glistening silver–it looked almost beautiful until I realized it was a knife with a six-inch blade.

"A sacrifice, O father," Heather said, holding the knife up in both hands, "so you will grant me the daughter I seek."

In the grip of this surreal scene, something surreal formed in my head. "It was you," I said to Heather. "You were the one who killed Rae Patino. She was going to have a child for *you.*"

Heather froze. Warren Hazelton looked stunned. "Who else knows about this?" he wheezed at Tolletson.

"No one, I'm sure," Tolletson said defensively.

"Everyone," I said. "I've been feeding this to the FBI and a reporter on the *Hinton Valley News.*"

"He's lying," said Tolletson.

"Try it, Heather," I said.

She intended to. She gripped the knife in a plunging position. Then she took a step toward me.

"*Adeste diaboli!*" she cried, raising the knife even higher.

The boom was like the sound barrier being broken, only right next to my ears.

I was knocked backward in the chair, feeling like every part of my body was being hit simultaneously by some colossal compactor. As I hit the ground, I saw a pillar of fire, shooting straight up through the roof.

CHAPTER FORTY-FIVE

I THOUGHT I'D lost consciousness. I was just numb. My head was bonging so loudly, I thought it might crack. My lungs started to fill up with smoke.

And I felt the heat of the fire.

The place was in flames.

Instinctively, I thrashed out with my legs, trying to move away from the danger. I moved only a little.

I thrashed some more and turned in a half circle. And came face to face with Benton Tolletson.

I shrieked.

He was covered with blood. His eyes, though open, seemed sightless. His body twitched in some wild paroxysm, as if he were trying to escape his own body.

Sensing the flames growing hotter, I tried to move again. It was useless. All I did was roll over on my back.

Black smoke swirled around me.

And then, out of the smoke, she appeared.

Heather Hazelton.

I could tell it was Heather only because of the hair and the dangling pentagram necklace. Her face was another matter.

It was the most horrific face I had ever seen. It was as if another face had taken over her own, a visage from the pit of hell.

I realized then that this was the same face Howie Patino had seen on the night Heather murdered Rae.

Yellow teeth bared through lips that were dripping blood, and a bestial howl came out of her mouth.

She raised her hand. In it was the silver knife.

What I heard next sounded like a gunshot. It was hard to tell with the *whoosh* of flames all around me. But Heather Hazelton went down.

Stuck where I was, I couldn't see what was happening. My eyes started to burn, and I was sure I would soon be dead of smoke inhalation.

A knife flashed over my head.

I thought it would find my chest.

Instead, it cut the cords that held me. I strained to see who it was. I saw an unfamiliar face, an older man, who said, "Let's get out!"

I was aching all over but managed to struggle to my feet. My arms were still cuffed behind me. The man who freed me grabbed my shirt and led me out of the doorway, through the big hall, out the open front doors, and into the night.

I sucked in the fresh air, coughed so hard I doubled over, and went down on one knee.

"Easy there," the man said. "Take it easy."

After a minute or so, I regained some equilibrium. The man was standing a few feet away, looking at the house on fire, *admiring* it.

"Morris," I said.

"I told 'em," he said, and then he laughed. "They didn't think I could do it!" He clapped his hands in applause for himself. I saw the butt of a revolver sticking out of his pants.

In the distance came the sound of a siren.

"They're coming," Morris said with a smile.

"What are you going to do?"

"Wait for 'em, of course. I want 'em to know I did it!"

The cops took both of us in. They put me into a cell by myself, and a little while later, sent in a tray with a frozen chicken sandwich, a carton of milk, and an apple on it.

I sucked on the sandwich and drank the milk.

I was in no hurry to get out of there. The cell offered me a respite, which I desperately needed after everything that went down. I could spend the night and then figure out what to do.

After finishing my sumptuous meal, I lay on the cot and looked at the dull illumination of the ceiling. For what it was worth, I said, "Thank you" into the air.

The heavy door at the end of the hall swung open, and I heard footsteps coming my way. Two people.

I looked up and saw Sylvia Plotzske next to the officer on duty.

"Let me in," Sylvia said.

"I'm not supposed–" the officer started to say.

"Just do it, Mark, and leave me with him. I want to question him alone."

The authoritative tone in her voice was surprising. I'd never heard her like that before. Apparently, neither had the officer. He unlocked my cell, and Sylvia walked in. He then locked us in together and left.

"You look terrible," she said.

"Thanks."

"You want to tell me what happened?"

"Do you know?"

"Tolletson's dead."

"He looked it."

"Along with Mr. and Mrs. Hazelton."

"Wow. A clean sweep."

"What can you tell me?"

"Sylvia, it's going to blow your mind."

I told her the story.

When I finished, she shook her head almost like she had expected it. "I knew Tolletson was into something bizarre. I saw a pattern in the way he handled things relating to the Hazeltons. Refusing to file against Darcy, for one thing, on an assault. The evidence was pretty convincing, but he got rid of it. Then there was the lifestyle . . ."

"I got to ride in his Cadillac."

"His new one. He gets a new one every year. Or did."

"And Hazelton paid for it all. In return, Tolletson kept the Hazelton family legally safe."

"That's it."

"And kept people from knowing what they were into."

"That too."

"Sylvia," I said, "what do you know about the innocence of Howie Patino?"

She suddenly looked vulnerable behind her severe glasses. "A lot."

"Tell me."

Sylvia sighed and spoke quietly. "Howie happened to be the perfect victim, in the wrong place at the wrong time. Tolletson took over the case from me when you didn't make a deal, and he made sure you lost."

"How?"

"You remember that supplemental medical report, the one that said Rae Patino was pregnant?"

"Of course I do. So did the jury."

"I planted it."

That's when I stood up. I could not believe what I was hearing. I ran my fingers through my hair, shaking my head.

Sylvia continued, "I did it during one of the court recesses. It wasn't hard to do. Tolletson told me the best time to do it."

"Why, Sylvia?"

"I'm a night-school grad, Jake, not a fancy Harvard type. I wasn't going to any big firm. But I was going to make it; I was going to climb. Tolletson picked me because of that, I'm sure. And he had me convinced your client might walk and that we had to make sure we nailed him."

"Well, you did. Now what?"

"I tell what I know. He'll be out on a habeas in no time."

I looked at her. She was sitting very still. "But that'll be it for you as a lawyer."

"I know."

I sat back down across from her. "Why are you doing this?"

She looked at me squarely. "I haven't been able to sleep much. I guess I just want to be able to sleep again. Especially after Delliplane."

"My witness? Was Tolletson behind that too?"

"I think so. I think if I dig a little bit, I'll be able to connect him."

Then I did something I had never done to a prosecutor in my life. I reached out and patted her hand.

We sat silent for a few moments as I thought. "Sylvia, there may be another way." She regarded me quizzically. I said, "But first we have to do one thing."

"What?"

The next day Sylvia had Darcy Hazelton brought in for questioning.

He was, at first, combative. Having me in the same conference room as Sylvia and Detective Garth Watts of homicide didn't sit well with him. But it didn't take long to break him down. He *wanted* to spill it.

Yes, he confirmed, his stepmother was the one. Rae was Heather's surrogate since Heather was well past child-bearing years. The baby Rae was carrying was a boy, fathered by Warren Hazelton, conceived artificially.

"But the witch wanted a daughter," Darcy spat as he recounted it. "Had some crazy idea about raising a supreme goddess or something. When it turned out to be a boy, Heather told her to get rid of it. Rae refused an abortion unless she got more money."

And that was why Rae ended up dead. Darcy heard Heather spilling it all out to his father one night. Rae was holding them both up, Heather said. Threatening to go to the media. Heather went to see Rae one night to have it out–the night Howie came home.

Hearing him pound on the door, Heather grabbed a knife from the kitchen. She told Rae to get rid of him and hid in the bathroom. While Howie was pouring his heart out to Rae, Heather listened, then finally acted.

Heather was good with a knife. She got Rae and Howie both. Howie apparently passed out immediately. That gave her an idea. She gave Rae more whacks, wiped her prints off the knife, and went out the bathroom window–without her clothes. Soaked with blood, she balled them up and held them as she fled.

"One question," Sylvia said. "Why didn't Heather put the knife in Howie's hand, for fingerprints?"

Darcy shrugged. I said, "Howie may have been coming around, and she had to get out, or Heather may have thought one step ahead of the cops. Howie's prints could actually have bolstered a story of a setup. Could have argued the knife *was* put in his hand. With no prints, it looks like Howie was careful *not* to incriminate himself."

"That's it," Darcy said. "That sounds like Heather. She was a smooth one."

"Darcy," I said, "were they really into devil worship?"

Darcy laughed scornfully. "I guess they're getting their chance now, huh?"

Just before leaving Hinton, I met with Sylvia in her office. She told me I could plead to a misdemeanor DUI. I'd go into an alcohol program, which was fine with me. I needed it.

Then I told her I was going to take on the murder defense of Edmund Morris. Pro bono.

Sylvia smiled. “Thank you,” she said.

“No need,” I answered. No one would ever know about Sylvia’s planting of the medical report, at least from me. I figured it would be worth it to have a good prosecutor in the system, one who would not turn a blind eye toward justice.

CHAPTER FORTY-SIX

AFTER HOWIE'S RELEASE, he moved back in with Fred and Janet and Brian. He took a job with Fred's outfit, and last time I heard from him, he and Fred were planning to take a little camping trip with Brian next summer. "I'm going to show him how to make knots," Howie said. "Remember?"

He also told me that from the moment he saw his son again he hasn't had another dream of the devil. He says that God took the dreams away so he could be a father to his son.

And Brian *is* his son. A blood test confirmed it.

I patched things up with Barb and Rick. They didn't move east after all, and that has made my relationship with Mandy a whole lot easier. Mandy and I ate at Chippers again the other night, and she showed me her latest horse drawings. A few of them were actually looking like honest-to-goodness four-legged animals.

Partway through her liver and onions, Mandy said, "Daddy, you look happy."

"I am."

"You're a whole lot happier than you used to be."

"I know."

"How come?"

This is what I told her.

Exactly one week after the explosion in Hinton, I was back in my apartment, cleaning things out. I found three old bottles of booze and took them outside and tossed them in the dumpster. I was gathering up my linens when I heard a knock on the door.

It was Lindsay.

"Surprised?" she said.

"Yeah. How'd you know where I live?"

"I had some help." She looked left, and then Triple C, a devious smile on his face, stepped into view.

"We're tracking you down," he said.

"What's this all about?"

"Come on," said Lindsay, taking my arm. I didn't even grab a coat. All I could figure was that they were taking me out for a victory meal or something. Fine with me. I was hungry.

Instead they took me to church.

It was a middle-sized church in Northridge, just south of Devonshire. This night the place was packed.

"Well, you finally got your way," I said to Trip as they led me inside. I had never seen anything like it. Raucous music, people waving their hands and shouting out "Amen," and a big, female gospel singer with a voice that rocked the walls.

A few weeks before, I would have run out of the building screaming.

But I was interested now. Something I'd read in Pascal kept coming back to me–"There is enough light for those who desire only to see."

At one point during the preaching–a lively sermon by a man who had more energy than I'd ever dreamed of–Lindsay slipped her hand into mine. It was warm and comforting and made me finally feel all right about being there.

After the sermon, the people all stood and started singing. An organ played, and people started singing a hymn about "no turning back, no turning back." Several came out of their seats and started walking up to the front.

Next thing I knew, Trip was out in the aisle, smiling an invitation at me. He was like a magnet. I found myself stepping out to him, feeling something inside pulling me. Trip put his big arm around my shoulder, and we started walking down to the front. I looked back at Lindsay and saw her smiling at me too.

Then, when Trip and I were about halfway down the aisle, I realized the most incredible thing. I was crying.

ACKNOWLEDGMENTS

I'M INDEBTED TO Al Menaster for his legal knowledge, sharp editorial eye, and generosity with his time. This book would not have been possible, in its present form, without him. Others helpful to me were Beth Barrett, Valerie Carillo, and C. A. Winning.

Again, my great thanks to all the team members at Broadman & Holman who make an author's job so much easier.

As always, my wife Cindy gave me invaluable advice on storyline and style. She continues to give me belief in myself and my writing. Her support means more to me than I can adequately express, so I'll just say, "Ready for the next one?"